The Pagan Hammer

Andrew Clawson

Get Your FREE Copy of the Harry Fox story *THE NAPOLEON CIPHER*.

Sign up for my VIP reader mailing list, and I'll send you the novel for free.

Details can be found at the end of this book.

Chapter 1

The cops were coming for Harry Fox. Why? He'd called them.

They'd be here any minute, because Harry had called in an anonymous tip about a black-market antiquities deal going down near the harbor, withholding only the exact location. He was planning to buy two recently stolen Viking artifacts from a seller, but he was going into the deal with a secret. He wanted to get caught. Or, more precisely, he wanted the seller to be caught while he himself got away. That was his plan. If it didn't work, he'd be in a Norwegian prison for a long time. Harry exhaled, his breath making a faint cloud in the cool air. This had to work.

Harry stood motionless, watching ships glide across the pristine waters of the Oslofjord. Fishing trawlers, pleasure craft, tour boats and kayaks dotted the glassy surface, so many in places it was hard to track them all. A good place to get lost, if you were of a mind to do that. And Harry certainly was. He just had to stay one step ahead of everyone else.

The seller appeared from around a corner, his collar turned up against the chill. One hand clutched a backpack slung over his shoulder; the other was buried in a coat pocket. This seller had no qualms about double-crossing one of the most dangerous men in Europe. A man like that was unpredictable, dangerous. Harry touched the knuckledusters in his own pocket. Ceramic, light, and the only weapons he had. It would have to be enough.

1

The seller stopped just out of reach across from Harry. "*Hast du das Spiel der Yankees gesehen?*" Did you see the Yankees game?

"*Zusätzliche Innings. Harter Verlust.*" Extra innings. Tough loss.

The agreed-upon code. One Harry had chosen, just as he chose German as the language. He didn't speak much German, but he didn't speak a word of Norwegian, so it had to do.

The two men stood there, neither moving. It was the first time Harry had seen the seller. A man who stole from his boss to make a quick buck. Or a hundred thousand of them, in this case. A man who wasn't afraid when he should have been. Not the sort of man Harry liked to do business with.

"Do you have it?" Harry asked, switching to English.

"Yes." The seller's eyes landed on Harry only for an instant. He looked in every direction, unable to focus. His weight shifted back and forth.

Harry took a tiny step back. "Let me see them."

The man Harry knew as Jan finally looked at him. A fake name, the most common for males in Norway. Jan wasn't happy. "No." He shook his head. "Too many people around."

Enough people to provide cover, in Harry's opinion. "Fine. Over there." Harry inclined his head toward a vacant bench about 50 yards away, away from the main pedestrian thoroughfare. "Sit beside me and open the case." He walked to the bench without giving Jan a chance to argue. Jan wanted the money? Harry needed to see the merchandise.

Greed proved a powerful motivator. Harry's backside had barely touched the cold seat before Jan joined him.

"This is not smart," Jan grumbled.

"Giving you a hundred grand without seeing the artifacts isn't smart," Harry said. "Open it."

Jan muttered something in his native tongue Harry was glad he didn't understand. The backpack unzipped to reveal a rolled blanket. Jan dug through his pack until an object came into view. "Satisfied?" he asked.

Harry couldn't respond. *Incredible*. Decorative gold and silver bands covered with runic writing encircled the metal piece. A Viking drinking horn. The most impressive example Harry had ever seen. He tried and failed to decipher any of the runes inscribed on it before Jan quickly covered the horn again.

"Enough," Jan said.

Harry looked up. In the distance, dozens of people walked along the harbor, drinking coffee, admiring the opera house, enjoying the clear, sunny skies. No one paid them any mind. "Show me the other one," Harry said.

Jan dug through the pack again until a second horn emerged. Gold and silver like the other, though the runes on this one were different. That's what Harry needed to see. He had to be sure. "Very nice," Harry said.

The horn disappeared. "The money." Jan still couldn't keep his eyes on Harry.

Harry pulled an envelope from his pocket. A big one. Jan nearly jumped off the bench when it landed in his lap. "Count it."

Jan finally paid attention. The flap of the envelope opened to reveal ten stacks of fresh hundred-dollar bills. Ten thousand in each stack. Total? A hundred grand.

Harry reached into his pocket. Slowly, as though he had all day. He touched his phone and pressed a certain button, one set to fire off a text message telling the already alerted Norwegian detective the trafficking deal was going down outside the opera house. It even said Harry was wearing a bright blue coat. That was important.

"Don't follow me," Harry said. He grabbed one of the backpack's straps and pulled.

The bag didn't move. "You are not leaving."

Harry tugged on the bag again. "What's the matter with you? We don't need a scene."

Jan kept an iron grip on the pack. Harry's money had disappeared into the pack. "Do not argue," Jan said.

Harry was about to do a lot more than that when the gun appeared. Low, hidden under the bag and aimed at Harry's gut. Harry kept hold of the bag. "Jan, you don't want this kind of trouble."

"These horns stay with me," Jan said. "Leave." He jammed the gun into Harry's side. "I will shoot if I ever see you again."

Harry kept his voice level. "We can come to an arrangement."

"This is the arrangement," Jan said. "You leave. I keep the horns and the money." Again, the gun in the ribs thing. "Go."

The dusters were around Harry's fingers now, on the hand across his body, where Jan couldn't see. Harry shook his head. "I won't forget this."

Jan's mouth had barely opened when approaching sirens blared and blue lights flashed off the opera house windows. Jan's head twisted as he turned toward the noise. Harry dropped his elbow to knock the gun down and held it there, then threw a hook. The dusters cracked off Jan's jaw, knocking him off the bench. Harry grabbed the gun as Jan fell and tossed it into the waterway behind them. The backpack was still in Jan's grasp as he tumbled to the pavement. Harry bent and rifled a fist into Jan's gut and then pulled at the bookbag while Jan gasped for air. The pack came free. Harry slung it over his shoulder and straightened.

He had the artifacts and his money. Now he had to keep his freedom. The cops were looking for a man in a bright blue coat, so Harry ripped his coat off and dropped it beside Jan. He sprinted off toward the walkway and rejoined the throng, sliding between pedestrians on his way toward town until Jan was lost from view.

He walked rapidly, keeping it below a run so people didn't take notice. A half dozen police cars with flashing lights approached the pier now. Harry dropped his gaze as tires screeched and the cars shuddered to a halt. Uniformed cops jumped out and ran directly at him. Harry stopped. So did everybody else, turning and watching as the cops raced through the crowd. In courteous Norwegian fashion, they parted to offer a clear path forward. Harry played along, staring wide-eyed as two officers brushed past him en route to the bench, the blue coat and Jan. They didn't give Harry a second glance.

Now he really picked up speed. Getting the cops to show up was one thing. Escaping undetected was another. Harry had never planned to steal the horns from Jan. No, he'd intended to pay the man and close this deal. So much for the best-laid plans.

Harry kept moving at pace across the plaza, headed for a series of high-end shops and office buildings leading to a pedestrian bridge that crossed one of the fjord's many tributaries. A commotion sounded to his rear. Police were headed back this way. At least four of them, radios to their mouths as they ran. The crowd had thinned, so Harry had a clear view as one officer pointed at him and started shouting in Norwegian.

"*Ryggsekk!*" The cop kept pointing, shouting the word again. "*Ryggsekk!*"

Harry didn't have to speak Norwegian to catch that it sounded an awful lot like *rucksack*. They were talking about his backpack. Harry took off running again.

A sprint across the bridge sent people bouncing off each shoulder. Across the water the foot traffic was even lighter. The cops yelled and pointed at him as they ran, forming a narrow line through the crowds while Harry raced at full speed into the heart of Oslo's waterfront business district. Glass and steel buildings leaned over him as he ran down the sidewalk. He had to outrun them and hope his escape plan worked.

Halfway down the opera house's rear — the place was *massive* — he dodged through a couple standing beside a row of parked motorbikes. Vespas, the sort found all across Europe. A particularly unimpressive model was step one of Harry's plan. He jumped on, fired the engine and shot across the sidewalk into traffic. The shouts of policemen faded as his engine whined and Harry headed into the city. The cops chasing him on foot were nowhere to be seen when he looked back. Harry grinned and congratulated himself. *I've still got it.*

The grin vanished as two police cars barreled around the corner ahead of Harry and headed straight for him. He veered left across an open plaza, people shouting as his motorbike hurtled through. He thumbed the horn to warn them; the tinny sound it made was scarcely audible.

"Out of the way!" Harry shouted, waving one arm. The people didn't need encouragement, diving and falling. "Sorry!" he called over a shoulder.

He made it across the plaza without hitting anyone and bounced back onto the street. An electric streetcar appeared in front of him, forcing him to turn right, farther away from his pursuers but also farther away from his planned path. Police sirens grew louder behind him, too close. They'd spot him soon and come at him from either side if they were smart about it.

Time to improvise. The streetcar lanes ran down the center of the roadway, two tracks with fencing on either side. He gunned the Vespa to a cross street and zipped over to the other lane, dodging into oncoming traffic and earning a blaring horn for his trouble. Two city buses idled in one lane ahead as they waited for the light to turn. A small group of people had queued at the stop, waiting for their ride.

Harry glanced over his shoulder and saw one police car appearing two blocks behind him. He swung his gaze around to the front again and saw another veer around the corner only a block ahead. Harry darted between the two stopped buses and jumped the curb, bouncing to a halt beside the line of wide-eyed riders. He hopped off the Vespa as the light turned green and handed the keys to a man standing close to him. "Keep it," Harry said. The guy dropped his coffee.

Harry turned as the first bus motored off, its engine whining softly as it picked up speed faster than he'd expected. Harry took off at a dead run, came level with the passenger door and then leapt to grab hold of the bus's bike rack, keeping low so as not to be seen by the driver. The bus continued to accelerate, and he clung to the rack with one hand, his other clutching the backpack. The road whizzed beneath him as he fumbled for a better grip, finally hugging both the backpack and the bike rack tight with both hands.

The police car coming down the other lane zipped past. Harry held on as the bus bounced along the road, one foot slipping briefly off the metal grating. *Keep going. Just a few more blocks.* That was all he needed.

His bus slowed for a stop, and Harry dared a glance up. He groaned. He was only halfway back to the opera house, where the next step in his plan waited. He had a chance – if he could get there.

Harry looked up to see the bus driver staring at him with a radio to her lips. *She's ratting me out.* "Come on!" Harry shouted as he jumped off, sticking his head out into traffic before ducking back. Two cops were scanning the crowds from the other side of the street. They hadn't spotted him yet, but he couldn't stay here. A streetcar approached off to one side, headed the direction he needed to go.

He ran across the road as the streetcar pulled up and slid to a halt. The doors opened, and Harry slipped aboard as the doors slid shut behind him. One hand on a rail, he took deep breaths and exhaled. *This could work.* Jan in jail, Harry on his way home, merchandise and money in his pack. He looked around the streetcar.

A uniformed police officer stood at the far door. He hadn't reacted as Harry boarded. In fact, he'd barely moved, one hand on the safety rail, the other in his pocket. Only half the seats were occupied, so the cop could easily see him. Yet all he did was pull out his cell phone and look at it for a moment, then peck at the screen with two fingers. He never looked at Harry. In fact, he was looking out the window. Staring, to be precise. Clouds covered the sun outside, turning the window into a mirror. The cop wasn't looking out the window. He was looking at Harry's reflection.

Harry didn't move as the streetcar slowed. Didn't run for the doors as they slid open to let passengers out. No, he waited until they were almost closed again before exploding through them at the last second. The last image Harry caught of the cop was him pounding his fists against the closed doors as the streetcar pulled away.

The opera house was only a short walk ahead. Harry was nearly back where he'd started, a block from the bench where Jan had likely been arrested. Harry headed for a waterfront café. He was halfway there when he heard the streetcar screech to a halt. He looked back to find the officer shoving the door open, leaping to the ground and running in Harry's direction.

He had to lose this cop, and he had to do it now. More officers would be on the way, coming from the waterfront ahead of Harry. Harry looked left. No good. He looked right, to a pedestrian bridge leading around the café's far corner and out of sight.

That was his ticket. He held the backpack straps tight as he ran at full speed around the corner, putting the building between himself and the first cop. He darted onto the bridge, a brick-and-stone affair he'd walked over while reconnoitering the area yesterday. These pedestrian bridges had drainpipes running down the sides to keep rainwater from pooling on the centuries-old stonework, the thick pipes sturdy enough to hold a man. At least he hoped so.

He ran to where the bridge linked with the mainland and quickly checked behind him. No sign of the cop. Harry slowed, hopped onto the thick stone rail keeping pedestrians from falling into the water, and jumped toward the drainpipe. For a long second he was weightless, then gravity took hold and he plunged toward the pipe, grabbing for it with both hands. His own momentum carried him forward like a gymnast and he crashed into the side of the stone bridge with a jaw-rattling *smack*. He held on until his vision cleared, then shimmied down to where the pipe bent itself into the shadows underneath the bridge. He heard the sound of running feet smacking above him on the sidewalk as he moved hand over hand along the pipe, swinging out over the river far below, until the bridge concealed him from view.

His breath came in ragged gasps, the muscles in his hands and arms shouting for relief as he clung to the rough metal pipe, dangling out of view, listening to the cop above him unleash all manner of Norwegian invective. Harry didn't have to speak the language to get the message.

The cop paced back and forth, yelling into his phone all the while until he finally fell silent. Harry held his breath, listening to the water gurgling beneath him, until finally, rapid, heavy footsteps again sounded from above, this time fading away as the cop ran across the bridge toward the fjord.

Harry counted to five, then pulled himself hand over hand back the way he'd come. Muscles screaming now, he grabbed a lip on the arched stone support and hauled himself up, one foot finding purchase as he climbed the rest of the way up the pipe. He clambered over the railing and dropped in a heap to catch his breath before scrambling off the other end of the bridge and scooting behind a patch of bushes. He leaned out, risking a look back down the bridge path.

A small army of policemen milled about on the bridge's far side.

He stood and moved at a fast walk toward a coffee shop, where he stepped inside and walked between tables until he made it to a rear door. The sign on it declared *BARE ANSATTE. STAFF ONLY.* Harry twisted the knob and went through, passing a startled barista as he moved down the narrow hallway and ducked out a side door. He entered another doorway adjacent to it, one propped open by a plastic crate. The cook sitting on said crate smoking a cigarette barely looked at him.

A bustling kitchen greeted him inside. Waiters shouted, cooks cursed, and heavy steam filled the air. Harry kept his head down and hugged the wall until he emerged at the rear of the restaurant, which overlooked the Oslofjord waters. Harry headed straight for a family restroom, stepping inside and locking the door behind him.

Please still be here. Harry's breath quickened as he lifted the toilet tank lid. The package he'd taped there that morning remained in place. Harry pulled it free, unzipped the waterproof bag, and prayed to any gods who happened to be listening that the plan would still work.

Police officers entered the restaurant overlooking Oslofjord's picturesque waters, startling diners and staff alike. They gruffly asked about a man who had come in wearing a backpack. Vaguely Middle Eastern in appearance. European, maybe. Average height, dark hair, solid build. None of the clientele recalled seeing the man come inside, certainly not one carrying a backpack.

No one connected those questions to the man wearing outdoor clothes who walked out of the family restroom with a small dry-bag dangling from one hand. Typical apparel for anyone spending a day on the cold waters surrounding Oslo. He strolled away from the restaurant and down a walkway leading to the water's edge. There he retrieved a kayak from where it was secured by the dock, stowed his dry-bag in the bow, slipped into his tiny vessel and casually paddled away.

If the cops had looked out onto the water, they might have seen this man making his way determinedly into the distance, though it would have been hard to pick him out among the other kayakers. This man paddled alone, headed to a dock well away from this bustling waterfront where a motorcycle had been parked. The motorcycle would take him to Oslo airport and a flight home to New York City, where the two souvenir Viking drinking horns in his luggage would turn out to be something far different than what he told the customs officials.

Chapter 2

Brooklyn, New York

A ceiling fan spun slowly above the two men seated around a table. Cirrus clouds of cigar smoke drifted up and curled below a ceiling stained from decades of such fumes. One man's face was lined, his skin a roadmap of experience. The other man's cheeks were smooth with the vigor of youth. The dark circles under the young man's eyes showed he carried the weight of a family on his shoulders. The weight, in truth, of an entire city.

"I am sorry, Joey." Gio Sabella took a long pull on his cigar. "It is the best I can do."

"A month." Joey Morello looked at Gio over steepled fingers.

"You are lucky to have that," Gio said. "I suspect the decision would already be made if it were not for your father."

"Who would they choose?"

Gio shrugged. "It is not my place to say. You know I am not interested in replacing your father, God rest his soul." Gio crossed himself. "He led us well for decades."

"Until someone killed him."

"A killer who escaped." Gio laid his cigar in a crystal ashtray. He leaned forward in his chair. "Finding who murdered your father will not bring him back or put you in his seat. You need more."

Joey lifted an eyebrow. "I'm listening."

"The families follow strength *and* wisdom," Gio said. "Your father had both. You must show both as well. Your own family is under threat. If you cannot stand up to one man, and do it *wisely*, I cannot offer advice."

Gio's true message remained unspoken, and Joey Morello heard every word.

Gio stood. "Be safe, young man." Gio accepted Joey's embrace, pulling him close so none of the bodyguards around the room could hear. "I believe in you," Gio whispered. "Show the other families."

The words rang in Joey's ears as he departed Gio Sabella's office and got into his waiting Mercedes. The fall leaves stirred as his driver took him back to his headquarters in Brooklyn, the sunlight falling through the bulletproof windows doing little to warm his face. Right now his future hung in the balance, and the man who could push it in either direction? Gio Sabella. One of his father's closest friends, yet now Gio had given Joey an ultimatum. Business trumped friendship in this world.

Gio had made it clear. *Find who killed your father.* Joey had been trying to do that ever since the bomb exploded beside Vincent Morello's restaurant table months earlier. Joey would have been sitting beside his father if it weren't for a phone call minutes before the explosion. Joey knew who had done it. The same man who was now trying to push the Morello family off their turf. A man whose reckless ambition threatened the fragile peace among all of New York's crime families. A peace Vincent Morello had created.

The man? Altin Cana, head of the Albanian crime family bearing his name. The Cana family was now waging war on the Morello family, creating trouble at their gaming houses, selling product on Morello turf, even sending cops to raid their money-laundering operations. All of it hit Joey Morello's bottom line, but even worse, it made him look weak. None of the other family heads wanted Altin to do anything but crawl back into the hole he'd come from, yet they didn't intrude. They saw this battle as between the Morellos and Canas. Joey needed to prove he could lead his men as his father had. Vincent Morello had led all the families in New York and Joey wanted to do the same. Gio had made it clear. If Joey wanted to lead them, he needed to prove himself.

That meant crushing the Canas. If Joey couldn't put this upstart Albanian into his place and avenge Vincent's murder, how could he lead the other families?

Joey's thoughts still churned as he arrived at his headquarters in Brooklyn. One thought ran through his mind as he walked inside the compound of converted brownstones, greeting the armed guards at each door before entering his office and falling into the oversized chair behind his desk. The chair where his father used to sit. *What would Vincent do?*

Joey opened the crystal decanter on his desk and poured a drink. The bourbon warmed his throat, yet Joey found himself unable to fully savor the smoky heat. Vincent had spent years preparing Joey to take over the family business. To lead the families and maintain peace. Now that time was here and what was Joey doing? Failing.

Joey set his drink down. Was he scared? Not much, and he'd never admitted to being scared of anything in his life. That didn't mean he'd never been scared. Everyone felt afraid at one time or another. It's how you reacted that defined you. Vincent Morello had come to America with nothing but his heritage, yet he'd risen to the top of New York's underworld, become a force none could withstand. How had he done it? By working hard, sure, but there was more. He did whatever it took, and he didn't do it alone.

Vincent had built alliances. When needed, he'd fought dirty. Vincent won, no matter what, and he'd kept winning until he'd built an empire. Perhaps Joey couldn't do this alone either, then. He wasn't destined to fail, but he might need help, from people he trusted. Trusted with his life.

Joey's phone buzzed atop his desk. A name flashed on-screen, that of a man he trusted above all others. Harry Fox.

As the Morellos' antiquities hunter, Harry filled a role for the Morello family that few others in the world could. His experience and connections brought resources Joey never imagined existed. He had friends in the Manhattan district attorney's office, specifically the Anti-Trafficking Unit, a team of law enforcement officers dedicated to stopping the flow of illegal artifacts pouring into New York. The team, led by a no-nonsense woman named Nora Doyle, used a time-honored police method to stop the bad guys: If you can't beat them, work with them. Harry Fox wasn't quite a bad guy, not really, so he was perfect. Harry also knew people the anti-trafficking team didn't, got close to people they never would. He went where they couldn't. In exchange for his help, the Anti-Trafficking Unit looked the other way when Harry participated in questionable activities that happened to pad Joey Morello's bottom line.

Harry Fox was one of a kind. He was Joey Morello's closest friend in the world.

Joey connected the call. "Back from Norway?" he asked.

Harry's response made him shift in his seat. His eyes narrowed as he listened. "You found *what?*"

Chapter 3

It took a while for Harry to describe how two Viking drinking horns had nearly landed him in a Norwegian jail. Once Joey got over the shock of Harry being in Norway at the behest of the D.A.'s Anti-Trafficking Unit – a mission Harry hadn't shared with Joey before leaving for Norway – Joey let it slide, probably because he had enough going on. Joey didn't need to know all the details.

"Now I'm back in Brooklyn," Harry said as he finished the tale. "Sara is studying the horns."

"It never stops in your world. Is Sara still putting up with you? I thought she went back to Germany."

"Funny you say that," Harry said. "She's interviewing in New York for a job at the American Museum of Natural History. They need an Egyptologist."

"Holy smokes. Good for her." A pause. "New York is a long way from her life in Germany." Sara currently worked at Trier University in the same position.

"That's the hard part," Harry said. "Her family is still in Europe." Harry had met Sara barely a year ago, and now she was considering moving to New York. For him? She hadn't said it out loud, but Harry could read between those lines. "Right now she's thinking it through. We'll see."

"I always thought she was a smart lady," Joey said. "Staying here for a bum like you makes me rethink that."

15

"You're a funny guy."

"I'm just busting your chops. That's great news. She's a good one, Harry." Joey lowered his voice. "You having any luck with that other thing?"

Spoken like a true wise guy. Joey was asking about Harry's research into his mother's death.

"Not much," Harry said. "The detective I need to talk to is out of town. We're meeting when she gets back."

"Let me know if I can do anything."

Joey didn't pry further. This was a private matter. Harry would share if he wanted to.

"Thanks," Harry said. "I'll let you know how it goes." He chewed on his lip for a moment. "How are things with you?" Harry finally asked.

"*Va bene, ci penso io.*"

Fine, I'll handle it. Joey slipping into Italian was never good. That meant Harry needed to leave the topic alone. "I'm here if you need me," Harry said.

"Keep doing what you're doing with the D.A.'s office," Joey said. "I need all the friends I can get right now."

Harry assured him he would and clicked off. He tapped the phone against his chin as cars rolled down the street and people milled around the park across from him. The normal world Harry watched from his porch. Two years ago he'd been running around the world with his father, learning on the fly how to chase ancient relics and stay alive in the process. That he did it for the Italian mob was simply part of life. An odd family business, but not a bad gig, and if Harry were being honest, it had made him feel closer to his dad. Which meant something, because Harry's dad wasn't around any longer. After that, Harry had become the man and promptly got himself into all sorts of trouble. That he was able to maneuver into a partnership with the district attorney's office was either a masterstroke or the biggest piece of dumb luck in his life.

"Harry, get in here," Sara called through an open window.

He jumped up without thinking and went in to join her. Both drinking horns lay on the table in front of her, protective cloth beneath them. Sara's auburn hair was pulled back off her face as she looked at him, her eyes wide, then shot out of her chair as though a bomb had gone off beneath it.

"Look at this!" She grabbed his bicep and dragged him over. "These drinking horns tell the same story. The exact same one. It's incredible."

This clearly mattered. Her rushed words, tensed neck, how both hands gripped the table. Sara was primed for action. And Harry had no clue why.

"That's important?" he asked.

"Are you kidding? It changes everything." Arms and hands flew in every direction. "I can read the words on the first horn; they're written in Elder Futhark runes. Anyone can read those; they're no secret. But these runes on the second horn are different, indecipherable." Here she pointed to the horn she had been leaning over when he walked in. "But now *I can read them*. This is the Viking equivalent of the Rosetta Stone. All the runestones we couldn't read, now we can. The stories, the history." She pulled him bodily toward her and did her best to squeeze the life out of him. "It's all here."

Harry shimmied and twisted until he slipped free of her grasp. "Got it. Elder Futhark, runestones, all of it. Sounds great." He put both hands up, palms toward her, and stayed still until she stopped jumping around. "One problem. I have no idea what any of it means."

Sara threw her hands up. "We're sending you back to school. Sit down." She didn't give him a choice and hauled him into the chair beside her. "The drinking horns each tell the same story."

"I caught that."

"Here's the important part." Sara pointed to one horn. "This story is written in Elder Futhark runes, which I can read. Vikings wrote using runes, and over time, the runes changed."

"Like going from Old English to Middle English, to…" He grasped and came up empty. "Whatever we use today."

She smirked only a bit. "Yes." A pause. "Modern English. Early Modern English came before it. Just a note."

"Point taken." He gestured to the horns. "You were saying?"

"Elder Futhark is the oldest form of runic alphabet. I can date the horns using this, can even infer who may have written it. Any number of conclusions can be drawn because of the specific runes used. But that's not the point." She indicated the other horn, which had runes inscribed on it that looked nothing like the ones on the first horn. "The runes on this horn are unknown."

"You've never seen them before?"

"I didn't say that. I said they're unknown. As in cannot be deciphered. I've seen it a handful of times before, on runestones in Europe. Runestones no one can read."

The curtain finally lifted. "You can use the Elder runes to decipher the new ones. Neat."

Her eyes widened. "*Neat?* We can now read a previously indecipherable language, Harry. Do you realize how important that is?"

"I guess it depends on what the runes say."

She lifted a hand. She lowered it. "A valid point. Nonetheless, this is revolutionary. I know of at least one runestone in Germany that has these runes on it. No one's been able to decipher it."

All well and good, but Harry was a capitalist. He couldn't forget about profits. "As I said, it's neat." He ignored her withering glare. "Why do these odd runes even exist? They can't be a new language, not with only one other example of them around."

"An excellent question." Sara leaned closer so her hair brushed his shoulder. The scent of lavender followed it. "You've found the heart of the entire matter. I think this is a *code*. A code created by two brothers. I'm not certain why, though I can guess."

"What brothers?" Harry asked.

"Two kings. Alaric, known for sacking Rome, and his brother Ataulf."

"Hang on. *Rome?*"

"Rome stood for nearly twelve hundred years, until the Visigoths conquered the city in 410 A.D."

"I thought these were Viking drinking horns."

"Technically, they belonged to Visigoths, but you know that cultures don't start and stop: they blend. The Visigoths migrated to Scandinavia, and over time became what we call Vikings." She waved a hand. "But that's not the point. The story on these horns is, and it involves the two brothers. King Alaric, who led the Visigoths into Rome, and his brother Ataulf, who became king when Alaric died not long after sacking Rome."

"Neat story."

Thunderclouds crossed her face. "If you refer to anything as *neat* again, you will be sorry."

He failed to hide a grin. "Okay, okay. How do you know this is a code between the brothers and not a new language? You said it's only been found in a few other places, but couldn't it just be a local dialect?"

"I believe this is a code because of what the story says."

"I'm listening."

"Not yet – let me finish. These horns were stolen from a dig in Norway. One of my colleagues worked with an archaeologist at the site. This archaeologist told him the dig team suspected the horns were a linguistic key to unlocking unknown runes."

"They suspected it and didn't follow up?"

"The horns were stolen before analysis could be done. From what I understand, the horns were stolen before they even came out of the ground."

Harry had no idea how the man calling himself Jan came to have the horns. He didn't care. The reason he had agreed to recover them for Nora's team was that he owed her: she had connected him with a city detective who might be able to shed light on the truth behind his mother's disappearance.

Officially, Dani Fox had died decades ago and her body had been found near the Hudson River. Harry now knew that was a lie. He just had to prove it. The next step was a conversation with retired detective Jessica Barnes, who had originally investigated his mother's case. If you could call it an investigation. There were first-grade book reports thicker than her file.

Harry looked directly at Sarah. "You're the first person to make the connection. Nice work."

"Our work is only beginning."

"You know I have to give the horns to Nora. Her boss has a special interest in them."

The clouds gathered again. "I know. How fortunate for the dig team that one of their members is a relative of the district attorney. Quite the coup to have the D.A. assign you to recover these horns and avoid potential embarrassment."

Harry had learned long ago to expect the worst from politicians. That way you weren't disappointed when they inevitably lived down to expectations. One side of his mouth turned up. "Maybe I'll tell Nora I'm not back yet, that it will take a few days to get the horns to her."

A breeze with the first bite of fall floated through the open window. Sara walked over and closed it, then sat beside Harry and put a hand atop his. "Despite evidence to the contrary, you are a wonderful man. However, that won't be necessary."

"Why not?"

"I've already deciphered the code."

He stared at her. "Aren't you going to tell anyone? The dig archaeologists will eventually figure it out and take the credit."

"I can't. I'm not supposed to have seen these horns," she said. "And I'm not giving up on the mystery around this now. We're only getting started."

He only half-heard her. Connecting with Detective Barnes was what Harry cared about. To him, these horns were a distraction, but as Barnes wouldn't return for a few days, he wanted to support Sara until then. More than he expected, to be honest. "What do you mean?" he asked.

"The story on these horns is about what happened after Alaric sacked Rome." Sara indicated one horn. "This horn belonged to *King Alaric, Conqueror of Rome*. It's written in Elder Futhark. The other horn belonged to *Lord Ataulf*, Alaric's brother."

"I thought this was all about being able to translate the strange runes. Not about what happened to Alaric after they took Rome."

"Understanding what happened to the brothers and their people is useful. Initially, I thought these horns were created while Alaric was still alive. However, part of the story describes events after Alaric's death, so I believe Ataulf added the runes after his brother died. Perhaps to memorialize their code, perhaps for some other reason."

Sara could lecture with the best of them. Harry prompted her along. "The story the runes tell?"

"Alaric died not long after sacking Rome. This is documented. The legend is that there was a treasure tied to Alaric's death. Supposedly Alaric was buried in an Italian riverbed along with treasure from his sack of Rome."

Harry edged closer to her. "Any chance it's true?"

She laughed. "Likely not. Multiple attempts have been made to identify the site without success. Does that mean it's completely false? Not necessarily."

"What else do you have?"

"Newly crowned King Ataulf led his people north, toward Scandinavia. Ataulf had a son named Theodosius, who died in infancy. His death devastated Ataulf, who the horns say dreamed of being reunited with his son in Hel."

Harry's brain caught up with his ears. "The son went to hell?"

"One *L*, not two. Visigoths believed anyone who died from natural causes or disease went there. It's not like the Christian version, other than the Christians stole the name and repurposed it as the devil's home. To Visigoths it was simply a location in the afterlife."

"What about Valhalla?" Harry asked. "The Valkyries, daily battles and the massive mead hall."

"Only warriors and lords went to Valhalla. You had to be rich or die in battle to gain access. The simple version is Valkyries flew you to Valhalla after you died, where you fought and feasted and waited for a final supernatural battle. The full story is a bit more complex, but you get the idea."

"Ataulf was a king, so he'd go to Valhalla." Harry frowned. "His son wouldn't."

"That's it exactly. According to the horn, Ataulf wanted to reunite with the boy. But in the meantime, he buried his son in a silver coffin and continued north, where he established a Visigoth kingdom."

"Where they eventually turned into Vikings and pillaged northern Europe for centuries."

Harry grinned and then pointed to Ataulf's horn. "Knowing the code on this horn, now you can read the other runestones."

"Yes." She grabbed her laptop and set it on the table. "Care to help me?"

He sat beside her. A thought that had been buzzing in his head demanded attention. One he shouldn't be worried about, not with his mother's case in front of him. "Any chance this mysterious runestone could lead to Alaric's treasure?"

"There is always a chance."

His phone buzzed. "Hang on," Harry said, the thrill of the unknown making his nerves tingle. "It's Nora."

He connected the call and Nora Doyle's voice filled his ear. "Where are you?" she asked.

"My place," Harry said. He looked to the horns. "I'm preparing the artifacts for transport." Sara typed faster.

"Bring them to my office as soon as possible," Nora said. "My boss is waiting for them."

"Your boss who abused the power of his office to get these horns back."

"He's grateful. Which means he owes you one."

There were worse things than having the New York district attorney in your debt. "I'll remember that."

"I appreciate it too, Harry."

"We're on the same team." The words tasted a bit funny in his mouth.

"Right," Nora said. "We are."

"I'll get them to you first thing in the morning."

"No later," Nora said. "One more thing. Detective Barnes called me."

If a record had been playing, the music would have stopped. "What did she say?"

"She came back early. Give her a call."

All thoughts of Visigoth treasure vanished. "I will. See you tomorrow."

Chapter 4

Oslo, Norway

Corpses littered the grassy field. Horses whined, chafing under the weight of armored men astride them. Metal armor rattled as bearded warriors trudged to stand together in a great mass, battered shields slung across their backs, swords at their hips. The few survivors were too exhausted for words, yet when one man came to stand in front of them, a ground-shaking roar erupted.

All eyes were on the lone man. A beard thick enough to stop arrows erupted from his chin. His chainmail coat rustled with each step, one heavy boot stamping in front of the other until he stood at the head of the remaining warriors. Steam rose from a close-cropped scalp when his helmet came off. A bead of sweat fell from the nose guard onto the trampled grass. He looked at the assembled men and raised one muscled, hairy arm holding a battle-axe.

"*Sigr!*" His voice rang loudly.

The warriors responded in Old Nordic. "*Sigr!*" Their cry of *Victory* matched his own.

The leader spoke again. "Till Valhalla!" The warriors mirrored his cry, using English as well. Then a chant broke out. "Magnus! Magnus! Magnus!"

Straight teeth flashed through the beard. He raised both of his arms and the men fell silent. "You fought well. Now we feast!" the man in front of it all shouted, and with that the re-enactment ended.

His words brought the dead to life. Fallen warriors stirred, their death blows no longer mortal wounds as they gathered themselves from the dirt and rose to join their fellow combatants in a rousing battle cry. As one they turned, lifted their weapons, and shook them toward the crowds gathered to one side. The crowd broke out in cheers.

Over a hundred men and women embraced each other, the Viking re-enactors clapping backs and offering praise for a pretend battle well-fought. They had practiced for months, creating a choreographed slaughter in honor of their ancestors, rehearsing endlessly to hone swordcraft and tighten shield walls. Though thousands of spectators had turned out for the festivities and ensuing celebration, this was more than entertainment for the actors and actresses. This was a chance to pay homage to their forefathers, to keep traditions alive and share their glorious past with fellow enthusiasts, both fervent and lukewarm. And it was, if they were being honest, the group's biggest recruiting event of the year.

The Scandinavians were Norway's largest and most popular collection of historical re-enactors, though staging battles was only part of their mission. They were more than a social club, more than weekend warriors out for a good time. The Scandinavians were a historical society intent on keeping the past alive by any means necessary. They believed the past held the key to their future, not only that of Norway, where most hailed from, but also of Denmark and Sweden. Those three countries comprised historical Scandinavia, land of the Vikings, a people whose thirst for life could never be quenched. Though it could be quite a short life, given they tended to start wars with every culture they crossed.

One particularly brawny member approached the man in front, the one named Magnus, and thumped him on the back. "Well-fought, my lord. A great battle."

Magnus Dahl returned the bone-rattling whack. "You as well, my friend. What a crowd!" He gestured to the massed spectators now milling about the grounds, many headed for the authentic Viking village Magnus and his fellow re-enactors had constructed, replete with a working forge, distillery, farm and massive hall, all built using the materials and techniques of Viking times. "I hope we brewed enough mead!"

"Do not worry about that, my lord." The brawny warrior winked. "There is mead and food aplenty."

Another hearty thump and the men parted ways. Magnus noted two suited men approaching. Eyes hidden behind sunglasses, they were forced to bob and weave among the crowd of re-enactment warriors. Both men were well built and tall. Qualities you looked for in bodyguards.

Magnus headed straight for them. "Come." He threw an arm around each man; he was tall enough that his arms rested comfortably on their broad shoulders. "Join me for a horn of ale!"

Both bodyguards quickly shrugged out of his grip. "You know we cannot drink on duty, sir."

The touch of annoyance in the guard's voice brought Magnus no small pleasure. "If you cannot join me, then you are dismissed."

The guards didn't react. Magnus tried to get rid of them on an hourly basis. "You don't need to be here," he said. "These are my friends."

"Crowds can be unpredictable, sir." The response was remote, given on autopilot. "Better to be safe."

"If you insist."

Magnus Dahl left them to catch up as he moved toward the central hall, his progress halted seemingly every other step to greet a fellow warrior or have his picture taken. Meeting Magnus Dahl would be the highlight for many visitors here.

A cheer erupted when Magnus walked through the doors to the large hall, taking a proffered drinking horn and joining everyone in a rousing rendition of an ancient song praising the Norse gods and the Viking fighting spirit. After the song ended and he'd quaffed the entire horn, Magnus went for his seat at the head of the long table. He never made it.

"Sir." A man dressed like a priest pulled at Magnus's fur-lined sleeve. "You have a call."

Magnus frowned. "Take a message."

"It is urgent, sir."

Magnus's frown deepened. "Fine. In the office."

The priest was part of Magnus's inner circle. A lawyer by trade, Birger Thorsby handled Magnus's most private affairs, including one currently underway involving an artifact. Two artifacts, in fact. Items Magnus hoped would resurrect a nation from the ashes of history.

"Stay here," Magnus told the security guards. The door Magnus entered looked to be carved of roughly hewn wooden boards, but the room inside was a modern office. Overseeing a village required not only labor and materials, but also building permits, tax payments and any other number of modern headaches. All those administrative functions were completed in this room.

The office also served as a place for Magnus to conduct business of a more sensitive nature. He slipped off his chainmail coat and sat behind the polished desk. Magnus pressed the blinking button on the desktop phone. "*Ja?*"

"*Vi har et problem.*"

Magnus tapped the arm of his chair. "What problem?" he asked, continuing in Norwegian.

"The drinking horns are missing."

No. Two drinking horns from a Norwegian dig site. "Where are they?" Magnus asked. "Did someone betray us?"

The caller hesitated. "I am not certain where they are. I believe an American now has them. He purchased them from a man named Wilhelm who worked on the dig site."

"Find this American. Pay whatever is required to retrieve them."

"It is not that easy. The man appears to be connected. To the New York mafia."

"A *gangster?*"

"Yes. The Italian mob."

Magnus pulled at his beard. "Why would he want the drinking horns?"

"To resell for profit."

"Can we decipher the horns' message from the images you have?" He meant the messages carved on the horns. Messages Magnus hoped would change the world.

"We are working on that now."

"Work faster. Learn the secrets they contain. This is only the first step on our journey. On a Viking quest."

"Understood, sir. What would you have me do about our man?"

"Call the police. Report him as a suspect in having stolen from us. Make up a crime and blame him."

"What should I do if we find him?"

"Wilhelm is *flár*." The Norse word for *treacherous*. A coward who had only one fate. "Interrogate him first, then do what must be done."

The caller agreed and hung up. Magnus remained seated, tugging at his beard. He'd spent decades in search of the drinking horns, only to have them snatched away when he was so close to his destiny. He had been born for this. He would reunite splintered nations. Magnus Dahl was the only man who could restore Scandinavia. He needed the horns to do it. If not the actual horns, then the story they could reveal.

Vikings from centuries past were by and large illiterate, like most of the world in their time. Skalds, the Norse bards, sang the praises of warriors and of their people. This oral tradition kept Viking history alive. Magnus was a scholar of Viking lore, knowledgeable in the legends and tales stretching back to the earliest Vikings. Back to when one murky story had been told, one about how Vikings came to rule Scandinavia. Back to a time when Vikings were known as Visigoths.

Magnus had no idea if there was any truth to the legend, yet it never left his mind, never let him forget what might be. It was a story that, if true, could prove that Vikings were the chosen ones. A people favored by the gods and meant to rule in their ancestral homeland of Scandinavia.

The story began during the Roman Empire.

Rome stood tall against invaders for over a thousand years until the Visigoths arrived. Led by King Alaric, they sacked the eternal city in 410 A.D. and upended the existing world order. Other nations suddenly questioned their own security. The Visigoths were mobile. Where might they turn next, and could they be stopped? An army capable of bringing down Rome had never existed. Did that mean Alaric's Visigoths were the new Roman Empire? Alas, no. Alaric soon died and his Visigoths were assimilated by the cultural melting pot, yet the mystique of their strength never fully vanished.

Scandinavia was long gone now, but Magnus had dedicated his life to bringing this once-great nation back into the world. What better way to raise Scandinavia from the ashes than to hearken back to her most glorious triumph?

His ancestral country had splintered, yet it remained home to the descendants of those whose mere name had once made others tremble. Yes, Scandinavia had fallen, split into three as their people became known as Danes, Swedes and Norwegians. But to recapture their former glory, they needed only a spark, a reminder of their destiny. A destiny buried in the past but capable of restoring them to power. Magnus would use the spark hidden in two drinking horns to rekindle Scandinavia's flame and make it burn brighter than ever.

Magnus didn't speak widely of his desire to reunite Scandinavians, at least not yet. His plan included all of Scandinavia's people, though he knew not everyone would see it that way. Those who didn't understand what it meant to be part of Scandinavia would say he was elitist, that he fed only his own ambition. They couldn't be further from the truth. Magnus was a man of the people. The man who would return them to glory. He wasn't a crazed fanatic. Magnus was meant to succeed because it was his birthright.

How did he know? Magnus Dahl's first cousin was the king of Norway, and Magnus was his only living relative. The king had no children, and his wife had recently died in a skiing accident. This meant

Magnus was now first in line for the throne, a once-remote eventuality that suddenly became quite plausible. Magnus had no desire to see his cousin die, of course. He loved the man and would never hurt him. However, fate had intervened in the most unexpected way.

It began when Magnus was attending the University of Oslo. In freshman year he was randomly assigned a dormmate, a man with whom Magnus eventually shared his hopes for a reunited Scandinavia. The man had been drawn to the same idea, and was one of Magnus's earliest supporters. This same man later went into politics and became the highest elected official in Norway – the prime minister.

Ola Hanche was one of the most popular politicians in Norway. A charismatic leader whose party held the most seats in the *Storting*, Norway's parliament.

How did this alter Magnus's dream? Simple: the prime minister could, with enough support, install Magnus on the throne. The Norwegian constitution stated the executive power was vested in the king, but in truth it was vested in the government, controlled by the prime minister.

A knock sounded on Magnus's office door. "One moment," he said, standing from his chair. His plan wouldn't work unless he was right about the two drinking horns, and he wouldn't know either way until his team decoded the horn's message. Their work would allow him to read a mysterious runestone, one which could lead to the true treasure Alaric had liberated from Rome. Finding that treasure would bring Scandinavia back to life.

A Scandinavia for all Scandinavians. Led by Magnus Dahl.

Chapter 5

Brooklyn

Harry needed a second try at dialing the correct number. His fingers were shaking too much.

Ringing filled the air. He paced in his kitchen as Sara continued her work in his living room. She didn't come in and listen. This call was private, even from her.

A hard voice answered. The voice of a woman used to giving orders. "Barnes here."

"This is Harry Fox."

"You're Doyle's friend." What he could only describe as a *harrumph* followed. "Was wondering when you'd call. She said it's about an old case." Retired detective Jessica Barnes did not enjoy small talk.

"It's about my mother's death. You were the lead detective on the case." He didn't bother her with the details.

"I handled thousands of cases. Be specific."

Harry gave her the report date and an overview. "The body was found near the Hudson," he finished. "The report didn't give much more detail."

"That's 'cause there were no details to report," she fired back. He had no idea what to say next. He kept quiet. "I remember the case," Jessica said eventually. What sounded like papers shuffling came through the phone. "Says here there were no signs of a struggle or evidence of a crime."

She had the file in front of her. "Correct," Harry said. "I know this is an imposition, but could I meet with you? I have questions about my mother's death. I was young when it happened."

"Take it your father isn't around."

"He was recently murdered."

Jessica Barnes didn't miss a beat. "Sorry to hear that." It also wasn't exactly foreign in her world. "Why do you want to meet?"

"What I want to ask isn't the sort of thing you talk about over the phone."

"Doyle said you live in Brooklyn. I'm in Queens. You want to talk? Come to my part of town."

"I can be there in an hour."

Another *harrumph*, this time with less hostility. "Thought you might be antsy. Fine. I know a place." She rattled off a name and address. "I'll be there in an hour." The line went dead.

"I have to go," Harry said as he walked past Sara and grabbed the messenger bag containing everything he had on the case. "Detective Barnes agreed to meet me."

Sara turned from the drinking horns and stood without a word. She embraced him, only for a moment, then let go. "Good luck."

He wasn't good with this sort of thing. "Thanks." He indicated the drinking horns. "I have to take those to Nora tomorrow."

"I'll be finished tonight."

"See you later," he called over a shoulder. He didn't look back as his front door closed behind him. Harry engaged every last deadbolt and lock. He knew Sara understood why he didn't have much to say.

Forty-five minutes on the train later he bolted up the subway stairs into a gloomy Queens afternoon. The brisk wind snuck beneath his coat collar as he barreled around people on the sidewalk, shouldering aside those too slow for his purpose until he reached the address Jessica had given. Harry looked up and frowned. Jessica Barnes wanted to meet at a barbeque joint?

Any doubts he had were pushed away by the mouthwatering smells emanating from somewhere in or behind the building: a barbeque pit in full swing. Harry pushed through the door and found most of the red-and-white-checked tables filled and a line of customers at the counter. He kept walking because he had no idea what else to do.

"Hey, Fox."

A voice rang out in the crowd. The sort of voice that could give a wonderful *harrumph* when needed. Harry looked over his shoulder.

"Over here."

He finally spotted her. An older Black woman with one hand in the air, seated at a secluded table along the wall. An open door revealed glimpses of employees out back tending a smoker large enough to handle a woolly mammoth.

Harry made his way to the table. "Detective Barnes?"

She waved at the other chair. "Have a seat," she said.

He joined her, his back to a half-wall that blocked most of the noise. Even though fifty people were digging into ribs, chicken and brisket behind him, he and Jessica were in a little oasis of quiet back here. "Interesting place," Harry said. "You a regular?"

"Something like that." A closed accordion folder sat on the table. Jessica made no move to open it. "How do you know Agent Doyle?"

Harry let a beat pass. "We work together."

Barnes raised an eyebrow. "You're an informant."

Harry bristled. "Not exactly."

"Then what?"

"I go where she can't. Unofficially."

"Sounds sketchy," Jessica said. "But Nora vouched for you. That's the reason I'm here."

Add that to the short but weighty list of what he owed Nora Doyle. "I appreciate it. This is about my mother."

"Her *death*." The way she said it made her feelings clear.

"I just want to talk."

Jessica's lips pursed. She pulled a stick of gum from her pocket and began chewing on it like it offended her. She did not offer Harry one. "That was one of my first cases. Got promoted to detective hardly a month before we found her. Had an older detective working with me on it."

Given how much salt was in Jessica Barnes, perhaps now was the time to introduce something sweeter. "From what I hear you succeeded pretty quickly. Nora said you had the most commendations ever awarded to a female detective."

Jessica's reply would have sliced through iron. "To *any* detective." The heat in her eyes cooled. "But I'm retired." She chomped the gum. "And you shouldn't believe everything you read."

Harry lifted an eyebrow.

Jessica looked at a spot over his shoulder as she continued. "I'm sure you heard the NYPD Medal of Honor story."

"Yes," Harry said. "Highest medal the department awards."

Jessica had been off-duty making a deposit at her local bank. Three gunmen walked in, fired shotguns at the ceiling and told everyone to lie on the floor. Jessica complied along with the rest, and listened until they threatened to shoot a young mother whose child wouldn't keep quiet.

Jessica told the robbers she was a mental health professional and could calm the child. What she did instead was get behind them, pull the service pistol from her waistband and shoot all three robbers. The NYPD brass called her a hero, and so did most of New York. Jessica became a city celebrity, and for decades after, politicians wanting to appear tough on crime took photos with her, keeping her front and center in the city's mind.

Harry narrowed his eyes. One of those photos was hanging on the wall behind her. "Is that you?" he asked, pointing over her shoulder. "With the old mayor."

She didn't turn. "Yes."

"Nice afro," Harry said.

Jessica started to reach for her trim gray hair, then stopped. "A younger woman's style."

Harry looked across the wall, past other framed photos. "Those are *all* pictures of you. There's at least a dozen of them." The pictures ran the gamut of Jessica in her teen years through a photo of her retirement ceremony. The cover of the *Times* issue showing her Medal of Honor ceremony was framed and displayed in one corner.

"My parents like pictures," Jessica said.

Harry sat up in his chair. "This is *your* restaurant?"

"My parents'," she said. She indicated the messenger bag. "You want to talk about your parents or mine?"

"Right." Harry fumbled with the straps until his thin folder emerged. "This is everything I have."

"How did you get a copy of this?" Jessica's glare was like a physical punch. "Where?"

"A friend."

Jessica tilted her head. "Is that so? I wondered if you'd be trouble. I was right." Her chair squeaked as she shifted. "Ask your questions."

He didn't care if she liked him. Harry had come for answers. "Were you the lead detective on the case?"

"I already told you yes."

"This report seems short. There's almost nothing here."

"It was a crap case. Don't take it personally." She sighed, leaned closer, and began ticking items off on her fingers. "Bodies wash up on the shores of the Hudson all the time. It wasn't priority, so we got there a few hours after they found her. Time in the water destroys most evidence, which is why we didn't find much. The medical examiner returned drowning as the cause of death and the case was closed." Her eyes softened a fraction. "I'm sorry, Harry."

He didn't shout, didn't pound the table, didn't blink. "I'd be satisfied if it were the truth. It's not."

"What?"

"The person you found wasn't Dani Fox. Someone messed up."

Jessica's voice got low. "I'd be careful throwing around accusations."

"I am careful." Now he leaned closer and tapped one finger on the report. "How do I know you're wrong? The report." He opened the file and flipped it around so she could see. "Look." He pointed to the medical examiner's jotted memo that the dead woman had never given birth.

He waited. Her eyes ran over the paper once, twice. Jessica sat still. "Take it you weren't adopted."

"Nope."

Jessica closed her eyes as the muscles in her neck tightened and she took in a long breath. "It always catches up with you. Every time." Something in her expression had changed when she looked at Harry now. If he had to put a name to it, Jessica seemed tired.

"Come with me." She rose without giving him a chance to argue. He was still stuffing his file in the messenger bag when Jessica was halfway to the door, which he caught just before it closed behind her. She had nearly disappeared in the pedestrian traffic, forcing him to shoulder through the crowd to catch up.

"Where are we going?" he asked.

"A safe place."

"Safe? That was your restaurant. How's it not safe?"

"Because I know everyone there."

She didn't speak for several blocks, then turned abruptly and pushed through the door of a small bar. Harry followed her, blinking rapidly in the dim light. Round stools stood in front of a long wooden bar polished by countless elbows. Neon beer signs flickered on the walls while a jukebox played in one corner. The sounds of a pool game came from somewhere in back. One bartender stood leaning against the counter, his arms crossed. He dipped his head when Jessica walked in.

"Keep up," Jessica said.

Harry followed her. "Two beers," she called out as they passed the bartender. He delivered them a moment after Jessica and Harry had settled into a tall-backed booth. Jessica took a long pull on hers. "And two more," she yelled.

She met Harry's gaze only after the second round arrived and they were alone. "We can talk better here."

36

"That bartender seems like a friend."

"He can keep his mouth shut. Can't say the same for my parents' customers."

He took a drink. He waited.

Jessica twisted her beer bottle slowly. "I had a bad feeling about the older detective training me from the start. His name was O'Sullivan. Connor O'Sullivan. Irish as they came. Old school, learned how to be a cop from men who fought in the war." She waited. "World War Two."

Harry nodded and took another drink.

"Connor was close to retirement. A lot of those men were at the time. It was a changing of the guard, and let me tell you, the guard needed to be changed. Connor already had one foot out the door. He just didn't care anymore. The world Connor came from didn't see anything wrong with taking a few bucks on the side here and there. Never too much, and never in a case that mattered."

"Like a woman's body washed up by the river."

"Connor O'Sullivan never did anything he thought would hurt anyone. He was right, for the most part." A long beat while Jessica appeared to wrestle with her thoughts. "I didn't see what happened. I only heard it."

"We were at the scene," she continued. "If you can even call it that. There were a couple uniforms, the two of us, and the team from the morgue. It was night and we were beside a bridge. I remember one of the uniforms called Connor over, said someone needed to talk to him. I didn't think anything of it. I was canvassing the scene while he talked over by the bridge abutment. I never saw the man he spoke with."

"What does this have to do with my mother's case?"

"I couldn't see the guy, but the wind was blowing the right way. It carried their conversation to me. I heard the man offer Connor money to misidentify the body. He agreed to do it."

Harry nearly launched himself out of the booth. "Who was the guy?"

Jessica held his eyes until he sat down again. "Beats me," she said. "I only heard his voice. Never saw his face."

"Did you ask Connor about it?" Jessica's face made it clear she had not. "Can you describe him?" Harry asked.

"Average height, average build. No accent." Jessica shook her head. "He looked like any other guy. I don't know who he was."

"But you heard him talking. Would you recognize his voice if you heard it?"

"You're talking twenty years ago, kid." Jessica called for another beer. "I might. I have a good memory. But you'll never find him. Never. I tried."

"How hard?"

"It was wrong, and I let it happen. The worst part is I have no idea why Connor did it. Greed, sure, but why lie? I thought it was just another drowning, nothing special."

"Why do you think someone would bribe him to misidentify the body?" Harry asked.

"That's easy. Whoever paid Connor wanted people to think your mother was dead."

The truth smacked him square in the chin. *Someone faked her death.* Or at least it seemed that way.

"I can see your mind going. Does all of this mean your mom was still alive when we found the body? The answer is it doesn't prove anything."

"How can you be sure?"

"What I can tell you is when someone fakes a death, it doesn't usually mean good things. Somebody wanted her to disappear."

A wave of emotion had rolled over him, leaving in its wake a deep emptiness. He had always been certain his mother had drowned in the Hudson. Now, he knew she hadn't.

Jessica's words were softer when she spoke again. "It's a lot. You still want to know why."

"Yes."

"Tell me about your mom. If I know more about her maybe I can help you figure out who might have wanted her to disappear."

Another wave of emotion rolled over him, one he didn't want to examine too closely. "I really didn't know her that well. I was too young." Where to start? "She came from England. Her father was English and her mother was Pakistani. They relocated to America when my mom was little. She met my dad through his work in archaeology when he spoke at the college she attended. He wasn't much older than the students."

The memory of this story lifted his spirits. "Apparently my mom knew what she wanted from day one. She asked him out, and before long they were engaged. Her parents weren't thrilled, from what I understand."

"Bad blood between her parents and your father."

"Something like that. I never met them."

"What about your father's parents?"

"They died when I was a baby."

"How did your mom deal with your father's legal trouble?"

"You mean how did she take it when he was arrested for dealing in stolen antiquities."

Jessica didn't blink. "That's what I mean."

Harry shrugged. "Beats me. I thought she died before it all happened, so I don't think she ever knew."

That got Jessica's attention. "Your father never told you the details?"

"He didn't." Harry found his jaw was clenched. "Said it was over and nothing could change it."

"Seems you have thoughts on the subject."

"My dad wasn't helping those antiquities thieves when he was arrested. He was framed." Harry didn't say he knew this because the former head of the New York mafia had told him. "But I can't prove it." *Not yet, at least.* Clearing Fred's name was still on his list.

"I believe you. It would help if you told me what did happen."

"My dad was hired to authenticate a Greek artifact tied to Archimedes or Zeus, which he did. When he went to the sale, the cops showed up and busted everyone. That's right around when my mom supposedly died."

"Was it before or after?"

Harry frowned. "Before. He wasn't in jail when she died."

Jessica closed her eyes, as though taking mental notes. "Go on."

Harry shrugged. "He was there when the cops showed up. Everyone was arrested. The cops threw the book at them all." He paused. "Do you guys actually say that?"

"Not really. What happened next?"

"They charged him with anything they could, serious jail time. With my mother gone, he took a plea. Ninety days for artifacts trafficking."

"And your mother was dead at this point?"

"I think so, but like I said, my dad never talked about it. And if I'm being honest, I really didn't want to talk about it either. Not the best time in my life."

"It's interesting." Jessica looked past him as though she'd find the answer inside this murky bar.

"You think any of that matters?"

"Maybe. Maybe not." She glanced at him, then looked away. Lost in thought, perhaps bored. He couldn't tell.

"It's been too long," Harry said, stirring the pot. "Maybe if you'd reported O'Sullivan back then you'd have actually found the truth."

She swung her gaze back to him. Steel flashed in her eyes. "I was wrong, kid. Damned wrong. I made a mistake and I've never forgotten it." Jessica sat up straight, her face a mask. "You should know a few things before you judge me. I started as a patrol officer. Eventually I worked my way up – on the level – to be the only female detective in the precinct. A Black female to boot."

"I'm sure that wasn't easy," Harry said. "Doesn't mean you get a free pass for looking the other way."

She went on like he hadn't spoken. "I hadn't been on the job for three months when we got this case. Connor was on his way out, like I said. He was pissed about babysitting me, used to joke about it. An old

Irish guy waiting on a little Black girl. How times had changed, he'd say. He was an ass, but he was smart. He showed me the ropes. Care to guess what he told me most often? To keep my head down. Don't make waves. He may not have liked me, but he cared about the force, and in his world the fastest way up and the way to stay alive was to not rock the boat."

"Which meant you didn't rat anyone out."

"That's the gist of it." Jessica lifted her beer bottle. Empty. "I wish I'd had the guts to say something back then. I didn't, and now you're here."

Harry jumped when she shouted at the bartender for another round. "Want to make it right?"

She barked the furthest thing from a laugh he'd ever heard. "How? You gonna tell me it's okay? That the biggest mistake I ever made doesn't matter?"

"No." The quiet force in his words made her go still. "You seem like a decent cop, so living with it will have to be enough. Can't change it now." The waiter appeared, set two more bottles down and did not linger. "But we can move ahead. There's a way you can make it up to my mom."

Her eyes narrowed. "What do you want?"

"Help. You're Detective Jessica Barnes. One of the most decorated the city has ever seen. I read about you. You're for real. The kind of person who can find a crack in a twenty-year-old case." He took a pull on his beer. "You're exactly the person I need."

Pool balls cracked. Music rang out from the jukebox. "That thought would touch my heart if I had one left." Jessica sat back as far as the booth allowed and crossed her arms. "I'll help you. I'm retired, got nothing else going on. Now, listen up." She leaned forward again and stuck a finger in his face so fast he jumped. "You tell anyone about me helping you, I'm done. You mention my name to anybody I don't approve, I'm done. Understand?" He said he did. "I'll dig around on my end. Cops don't like it when you poke around in their business.

Even less when you suggest they did something wrong. I'm guessing Doyle told you this too."

"She did. She also said you were the best."

"Tell her to stop kissing my backside." Jessica paused. "Start kicking someone else's instead."

Harry's lip curled up in a smirk. "She's doing plenty of that."

"Good. I'll handle my side. You go talk to a guy." Jessica pulled a notepad and pencil from her pocket like a true detective. "This is the medical examiner who handled your mom's case. Tell him I sent you. He's still active." The sheet of paper ripped out and came at Harry. "The guy's brilliant. Memory like an elephant. Ask him about the person who identified the body. O'Sullivan knowingly misidentified the corpse at the scene first, but someone else had to confirm the identification."

Harry nearly fell off the bench. "How did I miss that?"

"Because you're not a cop." Jessica tapped the paper. "Now's the time to start thinking like one. Call me after you talk to this guy. We'll get to the bottom of this. Together."

Chapter 6

Brooklyn

A red leaf floated toward the sidewalk outside Harry's apartment. It hung for a moment outside the window, almost as though it were looking in on the woman with honey-colored eyes seated at a table staring unblinking at a computer screen.

Sara Hamed was a trained academic. She believed in the laws of nature, the rationality of science. Yet for one very brief instant, she couldn't believe her eyes.

"I can read it." Which is exactly what she expected, though thinking you could do it and actually unraveling a centuries-old mystery were two different things.

A runestone stared back at her from the computer screen, one from a long-forgotten town in Germany, a runestone that had been built to last and still stood among the skeletal remains of foundations and a tiny graveyard. That the runes were considered unreadable had been more of a curiosity than anything. Until now. The scholars who had looked at this stone and then turned away had no idea what they concealed.

A clean sheet of paper lay in front of her. Another page filled with translated runes lay beside it as Sara methodically worked through the German runestone, translating each rune in turn, checking her work after each line. Time seemed to stop, the world fading away, and Sara acknowledged a thought, one she had pushed away before. She loved being an Egyptologist, with a front-row seat at the rich pageant of her nation's history. Sara actually got dirt on her hands as she worked. She had never thought it could get better than that. Until she met Harry Fox.

Recovering history was nothing like revealing it for the first time. That's what she did with him, and what had brought her across an ocean. For how long? Time would tell. An email she'd received from the American Museum of Natural History's human resources team this morning would play a role either way.

She blinked and tilted her head. The first few lines on the runestone told her a familiar story. After that, everything changed. One formerly indecipherable rune after another was now translated on her sheet. She wrote, on and on, until at one rune her hand stopped moving. The pencil slipped from her hand, rolled across the paper and dropped out of sight.

Harry barged through the front door and Sara jumped out of her chair. He looked over at her face. "You okay?" he asked. She didn't respond, so Harry asked if she wanted a drink.

She just nodded. *This has to be a mistake.* She picked up the fallen pencil and continued translating while Harry noisily stomped about the kitchen before returning with two beers in hand. She didn't acknowledge hers when he set it before her.

"I met that detective," Harry said.

The words entered her ears but didn't make it to her brain. She retrieved the pencil and kept writing. He said nothing, sipping his beer, until she laid her pencil down again. "This is incredible," she said.

Harry sat down at the table. "What is?"

"I'm deciphering the runestone in Germany. The one nobody could read before now." She tapped the page. "Ataulf left it."

"That's neat. No, wait," he said quickly. "That's incredible."

She looked up for the first time. His face gave her pause. Harry, who had survived being shot at or otherwise nearly killed on a weekly basis, looked different. He looked *excited*. "Where were you?"

Lines creased his forehead. "To meet the detective. Listen to this."

"I'm all ears." She turned to him, picked up her beer and took a sip.

"Another detective on the case took a bribe to misidentify the body as my mom."

That broke through her runestone spell. "Bribed?"

Harry relayed Jessica's story, along with her instruction to contact the medical examiner who had handled the case. "I'm meeting him tomorrow morning," Harry said. "He still works for the city."

"Hopefully his memory is as sharp as Detective Barnes said."

Harry stood, took a few steps, then returned to his chair. "I can't do anything else right now." His hands balled into fists. "I'd go to his house tonight if I knew where he lived. He has to remember something. Anything."

Sara reached out and took Harry's fists in her hands until he relaxed. "You're doing all you can, and it's working. Give yourself a break."

"You think I can relax now? I'm certain my mom didn't drown in the Hudson." He nearly stood again, but she squeezed his hands and he sat back. "So what happened to her?"

"One more night and you may know." Sara patted his arm. "You need a distraction. Lucky for you I have a story of my own right here."

He frowned, then it seemed to hit him. "The runestone. You translated it." Harry ran a hand through his hair. "I'm sorry, I wasn't really listening."

She pulled him over and kissed him. Quickly, because she had things to say. "I forgive you."

Harry was grinning when she pulled away. Sara tapped the papers in front of her. "This runestone tells a story you won't believe."

"Try me."

She turned the paper so he could see it. "I was right about the drinking horns being a code. A code that allows me to read these runes."

Harry jumped up. "I have to take those horns to Nora in the morning."

"She can wait until after your meeting with the medical examiner. Sit and listen." She waited until he did. "Ataulf created this German runestone. It talks about the Visigoths, beginning with their sack of Rome and continuing on with their migration north." She looked up from the paper. "These runes couldn't be deciphered, but that doesn't mean scholars didn't learn anything at all from the stone. We know the messages were carved at different times. The weathering on the rock indicates part of the message was written around the time Alaric died, while the rest was added centuries later. What does that suggest?"

"I don't know," he said.

"That this runestone is not just a story. The Visigoths returned several centuries later and added to the story. That suggests it's meant to serve at least two purposes."

Now he was with her. "To tell their story, and to stand through time."

"Yes. This stone is larger than most others." She pushed a lock of auburn hair behind one ear. "This stone is a marker."

"For what?"

"The first section of runes tells the known story of King Alaric sacking Rome, and tells it in greater detail than the horns. For instance, it mentions a portion of the treasure they stole." Sara pointed to the translation on her paper. "Look at this."

Harry leaned over. He went still. When he looked up again he was no longer wearing the face of a man wrestling with the demons of his past. It was the Harry Fox she'd met in Germany. "Could it be a different menorah?"

"Unlikely. How many other Temple Menorahs did the Romans steal?"

In 70 A.D. the Roman army laid siege to the city of Jerusalem for five disastrous months until they breached the city walls and burned most of Jerusalem to the ground. One of the buildings destroyed was the Second Jewish Temple. The city's treasures were plundered, including the famed Temple Menorah, a seven-branched candelabra of pure gold that stood over five feet tall and weighed hundreds of pounds. Forgetting the monetary value, the menorah's worth as a cultural pillar couldn't be measured.

Sara pointed at the runestone on her computer screen. "This stone tells us Alaric and Ataulf stole the Temple Menorah, which confirms what historians have long suspected. You know the Arch of Titus depicts Romans carrying the menorah into the city after the defeat of Jerusalem."

Harry knew this story. "The arch was built ten years after the parade Rome threw to show off their new treasures. Contemporary evidence, and it's still standing. The evidence is," he suppressed a grin, "rock-solid."

"The arch shows the menorah was taken from Jerusalem to Rome in 71 A.D., where it likely remained for over three centuries, until the conquering Visigoths arrived in 410 A.D."

"I'm guessing there's even more to your story than the menorah," Harry said.

"This German runestone was placed not long after Alaric sacked Rome. The Visigoths left Rome and traveled north to Scandinavia on a route passing through Germany. This stone also references Alaric's death."

"Which happened shortly after he left Rome."

"That also fits the known timeline. However, the latter parts of the stone were written hundreds of years later. I think descendants of the Visigoths returned and added to the stone using this code."

"Why?"

"The top portion of the stone talks about taking Rome, while the lower portion focuses on Ataulf as king. He became king after Alaric died and led most of their people north. Some Visigoths went to France, others to the Iberian peninsula, though most followed Ataulf north to Scandinavia."

"Where they eventually became known as Vikings."

"Yes. The stone talks again about Ataulf's intense desire to be reunited with his dead son. It says Ataulf planned a massive burial mound for himself."

"Not unusual for a king."

"No, but the phrasing is odd. It says *story*, not *memory*."

"Why is that odd?"

Sara couldn't explain her intuition, but years of experience had taught her to ignore such feelings at her peril. "I'm still working on that. What's more exciting is that the stone specifically references Ataulf's burial mound." Harry appeared unimpressed. "That's important," Sara continued, "because Ataulf's tomb has never been found. Now we know it exists."

"I see. Good thing you know a guy who might be able to help find it."

"Good thing you know a trained Egyptologist who can find such locations without getting shot at."

Harry was undeterred. "The shots usually miss."

"Until they don't. What we need to decipher are the directions left in this stone. The runes say much more than it appears at first read." Here she put her finger on the page, following the words as she read.

King Ataulf holds Thor's hammer and the gods' power. Thor led Ataulf to the island of Norse trade where no Arabs can plunder. Ataulf lies in the center hill above where Njoror claimed the warship Orn. Thor's power is with Ataulf.

"Thor's hammer?" Harry asked. "That has to be a metaphor. Thor was a god. He wasn't real."

"Of course it's a metaphor, but for what? Ataulf followed the Norse gods. *Thor's hammer* would be considered sacred words, receiving the utmost respect."

"If I had something like that, know what I'd do with it?" Harry asked. "Put it somewhere safe."

"A hidden burial vault, perhaps?"

"You said the German stone was a marker. That makes it a starting point." He indicated her scrawled translation. "Any idea where it tells us to go?"

She was just coming to terms with having pulled back the curtain on this dark portion of history, and here was Harry, ready to give chase. "Why is it everything you touch leads to gold?"

Harry shook his head. "Just lucky, I guess. And don't forget the bullets, spears, deep pits and bad guys that usually show up."

"Any bad guys on this trail are long dead," Sara said. She closed her eyes, took a breath to focus. "Right. What does it all mean? The latter part of this runestone was inscribed long after Ataulf's death. That's confirmed in the line saying he *lies in the center hill*. But I'm getting ahead of myself. What is the *island of Norse trade where no Arabs can plunder*? To understand this line, we need to remember what the Vikings did best."

"Plunder and pillage?"

She gave him a look. "*Sail*. Vikings were arguably the world's most successful seafaring explorers. They traveled to North America centuries before any Europeans. While some view them as brutes who spent all of their time raiding, in truth Vikings were proficient traders whose exploration enabled them to build trade routes across the globe." She took a breath. "When Ataulf led his people to Scandinavia, the Visigoths, or Vikings, weren't a large enough group to compete with the existing Arabic trade network. Arabic traders controlled the Mediterranean. The Visigoths were fierce, but they didn't have enough men or sufficient knowledge to defeat them. In order to avoid fighting a losing war, they established alternate trade routes through the Baltic Sea and the surrounding river networks. Those new routes took them past the coast of what we now call Sweden."

"And also past the coasts of quite a few other countries. Why does Sweden stand out?"

"Ataulf is buried in a place safe from Arabs. That's what *the island of Norse trade where no Arabs can plunder* references. We have to find a location that the Visigoths would have deemed safe, a place they wouldn't be threatened. Sweden is far enough removed from the center of Arab Mediterranean dominance that the Visigoths, and later Vikings, would have been relatively safe from attack there."

Harry wasn't buying it. "There has to be more than that."

"There is. The reason I'm so confident is here." She tapped one word on her translation. "*Orn.*"

"A warship?"

"Not just any warship. One I've heard of before. The stone tells us *Ataulf lies*, or is buried, *in the center hill above where Njoror claimed the warship Orn.* Njoror is the Norse god of the sea."

"The *Orn* sank," Harry said. "Njoror claimed it."

Sara stood. "The Vikings left their mark on the world in many ways. Runestones are perhaps the most familiar example, as they've provided a major source of modern knowledge about the Viking culture. Runestones also served as tombstones, historical markers, memorials." She pulled up a new image on her computer screen, that of a weathered runestone on a grassy hillside. "This is one of thousands that still stand."

"What's so special about this one?"

"It sits on an island in the Baltic Sea just off the coast of Sweden. The island is Gotland, and it has Viking burial grounds, along with the ruins of Viking settlements. Today it even has a functioning Viking village for tourists. Most importantly, this runestone is on Gotland." She pulled up another image of the runestone. "What do you see in the background?"

"The ocean."

"This runestone overlooks the sea because it sits on a hill. If you stand in front of the runestone and look past it toward the sea, you're looking at the very spot where a Viking warship sank fifteen centuries ago."

"How in the world can you know that?"

"Because this runestone is a memorial to the sailors who died when that warship sank. It happened in Ataulf's time." Her voice dropped. "Their warship? The *Orn.*"

"You think it's a trail the Visigoths left marking *Thor's hammer.* They didn't want it to be lost."

"The Visigoths clearly valued this *Thor's hammer* enough to leave markers leading to it. Markers built to last. Norse mythology holds that when the world ends there will be a great battle or similar calamitous event called Ragnarök. Slain warriors will return from Valhalla, gods will fight and it will be chaos. Once this battle ends, the world will return, cleansed and ready to start anew."

"Ataulf wanted the trail his people left to last through Ragnarök."

"Or perhaps he believed his son would be reanimated, either alone or alongside him. Either way, he left a trail. A path to find a great treasure. A path going through Gotland."

"Ataulf's burial mound is in Gotland. And no one's found it yet."

Sara pointed at the screen. "Do you want to go to Sweden with me?"

Harry's face lit up. "I do. But not now. I can't leave my mom's case behind again."

She'd expected nothing less. "Ataulf has been waiting for over a millennium. A few more days won't matter." Sara picked up her notes. "We're the only people who can read this. It's not as though anyone else is looking for him."

Half of a smile returned to his lips. "You're right. So let's go to Sweden – as soon as I know what happened to my mother." He stood. "I'm going through the case notes on my mom's file again before I see the medical examiner tomorrow morning. I can't miss anything."

Sara wanted to say something else, to share a more personal victory. One with implications for them both. She started to, but Harry's mind was already elsewhere, focused on his personal quest. She understood. Harry's entire past had been upended. Picking up the pieces mattered, almost as much as figuring out how to put them together again to reveal the truth.

Telling him she'd been offered the position at the American Museum of Natural History could wait. She needed time to decide if it was the right move. Not for him. For her, and whatever she wanted to come next.

Chapter 7

Manhattan

Harry stood outside the medical examiner's office door holding a cup of overpriced coffee hot enough to scald, a heat he didn't feel. He'd left Sara sleeping when he slipped out the door just after sunrise. Although the medical examiner's office was open for business around the clock, the man himself didn't get in until around nine. Harry would wait.

He sipped his drink, yelped at the heat, then blew on it until it finally cooled. The caffeine kicked in and he forced his thoughts elsewhere, if only for a moment. At any other time, Sara discovering a lost Visigoth message would have had him preparing for a trip to Sweden. The reference to *Thor's hammer* could be many things. A treasure. A weapon. A manuscript or another runestone. The one thing he knew for certain was that it would be valuable, the sort of relic Joey Morello would approve Harry chasing without hesitation. Goodness knows Joey needed something positive in his life, with his father's killer still free and the Cana family pushing more and more into Morello turf. Precarious didn't begin to describe Joey's hold on the seat of power.

To find Thor's hammer, whatever it was, would bring a shot of prestige to the Morello crew, along with an injection of cash. Nora wouldn't be happy, but he'd just found those drinking horns for her – horns he would drop off at her office today – and she couldn't argue with the truth that this relic hunt could be considered part of his "undercover" work for her. Which, all of a sudden, was something he actually did.

"May I help you?"

Harry nearly launched his drink onto a man who had approached on silent feet and now stood beside him.

"I'm here to meet Dr. Kerr. I'm Harry Fox."

The man was clean-shaven, sporting a bow tie visible at the collar of an overcoat that stretched nearly to the floor. The briefcase he carried looked to have survived several wars only partially unscathed.

"Come in." Keys rattled as he unlocked the door, a clouded glass affair with *Dr. Jerry Kerr, Medical Examiner* stenciled across the front. The man pointed to a chair. "Have a seat."

A sterile waiting room welcomed him; there were no magazines or complimentary coffee machines in sight. Two battered plastic chairs sat next to a water cooler. A large clock hung on industrially painted walls of a color best described as upchuck green. Harry took a seat and avoided looking at the clock. His messenger bag went on the chair beside him.

The man disappeared down a hallway. Perhaps two minutes passed before he returned, walking with a slow, deliberate pace. The muted sodium lights flickered overhead. The man stopped inside the doorframe. "I'm Jerry Kerr."

Harry shot out of his chair. "Thank you for seeing me. I know you're busy, and I promise I won't take much of your time."

"Jessica told me it was important," Jerry Kerr said. "She didn't say why."

"It's a personal matter. I want to speak with you about a case you handled."

"When was it?"

"Roughly twenty years ago."

To his credit, Kerr didn't laugh. "That's a long time."

"Detective Barnes said you have an impressive memory."

Kerr chuckled. "She may have exaggerated a tad. However, when she asks for a favor, I do it. Come back to my office."

Harry followed the doctor down a hallway of the same enchanting

53

color as the outer office. More sodium lights were overhead, and as they passed several closed doors the faint scent of industrial cleaning agents hung in the air.

"In here." Kerr led Harry into a spacious office. Bookshelves lined the walls, wooden shelves filled with medical tomes and other books Harry couldn't begin to decipher. A computer sat atop the doctor's desk, beside a single notepad and pen. No files, no folders, nothing even remotely approaching clutter. The degrees and other assorted testaments to Kerr's achievements hung neatly in one corner. Framed photos of Kerr at varying stages of life covered one wall. The older Kerr got, the more children and grandchildren appeared alongside him.

"Have a seat." Kerr gestured to a chair across from his desk. "What case brings you here?" he asked as he lowered himself into a well-used chair.

"My mother's."

"I see. I'm sorry for your loss."

"Did Detective Barnes tell you anything about this case?"

"Jessica told me this should be handled in the strictest confidence. Nothing you say to me will leave this room." Kerr stretched his arms to either side. "You may speak freely."

Harry met Dr. Kerr's eyes. His hands tightened on the chair arms. *Just go for it.* "A body was found by the Hudson." He gave the specific date. "Female, around thirty years of age, no sign of foul play. Detective Barnes and her partner responded. His name was—"

"—Connor O'Sullivan." Kerr closed his eyes, as though watching a reel of the experience play on the back of his eyelids. "It was a routine examination, if memory serves. Adult female, perhaps thirty years of age. Dark hair, skin tone suggestive of Middle Eastern heritage. No signs of trauma. My report identified drowning as the cause of death. Accidental." Kerr opened his eyes. "I believe those are the relevant points."

"Did you review the file before I came here?"

"No."

"Your memory is incredible."

Kerr shrugged. "So I've been told. What questions do you have?"

Harry did not pull out his copy of the file. A feeling in his gut told him to keep that hidden for now. "Are you able to tell if a woman has given birth when you complete an autopsy?"

"Yes, in several ways. I inspect the cervix, locate a scar from a cesarean birth or perhaps marks on her hip bones. It's quite rudimentary."

"You couldn't miss those signs?"

Kerr frowned. "No, I would not miss them."

"That's why I'm here." Harry waited for his heart to stop thudding. "I'm not here to question your work. I just want to find the truth about my mother."

Lines creased Jerry's forehead, his eyes narrowing. "The deceased woman had not given birth. I made a note of it on my report."

"Which proves that woman wasn't my mother."

"You were not adopted?" Kerr asked. Harry shook his head. "You're certain?"

"My father told me the story about how my mother spent twenty-four hours in labor with me. I'm certain."

"Then the identification of the body as Dani Fox was incorrect."

"Do you remember who made the identification?"

"Detective O'Sullivan would have made the initial identification," Kerr said. "Then an individual familiar with the deceased would provide confirmation. That's protocol."

Harry leaned closer to Kerr. "Do you remember who it was?"

"I don't. You would have to review the autopsy file."

"Do you have it?"

"Of course. Records from that time are in hard copy in storage here."

Harry's chest grew tight. "The report would include the name of the person who came to identify the body, wouldn't it?"

"It would."

"May I see it?"

"As soon as you have a court order."

Harry blinked. "What?"

"Autopsy reports are confidential. Only immediate family can receive them without a court order. And we have just established you are not immediate family to the woman I examined."

Harry's stomach dropped. The doctor was right. Harry had just torpedoed his own request. "Can you look at it for me?"

"Not if I want to keep my job."

"Can't you look and tell me who it was? I don't have to see the report."

Kerr folded his hands and leaned over the desk. "I sympathize with you. Truly. If I could assist, I would. The best thing I can tell you is to go to the police and tell them what you told me. I won't ask how you learned about the note – which I wrote by hand on the autopsy report – but I will say you have a very persuasive case. Detective Barnes can advise you on how to get an order. Get one, come back and I will be happy to share the file with you."

Heat flashed in his gut, urging him to do something unwise. "I see." It took every bit of self-control for him to stand up from the chair. "I'll do that. Thank you."

Harry let himself out. The hot anger in his stomach hadn't dissipated, so he gave it an outlet. Stepping into the corridor outside the waiting room, he walked out of earshot and called Detective Barnes. She answered on the first ring and Harry told her the entire spiel. "Any idea who I can ask to get a court order?"

"That's garbage and he knows it. Getting an order could take months." She groaned. "I can't believe he's making you do this."

"I just walked past the records office," Harry said. "The autopsy file is behind that door."

"You're still at his office? Inside the building?" Harry said he was. "You seem like a man who takes advantage of opportunity." Harry couldn't argue. "Go back towards Kerr's office and wait around the corner," she said.

Jessica explained what to do next. Harry didn't have a chance to agree or even question her before the line went dead. Hustling back through the door with Jerry Kerr's name on it, Harry turned and moved to a corner just down the hall, rounding it and then pressing his back to the wall. *Make this count.* He checked his shoes were tied, then waited, one eye poking around the corner, locked on Jerry Kerr's office.

Moments later Kerr's door opened and he raced out – running like a doctor who had just received a phone call from a former colleague telling them about an accident outside the building where multiple victims required immediate medical attention.

Kerr dashed into the stairwell and vanished. Harry bolted for the medical examiner's office door, which was slowly swinging shut again. Harry hit the gas. It was going to be close. He dove for the door and wedged two fingers between it and the frame an instant before it shut.

He bit back a yelp of pain as his shoulder collided with the door, shoving it open again. He shoved his wounded fingers under an armpit, slipped into the room and pulled the door shut behind him. The lights were still on inside. Harry paused, listening. Silence.

He looked at the clock on the wall. "Two minutes."

Down the hall he ran. He'd been skeptical when Jessica had told him she could get him into the records room right then, that she'd later tell Kerr that her call had been a mistake. Jessica had bought Harry a few minutes of time. He had to make it count.

"The records should be organized by last name," Jessica had told him. "If they're rearranged or he's moved them around, you'll be in trouble. Don't take the file. Jerry Kerr might buy me mixing up streets, but if he suspects your mother's file was tampered with, we're both cooked."

"You get him out of there," Harry had replied. "I'll handle the rest."

He pushed through the door with *RECORDS* inscribed across it, reaching for the switch. The overhead lights burst to life, and Harry stopped.

He was in an airplane hangar. Filing cabinets stretched to the horizon. The hangar may have only been one story tall, but there were hundreds of filing cabinets in here, each one six feet tall and half as deep.

"Two minutes," he reminded himself. With a quiet sigh of relief, he found that the files were in alphabetical order. The closest cabinet had a large *Aa – Ac* on it. Harry sprinted down the aisle, weaving between rows until he found a cabinet with *E* on it. A quick turn back toward the front of the room brought him to the *F* row, and then it was a mad dash to the first cabinet with *Fo*. Three entire cabinets were devoted to that sequence. He went to the last one and opened the bottom drawer. "It's gotta be at the end."

File folders dusty with age rustled as he scanned names until he hit a *Fowkes*. Next came *Fowler*, then *Fowles*. He jumped to the middle drawer. *Fowling, Fowlinger*, so many wrong names. A glance at his watch found one minute gone. He looked down and stopped.

Dani Fox.

Slimmer than most, her entire report fit into a single weathered folder. Out it came. Harry had thirty seconds left and no clue where to start. He flipped to the end. The last page had a number of signatures on it, a row of them scrawled beneath lines of text. A heading over one of the lines screamed to him. *Identification.*

The name *Connor O'Sullivan* came first, his title and badge number beside a scrawled signature. After that, *Jerry Kerr*. The next line was labeled *Verification*. The name written above it made no sense.

"Wyatt Fox?" He'd never heard that name in his life. A comically simple signature was beside it, what looked like an elementary student's attempt at signing their name. The line beside it turned Harry's guts to ice. The line labeled *Relationship to Deceased*. On the line was a single word, written by the same person who claimed to be Wyatt Fox. *Brother.*

Dani Fox's body had been identified by her brother. Except Dani Fox was an only child.

Time was up. Harry snapped a picture of the signature page on his phone before shoving it back into place, closing the file drawer and running.

Chapter 8

Oslo

It began when Magnus Dahl received the analysis of the stolen drinking horns. An analysis completed by men on The Scandinavians' payroll, experts on Viking and Visigoth history. The two experts verified that the writing on King Alaric's and Lord Ataulf's two horns told an identical story in two different languages.

The re-enactment after-party had become a members-only gathering, families having departed, leaving only the re-enactors, men now intent on filling and emptying their beverage containers as many times as possible. Magnus could handle his mead, yet he didn't enjoy losing his senses, so most of what he drank was water. When the message from the two Scandinavian historians came through, Magnus ducked out a side door and into a waiting car.

"Let's go home," he said to the driver.

Magnus opened the email and read it twice. Why would Alaric and Ataulf create a secret language? The horns told the same story, one in runes any historian could read, the other in a previously unreadable language. A code his historians had cracked by comparing the two horns. The code must serve a purpose. As he read it again, a nagging thought came to mind. The encoded words from Ataulf's horn somehow looked familiar. *I've seen this writing before. Where?*

He was halfway home when it hit him. "Germany," Magnus said. "It's in Germany."

He'd seen these runes before – on an indecipherable runestone in

Germany. Magnus nearly smashed his phone when it couldn't locate a readable image of the runestone. When his car pulled to a stop outside his home, he threw the door open and ran inside, not even taking his muddy period Viking boots off before rushing through to his office and flinging himself down at his desk. It was the work of a minute on his laptop, to locate a clear image of the German runestone.

"Praise Odin." Magnus picked up a pen and, using the translation summary sent to him by the historians, began deciphering. Methodically, one word at a time, until the end. Then he sat back, one hand pulling on his beard. "This story is only the beginning."

He read the message again. The Visigoths sacking Rome and making off with countless treasures, including the Temple Menorah. Alaric's death, the new King Ataulf leading the Visigoths to Scandinavia. Theodosius dying and Ataulf's desire to reunite with him. Magnus stared at the phrase *Thor's hammer* for several long seconds, and his jaw tightened as he read about Ataulf's burial mound and the ship *Orn*. A ship wrecked near Ataulf's grave.

Magnus was a student of Viking history, the past of his nation and people. He knew of the ship *Orn*. It was mentioned elsewhere in the world of Viking history, including on a runestone in Sweden. A stone that told Magnus where he could find Ataulf.

"Gotland," he said to himself, referencing a Swedish island where Vikings once ruled, and where the ship *Orn* sank long ago. An island on which a runestone memorial to the lost sailors still stood, on a hill overlooking the sea where the ship had foundered. That's where he would find Ataulf. He stood to pack his bags for the trip before he remembered.

His fist slammed on the desk like one of Thor's thunderbolts. "The ceremony." One of the royal family's annual celebrations, a chance for the country to gather and celebrate their nation. He couldn't miss it. Prime Minister Ola Hanche wouldn't hear of it. Without Magnus staying in the public eye, his chances to resurrect their nation in the future would diminish.

Magnus twisted his coarse beard hair. "I will send Jacob." Jacob Pedersen was one of Magnus's most trusted employees, a capable man in whose veins Viking blood ran strong, a man willing to do anything to help Magnus reunite Scandinavia. A level-headed man Magnus trusted with any task, for Jacob possessed an uncannily even keel, no matter how tempestuous the waters surrounding him.

Yet even Jacob couldn't achieve this alone. Jacob had a broad knowledge of his ancestors, but this mission required an expert on the history of Scandinavia. Magnus knew such a man. A man he did not want to trust, but now he had no choice.

Magnus first dialed Jacob's number. "Are you alone?"

"I am," Jacob said.

"The two drinking horns," Magnus said. "They are the key to a puzzle I need you to help unravel." Magnus relayed his decoding of the horns, the message about Alaric and Ataulf's travels, and the connection to a previously unreadable runestone in Germany. "I want to send you to Gotland to investigate the stone."

"I can leave at once," Jacob said. "Are you coming?"

"My presence is required at a ceremony in Oslo. The prime minister would not be pleased if I skipped it."

"Should I wait until after the event so you can join me?"

"No. I need you to go as soon as possible."

"I can leave tonight. Do you anticipate anyone else will be searching? People outside our organization?"

"As you know, our man Wilhelm tried to sell the horns to American mobsters. I doubt gangsters have an interest in our story, though they may try to sell the horns. Leave tomorrow to ensure our advantage." Magnus bit his lip. "I want Ingvar Larsen to join you. His knowledge of Scandinavian history is second to none."

A pause. "Are you sure his involvement is wise? His appearances have been creating more backlash recently. More crowds as well."

Ingvar Larsen was a frequent speaker at events hosted by fringe elements ideologically adjacent to The Scandinavian organization, though officially Magnus had no affiliation with Ingvar or the extremist audiences who cheered him on. Ingvar talked out of both sides of his mouth, always depending on plausible deniability when his followers went too far. Ingvar never explicitly advocated for actions Magnus found distasteful, but neither did he disavow those positions. As such, the extremists were emboldened.

Magnus and Ingvar had had a few public disagreements, none too serious, for Ingvar knew Magnus was his ticket to the mainstream. Compromise was the currency with which one purchased leadership. If Scandinavia were to ever become a reality, Magnus needed allies. And Ingvar Larsen didn't have followers; he had acolytes. Scandinavia's rebirth was much further away without Ingvar's support.

In time Magnus believed Ingvar would come around, see how moderating his beliefs and actions would make for a better future.

"Ingvar has his faults," Magnus conceded.

"His last speech ended in a riot," Jacob said. "People were injured, four critically. Many were arrested."

"With time he will realize his fierier comments are not helpful."

"Last week he spoke at a rally organized by the National Alliance."

The National Alliance had been labeled as a hate group by the Norwegian government. Their members routinely protested outside of mosques and organizations supporting people of color. Their protests often drew counter-protests. Some ended peacefully. Others did not. The last rally where Ingvar had spoken was an evening march to government offices processing immigration requests. The National Alliance members had eventually dispersed after riot police arrived, but few of them had extinguished their burning torches.

Magnus had seen it on the news. "I will talk with him about the company he keeps. We disagree on how he conveys his message and who he welcomes to the cause, but at the core, we are aligned."

Jacob knew when to fold. "I am ready to leave at any time."

Magnus said he would be in touch and clicked off. His chair protested as he slumped back. Why did Ingvar have to be so difficult?

Most of the people who followed him were decent Norwegians, men and women who wanted the same thing as Magnus. Not a return to the past, as many claimed, but a reunification for the future.

This new Scandinavian movement required a spark. Magnus suspected he might have found it in Ataulf's message, yet to nurture it from a brief flash into a roaring blaze heralding Scandinavia's rebirth, he needed a man like Ingvar Larsen. Didn't he?

"I do." Magnus picked up his phone to call the man. Ingvar would likely do a backflip when he learned Magnus needed him, so this needed to be played carefully. Manage Ingvar and remind him who needed whom.

The phone buzzed in his hand. An Oslo number. Magnus connected it with a frown. "*Hallo?*"

"This is *Politiinspektør* Hans Gangas of the Oslo Police District. Is this Mr. Magnus Dahl?"

A fellow re-enactor, and a man Magnus had met before. "Good evening, *Politiinspektør.*"

"Good evening, sir. It was a fine battle today."

"That it was. I am certain you fought well."

"I was sent to Valhalla, sir."

"Then you are a true Viking. How may I help you?"

The *Politiinspektør* cleared his throat. "This is an informal call, sir. Regarding a man recently taken into custody. The man is now at our station."

Magnus gripped the phone harder. "What is this man's name?" Magnus knew the answer before he heard it.

"Wilhelm," Hans said.

Finally. "Why was he detained?"

"Suspicion of trafficking in stolen artifacts, sir."

"Did you recover any artifacts?" Hans Gangas said they had not, which meant one thing. "Wilhelm is talking," Magnus said. "What is he saying?"

"He has made unsubstantiated allegations regarding certain

individuals." Hans let that hang on the air. "Who shall remain nameless."

Wilhelm was naming people in The Scandinavians. Magnus didn't have to ask who was being hung out to dry.

He closed his eyes and made a hard decision. Wilhelm was *flár*—treacherous. He deserved his fate.

"Wilhelm will have a visitor soon," Magnus said. "A man who will request to speak with him privately. Is it possible for Wilhelm to be kept isolated in a cell after his meeting?"

"It is."

"You are a true Viking, Hans. I will not forget this."

Magnus clicked off. Scandinavia would be free, united and strong. *Flár* bastards like Wilhelm could not be part of it.

Chapter 9

Brooklyn

Tendrils of black smoke drifted from the broken windows. Flashing red lights spun atop the last remaining fire engine, painting a brick wall the color of blood. Police sawhorses with yellow caution tape strung between them blocked either end of the sidewalk, and crowds had gathered at the end of each block to gawk at the carnage.

Shattered glass crunched underfoot as Joey Morello approached the uniformed officers keeping bystanders at bay. Yes, that was his building. Yes, he could prove it. No, he wasn't injured.

It took some effort, but Joey was eventually granted access to the site, with the warning that he couldn't enter the building. He walked up to the empty windows and peered in at what used to be a pawn shop specializing in precious metals. It had been a respectable business where people who needed cash could get it quickly. The building was insured, of course, and anything truly valuable was kept in a massive fire-proof safe. The physical damage didn't worry Joey. What made his teeth clench tightly together was the message it sent.

An open declaration of war. The Morello family owned this pawn shop and everyone knew it. Fewer knew it was one of their busiest money-laundering operations, with profits from any number of illegal enterprises flowing in the back door, clean money moving out the front. Losing the pawn shop would cost Joey Morello tens of thousands of dollars every week until it was back up and running. Were this the only dent in his cashflow he could afford it. But this was the third money-laundering operation to suffer catastrophic damages this month.

Joey found the fire marshal. "I'm the owner," he said. "Any idea yet what happened?"

The man studied Joey over the top of his glasses. "Looks like a gas leak."

Another gas leak. The Canas weren't even trying to hide it. "Nobody was injured?"

"Nope," the marshal said. "It's a miracle. Both employees were outside having a cigarette when it blew. Someone was looking down on them."

More likely someone had called and told his employees they had thirty seconds to get out. That's what had happened with the other attacks.

"You're right," Joey said. "Any sign it wasn't an accident?"

"If there are traces of accelerant or explosive, we'll find them." The marshal turned back toward the blackened building. "I'm sorry for your misfortune, sir."

Joey wondered if black smoke was coming from his ears. There was no doubt this was deliberate. And Joey even knew the name of the man responsible. The man responsible for the *gas leak* at Joey's laundromat a few weeks earlier, the man who had set fire to one of the Morello gentlemen's clubs. All fronts for the Morello family through which they laundered cash. Altin Cana, intent on weakening Joey's operation so he could take over Morello turf.

Joey spat at the ground. An upstart Albanian punk who wanted to rise above his station. A man with no respect, no sense of decency. This chump didn't play by the rules – and now Joey had to stop him.

Joey turned his back on the wreckage and walked to his car. He had men to reassure and soldiers to send out. The sort of thing a man who led all the families did when attacked.

Vincent Morello's murder three months ago had created a power vacuum, one Joey now struggled to fill. Because of the other crime bosses' respect for his father, Joey wasn't yet out of the running to be the next *capo dei capi*, boss of the bosses. Now Joey had to show the other families he could handle his own business. Only then would he be anointed his father's successor. To do that, justice must be dispensed. The man who had killed his father must pay.

One of Joey's bodyguards waited beside the running Tesla SUV. A brand-new one, as the last one he had was now full of bullet holes. The man was roughly the same size as the vehicle. "You okay, boss?"

Joey put his hand on the man's shoulder. It felt like bricks. "I'm good, Mack. Let's go home."

Mack closed Joey's door, climbed into the driver's seat and the vehicle whizzed off, so silent Joey hardly knew it was on. Half the trees they drove past had no leaves. The other half would soon follow as winter approached. Joey closed his eyes and sat back in his seat. He opened his eyes again and watched the city pass by his window for a minute before pulling out his phone to call a man he trusted with his life.

Harry was standing outside his front door when his phone rang. Joey Morello. Harry turned and sat down on the steps. "Hey, Joey."

"They hit a third one."

Harry's stomach clenched. "Where?" Joey rattled off the address of one of his pawn shops in Brooklyn. "Anybody hurt?" Harry asked.

"Same as the laundromat. Someone called right before the explosion and told them to get out if they wanted to live."

"Just like the club," Harry said. "Early in the day, before any business showed up, and they gave a warning. Only the building burned. No injuries."

"You know who this is."

"Altin Cana." Harry looked around without realizing it. "We'll get him."

"We need to fight back. Speaking of a fight, you ever get word about that chump in Greece? That guy you took out with, what was it, a trident?"

Harry shuddered at the memory. "Stefan Rudovic. He had a sword. It was a fair fight."

"He still in the hospital?"

"Nora has a contact in the Athens police department keeping tabs on him. Stefan was released two days ago. That broken ankle is healing."

"He'll be out for revenge, Harry. You watch your back."

Two times in the past year men had come for Harry at his apartment. The first time a man ambushed him at the front door in pursuit of a recovered relic. That guy was gone in a permanent way, and Harry had his muscle car – thanks to Joey. The second time, three goons ambushed Harry in the field. Those three were still on ice in an English morgue as far as Harry knew.

"I can handle myself," Harry said.

"You're a known Morello man," Joey said. "That's dangerous these days."

"We'll be back on top once you get Altin Cana sorted."

"Not if I don't have support from the other families," Joey said. "That won't happen until I avenge my father."

Harry looked up and down the street again. Nobody looked back. "You could go after him."

"I could, but I won't. You know why."

"It looks reckless without proof."

"My father only used force if diplomacy failed. And only *if* he could prove who the enemy was. Altin Cana is a *bastardo*, but he's smart. None of the men he's used were Albanian. He brings goons in from out of town, then they vanish. He's not dumb enough to send his own men."

"He sent Stefan after me."

"Stefan was chasing the same relic as you. Speaking of that, have you heard from Evgeny Smolov?"

Evgeny Smolov was a Russian expatriate who had left his homeland after running afoul of the madman in Moscow. With a reported net worth in excess of eleven billion dollars, Evgeny had ample cash to pursue his favorite hobby – collecting cultural relics. He either paid cash on the black market or hired mercenaries to seek out the relics for him. A month earlier Evgeny had hired Stefan Rudovic to find a legendary Greek artifact, a relic Harry Fox was also chasing. At the end of that adventure Stefan lay in a Greek hospital with a burning desire to see Harry Fox dead. Evgeny ended up with the artifact and Harry went home empty-handed, along with a somewhat uneasy alliance with Evgeny, who told Harry he'd be calling him soon. Evgeny appreciated a man with Harry's skills. Might even want to hire him.

It would be hard to turn down a man who could bury you in a mountain of cash. "Nope, and I hope I never do. That guy scares me."

"Be nice if he calls," Joey said. "We can use a friend like him."

"Have you talked to Gio Sabella?" Gio headed another New York family, a man who had come into power at the same time as Vincent Morello and who commanded respect among all the leaders. If Gio openly backed Joey Morello to fill his father's seat, the other leaders would follow.

"He's too cagey to commit," Joey said. "Doesn't matter if I know Altin Cana did it. He says I have to prove it first, then handle my business."

A cool breeze pushed fallen leaves past Harry's shoes. A question he'd been holding back for weeks now came to mind. He took a breath. "Why don't you create the proof you need? You know he did this."

"I could," Joey said. "But I'm expected to take him down the right way. The way my father would. With honor."

Harry had thoughts about mixing honor with murder, but he kept those to himself. "Let me know what I can do to help."

"You're on Evgeny Smolov's good side. You have an in with the D.A.'s office. You're doing plenty. Any luck with the retired detective lady?"

"Yes and no." Harry relayed how Detective Barnes revealed her partner had taken a bribe to misidentify the body found by the Hudson.

"Crooked cops are the worst," Joey said. "Unless we're paying them. But that's good news for you. It means you're making real progress."

"Maybe, maybe not." Harry went on about speaking with the medical examiner, needing a court order, and then Detective Barnes running interference so Harry could sneak into the records room. "The report said her brother identified the body. She never had a brother."

"So who the heck identified the body? Maybe it was the same guy Barnes saw talking to her partner at the scene."

"Maybe. Or someone else entirely. Barnes never got a look at the guy, only heard his voice. She said she'd recognize it if she heard him again."

"What about that Irish cop?"

"Connor O'Sullivan died years ago. He's no help." Harry ran a finger over the rough concrete under his backside. "Right now I'm at a dead end."

"Keep the faith, Harry. Look how much you learned. That body wasn't your mom. Someone paid for that lie."

"Nobody I talked to." A memory had surfaced on his way back from trespassing at the medical examiner's office. "I was thinking about your father today."

Joey perked up. "Why?"

"Something he said to me. About my mother. He said my dad used to keep in touch with my mom's cleric after she supposedly died." Dani Fox's Pakistani heritage gave her beauty, midnight black hair, and her Islamic faith. Fred Fox had had no interest in religion, so Harry had been surprised to hear his father had kept in touch with her cleric, Abdul Jalali. "It's curious."

"You should talk to the cleric," Joey said. "I would."

"I will. It's not like I have many options." Harry knew the mosque's name, so finding the cleric was probably the easy part. Figuring out if he could help at all would be the trick. "Let me know if you need anything," Harry said. "Anything at all."

"Good luck," Joey said, and clicked off.

Harry pulled up the cleric's contact information. Harry couldn't recall having met the man, though apparently he had as a child. Abdul had been his mother's spiritual leader. But why would Fred have kept in touch with Abdul after his wife supposedly died? This was the longest of shots. The sort a desperate man took.

A man answered. "*Assalamu alaikum.*" Peace be upon you.

"*Wa alaikum salaam,*" Harry responded. And unto you peace. He continued in Arabic. "My name is Harry Fox. Is the imam available?"

It took a minute, but eventually a voice steeped in years came on the line. "Harry Fox?" The man spoke in English.

"Thank you for taking my call." Harry's phone beeped with an incoming call. He ignored it.

"It has been over a year since your father's passing."

"It seems much shorter."

"I understand. Your mother was a member of our mosque. I always have time for our believers. However, right now I have only a minute."

He didn't have any idea where to start. "You used to speak with my father after my mother died."

"That is correct." A long silence ensued. Harry's gut told him to keep quiet. "Your father missed your mother greatly. I offered my support."

The way Abdul Jalili said it made two things clear. One, he had been in contact with Fred after Dani's supposed death. Two, Abdul was holding back. The man sounded *nervous.*

"Is there anything you can tell me about my mother?"

"I could tell you much."

"I have reason to believe my mom's death isn't what it seems."

Another pause, shorter this time. "What do you mean?"

"The body they found wasn't my mom."

"Have you told the authorities?"

"I'm working on it," Harry said. "Is there anything you remember involving my parents that seems out of the ordinary? I really don't even know what I'm asking for."

"You must take time, Harry. Examine what you know, and just as importantly, what you do not yet know. Much may still remain outside your view."

"I know my mother didn't drown in the Hudson River."

"I am sorry for your pain," Abdul said. "I wish I could be of help. Now I must go to prayer."

"Are you sure there's nothing?" Harry asked quickly. "Anything at all. I'm calling because my father trusted you."

Ali didn't respond. He didn't hang up. He must have been holding the phone tightly, for the sound of his breathing filled Harry's ear.

"Please, Imam."

"There is much you do not know about your parents. That is all I can tell you."

The line went dead. Harry stared at the phone in his hand. The imam knew more than he was saying. But what?

Chapter 10

Manhattan

Nora Doyle resisted the urge to throw her computer out of a window. It wasn't the computer's fault the district attorney's financial team wanted detailed receipts for her most recent expense report. However, were the computer a sentient being, it would be very frightened right now.

She ground her teeth. "I bought a cup of coffee. They want a receipt for *coffee*."

Someone walking by stuck their head through her office door. "What's that, boss? You need coffee?"

Nora glared at the monitor. "No, I do not need coffee. I need five minutes with those finance jackasses and a 'get out of jail free' card."

The man's head vanished faster than she could blink. Nora gave up on the expense report and turned her attention back to an email Harry and Sara Hamed had sent her late last night. A summary of what Sara had translated on the drinking horns, and their suspicion the two stories might say more than it appeared at first look. Harry promised to explain more when he dropped the horns off. The way he phrased it made it clear this wasn't the end of the drinking horn story.

Her phone rang. She jabbed at the speaker button with murder in her finger. "Doyle."

"Guess who is talking?"

It was her contact in the Oslo police department. A detective named Henning who specialized in cultural crimes. Nora had asked him to

74

keep an ear open for news on the man who'd tried to rip Harry Fox off. "Is Wilhelm talking?"

"Yes. *After* his lawyer arrived."

"That makes no sense. Lawyers tell you to shut up."

"It is odd, though this Wilhelm is a very nervous man. Even more so after his attorney left."

"Any idea what the attorney said to him?"

"No, Agent Doyle. We respect their privacy."

As did Nora. Usually. "What's Wilhelm saying?"

"He is still speaking to a detective," Henning said. "Naming names."

"Anybody I'd know?"

"Have you heard of The Scandinavians?" Nora had not. "They are a group based in Oslo. Men and women who fervently revere their Viking heritage and offer battle re-enactments along with educational seminars. They even built a working Viking village."

"You think they were trying to steal the drinking horns?"

"I doubt it. The Scandinavians have grown influential recently. They have connections to high-ranking politicians and the monarchy."

Henning explained that a man named Magnus Dahl was related to the royal family, and that Wilhelm had mentioned Magnus's name. "Is this Magnus a good guy or a bad guy?" Nora asked. "As best you can tell."

"Many people are both," Henning observed quite reasonably. "Though not in this case. Magnus Dahl is one of the most well-regarded citizens in Oslo and the informal leader of the group. I am not certain why Wilhelm says he is frightened of Magnus. Wilhelm is a member of The Scandinavians. Beyond that, there is nothing to connect the men."

"You think he's desperate, just playing for time?"

"That is my suspicion. I cannot begin to guess whether any of what he says is true or not."

Nora looked out her window. Across the street were row upon row of other office windows framing miniature-sized people going about their professional lives. People who looked completely normal. People who could have secrets no one would ever suspect. It happened all the time. "Ever have an inkling this Magnus Dahl is more than he seems?" she asked. "Oslo is a big city, and you say he's a big fish. You're a detective. You hear things. Ever hear anything about Magnus?"

Henning didn't answer at first. Which was all the answer she needed. "There have been rumors," Henning finally said. "But only rumors."

Right now, Wilhelm had his back against a wall. Anything he said should be taken with a boulder-sized grain of salt. Still, Nora had to ask. "What sort of things did you hear?"

"Magnus was once rumored to be involved in acquiring rare antiquities with ties to ancient cultures."

"Like Viking drinking horns."

"No," Henning said. "This involved items tied to Greece. There was never hard evidence of his personal involvement. I have strong reservations about anything Wilhelm is saying, including allegations involving Magnus."

Henning was probably right. Almost certainly. That didn't mean Nora would let it drop without doing her own digging. "What exactly is Wilhelm saying?"

"That Magnus purchases artifacts illegally. He refuses to provide more details without a cooperation agreement."

"Which means he's probably lying. 'Give me the agreement first, then I talk. Tough luck if what I tell you turns out to be bogus.'"

"You have traveled this road before," Henning said.

"Many times. What are you going to do?"

"Nothing, unless he provides concrete details that prove to be true. Without those, Wilhelm will almost certainly remain a guest of the city of Oslo for some time."

Henning promised to keep Nora updated, and they hung up. Her chair squeaked as she leaned back and rubbed her eyes. Magnus Dahl being accused by a man in custody was hardly anything to get excited about. Yet Nora knew it was a mistake to ignore such claims entirely. A few taps on her keyboard and Nora had the bearded, smiling face of Magnus Dahl on her monitor. His thick neck supported a head on which a battle helmet would fit nicely. He wore a suit and tie, but it didn't take much imagination to picture Magnus with his ancestors rampaging their way across Europe.

Nora picked up her phone and began scrolling through her contacts. A career tracking down missing antiquities had brought her a global network of connections, men and women who knew Nora fought to protect their cultural heritage. People who, if she ever needed help, were happy to offer it.

This network included Detective Inspector Guro Mjelde. Guro worked out of Interpol's National Central Bureau in Oslo, where she focused on financial crimes, including money laundering, committed by global criminal organizations. One of Nora's cases had involved liaising with Guro to locate and repatriate a gold Incan statue. Guro couldn't have been more different than Nora on the surface, though they were kindred spirits when it came to bringing down the bad guys, so their brief partnership had created a rock-solid bond between the two women. Guro had promised she'd be there for Nora any time. Nora was about to see if she meant it.

"D.I. Mjelde speaking." Her bubbly voice was unlike any other.

"Hello, Guro. It's Nora Doyle."

"Nora! My goodness, it is wonderful to hear from you."

Nora grinned despite herself. "You too, Guro. Have a second?"

"I always do for my favorite American." The hectic sound of phones ringing and people talking in the background suggested otherwise. "What is it?"

"I need a favor. An off-the-books favor."

"Oh, my favorite kind."

"Do you have anything on a man named Magnus Dahl?" She spelled it for Guro. "Look back at least two decades."

Keys clicked rapidly. "Do you have any other search parameters?"

"It would involve a Greek artifact."

Background noise, a keyboard under attack, and phones ringing filled Nora's ear as she waited. It didn't take long.

"Found it," Guro said. "Wait. Perhaps not. Why can't I open this file?"

"You can't read it?"

"Not without using my administrative credentials."

"What does that mean?"

"This file is classified," Guro said. "Fortunately for you, I have top-level clearance."

"I promise this stays between us."

Guro's voice dropped when she spoke. "Magnus Dahl is a member of the royal family."

Nora was silent for a beat. "They're not above the law."

"No, they aren't." Silence on Guro's end for a moment. Nora forced herself not to get up and pace. "To be clear," Guro finally continued, "nothing was ever proven. In fact, this file seems to be little more than conjecture."

"What can you tell me about it?"

"Is this part of an official investigation?" Guro asked. "I am not permitted to release classified files for any unofficial reason. However, if it relates to an ongoing inquiry, then it is my duty as your international partner to assist. As we have collaborated in the past, I do not need verification."

"It relates to a case I'm working on."

"Then I can assist. I assume this will not be shared with anyone?"

"I swear." And by that, Nora meant she probably wouldn't. Unless she did.

"Then check your inbox."

Nora reminded Guro she was the best person in the world before hanging up and opening the file. A massive red *CLASSIFIED* stamp across the top made it clear Guro had no qualms about playing fast and loose with the rules for her friend Nora.

The file turned out to be about a single case. It revolved around a pair of artifacts Magnus may or may not have paid a group of men to locate, though the venture had backfired on him in spectacular fashion. The facts were as such. A group of international thieves had been hired by an unknown individual to locate a Greek artifact. One Interpol agent theorized the money funding this venture came from Magnus. Allegedly, the thieves weren't able to locate one of the two artifacts, so they had created a fake to pawn off on the buyer. The scheme had unraveled when an NYPD and FBI joint task force, in partnership with Interpol, arrested one of the crew. Magnus was never formally tied to any of this, and from what Nora read he'd never even been questioned.

That was all the file contained. There was a brief note about what happened at the bust, pointing Nora to another file if she wanted to know more. It turned out the only person arrested looked to be a fall guy, a man whose only crime was being hired to authenticate the potentially forged artifact. An academic named – *no way.*

Nora shot out of her chair. She rubbed her eyes, looking again. The name wouldn't have meant anything a year ago. Today it nearly knocked her over. The academic who had been hired by the thieves and who had taken the fall was a man she'd never met, yet she felt as though she knew him well. His name?

Fred Fox. Harry's father.

"Where are those interview summaries?" A firestorm of questions swirled in her head. She pushed them aside. First, figure out exactly what happened. Then deal with the fact this was Harry's father. "Here they are."

Only a few short pages. Summaries of two rounds of interviews conducted after Fred Fox was arrested.

During the first round of interviews the thieves had pinned the blame on Fred, and the cops bought it. Fred had been physically in possession of the artifact, and the cops didn't buy his explanation of being hired to authenticate it. The thieves flipped the script, saying Fred had actually hired *them* for protection. They claimed to have no clue about the artifacts deal.

The cops bought it and had pinned everything on Fred, despite him telling the cops he'd been hired to authenticate not one, but two artifacts. The first was an authentic statue of Zeus. The second was a notebook supposedly written by Archimedes, the renowned mathematician. Fred told the cops that notebook was a forgery, and further told the cops that the thieves who hired him had lied to Fred about the meeting. The thieves told Fred the meeting was for Fred to disclose his findings about the artifacts. They never told Fred it was actually a meeting to close the deal, his analysis be damned.

Fred was adamant the facts were obvious, going so far as to decline legal representation at first. After the first round of interrogations, Fred had obtained an attorney, and then his story had changed. Fred went from saying he'd been set up to *admitting* his guilt. He even claimed to be the mastermind.

Nora typed the attorney's name into her search bar. The guy was high-powered, from one of those white-shoe firms kept on retainer by Wall Street types. The guy's fees would have been exorbitant. Either Fred Fox had had a stash of gold bars in his basement, or someone else had been footing the bill.

Sinister thoughts filled her mind, prime among them that someone had not wanted Fred to talk. Who better to send to shut him up than an attorney like this one? A man skilled in delivering messages of all stripes. What had the attorney said? Impossible to say, but it had made Fred change his tune and profess guilt.

Fred had confessed and was granted bail until sentencing. The file ended there. Nora knew Fred had spent a short while in prison, then had become Vincent Morello's go-to man in the black-market antiquities trade. Vincent funded Fred's work for decades, and when Fred died violently in Rome, his son Harry had taken on the mantle of Morello relic hunter. What Nora didn't know was what had happened between Fred getting out on bail and him joining forces with Vincent Morello.

The question gnawed at her. The last thing she wanted to do was nose into Harry's past. They had a good thing going, Harry working on Nora's team as her inside man with the mob. In exchange, she looked the other way at times. An imperfect relationship for an imperfect world, one that had helped her recover the two stolen drinking horns.

Nora wanted to know more for one simple reason: there was more to these drinking horns than she understood. Harry had made that much clear. If she could tell Harry what happened to Fred after he'd made bail, perhaps Harry would share the full story and what it led to. She knew him. Harry never did anything halfway, and if those horns had his interest, they had hers as well. Using Fred Fox's past could lead to a gold mine of opportunity.

An unfamiliar feeling flashed through her chest – hesitation. She turned from the screen and stood. What was she thinking? *Look at the long game.* Using this information to manipulate Harry into talking to her might help in the short term, but eventually he'd figure it out, because he was sharp. Occasionally too sharp for his own good. A career working against organized criminals and losing nearly every time had honed her cynicism to a deadly edge. Times were changing. The past year proved that more than anything. Harry was her in to the artifacts underworld, but he was more than that. Harry and Nora were teammates. Harry had saved her life in the field. Teammates didn't treat each other like disposable assets.

Nora reached up, stretching a knot from her back. This was a chance to play it straight, to make the team stronger. Telling Harry what she knew might help him sort out the tragedy that was his family story. It was the right thing to do. If he told her about his father in return, wonderful. If not, so be it. She grabbed her phone and called Harry before she could change her mind.

It went straight to voicemail. She left a message telling him to call her at once. About the horns, and about another matter.

The phone clattered on her desk. A very slight sour note took root in her stomach as she continued to second-guess herself. Was she doing this purely to help Harry come to grips with his past? Or did she really want to reel him in, bait him with information about his father, use it to convince Harry that this job wasn't done yet and he needed to take her along for whatever came next? Or was she getting greedy and trying to leverage painfully personal information against her ally because he could go places she couldn't, do things the law didn't let her do?

Nora kicked at her garbage can and sent it flying. "Stay focused," she told the walls.

"Focused on what?"

Nora spun around. "Jeez, Mom. Knock next time."

Jennifer Doyle looked toward the fallen garbage can. "Perhaps I should bring a shield."

"Very funny."

"Do you have a moment?"

Nora grinned for the first time in hours. "Sure. Come in."

Jennifer walked into her daughter's office, heading straight for Nora to wrap her in an embrace. "I would ask if anything is wrong, but the clues are hard to miss."

"I'm fine. Have a seat." Nora took her mother to the room's lone table and joined her on the other side of it. "A case is getting to me, that's all."

Anyone who happened past might mistake the two for sisters. Both trim, average height, with an intensity to their gaze that you couldn't miss. A gaze that, if you looked closely at Jennifer's face in particular, had storm clouds beneath the surface. Other than that undercurrent, their only physical difference was Gary Doyle's Irish heritage, which had given Nora her auburn hair.

"Care to talk about it?" Jennifer asked.

"I won't bore you."

"What you do is far from boring." Jennifer leaned closer and whispered conspiratorially. "Your father is the one whose work bores me. Yours I love."

"I'll tell him you said that."

Jennifer leaned back. "I tell him every day."

"Okay, you asked for it." Nora got up and closed her office door. "I could use your advice." She sat back down as Jennifer gestured for her to go on. "It involves a confidential source with ties to the antiquities black market. He's an inside man, a person who can go places I can't and who knows people I don't. We have a mutually beneficial arrangement."

Nora never revealed information that could identify or compromise her sources, not even to her mother. Jennifer Doyle, wife to a prosecutor in the D.A.'s office and mother to this anti-trafficking team leader, knew not to ask. "I see."

"As part of a separate investigation I received personal information this source would want to know. If I don't share it with him, he'll never know I have it, but I'm tempted to do it for the wrong reasons."

"How so?"

"If I tell him what I have it will compel him to take action." It was the best she could do without being specific. "Right now he's working on a project that's more important to him than anything he does with my team. There's no chance he'll drop it to keep helping me."

"You require his help now?"

Nora nodded. "He's already helped me with my current case, but there's more to do, another layer to peel back, and I can't do it myself."

"Which gives you the problem of deciding whether or not to reveal this information now. This man is an ally of yours. Do you value this partnership?"

Nora said she did. "He saved my life."

Jennifer's face was a stone mask. "So you tell him and distract him from his personal case, or hold the information back until a later time."

"There's more," Nora said. "I could use the information I have to force his hand, make him keep working on my case."

"Which also risks the foundation of your partnership." Jennifer crossed her arms. "Trust."

Nora's eyes narrowed. "Yes."

Jennifer laid her hands on the table. "You are an incredible woman who works tirelessly to recover lost artifacts and bring criminals to justice. You are also a decent human being. You understand the value of doing not what is convenient, but what is right." Jennifer leaned closer. "Ask yourself: what is the right thing to do?"

"I should never have invited you in here."

Jennifer didn't let her go. "I'm waiting."

Nora sighed. "The right thing is to tell him now. If he decides to keep helping me, he does it of his own accord. If he doesn't, then I still sleep at night knowing I helped him."

Sunlight falling through the window sparkled when it hit Jennifer's wedding ring. "You do not need me. And I hope you do not realize that any time soon."

"I'll always need you, Mom. At least to keep Dad out of my hair."

Jennifer smiled. "Deception can have unintended consequences." Her voice softened, and those clouds that sometimes hovered in her eyes appeared. "Ones you could never anticipate."

"You're right," Nora said. "I'll tell him."

"Don't allow greed to change your values. Treat this man with the same respect you show everyone."

"He's used to dealing with far different people than me. That also means he isn't squeaky-clean."

"Who of us is?" A flash of the clouds again. "The world is often gray, not black and white."

Her mother had never said it that way before. "I guess it is," Nora said. "Thanks, Mom."

"Thank *you*, dear." Jennifer glanced at her watch. "Now, I've taken enough of your time."

Jennifer stood, and Nora walked with her to the door. "Thanks for stopping by, Mom. I mean it."

Her mother stopped inside the doorframe and turned. She put both arms on Nora's shoulders and pulled her close. "Be careful."

"I'm in the office today. I'll watch out for papercuts."

"Nora."

Nora rolled her eyes. "I promise."

"Thank you." She let Nora go. "I know you will make the right decision. The world is often unkind. Do your part to make it better."

Chapter 11

Brooklyn

A trio of teenagers strolled past as Harry sat on his front porch. Their muffled laughter barely registered, not with imam Abdul Jalali's words filling his head. *There is much you do not know about your parents.*

What did he mean? The cleric counseled people of all types, many of them facing incredible challenges. Abdul had to be a pillar of support for them, the sort of man who didn't frighten easily. Yet on the phone with Harry he'd sounded nervous, uneasy. It made no sense — unless Abdul was hiding something.

Harry stood to go inside when his phone buzzed with a new voicemail. The call he'd received while talking to Abdul. He checked the number. What did Nora Doyle want? Harry listened to the message, then listened to it again. He sat back down on the porch. He looked both ways, then looked in his window. No one on the street. Sara remained inside. He was alone. He called Nora back.

"Doyle."

"What's the *other matter* you want to talk about?"

"First, where are the drinking horns?"

"Coming over shortly. What else do you want to talk about?"

"It's personal."

"For me or you?"

"You, Harry. Definitely you."

"I'm listening."

"It started with the drinking horns."

"How's that personal for me?"

"Here's how." She dove into the story, telling him of Magnus Dahl, a black-market deal from twenty years ago to acquire a pair of Greek artifacts, and a scheme gone wrong. Nora didn't give any names besides Magnus's.

"How do you know all of this?" Harry said. "I thought the horns came from a dig site."

"They did," Nora said. "Stolen by a man affiliated with Magnus's group. One called The Scandinavians. I believe Magnus was involved, but there's no proof."

"If the guy was illegally purchasing artifacts twenty years ago, he's probably still doing it. It's not a hobby you lose interest in." Harry ran through it in his head. "How sure are you Magnus was even involved back then?"

"Interpol suspected he was involved," Nora said. "I have their file on the incident. Magnus was a person of interest."

"An Interpol file? Nice connection."

"You're not the only one with friends."

"What aren't you telling me?" he asked. "How is any of this personal?"

"Where are you?"

"Sitting on my porch."

"Stay there. I'm coming to pick up the horns. Then we'll talk."

She clicked off before he could argue. Harry called her back and it went to voicemail. He loosed a string of invective toward her office in Manhattan before pushing through his front door. Once Nora made a decision, forget about changing her mind. His only choice now was to wait for her.

"Nora's coming over," Harry called out to Sara as he walked inside. "We have to pack the horns."

"Already done." Sara pointed to a box on the table. She managed to keep her voice casual when she asked a question. "How did it go with the medical examiner?"

He relayed how the medical examiner had told him a court order was required for him to get the autopsy report. "Detective Barnes didn't like that," Harry said. "She helped me out."

Disbelief filled Sara's face when he explained. "She lied to the medical examiner so you could break into the records room?"

"The door was open," Harry said. "I only trespassed. The report said my mom's brother identified her body."

"Your mother did not have a brother."

"Which means I'm stuck." Harry resisted the urge to smash his hand against the table. "Someone bribed Connor O'Sullivan to misidentify the body as my mom. Detective Barnes heard the man who offered the bribe, but she never saw his face. Then the body was formally misidentified a second time at the medical examiner's office, maybe by the same man, possibly by an accomplice. I have no idea who did it. If I could figure out the why, the who may be obvious."

He fell silent. A terrible certainty had filled most of his life until today: the unshakable knowledge that his mom had died all those years ago. Now he knew that was a lie, and it seemed as though the ground was shaking beneath him.

Sara squeezed his forearm, the warmth of her hand pleasant in a room gone cold. "Look how much you learned. A week ago you knew your mother drowned in the river. Now you know the body they found wasn't hers. That tells you there is hope. You'll find out what happened to her."

Nice thoughts. Useless as well. "Anything could have happened since then. She could have died any number of ways. The one thing I know is she's not alive."

Sara's nails dug into his arm. "Don't say that."

"She's gone. That's one thing I'm certain of."

"How can you be certain?" Sara asked.

Harry couldn't stop the words from coming out. "If she was alive, my mom would have found me."

Sara didn't respond.

"I need a beer." Harry stood and headed for the fridge, the warmth from Sara's hand lingering on his arm. He cracked a bottle and downed half of it.

Sara turned back to her laptop as he stared out the window, trying and failing to keep his mind empty. Barren tree limbs bounced on a cold wind, their lost foliage swirling in rustling waves on the sidewalk and down alleyways. He finished his drink as a thunderous pounding sounded on his door. Only one person knocked like that.

Nora glared at him when he pulled the door open. "Come in," he said.

"Sara Hamed." Nora bypassed Harry and went straight for the Egyptologist. "Good to see you."

"You as well," Sara said and hugged her. "The drinking horns are ready to go."

"Thanks." Nora made no move to get them. "I need to speak with Harry."

Sara made to leave the room. Harry lifted a hand. "Stay. We're a team, remember?"

"We are." Nora's hands found her hips. "This is a personal matter. About the Interpol case we discussed."

"Then we'd better get Sara up to speed."

"Fine by me." Nora sent another silent apology to Guro Mjelde, then recapped the story she'd told Harry earlier.

Sara listened in silence until the end. "You trust this information from Interpol?" Nora said she did. "What part of the case pertains to Harry?"

Nora looked at Harry. Then Sara. She crossed her arms on her chest, looked out the window and then back to Harry. "The expert who was there to authenticate the artifacts was the only person arrested in the bust. He was a professor."

Harry's world went black. He couldn't think, couldn't move. "No."

"They arrested your father."

Somehow Harry's hand found the back of a chair. He felt but didn't

89

see Sara grab hold of his shoulder. "Sit down."

He didn't move. This was the case Fred had never talked about. The moment Fred's life had changed forever, when his son's life had changed. The men who had stolen a Greek statue and fabricated an Archimedes text had stolen their family's future before it ever started. Men paid by Magnus Dahl.

"Your father was interviewed twice," Nora said. "The first time was right after his arrest, when he said the text was a fake and he had been set up. He believed he was there to verify the Zeus statue. He had no idea the fake Archimedes text was involved. When the police showed up, your father was suddenly the fall guy."

"He never told me," Harry said. "There must have been evidence he wasn't lying."

"Your father's story changed dramatically after an attorney showed up to represent him." A pause. "An attorney he never requested."

"What?"

"Your father changed his story after the attorney came in."

"My dad was honest. He would have told the truth. The attorney probably told him to be quiet."

"That's the thing. Your father stopped saying he was innocent and told the cops he was *guilty*. He said he hired the men for protection because *he* was trying to sell a fake artifact."

Now Harry stood up. "Why would he take the fall?" He sat down again, not waiting for an answer. "The attorney must have put him up to it."

"Another thing is that the attorney's rates would have been astronomical. Your father wasn't wealthy, was he?" Harry said he wasn't. "Your father couldn't afford an attorney who charged over a thousand dollars per hour."

Harry's eyes widened. "Never. Someone sent that attorney. Someone who wanted my father to change his story."

"Do you think this relates to Detective O'Connell's lies?" Sara asked.

Nora pounced. "What lies?"

Harry spilled it all. "My mom didn't have a brother," he finished. "Whoever that person was, he lied to the medical examiner, possibly with Detective O'Connell's help."

"Wow." Lines creased Nora's forehead. "Let's start with the Magnus Dahl angle. We have actual evidence for that. Well, circumstantial evidence."

"What happened after my dad changed his story?"

"The file ends after he confesses. Interpol handed it off to the local authorities. I thought you might know."

"I think my father was released, although it may only have been for a short time on bail. I'm not sure." The memories were still a blur. "That's when my mom died and everything changed."

Harry had always suspected his mom's death drove Fred Fox to collaborate with Vincent. Fred had eventually beaten the antiquities-related charges with the help of Vincent's attorney, but by then his professional reputation was in tatters and his wife was gone.

"My dad took the only job he was offered after he was acquitted," Harry said. "Working for Vincent Morello."

Nora had the heart to let that slide. "Which he did – quite successfully – for decades."

They all fell silent. Harry sat still, letting his mind go. It didn't take long for him to realize what had to happen next.

"I need to figure out what the heck Magnus Dahl knows. You said he may be tied to these two drinking horns. We have an idea why he might want them."

Nora raised an eyebrow. "Go on."

Harry nodded to Sara. "Tell her."

"I discovered this yesterday," Sara said, turning her laptop to face Nora. "The drinking horns tell a story. I'm convinced it's a marker."

"What sort of marker?"

"A marker leading us to the full story behind Alaric and Ataulf's treasure."

Nora leaned over the table. "You have my attention."

Sara offered a summary of her findings. Nora, in one of the few instances Harry could remember, had no response.

Harry watched her face. He got a funny feeling. "I think you'd be worried we're going to go after this treasure. But you're not." Now Harry leaned toward her. "Why?"

Nora looked at the ceiling, then the table, and finally out the window before she turned to Harry. "I didn't come here to take you away from your search. I had no idea it involved your mother's death, but I do know our interests align here."

Which was true. Harry had purposefully kept it a secret from her. "And now?"

"It appears we have a common goal. To find the truth behind the story of these drinking horns."

"And if it leads to revealing a certain royal Norwegian is an international smuggler, possibly with all sorts of relics hidden away, all the better."

Nora shrugged. "You said it, not me."

"If this is a chance to find out more about what happened to my mom and dad, I'm in." He paused, then looked at the woman beside him. "If Sara wants to, that is."

Sara hesitated for a fraction of a second. "Of course," she said. "I'm still on leave from university. Why not?"

Harry noted and immediately forgot her hesitation. "Magnus Dahl had better watch out."

Nora waved a finger at him. "No, Harry. *You'd* better watch out. Magnus is wealthy, a member of the royal family, and is basically a Viking. Follow the trail, and try not to attract his attention in the process."

She had a point. "We'll see."

Nora muttered something Harry was glad he couldn't hear before looking to Sara. "What do you recommend?"

"Do we officially have your support now?" Sara asked. "This was

Harry's private mission before."

"If you agree to give me anything you find on the way," Nora said.

"Within reason," Harry said quickly. "Which we will discuss after I know what it is I'm giving you."

"Any discovery tied to your family stays private. Any relics or information about them comes to me. Deal?"

Harry frowned. If he were ten, he would have crossed his fingers behind his back. "Deal."

"Now, what do you need?"

Sara jumped in. "Two tickets to Sweden. First class would be nice."

Chapter 12

Visby, Sweden

Gotland was Sweden's largest island. Accessing it from Sweden's mainland required a three-hour ferry ride from Stockholm to Gotland's largest city, an ancient town called Visby.

A few of those on board the ferry from Stockholm to Gotland had also been on the plane from New York with Harry and Sara. Before falling asleep on the plane, Harry had opened a new book, a biography of Al Capone. Cliché, yes, but a friend had recommended it and he needed to take his mind off the case for a few hours. The story of Capone's meteoric rise and equally dizzying fall from power gave him an idea. An idea he needed to think about before he said anything out loud. That didn't stop him from firing off a text to Joey, a message his boss might not understand. Harry wasn't sure he did either.

Harry leaned on the ferry's rail. The Baltic Sea stretched to the horizon all around them, though in truth they were surrounded by Europe on all sides. Cold saltwater spray shot up and hung in the air, misting to land on Harry's tongue, which he stuck out without thinking.

"Do you know how much diesel fuel is in the ocean?" Sara asked, watching him with distaste. "It's an abomination."

"Good point." He drank plenty of coffee. Hopefully it neutralized toxins. "Anything besides Visigoth hoards you want to tell me about before we get there?"

He said it in a joking manner, only there was more to it. Sara had seemed to hold back a few times during their journey. Hard to be sure, but he had to ask. "Is something bothering you?"

She kept looking out over the water. "Other than us once again heading into danger?"

"Adventure. Not danger. You used the wrong word. Besides, that's what you like about me."

That got a smile. "No, nothing is bothering me." She didn't offer anything further.

Harry checked his phone again. Nothing from Detective Barnes. And still nothing from Joey Morello. They had chatted briefly before Harry got on the plane in New York. His boss had barely responded when he'd learned of Harry's trip. "Good luck," was all Joey had said.

"You need me for anything?" Harry had asked him.

"No. I'm working on diversifying our operations."

"Your father would be proud."

Joey sounded like he was holding the world on his back. "A few more of my washing operations get hit and we're in trouble. Real trouble."

The washing operations were Joey's colorful euphemism for businesses he laundered money through. With three currently out of operation, Joey had cash stacking up in basements and falling out of safe deposit boxes. Without clean money to pay his men or run the family, the pressure was growing. Cash made Joey's world go round. Clean cash, and loyalty. Both were in short supply.

"Any word from Gio Sabella?" Harry asked.

"Still the same message. Show them I can handle this. Then they'll think about supporting me."

Handling it meant avenging his father, but not starting a war. Joey needed solid proof to do that and satisfy the old-school Italians that Altin Cana had, in fact, ordered Vincent Morello's death.

"You'll get it," Harry said.

"Keep your eye out for that Stefan Rudovic punk," Joey said. "He seems to show up when you're out in the field."

"He can limp after me all he wants. I'll handle him."

Joey chuckled. "Good man, Harry. See you soon." When he clicked off, Harry had the distinct impression Joey's fortunes would soon turn. For good or bad, he didn't know.

"Ready?"

Sara's voice pulled Harry back to the present. "Yeah. Let's find this runestone."

With the ferry not even half full, it took only a few minutes to drive their Volkswagen off once it docked. Harry headed into the medieval city of Visby. Houses with red tile roofs hugged the coastline; stone houses built centuries ago whizzed by them on either side. Three black pointed roofs atop white stone towers lorded over the city, their uppermost points reaching nearly two hundred feet high.

Sara noted him craning his neck for a glimpse. "That's Visby Cathedral. It dates to the thirteenth century."

"Looks like most of the town does. I wonder if Ataulf's runestone is the only old secret this town is hiding."

"One mystery at a time, Harry."

"No fair using my own advice against me." Harry rounded a corner and headed for a wall of mortared limestone, thick enough to withstand cannon fire, that surrounded the city. Towers rose in the distance on either side, while a narrow gate had been cut in the wall ahead wide enough for two cars to pass through at once. Anything bigger than a pickup truck and you had to wait your turn.

"Think skinny," Harry said as he rolled through the opening, and then his eyes widened. One moment they were in medieval times; the next, civilization abandoned them completely. Green fields and hills stretched to the horizon. A two-lane road weaved briefly ahead before massive trees with barren limbs crowded in close on either side. "How far to the runestone?"

"Twenty minutes." Directions spouted from the car speakers when Sara punched their destination into his phone. "It's near what was once a large settlement. Evidence suggests that for a brief period, perhaps a decade, that settlement thrived as a center of trade on the island."

"Any chance there are parts of the town people haven't excavated yet?"

"There's an excellent chance. The town vanished as quickly as it started. One year it was vibrant and well; the next, deserted. No one knows why." Sara tapped the side of her head. "Though I have a theory."

"Ataulf's people moved on," Harry said. "It was a Visigoth settlement, and when he continued north or died, they all left."

"My thoughts exactly. Gotland Island is rich with historical sites. This specific one is, to be blunt, viewed as less exciting. With limited funding for digs, more promising locations have been excavated."

"Good for us."

Gray clouds crept in during the remainder of their short drive, giving the crisp air an extra bite as they crested a sloping rise and their destination came into view. If you could call it that. A few signs, some rocks that might once have been building foundations, and an incredible view of the sea.

"Head for the car park," Sara said.

"You mean that gravel patch?"

"Yes, the car park."

They were the first, and, Harry suspected, last people to arrive that day. Several cars were parked together in the distance, farther down by a narrow beach. His tires crunched as he wheeled onto the gravel lot and stopped. "This is where the *Orm* sank?"

"Yes, off the beach ahead. The wreck was discovered decades ago."

She jumped out of the car, leaving him to grab their pack and follow. Sara had brought several items she usually found helpful in the field, some of which had required explanation at the airport before she checked her bag. The crowbar had been of specific interest to several T.S.A. agents who gave Sara's professional credentials a thorough vetting before allowing her to pass. Thankfully, they never spotted the ceramic knuckledusters in Harry's luggage. He touched his pocket to confirm they were still there, then reached for the amulet hidden under his shirt, which he almost never took off.

Harry sped up to catch Sara as she power-walked toward the single runestone jutting above the ground. His thighs protested as he ascended yet another rise, finally catching her at the very moment she stopped. Right in the middle of an open area.

"Whoa," Harry said, dodging to one side. "What's wrong?"

Sara pointed at the ground. "No grass is growing here. These brown spots form a rectangle."

Only once he was right on top of it did Harry notice. A wide rectangle of brown oblong patches in the lush green grass. Each was roughly the size of a foundation stone. "Big place," Harry said.

"I expect this was the mead hall. The lord would have lived here."

"Ataulf?"

"Perhaps."

Wind off the sea whipped her hair as she lingered for a moment before setting off again. He followed her to the base of the single runestone. Harry craned his neck and took a step back. "This thing is huge." It was easily ten feet high and half as wide. Harry looked around the side. "It's three feet thick. This thing must weigh a ton."

"Likely more," Sara said. "I wouldn't want to be one of the Visigoths who raised it."

This was a heck of a lot bigger than he'd expected. Then again, he'd never seen a runestone up close before. "Are they all this big?"

"Depends on the riches of the lord who built it. The one who raised this was clearly wealthy. That fits with the idea that this town once thrived."

"Ataulf had a fortune. His brother looted Rome and then died."

Sara pulled out a notebook. "Remember, no one has connected Ataulf with this site. We're the only people who know."

"Because no one could read the runestone in Germany." Harry peered at the stone. "Can you read this one?"

"Yes. These runes are well known. It was built as a memorial to the Vikings who died on the *Orn*."

He fell silent as she studied the stone. Whitecaps made the sea come alive as he looked around. The wind had turned cold, blowing hard enough to make his eyes tear up. He squinted against the breeze, gray clouds overhead casting wide shadows on the ground. A person down at the beach was trying with minimal success to fly a kite.

"There's nothing unusual here." The wind snatched Sara's words away as soon as he caught them. "The stone tells of a tragedy and laments the Vikings dying. This is important because it ties in to the German stone."

"Which contains a story with two parts," Harry said.

"The first written during Ataulf's lifetime. It tells of their sacking Rome, Alaric's death, and Ataulf leading his people toward Scandinavia. The second half was written centuries later, and it focuses on Ataulf and his son. Specifically, his desire to be reunited with the boy in the afterlife." She hesitated for a half a breath. "It also describes Ataulf's burial tomb."

"A tomb no one could prove existed until you broke the code."

"It helped to have the drinking horns." She looked away from the sea, beyond him, toward the small hills in the distance. "This ground is telling us a story. It's telling us where to look." She recited a passage from memory. "*Ataulf lies in the center hill above where Njoror claimed the warship Orn. Thor's power is with Ataulf.*"

Harry slowly turned. "It's right here."

Undulating ground stretched ahead of them, interspersed with patches of trees, some thick enough to prevent you from seeing past them. Funny thing. No trees sat atop the high ground. Only around it. Harry voiced his thoughts.

"Why do you think that is?" Sara asked.

"Someone cleared the trees when they started digging. And they left something behind that prevents trees from growing."

"Let's follow that lead." She started toward the hill. "Get those shovels out."

They walked around a copse of trees tall enough to obscure them from the view of anyone at the beach. "You ever excavate an untouched grave like this?" Harry asked.

"Never. If we're correct and this is a grave, it's technically called a burial mound. Larger ones can contain a series of rooms dug out of the ground and supported by wooden beams. Others are simple coffins covered by earth and stone." She walked behind him and reached into the pack he was carrying. "This is a large one."

He was pushed and pulled off balance as she dug in the bag. "What are you looking for?"

"This." A slender metal rod appeared in front of his face. "It will save us time."

"It's a stick."

"A stick that extends." She fiddled with the ends, then stepped back and whipped the device around. The bottom fell out as it flew, the metal rod elongating to over eight feet. He wouldn't want to be on the wrong end of it.

"It's a *long* stick." Harry raised his hands, palms up. "What do you do with it?"

"Push it into the ground. Any sustained resistance suggests there's something solid beneath the surface. If the stick goes easily into the ground, we keep looking for a place to dig."

"I like this stick."

She shoved it against his chest. "It's yours. Push it into the ground where I tell you."

Sara began walking around the short hill. Harry followed her until they returned to the same place they'd started. "Done already?" he asked.

"Funny. I didn't see anything to suggest an underground entrance." She pointed at the ground in front of them. "Do you see how this hill is oblong?" Harry said he did. "That could mean the entrances are on the shorter sides. Any rooms inside the mounds would have had wooden pillars or roofs to support them."

"Hold this." Harry slipped the pack off and tossed it to her. "Any tips for using this stick?"

"Don't impale yourself."

Fair enough. He set one pointy end of the surprisingly sturdy rod against the ground, stepped closer so the other end was behind him, lest he slip and ram it through his guts, then leaned on it. He pressed tentatively at first, then pushed harder until it started sliding into the dirt. "Throw me some gloves," he said. With those on he had a real grip and went back at it. Slowly and steadily, the stick kept going down into the dirt, bouncing off a few rocks but always managing to make further progress after an adjustment. One foot in. Two feet. Harry maneuvered it past another rock and shoved again. This time the rod didn't move. Harry did.

He lost his grip and spilled to the ground. The rod stayed in place, bouncing from side to side. "It's stuck," he said as he stood.

"Excellent." Sara grabbed his shoulder and pushed him back toward the rod. "Try again. Really push this time. We have to be sure it's not another rock."

The stick was barely two feet into the dirt. It went no farther no matter how hard he pushed. "That's it," Harry said. "Whatever's in the way is solid." He stood and wiped his hands. "Give me a shovel."

"No." Sara took off. "First check the other side as well."

He was left to fight with the rod until he could pull it free, then grab the pack and fumble to get around the far side of the mound without impaling himself. More pushing and grunting and swearing, same result. About two feet into the ground the stick stopped moving. "Satisfied?"

"I am," Sara said. "Now we dig."

"Which side?"

Sara touched her chin. "I suspect Ataulf would have been buried so he could face the ocean." She pointed to the far side. "We start over there."

The kite still fluttered over the treetops. No more cars had arrived. They still had the place to themselves. "What do we say if someone shows up?"

"We ignore them. If they ask what we're doing, we tell the truth. Excavating."

"Even if it's a cop?"

"Then we lie and say we're digging for treasure."

He did a double-take. "That's sounds crazy."

"Which is the point. The police will tell us to go home. We leave, then come back later. It's better than getting arrested."

Sara was speaking his language now.

"I like it."

A shovel handle went into his chest. "Dig." Sara tossed the pack aside and rammed her shovel into the dirt. Harry shook his head and did the same. Jam the shovel down, step on it for good measure, lever the dirt, repeat. They worked in silence, spreading the dirt around so it wasn't obvious how much they'd moved. A single car drove past, headed away from the beach back toward Visby. The kite still floated on the wind.

The first bead of sweat formed on Harry's chest and trickled down to his navel. He stopped digging, taking a long drink from a water bottle. He offered it to Sara. "We're nearly two feet down," he said.

She drank greedily. "Keep digging."

His back protested as he picked the shovel up once more. Thank goodness this dirt was mostly that – dirt. Only a couple of rocks had come up. No tree roots had blocked his efforts. Smooth going for such manual labor. So smooth it made him wonder. Harry jammed his shovel down once more. *Thunk.*

Even his teeth shuddered with the impact. Sara stopped digging. "Did you hear that?" he asked.

She hefted her shovel and smashed it down next to his, nearly taking a few of his toes off in the bargain. *Thunk.* "I like that sound," she said.

Earth flew as they dug with abandon, the soft mixture of sand and dirt flung aside to reveal a wooden beam beneath the surface, roughly two feet down. "Those are tool marks," Sara said, peering at the exposed wood.

"Should I go up or to the side? We need a door."

"If this is an actual tomb," Sara said. "It could be many other things."

He stopped digging. "Like what?"

She bit her lip. "I have no idea. I'm trying to keep a level head."

"Forget that nonsense. We *found* it, Sara. This is Ataulf's tomb."

"Dig to the side for a few feet. An entrance would at least be high enough for a person to walk through if they crouched. That would require some kind of frame for a doorway."

Harry's progress accelerated now that he could dig from below and lever the dirt out. A distant rumble rolled across the land. Darker clouds hung heavy in the distance far out to sea, moving parallel to the shore. It seemed they'd be spared a dousing. He bent over, ignoring the fire in his thighs, scraping his shovel along the wooden beam to bring more of it into view. Rough plane lines showed that it had been cut, a solid hunk of wood turned into what was likely a supporting beam. Harry rammed his shovel along the board to scoop earth. It stuck fast and his momentum sent him sprawling over the handle to eat a face-full of grass.

"Did you find the edge?" Sara asked.

The grass muffled his response. "I think so."

"Move." She gave him a softish kick and threw a few shovelfuls of dirt aside as he grumbled and got up. "You did. Nice work, Harry."

"Thanks." He brushed himself off, chose to forget that kick, then helped dig. Another board had been laid perpendicular to the one below, rising at a forty-five-degree angle toward the hilltop. "This could be a doorway."

"It is. Look, this metal strap runs the width of the door. I bet it's holding several boards together to form a door."

Harry shoveled dirt from atop the bottom board until he found where it met another perpendicular board on the other side. "It's about three feet across," he said.

Sara flung another shovelful of earth aside. "We're lucky no one has come by yet."

They were exposed to anyone who happened past. Harry looked back toward the car park to find no new arrivals. The copse of trees partially shielded them from being seen by beachgoers; above them, the solitary kite still flew against the dark sky. He dug faster.

Ten minutes of furious shoveling revealed a wooden door two feet below the surface, three feet wide and half again as tall. Sweat rolled down his neck as he tossed the last shovel of dirt aside and collapsed to his knees. "That's it," he said.

Sara drained the water bottle and kicked him again. "Get up and help me open this door."

Harry grumbled loud enough to be sure she caught it as he stood, reaching into the pack for their crowbar. It was the only thing sturdy enough to lift the door, which consisted of wide boards banded together with corroded metal strips at the top and bottom. "Looks like iron." Harry nicked one strip. "Iron's heavy."

"All we have to do is get it open a few inches, then the car jack will do the rest."

Harry dropped his shovel. "Stay here." He ran to their rental car, fumbled in the trunk for a minute, then returned with the jack, handing it to Sara. "Stay back when I lift this. The wood could crack. You'll lose a hand if it drops on you."

The crowbar bit into the wood frame when he tried to slide it between the boards. Splinters flew. "I can't get under the door without tearing up the wood."

Sara frowned. "Keep trying."

He hefted the crowbar. It slammed down, shards flew and he now had a space between the boards where he could insert his fingers. Wriggling it caused further damage but also gave him more purchase, enough to lean back and forth until the door budged. "I think the door will hold," Harry said. Back and forth, to and fro, he moved up and down the length of the opening to break the door free. He managed to get the crowbar in and lever up the door enough to create a gap of a few inches. No way could he get the jack in there.

Harry stood, stretched the ache out of his back until it popped like a firecracker, then waved Sara over. "Get me some rocks. I need to prop this door open."

"Where am I going to find rocks in sandy soil near a beach?"

"Where the Vikings left them." Harry pointed toward one of the building foundations they'd walked past. "There are loose stones over there. Get me sturdy, flat ones."

Her mouth opened. "You want me to ruin this site?"

Harry gestured to the mounds of dirt and damaged wood around them. "You're joking."

She raised a finger, opened her mouth and said nothing. Her finger dropped. "Fine. But you are helping me put them back after we're done."

"If you say so. Now move it. I need those stones to prop the door open enough to use the jack."

Sara went at it. As Harry continued working the crowbar and keeping an eye out for any unwanted attention, she gathered enough stones to prop the door up high enough in two places. He leaned on the crowbar as she stacked the stones, alternating ends until the frame stood open just enough for the jack to slide in. Harry resisted the urge to look inside with a flashlight. Sara did not. "I see steps leading down."

"You won't see anything if these stones slip. Get back." Only after she moved, grumbling all the while, did he lever the jack up until it was snug against door and frame. "Keep your eyes open. There's still someone on the beach." He pointed to the kite fluttering against the dark clouds. "They might decide to come here."

"What would you have me do?"

"Just keep watching." The jack lever pumped up and down, causing the metal machine to bite into the doorframe at first, pushing the wood up but not moving the door. Harry closed his eyes and sent out a prayer to any deities in the vicinity. *This wood had better hold.*

Another pump, then another. The frame was solid. Maybe there was a god of sturdy wood out there. He said another silent prayer. Inch by inch he levered the door up, its iron hinges groaning, until the jack reached its limit. Harry stepped back, holding his hands steady. It had worked.

"I'm going to try and lift it up," Harry said. "Get back so it doesn't smash you flat."

"You can't lift that," Sara said.

"Watch me." He knelt before the black opening in the door, nothing more than two feet of pure darkness into which he had to stick his legs. That was the only way to get this thing open. An utter lack of confidence didn't stop him from squatting on the edge and putting one leg after another into the opening. His feet found purchase, and Harry stuck his arms through now, pulling them tight against his chest. The door was big, but he knew two things. First, most of the muscle mass in your body is in your legs. He could lift a heck of a lot more with his bottom half than his top. Second, doors were meant to be opened. Ataulf wouldn't have built a door if he didn't intend for someone to eventually open it. Maybe a massive Visigoth warrior, though they were in short supply at the moment, so Harry would have to suffice.

He took a breath, gritted his teeth, and stood. Or tried to. He went nowhere. "This is heavy."

"You are the dumbest smart person I know." Sara looked all around. "At least no one has heard us yet."

"I'll get it." Muscles strained, Harry grunted, and the door shifted. He nearly shouted with joy before the sound of rocks falling made his stomach turn. The rocks Sara had piled. The ones keeping this door open. Now the only thing holding it up was Harry.

He lifted again. Ancient wood bit into his hands and bottom like long knives, cutting off the blood flow. He kept the door going, inches at a time, never stopping to think what could happen if he slipped, how quickly his legs could be sliced off if the door slammed down on them. Harry closed his eyes and gave it everything he had.

He opened his eyes and nearly fell over when Sara bulled her way into the opening, the same as he had, and started lifting alongside him. If he had an ounce of strength to spare he'd have yelled at her. He didn't, so he pushed.

The door moved. A bit more, then faster until they both let out a yell as they stood up and heaved the door open ahead of them, the big wooden block pivoting on ancient hinges before it flipped over and crashed into the sandy earth with a muffled *thud*. Harry kept going with it and slipped. He tumbled, tucking and rolling as the ground went out from beneath him, until he fell into an open void and crashed down in darkness.

He lay on his back, the wind knocked out of him. Dirt filled his nose, the gritty sand making him sneeze until he could draw a breath and open his eyes. Harry had descended into absolute darkness, the air so heavy he could scarcely breathe. He sneezed again, and the world returned for an instant, giving him a glimpse of the now shattered entranceway above.

Harry sneezed again. It wasn't just the dirt. There was something fuzzy on his face. He ripped it away as a searing light stabbed his eyes. He turned his head away and threw a hand over his face.

He felt Sara's hand on his shoulder. "Are you okay?" she asked him.

"Get that light out of my eyes." Harry pushed her hand away and the light vanished.

"Stop pushing me." Sara stepped back, pointing her flashlight away so it didn't blind him.

Harry looked around, dots dancing on his vision from the flashlight. He rolled to get on his feet and smashed into something else.

Sara's voice boomed again. "Stop moving around."

He had no choice but to obey, lying back in the dirt. "Are we inside a tomb?"

"What's left of one. Get up." She didn't speak until he was on his feet, moving more carefully this time. "You smashed through the door."

Which explained the wood shards everywhere. But what about the fuzzy thing that had touched his face?

Sara grabbed his shoulder and twisted him away from the broken entrance door. "We found it. Ataulf's burial chamber."

He swiveled his head around to get his first look at a room buried for nearly two millennia. Sara's flashlight played over the chamber. A chamber filled with treasures. A metal shield sat atop a low table, with a terrifying double-edged sword, rusted chainmail and a scepter beside it. Thick pelts hung on the wall behind him. *That's what fell on my face.* He looked down. A cloak of bear pelts lay balled at his feet. No doubt a warrior's prized possession. Harry turned and continued to study the room.

Thick wooden beams ran the length of the floor, as well as up the side walls, and arched overhead for support. It resembled a personal mead hall for Ataulf's journey to Valhalla, a hall filled with Ataulf's worldly goods. Harry's gaze dropped back to what lay on the table in front of him. His eyes narrowed. *Why the weapons and scepter?*

"Look back there." Sara aimed her light to the chamber's rear. "Those are all chests."

Harry followed her gaze. Wooden chests held together with metal bands. The sort used for storing clothes or goods. Or something more valuable. "Those are big locks on them," Harry said. He did not move toward them. "I'm more interested in this." He picked up the scepter. It was over a foot long and made of iron, the lower end flat and studded with gemstones – sapphires, emeralds and several diamonds. The upper end crooked in a ninety-degree turn, a pair of identical runes carved into the silver on either side.

"What does this say?" Harry asked.

Sara leaned over it. "It's the rune for *Thor.* This other symbol is a lightning bolt."

"Is it a ceremonial scepter?"

Sara shrugged. "Possibly. Or a repurposed treasure stolen during a raid." She turned away. "The chests should tell the story. I hope they left keys."

He doubted that. "I have another idea." Harry laid the scepter down and walked over to the side table, which was apparently an armory. A double-headed battle-axe called to him. "This will take care of those locks."

Sara didn't acknowledge him. "This is wrong."

"What part?" Harry hefted the axe. Intricate carvings adorned the blade. A four-pointed star was at the top, as though a throwing star had been added. The darn thing was *heavy*. "Breaking into this tomb? Not calling the authorities? Or a different part?"

"The burial chamber is wrong."

He looked around. The room had been dug into the ground; wooden beams surrounded it, from the floor to the curved ceiling overhead. "Isn't it supposed to look like this?"

"Burial chambers are for burying people." She pointed to the long, empty table in the room's center. "Where's Ataulf?"

She was right. They were in a burial chamber with no body. "Do you think his body was stolen?"

"Give me a minute." Sara motioned for him to stay put. She began walking around the room, first stopping at the table beside him and checking the armor and sword, then moving on to the chests lining the back wall. Each lock held when she pulled on it. Still she said nothing, moving around to the far wall, one with pelts hanging on it above various tools and what looked like a board game with pieces of horn and carved stone scattered on the floor. Finally, she returned to the vacant table in the room's center. "Yes, I do think the body has been moved."

"Why would the Visigoths move his body?"

"It's hard to say. Perhaps he gave them instructions to move it. I suspect the Visigoths took Ataulf with them when they migrated."

"They'd travel with his body?"

Sara turned to him. "Don't be surprised. Vladimir Lenin's body has been on public display in Moscow since 1924." She pointed around the room. "But there's another reason why I think this. The chests that are still here. Grave robbers wouldn't steal a body and leave unopened chests."

Which raised another question. "What do you think is in those chests?"

"I don't think I want to know how you intend to find out."

"Ataulf isn't here. The German runestone said *Thor's power is with Ataulf.* This armor and the rest of it is interesting. It's also not *Thor's power.* We need to open those chests."

Sara fidgeted, the battle playing out on her face. She bit her lip. "Please open them gently."

Harry glanced at his watch. "I don't have time for that." He grabbed the battle-axe, thought better of it and set the axe back down, then hefted the crowbar, which had fallen in with him. "This will do the trick. It opened that door."

He strode over to the four large chests that lined the back wall. Each had an iron lock on it. Harry paid no attention to those ancient locks. His crowbar had no chance against them. However, it was a match for the wood the locks were bolted to. He lifted the crowbar, took aim at the first chest, and crashed it into the wood, turning his head away to avoid the flying splinters.

The crowbar bounced off and his teeth rattled. "This wood is like stone," Harry said. Again he tried, and again it did nothing. "I can't break through it."

Sara pointed to the far wall. "One of those tools may work."

He walked back to her, handed her the crowbar and grabbed the battle-axe that had been his first choice. "This one will."

Before she could argue he moved back to the nearest chest and went for it. Up went the axe, down it crashed and the lock went flying. "Wow." Harry tugged and pulled until the axe came free. "That worked."

Sara nudged him out of the way. "Don't break the others open yet."

He watched as Sara lifted the remaining piece of lid. "My goodness."

Harry looked over her shoulder at the largest silver dish he'd ever seen. Two feet in diameter, with Roman gods cast into the edges and Latin lettering etched into the center. Sara picked it up with a grunt. "It's solid." The plate thumped on the table when she turned and set it down. "That's the owner's name written on it. Oh, my."

Harry studied the Latin text. *CAESAR AUGUSTUS.* "Augustus," he said. "The first Roman emperor."

"I've seen a few others like it in museums." She turned and pointed. "Open those other chests."

The axe worked its magic. Three swings, three more locks sent flying. Harry set the axe down with care, lest he lose a toe, then stood back as Sara lifted the first lid. Dazzling light washed across the chamber. Harry leaned over before he could stop himself. "Rubies. Sapphires." He coughed. "*Diamonds.*"

Sara reached in and lifted a bejeweled goblet. "The cup of a Caesar," she said. "Augustus again."

She handed it to him. Harry briefly considered whether it would fit in his pack and how he'd get it back to America. Until Sara opened the next chest. "Here are the pitchers." She lifted out two towering pitchers, each big enough to hold several liters of water or wine. Gemstones dotted the silver surface of each. "These are worth a fortune."

"More than that to the right buyer," Harry said.

Sara spun to face him. "We cannot keep them. We promised Nora. These relics belong to the Swedish people."

He groaned inwardly. "I was just kidding."

"There's one more chest," Sara said. She didn't hand him the pitchers, instead putting them back in. "It's the biggest one."

Harry reluctantly put the goblet back into the other chest. She lifted the lid on the last chest, her body blocking his view.

"What's in it?" He moved to her side to get a look. "That's not Roman."

"Hold this." Sara handed him her flashlight and knelt down to retrieve the object inside. Metal flashed when it came out. "This is a Viking relic."

"Another drinking horn?" Harry tilted his head.

"A king's drinking horn." Sara turned the horn so he could see it, her face coming alive in the light. "King Ataulf. Look at the writing. Ataulf left us another message."

Harry's breath caught in his throat. "It's the same code that's on the horn you deciphered."

"Get another light from your pack." Sara turned and set the drinking horn on the room's center table while Harry grabbed a second light, aiming both at the horn. "It looks like a ceremonial horn," she said. "Too large for everyday use."

This horn resembled the earlier pair they had uncovered. It was much taller, made of silver with gold trim all along its rim. Etched runes covered the entire surface. "What does it say?" Harry asked.

Sara had her phone out, using her digital notes to translate. "Listen to this." She began reading from the upper edge, turning the horn as she went.

These treasures are to serve King Ataulf in the afterlife and to honor his memory in his first resting place. The king wished to leave a mark if his body ever moved. A path to follow him forever. King Ataulf moves with the power of Thor and his people to the top of this land where it touches the sky and watches Njord's home. Thor's power will be safe under King Ataulf's lost treasure.

"I was right." Sara set the horn down. "It was the Visigoths who moved Ataulf's body. That's why this settlement vanished. Everyone left after Ataulf died."

"Why?"

"It is difficult to say. Regardless of why, this *was* Ataulf's grave before his body was moved. Norsemen believed the souls of departed warriors could collect burial goods from any chamber dedicated to the warrior. This was the Visigoth way of providing Ataulf with enough material possessions to live as a king forever."

"Why not take it with them and build a new gravesite?"

"Good question." She wiped dirt from her cheek. "One I can't answer. What we *can* answer is the riddle on this horn."

"Which points us to the location of his new grave," Harry said. "Any idea where *the top of this land where it touches the sky* is?"

Her teeth flashed in the dim chamber. "The Vikings were explorers and warriors, but also traders. I doubt they would abandon this location without reason. They enjoyed prosperous trade on an easily defensible island."

"*This land* actually means Gotland?"

"I believe so. It's a relatively flat island, as well. There are only a handful of actual mountains close to the water."

She thought for a moment. "*Njord's home.* Of course. *Njord* is the Norse sea god. They're talking about a location beside the ocean."

"Which narrows it down for us. There are perhaps five possible places."

"We have to check them all." Harry forced himself to forget about the Roman treasure. "Come on. We need to figure out—"

"I know where to go."

He spun, slipped, and caught himself just in time. "How?"

"Five possible locations, at best. Only one of them has a runestone on the top."

Harry shook his head. "Thank goodness you came along. Where is it?"

"About ten miles from here."

"Let's get moving." He headed for the stairs and the gloomy daylight framed between the two broken doors, grabbing the scepter along the way. The hooked end made him think of a key, and years in the field told him not to ignore his gut. Why else would it have been left behind, other than to serve a purpose? "I have a feeling about this," he said as he picked it up and kept moving. "I promise I'll give it to the government when we're done."

Nothing but silence followed him. "What's going on?" Harry asked over his shoulder.

Sara stood over the drinking horn chest, looking down into it. The horn was in her hands. "We missed something."

Harry bolted back to the chest. "More treasure?"

"Of a sort." She reached into the dark box and came out with a hunk of wood. "This is different."

His flashlight beam played over it, and even so, it took a few seconds to register. "It's a wooden carving." He squinted. "An eagle."

"It's a toy."

"Why would Ataulf put a toy eagle in a chest with his drinking horn?"

Her words were hard to catch, as though Sara spoke to herself. "This is for his son. Ataulf's dream was to reunite with Theodosius. The Visigoths believed the son might try to find his father in the afterlife. This toy is a marker for Theodosius. Ataulf wanted to help his son to find him."

Harry considered the horn's message. "Could his son be the *power of Thor* Ataulf keeps mentioning?"

"I doubt it. Thor has no association with children. I believe the phrase is a metaphor for something physical, a permanent object. I'm not sure what, though."

Harry put an arm around her shoulders. "We're one step closer to finding out. Thanks to you."

"Your small contributions have been noted."

"I feel the love. Ready to go?"

Sara didn't answer. She studied the toy eagle in her hand for a long breath. The look in her eyes kept Harry silent until Sara leaned down and gently placed the eagle back in the open chest. She kept the drinking horn and walked away. "I hope they found each other."

A kite danced on the ocean wind, zipping back and forth across the sky.

One man held it tightly, though anyone watching would find the joy usually seen while flying such a carefree toy was absent from his face. Rather, this man seemed intense. As though keeping the kite airborne was a mission to be completed, not a game to be enjoyed. The man stood alone on the beach, an earpiece in his ear. His name was Niko Sparv, and he never turned around to look behind him, toward the hills above. Toward where two people had just uncovered a Viking burial chamber.

Niko also never turned to look at a specific spot in the distance. A spot atop a slight rise, which would serve as the perfect vantage point to watch the two people who had been digging with abandon for over an hour. A spot where, if the watchers lay flat, the people digging would never see them.

Atop the rise Jacob Pedersen lowered his binoculars. "The man and woman are back on the surface." Jacob spoke softly into a cell phone on the ground in front of him. The line was open, Magnus Dahl listening as Jacob provided real-time updates. The man flying the kite also listened via his earpiece. "The woman is holding something," Jacob continued. "It resembles a drinking horn."

Ingvar Larsen lay on the grass next to Jacob. He too had binoculars. "A large one," Ingvar said.

Magnus's tinny voice came out of the phone. "Is there any chance you can recover it?"

"Not without conflict," Jacob said.

"We cannot take that risk without knowing who they are. Can you take their photograph?"

"We do not have the proper equipment."

"Then follow them," Magnus said.

Ingvar frowned. "Do you think it is wise to leave this new site unattended? Other artifacts may be inside."

"Leave Niko behind. Have him inspect the site. You two follow the man and woman. Send me their license plate so I can check who owns the vehicle. Tell Niko to leave the site as he finds it." Jacob and Ingvar said they would. "Where are the two intruders now?" Magnus asked.

"Getting in their car," Jacob said. "We will follow them."

Jacob radioed Niko with instructions to inspect the newly opened ground as they took up pursuit of the two intruders, staying well back so the pair would never see them coming until it was too late.

Chapter 13

Gotland

Harry's phone vibrated as he turned off the main road and drove toward their next destination. "It's Nora," he said, and connected the call. "Hello. I'm here with Sara."

"Did you find anything?" Nora asked.

Right to the point, as always. "Sara can explain."

Sara recapped what they had just discovered. "We're at the second site now," Sara finished.

"Darned lucky how close you were," Nora said.

"Luck isn't the entire reason," Sara said. "These runestones were left here a thousand years ago. At that time, few people traveled more than ten miles from where they were born during their entire lives."

"Any idea what's there?"

"Nothing I care to say out loud."

"Signs of danger?"

Harry took this one. "None, and we've been careful. There was hardly anyone around at the first site. This one looks deserted too."

They were at a Viking archaeological site; this place didn't even have a gravel parking lot. At least the trees had been cut back from around the stone and the grass had recently been cut. "This runestone is big," Harry said, craning his neck to look. "Twice as tall as me."

"Is it another burial mound?" Nora asked.

"Possibly," Sara said. "I have to read the stone first. There are small hills around us, so it's possible."

Nora said. "I can call the local police if you'd like, have them come help."

"We just removed a Norse artifact from the last site," Harry said. "Better we see this through first."

"Harry," Nora said. "I need to tell you something. The man who sold you those drinking horns has started talking."

"Jan," Harry said. "What did he tell you?"

"His real name was Wilhelm."

Harry missed it at first. Sara did not. "What do you mean *was*?"

Harry drove in silence for several moments until Nora spoke again. "He was found dead in his jail cell today. They think he was poisoned. Preliminary evidence suggests botulinum toxin."

Sara jumped in. "What is botulinum toxin and how did it get into his system?"

"Botulinum toxin is better known as Botox."

"The injections that eliminate wrinkles?"

"Yes," Nora said. "The cosmetic treatment utilizes only a minute mount of a single protein extracted from the bacterial toxin. The entire toxin is incredibly lethal. Oslo police believe Wilhelm ingested the toxin orally. However, they aren't certain on that point."

"He either ate or drank it," Harry said. "How did he get it?"

"The police don't know yet. Wilhelm's attorney was his only visitor and claims he didn't bring any food or drink into their meeting."

"So Wilhelm started talking and now he's dead," Harry said.

"Now you understand there's more going on than you realize," Nora said. "Keep your eyes open. These drinking horns are dangerous."

Harry promised they would and clicked off. He looked in the rearview mirror as a car drove past the turnoff for this site. Drove past slowly. He watched as the car kept rolling and eventually picked up steam before rounding a turn and moving out of sight. Harry shook his head. No time to get jumpy now.

"It's getting dark," Sara said as he parked in the grass. "Bring your flashlight."

She got out and he followed. The runestone stretched above them, this one as wide as a car. "I thought the last one was big," Harry said. The stone ahead dwarfed the previous one.

"It's one of the largest stones I researched." Sara pointed around them. "See how it's out in the open? That means the Vikings who raised it used movable tools, pulleys and hooks of some sort. You couldn't move it without them."

"They weren't just shipbuilders."

"Far from it." Sara pulled out her flashlight and lit up the stone. "These runes aren't in any sort of code."

Harry's fingers grazed the ceramic knuckledusters in his pocket. He looked around. Nothing but open fields and trees. "What does it say?"

Sara didn't respond as her flashlight beam moved across the stone. Harry kept watch as they stood in silence. The gray clouds overhead had darkened to a metallic hue, the sun having given up hope on today before slinking off to call it an early night. A chill wind snuck up his shirtsleeves. Harry crossed his arms and flexed his fingers.

"Look at this."

He twisted to find Sara standing inches from the runestone with her light aimed at a single rune, one she traced with a finger over and over. "Right here."

He tilted his head. "It's a rune."

"More than that."

Harry spoke multiple languages, but he couldn't read a word of this. "Help me out here."

"Get your light out." Only after he followed orders and had his light on the rune as well did she look at him. "This rune isn't a word. It's a *name.*"

He hazarded a guess. "King Ataulf?"

"Close. It says *Theodosius Ataulfsson.* As in *son of Ataulf.*"

"Why mention him?"

"I don't know."

Harry played his light over the stone. The wind had picked up, carrying with it a sound that made him twist around. The sound of an approaching car. "Get down," he said.

Sara did not get down. "Because you see headlights?"

On cue, a pair of headlights came around the bend of the road ahead. The car slowed as it passed the entrance to the site and then rolled slowly onward, out of view.

"I've seen that car," he said. "It followed us here."

"Harry, every other car on the ferry looked like that one."

"I'm telling you it's the same one," he said. "A small sedan, dark-colored."

Sara waved a dismissive hand. "You're the last person I expect to be jumpy. It's only a car on a quiet road. Don't let Nora's warning about a poisoned turncoat make you nervous."

He wanted to tell her it *should* make them nervous. "Fine. What's special about Ataulf's son being mentioned here?"

"I'm working on it."

Sara kept reading. Harry held his light up and angled his head. "The rune of his name looks odd." Harry reached out. "Almost like it's outlined. See this?" He traced a faint line encircling the rune. "It's set apart from the other runes. There's more space around it."

"You're right." Sara took several quick steps back. "*Theodosius Ataulfsson* doesn't align with the other runes."

"These runes aren't the straightest words ever written. The guy wasn't writing on lined paper."

Sara agreed. "Look at every other rune. None of them are written so haphazardly." She touched her chin. "Perhaps I'm wrong. Why would this particular rune be carved in such a manner?"

Harry peered at it again. The rune didn't just stand out. It had a purpose, a reason for looking like it did. He rubbed the stubble on his chin, an idea taking shape. He walked around the stone and ran his light over the rear side. No runes adorned this part, the only engraving a jagged line carved above the feature Harry secretly expected to find. "Got you."

Sara's voice sounded from around the stone. "What?"

"Come here." She walked around to join him. Harry pointed at what he'd found.

"It's a hole – probably a handhold," Sara said. "Likely created to help lift the stone. Perhaps it's natural."

"I don't think it's an imperfection or part of the moving process. Why carve this image above the hole?" He pointed to what resembled a bolt of lightning.

Sara frowned. "What are you suggesting?"

"Wait." Harry jogged back to their parked car, popped the trunk and retrieved something before returning to Sara's side. He held it out. "I think this is part of it."

She reached out and took the scepter from him. "The iron scepter? I'm not sure it's even a Visigothic artifact. It's certainly not tied to this runestone."

The corner of his mouth turned up a smidge. "Want to bet?" He took the scepter from her unresisting hands. "The rune for Ataulf's son is on the front. It's roughly level with this hole here on the back side."

"What does that matter?"

He pointed. "Does this carving above the hole look like a lightning bolt to you?"

"I suppose it does."

"You know anyone who uses lightning?"

"Thor."

"Lightning is *Thor's power.* That's what we're trying to find. And where is it? *Under King Ataulf's lost treasure.*"

"You believe this runestone is Ataulf's lost treasure?"

Harry shook his head. "I believe Ataulf's treasure is *on* the runestone." He moved to the front side and pointed to a rune. "Right here."

"Theodosius Ataulfsson," Sara said. "His son. His lost son." Lines furrowed her brow. "How does this tie in to the scepter and the hole?"

He held the scepter up. "This isn't a scepter. It's a key, and the keyhole is right here."

The furrows deepened. "The key to what?"

"No idea. Let's find out." The wind whistled around him. The road was clear to one side, while a short rise shielded them from view in the other direction.

He didn't force the key into the opening, which was about the size of a deck of cards. Exactly the same size as the scepter's top end. It slid in with hardly a scrape until it suddenly stopped and held fast. He shone his light on it, wiggling the scepter from side to side. If this was a keyhole, there should be a smaller slot for the end to slide in. Like teeth on modern keys. He twisted and prodded, feeling his way around with chilled fingers until the key slipped to one side and locked in place. *There's an opening in here.*

"It fits," he told her. "I'm trying to turn it."

He twisted, slowly at first, then with more pressure. First in one direction, then the other. The jagged line above the keyhole tied back to Thor, he remembered, to a power of some sort. Would lightning flash down from the sky? No, that was all mythical mumbo-jumbo. At least he hoped so. Harry looked to the clouds, then leaned hard on the key and pushed.

It slipped, moving a few inches. He redoubled his efforts, gritting his teeth as he twisted and grunted, giving it all he had.

Stone scraped again. The key twisted. Harry groaned between clenched teeth and kept pushing. The muscles in his arms screamed and the grating sound of rock sliding over rock filled the air until he lost his grip and fell headlong against the runestone, scraping skin off his face. A thunderous crack split the air, the rock groaned and Sara screamed. Harry turned to her, only to be taken clean off his feet as she barreled into him like a linebacker, taking them both to the ground as the towering runestone split in half, the front end falling as though Thor's mighty hammer itself had come down upon it.

Harry's brain rattled as he hit the ground, Sara's weight crushing the air from his lungs as she landed on him. He twisted free. "Are you okay?" he asked, trying to rise.

She grabbed his shoulder and pulled herself up, knocking him down again in the process. "You were right." Sara stood over him, breathing hard. "The scepter was a key. It actually worked."

Harry scrambled to his feet. "You're lucky it didn't crush you." In front of them lay half of the stone, now lying flat on the ground where Sara had been standing moments ago.

"It clipped my foot on the way down." She grabbed his arm and turned him. "The runestone isn't solid. Look."

He did. "Just like I thought."

The runestone was not only a marker. It was a huge, hollow chest containing one incredible object. "That's a battle-axe," Sara said. "You thought it would be here?"

Harry nudged her aside and reached down. "The outline behind the *Ataulfsson* rune made me think this stone might be hollow. Add in that the scepter looked like a key and it wasn't hard. I had no idea about the axe, though."

"Why didn't you say anything?"

"It was only a hunch."

Sara grabbed his arm and pulled back on it. "Give me some light."

Harry pulled his flashlight out and aimed it at the fallen stone. A fearsome double-headed axe lay in the inner chamber, measuring a full three feet from base to pointed tip. Dazzling jewels reflected Harry's light over everything, and he could see that runes had been carved on the blade. It was both awesome and terrifying. "This isn't a fighting weapon," Harry said. "The shaft is silver and the blade is gold."

Sara grunted as she reached in and lifted the axe. "Only the wealthiest chieftain could afford such an opulent weapon. These jewels are real. I expect they came from Rome." Her gaze moved up the handle to the double-headed blade. "It's exquisite."

"Are the runes in Ataulf's code?"

"No. And there's writing on both sides." She laid the axe down, studied it for a moment, then began reading aloud.

King Ataulf's axe, a gift from Thor, who gave Ataulf's people power to defeat the White God and make his power theirs.

"Turn it over so I can read the other side," she said.

The roar of a racing engine filled the air. Harry jumped up as a pair of headlights came around the low rise. A car veered off the road toward them, zooming up the entranceway before skidding to a halt in the parking area. Two men got out, lit by the day's last light.

Both men moved toward Harry and Sara without speaking. Sara backed up and bumped into Harry. He stepped in front of her. "Tell them we found it this way," Harry whispered.

The men closed in. "Are you injured?" the driver asked in English, his words accented. A local accent. "We saw the stone fall."

"We're fine," Harry said. He studied the man: thickly built with a very respectable beard. A chill ran up Harry's neck. It wasn't from the wind.

The passenger, smaller than his companion, moved past Harry. "Good," he said. "Look at this runestone. How did this happen? These stones are – *prise gudene*." He had spotted the axe.

Harry frowned. "What?"

The driver hurriedly jumped in. "He is relieved you are safe."

The driver kept talking but Harry didn't listen. His mind was in overdrive.

How did they know we speak English?

Harry looked down the road, back toward where the car had appeared from. He couldn't see more than a few hundred yards. The sloping hill would have hidden the runestone from view.

"How did you see us?" he asked.

The passenger ignored Harry, clutching the battle-axe as though it were a gift from the gods. The driver spoke. "We were driving this way," he said, again in English. "We saw it fall."

Harry's hand slipped into his pocket, his fingers threading through the knuckledusters. He pointed at the mound in question. "You can't see us from the road."

Now the passenger turned around. He looked at Harry and Sara as though for the first time. It was a look Harry had seen plenty of times before. Disgust.

Harry backed up a step, pushing Sara along behind him. "Who are you? And how did you know we spoke English, not Swedish?"

The driver balked. The passenger did not. "If you are smart," he said. "You will leave."

Sara spoke to Harry softly in Arabic. "*Yajib 'an narkud?*" Should we run?

The passenger's face twisted. "Heathen scum." The man reached under his jacket and brought out a short, strange-looking axe. "Leave now."

Sara jumped back when the strange weapon appeared. The driver moved toward his colleague, arms out as he shouted at his colleague. "No!"

This wasn't the first time Harry had faced down a blade. This axe had one sharp side, currently aimed at Harry's chest as the passenger advanced. Harry flexed his fingers in the knuckledusters. His other hand, still holding his flashlight, pointed down, and as the armed man moved toward him, Harry did what seemed like the dumbest thing.

He charged. Screaming, Harry lifted the flashlight up and aimed it at the man's eyes. In the dim light it blinded him. He lifted an arm to shield his eyes as he took a wild swing with the axe. Harry stepped out of reach, let the blade whiz past, and wound up his other hand. The passenger stumbled forward and Harry laid into him with his reinforced fist. He'd landed better punches, but not many.

The passenger flew backwards as though from an explosion. The axe dropped to the ground, landing at the same time its owner did. Both lay motionless in the grass.

Sara shouted from behind him to watch out. The driver was running at Harry now, unarmed but big enough to plow him over. Harry feinted left, the driver bit, then Harry slipped past the bullrush and kicked out a leg to trip his assailant. The man stumbled and went to one knee. *Got you.* He turned and loosed another punch with the dusters.

The driver's hand shot up and knocked Harry's incoming blow aside. He grabbed hold of Harry's arm and pulled him down, using his shoulder as a fulcrum to send Harry tumbling. Harry rolled, jumped to his feet and put his fists up.

The bigger man moved in fast. No feints, no bluffs, only a straight-on attack. The first punch glanced off Harry's head. The second Harry blocked with a forearm. Harry leaned in and headbutted the guy's nose and followed with a shot to the stomach. The guy hardly budged before throwing another punch that knocked Harry down.

He fell heavily on top of the opened runestone, his entire body vibrating with the impact and the breath leaving his lungs. The driver came toward him. A high-pitched scream stopped him in his tracks.

Sara flew out of the darkness, her foot a blur as it snapped up and caught the driver under the chin. He stumbled, unable to avoid her follow-up jab to the ear. Disoriented, he stumbled to one knee. Sara kicked for his chin again but he blocked it with an elbow. As Harry scrambled to his feet the driver grabbed Sara's hair and tossed her aside.

Harry scrambled to his feet, pulled back his fist and aimed for the guy's nose. This time he connected. A direct shot that sent the big man down for good.

Harry gave him a kick in the ribs for good measure as he leapt over the prone man to help Sara to her feet. "Are you okay?" he asked.

"I'm fine," she said. "You?"

"I'm good." He glanced behind him. Neither man was moving. "Time to go."

"Not without the axe." Sara ran for the broken stone and retrieved the battle-axe. Harry checked that his father's amulet was still tucked beneath his shirt before he scooped up the odd-looking smaller axe that had nearly cut him in two and rifled both men's pockets for their wallets. With a last look behind them, they ran for their car, but not before Harry made a quick stop. The strange axe made short work of the intruders' tires – a dark sedan, Harry noted wryly – before he and Sara hopped into their own car. Gravel flew as Harry floored it.

"I got their wallets," Harry said over the whine of the engine. "We need to know who's after us." Sara did not respond. "You okay?" he asked. Nothing. He looked over to find her studying the battle-axe. "What is it?"

"There are runes on both sides of the axe head. I didn't see that the other side is written in Ataulf's code." She looked up at him. "I know why the axe was in that runestone. Ataulf's path doesn't end here. Not even close."

Chapter 14

Stockholm, Sweden

The world slowly came into focus. Harry cracked one eye open, then the other. Horrible morning sunlight slipped around the hotel room curtains. What was that awful racket?

"Wake up. Our flight leaves in two hours."

Sara ripped the covers off him. Harry cursed her ancestors. "Very mature," she said. "Get up." A towel landed on his head. "You need a shower."

A glance at the bedside clock revealed he'd slept for only a few hours. After escaping from the runestone site without any axe holes in either of them, Harry and Sara had raced back to Gotland to catch the last ferry of the day to the Swedish mainland. They never left their car other than when Harry had stopped to grab food and throw the strange axe overboard. It was a replica Viking battle-axe, Sara told him. Why the man would possess it was beyond them until Sara looked at the contents of the stolen wallets.

"Ingvar Larsen." Her eyes widened.

Harry looked at her, puzzled. "Who?"

She explained Ingvar was a well-known Norwegian nationalist with a large following. A frequent speaker on the less reputable news platforms across Norway and the neighboring countries, he extolled the virtues of those nations' shared Viking heritage while advocating for a return to the past, when Norwegians, Swedes and Danes were one people. Homogenous, powerful, uncompromising. Qualities Ingvar claimed were absent in the modern world while contending that they were all the poorer for it. He urged Scandinavians to assert themselves, to lead for the future. That this also put them a step above anyone who didn't look or think as they did was of no concern to him."

"Is he connected to Magnus Dahl?" Harry asked in the safety of their car. "That group of his, The Scandinavians."

Sara shook her head. "Not really. Ingvar is an extreme nationalist who brings all the ugly parts of such rhetoric to the table. He says his people are better than others, more righteous, chosen by the Norse gods."

"And everybody else?"

"If by *everybody* you mean women, minorities and those who don't worship Odin and Thor? They can get in line, or find somewhere else to live. He's a flamethrowing culture warrior who supports intolerant behavior. And he has quite a following. Not as large as Magnus Dahl's society, but Ingvar should not be underestimated. However, his platform differs greatly from The Scandinavians."

"How so?"

"Magnus Dahl wants to reunite the countries based on Viking ideals of strength, courage, a sense of adventure. The big difference is Magnus's vision includes everyone. You can be different and still be a part of his future. There's room for all manner of people. That's not true in Ingvar's world."

Harry had digested all of this as the ferry swayed gently on the water. Sara studied the battle-axe, then pulled out her phone and began taking notes. Only after she finished did she speak. What she'd told him had almost knocked Harry flat on his back.

That had been less than twelve hours ago. Harry caught a glimpse of himself in the mirror as he stepped out of the hotel room's steaming-hot shower. He quickly looked away. Dark bruises covered most of his torso and face, a gruesome sight to behold. Muscles protested as he toweled off and dressed. Sara stood by the room's desk when he walked out. The battle-axe lay on it in front of her.

"Come over here," she ordered. "Listen to me one more time before we go."

It had become a ritual of hers. Review the evidence, formulate a theory, and only then share it with Harry, going through it step by step to see if it held water.

"The runes aren't encoded." She read aloud.

King Ataulf's axe, a gift from Thor, who gave Ataulf's people power to defeat the White God and make his power theirs.

"Sounds like a museum placard," Harry said. "Explaining what you're looking at. Most of it makes sense. Except the *White God* part and *his power.* Any idea what that means?"

"Yes. And no. It clearly refers to another deity, though it's too vague to pinpoint exactly which one. The phrase *White God* is used in reference to the possibility that ancient cultures were first visited by white people long ago. These cultures had never seen light-skinned people before, so they believed them to be gods. It's also used in reference to extraterrestrial beings."

"Aliens."

"Little green men. Or white men, in this case. I also know of a goddess named Leucothea in Greek mythology referred to in this manner." She looked up from the axe. "It could also be about Jesus Christ, who some cultures referred to as a White God. That's unlikely, though, given Jesus of Nazareth lived in the first century. Archaeological remains, period art and historical texts all indicate the people of Nazareth had olive-brown skin. Jesus was many things. A white guy isn't one of them."

"So *White God* wouldn't be an accurate description."

"It's difficult to say what deity this refers to without more information. What we can say with certainty is the Visigoths valued this battle-axe enough to hide it in the runestone. They also believed it conveys a power tied to this *White God.*" She turned the axe over. "This side is different." She began reading.

Ataulf honors Theodosius as Thor honors his father. Thor commanded Ataulf's people to return his earthly might to the site of Odin's power in Noregr.

"This message ties back to the drinking horns from the dig site as well as the horn from Ataulf's empty burial chamber."

"A continuation of the path we followed."

"A path leading to *the site of Odin's power in Noregr. Noregr* was the name for what we now call Norway."

"We need to find a Norwegian place of worship focused on Odin," Harry said. "The *site of Odin's power* would be where people worshipped him. That's how gods gained power, through worship."

Sara raised a finger. "Not necessarily. The Vikings' faith was decentralized, focusing on the family and maintaining societal connections. Vikings didn't have churches or houses of worship. That concept was introduced to them by Christian missionaries."

"Huh." Harry rubbed his chin. "Then there are potentially hundreds of sites for Odin's power."

A glint of mirth flashed in her eyes. "Yes, if you limit yourself with the idea of a *religious* location. We should also consider other locations of power or influence. What sort of place symbolized power back then?"

Harry snapped his fingers. "Castles. Or fortresses, if we're talking about Vikings."

"Including a Viking fortress known as the historical seat of Norwegian power. One standing since the Vikings ruled Scandinavia."

"Where is it?"

"Avaldsnes Kongsgård estate, in the Norwegian village of Avaldsnes." She wrapped the battle-axe in a towel. "I checked. It's a ninety-minute flight from here."

"Are you bringing that axe?"

Sara planned to pack the axe and check it on the plane as a declared historical artifact. "I don't want to leave it behind."

"Why not?"

"Call it a feeling. Ready to go?"

Harry drove at daredevil speed to the airport. Despite having to fill out a dozen forms in triplicate and pay an exorbitant insurance fee to protect the axe, they made it to their gate minutes before departure, sliding into their first-class seats with seconds to spare. An uneventful Lufthansa flight brought them to the Norwegian city of Haugesund, where Harry rented yet another tiny car for the ninety-minute drive north to Avaldsnes on Norway's west coast alongside the Karmsund strait. The three tallest transmission towers Harry had ever seen loomed in the distance for much of his drive. Sara informed him they were nearly five hundred feet tall.

"That's a lot of power," Harry said.

"Twelve hundred years ago Avaldsnes was the most powerful city in Norway. Now the village is home to a few thousand people and is more notable for its past than its present."

Green fields passed as the road hugged the coastline, taking them past low-slung stone buildings and more animals than people. Few cars passed in the opposite direction, and nearly all of them were dark sedans. Harry eyed each one with suspicion. "At least we'll see the bad guys coming first."

Sara remained very still in the passenger seat. "Do you think they'll follow us here?"

Harry was quiet for a moment. Not long ago he'd promised the lies would stop. About who he was and what he did. About all the rough edges he worried would push her away. He bit off the first response that jumped to his tongue and drummed his fingers on the steering wheel. "I hope not," he said truthfully. "We already beat them once. Maybe they'll take the hint."

"I doubt it." She kept looking ahead.

"Me too." Another mile passed in silence.

"Ingvar worries me," Sara said. "He and those followers of his are unstable. Perhaps he plans to send one of them in his stead."

Harry had no response to that. "I asked Nora to check on him and the other guy, Jacob Pedersen. No word yet." He reached over and touched her leg. "Don't worry. We're a good team."

She finally looked over at him and met his gaze. "Yes. We are."

Harry's phone buzzed on the console beside him. His heart accelerated when he looked at the number. "It's my mother's old cleric."

Sara gave him the universal sign for *Do It,* so he put the call on speaker and answered in Arabic. "*Assalamu alaikum.*" Peace be upon you.

"*Wa alaikum salaam,*" Abdul Jalali replied. And unto you peace. "I would like a minute of your time."

"Of course."

"Since we last spoke I have prayed to Allah for guidance."

The pungent scent of sea air filled his nose as Harry moved into the slow lane. "What were you praying about?"

"I am a man with two unenviable choices of what I should do. Should I honor a promise I believe is wrong, or should I go back on that promise in the hope of bringing enlightenment? Allah has revealed the path to follow. It is the latter."

"I see." Cows dotted the fields that passed his window. "What does that mean?"

"I have lied to you. But with only the best of intentions."

The exit for Avaldsnes appeared ahead. He would have zoomed past it if Sara hadn't pointed out the turn. "You lied?" Harry asked.

"At your father's request."

Harry pulled off the road onto the gravel verge and braked. "What did he ask you to lie about?"

"Your mother."

Harry's stomach turned to ice. A twisted, frozen ball that made his throat tighten. "What about her?"

"Before I tell you, know that I do not have the entire story."

Harry opened his door and stepped out, then motioned for Sara to come and take the wheel. Only after he was in the passenger seat and Sara had them moving again did he respond. "Tell me all of it."

Abdul paused. "Your father came to me after your mother's death.

He told me about a terrible secret, one I swore to Allah I would take to my grave." Another pause, longer this time. "Your father said a letter would come in the mail. Addressed to me, but not for my eyes. The letter was to be held for him. He asked me as a servant of Allah and the earthly steward of your mother's faith. I could not deny his request. He also told me a second letter would arrive with the first, one with my name on it. I was to read this letter and decide if I would help him."

Harry gripped the door handle hard enough to break it. "What did the letters say?"

"I only read the one addressed to me. The letter was from your mother. Written *after* she died."

Chapter 15

A tornado of rich scents filled the air – vibrant cinnamon and nutmeg with mint and smoky cumin, a promise to diners at this newly reopened Brooklyn restaurant that they were in for an experience guaranteed to bring them back time and time again. Among all the wonderful aromas, one could not be found, no matter how hard a patron tried to detect it: the dark smell of scorched wood.

That's because the dining room in Sanna had been rebuilt from the foundation to look exactly as it had before a bomb exploded in the middle of this Brooklyn eatery. It could have been much worse, as just one man had died in the blast. Two others were gravely injured, though those two bodyguards were merely window dressing for the name on everyone's lips. Vincent Morello, head of the Morello crime family, who had been the sole casualty of the explosion.

The restaurant's incredibly fast turnaround from crime scene to bustling locale came down to one man. Not Ahmed, the congenial owner, but Joey Morello. He had nearly been killed in the blast that had claimed his father, yet the day after he'd identified his father's corpse in the morgue, Joey had reached out to Ahmed with a message: "Sanna must come back as soon as possible. I'll pay for everything. Here are the contractors to use."

When Joey's guys got to work, miracles happened. Not only was Sanna back in business in record time, but business was, not to put too fine a point on it, booming. Exactly what Joey Morello intended. A destroyed building with dark windows and an empty parking lot meant the bad guys had won. Impressions became reality, and the good guys weren't going to lose this war, not on Joey's watch. So Sanna came back fast and took Brooklyn by storm. The same as Joey would do.

Altin had killed Vincent; Joey knew that in his bones, knew it with certainty. Now he had to prove it. And on that issue hung the future of his family.

"Mr. Morello, welcome." Ahmed held open the private entrance tucked around the corner of his rebuilt restaurant. An entrance Joey had requested be added in the blueprints.

"Good to see you, Ahmed." Joey wrapped the proprietor in an embrace. "Call me Joey."

"Of course, Joey." Ahmed led his most valued customer to a private dining room, available to Joey around the clock, no questions asked. "I will have the wait staff come at once."

Joey stopped outside the private room's entrance. "I'll have a drink at the bar first." He turned to his bodyguard and driver, a hulking brute named Mack who happened to be one of Harry Fox's closest friends. "What do you say, Mack? Care to join me?"

"You got it, boss."

Joey turned back to Ahmed. "Just one round. My guests will arrive shortly."

Ahmed cleared a corner spot at the bar for them. A buzz went through the room when Joey walked in, the nearby diners taking note of the dark-haired man with the angular face as he passed. If Joey's easy smile didn't draw their eye, Mack's tree-trunk biceps made them take note. Joey took his time, letting them all get a good look. He took his seat, and when Mack sat down beside him, the chair creaked with alarm.

"Mighty open out here, boss."

"I want them to see me."

"They know this is your joint. What if one a' them chumps is around?"

Joey shook his head. "The Cana punks know better than to come here. This is my place now."

But Mack was right, and Joey knew it. This wasn't smart. He'd decided, though, that that didn't matter one bit. Joey wanted to reinforce the message that this was *his* place. The Morellos weren't afraid of anyone.

Joey finished his drink, glanced at his watch and stood. "Let's go. Gio will be here any minute."

Joey had scarcely stepped into the private room when Ahmed whizzed past at full speed, headed for the rear entrance. Gio Sabella had arrived.

"Your table is in here." Ahmed showed a silver-haired man into the room. One person accompanied him, a man roughly the same size and shape as Mack. The two big guys nodded to each other, then took their seats at a table near the entrance. Joey Morello and Gio Sabella sat at a square table in the room's center.

Only after Ahmed took their orders and Joey opened a bottle of wine from his private stock in the manager's office did they begin chatting. Small talk at first. Joey had learned long ago that the old guard took life at their own pace. If Gio wanted to walk down memory lane with the son of an old friend, so be it.

Their meal came and went. Finally, when cigars were lit – an impressively direct violation of the city's health and safety code – Gio got down to business.

"Thank you for dinner," he said. "I would not have chosen this place on my own. I am glad you did."

"My pleasure," Joey said. "It's important for people to see me here, to see this neighborhood standing tall."

Gio puffed on his cigar. "Your father would be proud."

Joey sensed an opening. "I hope so. There is business about my father that remains unfinished."

Gio's drowsy eyes perked up a notch. "Do you have news to share?"

Joey did. News that could start a true war. "You have heard about our difficulties lately." Gio dipped his head a fraction of an inch. "I know who is behind them. The same man who has just experienced difficulties of his own."

Gio set his cigar on an ashtray. "The storage unit fires."

A series of storage units owned by Altin Cana had recently burned to the ground. Authorities estimated the losses at little more than structural value, given that few damaged items had been found in the ruins. What they didn't know was that Altin Cana leased those lockers to store his drug shipments, all of which had gone up in smoke. Joey estimated the street value of what he had ordered incinerated at over a million dollars. Nothing that would bankrupt Altin, but it sent a message.

Gio spoke. "I hope whoever dropped his cigarette in the wrong place cannot be tied to you."

The man was back in Brazil by now. Rich enough that he never had to leave again. "He is long gone."

Gio picked up his cigar and rolled it between his fingers, watching the smoke curl. Mack and his twin ate in silence across the room, eyes on the door. "I am disappointed, Joey."

Joey nearly spilled his wine. "Disappointed?"

"Your father would not have taken such rash action. It shows anger, not patience."

Joey's knuckles turned white on the chair's arm. He knew better than to interrupt, so he drowned his response with wine.

"As I said before," Gio went on, "this business requires proof. If you have that, then the other families will be on your side." He jabbed the smoking stogie at Joey. "*After* you give him what he is owed."

A bullet through the chest, most likely. "I'm working on it," Joey said.

"By burning a tiny slice of his profits? That will not stop Altin Cana. It will only make him angry. Angry men are not rational. They lash out and people get hurt." Now Gio pointed to himself. "It is possible I will be one of those people."

Joey cocked his head. "Altin Cana would never come after Gio Sabella. That would be crazy."

Gio stared at him through a smoky curtain. "As crazy as killing Vincent Morello."

Joey couldn't think of a reply.

"I know you are angry," Gio said. "You should be." He leaned closer. "If you say Altin Cana killed your father, I believe you. But I am one man."

"All the families listen to you."

"I must to able to prove what you say. They will not follow me without assurances. Listen to my advice."

"Always."

"The fire was a mistake. Altin will seek revenge, and people will die because of what you did. Yours was not the act of a true leader, of a man who can show others the way."

"What would you have me do, wait around for him to keep blowing up my washing houses?" Joey shook his head. "If I lose many more of my businesses, I'm in trouble. I had to hit back."

"That's where you are wrong." Now Gio leaned over the table. "The best punch is one your opponent never sees. A punch he never recovers from. Instead, you warned him, and he is ready. For what, to do what, I cannot say. I only know this will end in violence."

Joey pulled out a lighter, sparked it, and spent a long minute relighting his cigar, which hadn't gone out. He needed every second to cool his rising temper. "I appreciate this," he finally responded. "May I ask you a question?" Gio waved for him to go ahead. "What would you do?"

"That is simple. I would find proof Altin Cana killed my father. Then I would end him forever." Gio lifted a finger. "In a way that endangers as few of my men and my friends as possible. That is the mark of a true leader. A man who protects those around him." Gio stood and looked over his shoulder. "A moment, gentlemen."

Mack and his fellow bodyguard stood and walked out into the

hallway. "Help me with my coat," Gio said. "My bones are stiff."

Joey helped the elder gangster into his jacket. Sadness flashed across Gio's face when he took Joey by the shoulders. "Settle this within two weeks. It is the will of the families."

The words nearly knocked Joey off his feet. "What if I can't?"

Gio turned and picked his trilby hat off the table. "Then it is out of my hands. They will move in another direction."

Which meant Joey Morello would not succeed his father as the next *capo dei capi*, the boss of the bosses. The role Joey was born to fill, and his chance to live up to his father's name.

"I held the line for as long as possible," Gio said. He put his hat on, then pulled Joey in close and kissed him on the cheek. "Avenge Vincent." Gio stepped back, then tapped a finger lightly on the side of Joey's coiffed head. "But with this."

Gio took his leave, followed by his bodyguard. Joey remained standing beside the table, his mind racing, yet filled with nothing at all. Mack walked to Joey's side. "You'se okay, boss?"

"Two weeks." That was all Joey could say. "Two weeks."

"What happens in two weeks?"

"I either live up to my name or disgrace it forever."

Mack looked around the room. "You had too much wine. Let's get you home."

Joey walked through the door, past the waiting Ahmed and out to their car. As Joey sank into the rear seat and Mack closed the door, an image popped to mind of a text message from his closest friend. A message that made no sense. Out came his phone. Joey scrolled until he found the cryptic message Harry had sent less than a day ago.

I might have a way to get rid of our mutual problems. No stiffs. More to come.

Harry was telling Joey he might have a plan to get rid of their shared Cana problem. Altin Cana for Joey, and Altin's right-hand man Stefan Rudovic for Harry. A plan where nobody died.

Joey leaned back in his seat. Did his entire empire now hinge on Harry Fox? Joey shook his head. No. He had to do this on his own.

And to do that, he needed to think. Harry's plan could wait.

"Hit the gas, Mack. I need espresso. It's going to be a long night."

Chapter 16

Sara nearly swerved off the road. Harry sank back in his seat, the cleric's words filling his head. *It's not possible.*

"The letter was addressed to me," Imam Abdul Jalali said. "I am certain your mother wrote it, as she referenced private conversations. She also included recent news to confirm the date it was written."

"What did she say?"

"Your mother made one request: that I deliver future letters to your father. Letters she wrote. Letters no one else could know about. She said that should anyone learn of the letters, her entire family would be in danger."

Harry couldn't speak, couldn't think except for one sentence, over and over. *I was right.* She hadn't died back then. This was proof. Not conjecture and hope. Actual evidence.

Abdul continued. "The letters arrived once per year. Your father would come to the mosque, and I would give him each one. I never opened the letters. It was our unbreakable bond." Abudl let out a long breath. "I am doing this for you, Harry. And for your mother. You were the good in her world."

Abdul Jalali remained silent until Harry found his voice. "Is she still alive?"

"I do not know. The letters stopped after your father's murder."

"Did you ever see her?" Abdul said he had not. "Where were the letters from?"

142

"They were all posted in-state. Some from the city, others from places farther out. There was no pattern."

"You were curious too."

"I was. Then I realized it was not my place to question the path of a fellow believer who required my assistance."

A memory surfaced through the chaos. "The first letter, the one you read. What language was it written in?"

"Arabic."

The outside world fell away. Harry's mind flew back to when Fred Fox was alive and the coming nightmare seemed impossible. Back to their home in Brooklyn, the same place Harry lived now. Fred had been preparing to leave for Rome. Harry had found his father holding what looked like a handwritten letter. The only reason Harry even took note was that the writing had been Arabic.

His father had hurriedly put the letter away, and Harry had never thought anything more of it. Fred Fox communicated with people around the world in many different languages. At the time, Harry was more interested in Fred's impending trip to Rome. A trip from which he'd never return.

"I saw one of her letters." Harry shook his head. "My dad was reading it."

"What did you say to him?" Abdul asked.

"Nothing." *I had no idea what it was.* "Thank you, Abdul. I can't tell you how much it means to know this."

"I pray you find what you seek. Goodbye, Harry."

Silence filled the car as Sara made a turn. She leaned forward as a structure darkened the skyline ahead. A structure of stone and mortar. And holes, lots of them. It had stood for over a thousand years. Perhaps it held secrets still.

Harry barely noticed. "I have to go back to New York."

She turned to him for a moment, and then faced the road again.

"One of the last times I saw my father was right before he went to Rome," Harry went on. "He was reading a letter. I didn't think much of it at the time. Heck, the only reason I even noticed was because the writing was Arabic. I think it was a letter from my mother."

"Do you still have it?"

"I should. I didn't get rid of any of his stuff."

The dark buildings ahead grew taller as they drove closer. A massive structure by Viking standards, a fortress strategically located to control trade traffic through the strait. Control that would yield a fortune in taxes. The closer they drove, the darker and more ominous the buildings seemed. Half-crumbled structures forgotten to time jutted up from the ground, like the broken teeth of a giant's corpse.

His mind caught fire. "There have to be more letters. They came every year, and I can't believe my father would throw them away."

Sara's voice came to him at the edge of hearing. "Perhaps he did. For her sake, or yours. Abdul told you your father knew your mother was alive for years, but he never told you. Your father was a loving, caring man who wanted the best for you. He would only keep this from you if it was in your best interests."

It all came back to one question. "Why?"

"The answer may be in the letters. Or perhaps not. Your parents were careful, Harry. They kept this secret for decades."

"Abdul knew."

"Not all secrets can be kept alone. He broke your father's confidence. However, this doesn't give you answers. To either question."

Sara seemed able to read his mind. "Of why it happened, and whether she's still alive."

"Yes. You need to go back to New York and find out what's in those letters." She turned off the road and pulled to a stop. "We're here."

The fortress ruins stood before them. Broken archways fronted jagged walls that had once stood as tall as three men, with taller watchtowers dotting the length of it all. The ruins sat on an outcropping overlooking one of the strait's narrowest points, from which the fortress master could easily control shipping traffic. A ship paid the toll or it did not pass. Kingdoms were built around places such as this. Places of profit.

Harry barely saw it. "I need to go back."

She looked out the windshield at the fortress. "I understand. But consider these two things. First, your parents deceived you for a reason, one you don't know and may not understand. It's a question you may find the answer to if you go home."

"What's the second?"

"Do you *truly* want to know why this happened?" She raised a hand to cut off his protests. "Yes, of course you do. On the surface. But truly?" Sara twisted to look at him. "Your parents lied to you for two decades. What could have made them do that? Whatever it was, they let you live a lie. Perhaps revealing the truth behind their deception isn't the right answer." A beat passed. "They believed it wasn't."

If anyone else had said this, he'd dismiss it out of hand. For Sara alone, he considered it. "I need to know."

"There's one more question." She touched his forearm. "Why hasn't your mother contacted you since your father died? Because she either can't, or won't."

Harry ground his teeth. "You mean she can't because she might be dead."

"It's possible. Or she won't, because it would put you in danger." Her hand fell away. "Though I worry how you may feel if it is the former."

He shook his head. "I don't care. Whether she's dead or alive, I have to know."

"What happens after that?"

"After what?"

"After you learn the truth," Sara said. "If your mother is alive or not. And if she's alive, why she hasn't contacted you. You and your mother both may be in danger then."

"You don't think I should try to figure out the truth? That's crazy." His jaw tightened. "You'd do the same thing if you were in my shoes."

"Yes, and no." He frowned at her. "I would want to find out the truth," Sara said in response. "I would also be cautious."

"I'm always careful," he fired back. "Usually."

She pointed right between his eyes. "I can see it on your face, hear it in your voice. Don't let emotion cloud your judgment. You know better than most what the consequences of that can be."

"I'm thinking clearly. I want the truth."

"In the space of a few weeks you learn that not only was the body found in the river not her, but that she continued communicating with your father after she disappeared. Your world has been turned upside down, and your emotions along with it. Whatever the story, don't let your desire to know it get you killed." Her voice dropped a fraction. "What did your father say about moving too quickly?"

"You can be fast and dead, or slow and alive." Harry couldn't help but grin. "Unless you have to be fast. Then don't look back."

"There is no boulder chasing you down a hill to squash you flat." Sara tapped her watch. "Don't rush into this. *Think* first. Then act."

"I'm still going back to New York."

"Take a day to consider. Only one."

Harry scowled. "Why? So I can help Nora figure out what Ataulf's trail leads to?" He gestured toward the fortress. "She'd never even know this mattered if it weren't for us."

"It's not about Nora. It's about you being safe."

The unspoken part of her message rang loudest. Sara wasn't worried about the Viking mystery more than him. His safety mattered to her. She wanted him to tap the brakes, think about it, and she'd asked him to do so despite knowing how much this meant to him. Heck, his parents had brought them together; his father's amulet had been the spark that had grown into the bond they shared today. Sara didn't want him to stop for her benefit. She wanted him to stop for his.

"The past has controlled my life for as long as I can remember."

Harry tapped his finger on the dashboard as he looked at the fortress. "Chasing relics, losing my parents, living as an outsider with the Italians. All of it brought me here. It's why I'm happy."

"Are you sure?"

The hole in his gut shrank as he spoke. "This is awesome." He waved an arm to encompass pretty much everything. "Following a path through history, chasing treasures nobody knew existed to places I never imagined. And I get to do it with you."

Sara gave his arm a gentle squeeze. "All I ask is that you look to the future right now. Only for a day. If you still feel this way tomorrow, I'll support you either way."

To the future. Harry nodded. Yeah, he could do that. "Okay."

"Good." A wayward strand of her hair sparkled in the sunlight. "We should get back to town," she said as she tucked it behind an ear. "You need time to think."

"Where, at a hotel?"

Sara nodded. "We're already here and there are people on our tail. Close behind, far back – it's hard to say. Right now we're winning this race. It's no time to let up."

His door flew open, and he pocketed his phone and stepped out with renewed energy. "We'll see how I feel tomorrow, but today we focus on Ataulf." A brisk wind skimmed over the strait and smacked him in the face. Harry narrowed his eyes against it and studied the fortress.

Sara walked around the car, came right up to his chest, and wrapped him in a bear hug. "I know this can't be easy."

"It's not. But…" He paused, dragging it out. "I think you're right."

Her face was buried in his chest. "Say that again, please."

Harry pulled away. "Nope. Can't let you get a big head. I need you on point."

"Very funny." She swiped at his arm.

"I try." His pocket buzzed and he pulled out his phone. "Guess who's calling?"

Chapter 17

Manhattan

The phone on Nora Doyle's desk rang. She looked up from a stack of accordion file folders and resisted the urge to smash the thing, instead stabbing a button to connect the call. "Doyle."

"This is Detective Henning."

Her contact in the Oslo police department. "Did the attorney finally confess to poisoning Wilhelm?"

"Far from it. I suspect we will never know with certainty who poisoned him."

"If this isn't about a dead artifacts trafficker, what's on your mind?"

"Wilhelm was associated with Magnus Dahl and The Scandinavians. Why did he steal a pair of Visigoth drinking horns and attempt to sell them?"

Henning clearly had a theory. "I'm listening."

"The Scandinavians are dedicated to preserving and advancing Viking culture, yet Wilhelm steals a Viking artifact just to sell it? I can understand a theft with the intention of keeping it for himself, but trafficking? I do not buy it."

"Agreed. Problem is, Wilhelm's dead. Corpses keep their mouths shut."

Henning grumbled something under his breath in Norwegian. "I am not calling about Wilhelm. This is about Magnus Dahl. I have been monitoring him since Wilhelm's death."

"Why?"

"Intuition. This entire situation makes me suspicious."

"Isn't he untouchable? He's part of the royal family."

"As I said, quietly. Which is how I learned Magnus met with several high-ranking members in government circles within the past few days. Direct family members and prominent elected officials, including Prime Minister Ola Hanche. His party controls the most seats in our parliament."

"Not to mention his close relationship with the king's cousin," Nora said.

"Correct," Henning said. "You follow our politics?"

"I make it my business to know my suspects."

Nora got the impression Henning was smiling when he responded. "Ola Hanche roomed at university with the aforementioned cousin. His influence on Norwegian politics cannot be overstated. However, political winds change."

"You think Hanche may be out of favor soon?"

"Perhaps, and that is my concern. Politicians know public favor comes and goes like the tide. They are quick to act when their time runs short. The timing makes me wonder. A politician with great influence aligns himself not only with members of the royal family, but also with Magnus Dahl, leader of the nation's most influential cultural movement? I want to know why."

"I see what you mean." Nora chewed the inside of her lip. "This isn't the first time you've had your eye on what Magnus is doing. Am I right?" Henning's silence confirmed it. "What gives, Henning? You can be straight with me."

"Wait one moment." The sound of footsteps, then the creak of a door closing. "This must be kept in strict confidence."

"I can keep my mouth shut."

"I hope so. If this gets out I will pay a price." The rapid-fire tapping of a pen atop a desk clicked in her ear. "In recent years The Scandinavians have grown beyond being simply a regional group and gained a national following. The authorities take note of individuals who amass sizable political followings."

"Those groups can get out of hand."

"It is a situation for which we must be prepared. The Scandinavians are peaceful. They operate a working Viking village, organize battle re-enactments, and provide public educational experiences regarding Norway's heritage. On the surface, they are a benign group with perhaps too much testosterone and a love for edged weapons."

"Nothing to suggest they're a problem."

"I did not say that. The Scandinavians are but one of several culturally charged groups active in Norway. Our main concern is the lines between these groups will blur."

"As in the more extreme groups will radicalize parts of the larger, less charged one."

"Yes. One association in particular," Henning said. "Or rather, one man. Ingvar Larsen."

Nora frowned. "Why do I know that name?"

"You may have seen the coverage of him shouting from a podium about the impending demise of Norwegian culture. Ingvar is convinced that all of Norway's problems tie directly to how far we have deviated from our Viking roots. He believes that only by embracing those values will Norway and other Scandinavian nations return to their rightful place."

"Now I remember him. Short guy, shouts a lot."

"That is Ingvar."

"He makes no sense. Norway is consistently rated one of the happiest countries in the world."

"To you and me he makes no sense. To people with grievances of all kinds he is a cultural warrior intent on righting their long-ignored wrongs. He is divisive, hateful, and, unfortunately, persuasive to a certain mindset. His influence has only grown in recent years. Our government can no longer ignore him."

"I'm sure he's smart enough not to cross the line into any criminal behavior."

"Do not be too sure of that. He is the worst sort of opponent. Intelligent."

Nora pulled up a news article about Ingvar. "I see there was nearly a riot at his last rally." She read further. "Cars destroyed, businesses damaged, even a few assaults."

"Imagine a well-organized group of football hooligans embracing the worst aspects of humanity. To them, empathy and kindness show you are weak. Only strength is accepted. And diversity is evil."

"Only those who look and think like you are tolerated," Nora said. "I get the picture. Are Ingvar's people infiltrating The Scandinavians?"

"Recently we learned of communications between leaders of The Scandinavians and Ingvar Larsen. I believe Ingvar now has the ear of Magnus Dahl. That is a worst-case scenario."

Nora saw the dark picture. "If Magnus starts buying into Ingvar's rhetoric it could turn some of his followers into people more like Ingvar's. What we've seen so far wouldn't hold a candle to the damage and injury that could come about from a change like that."

"The Vikings Ingvar idolizes lived in a different time," Henning said. "It may as well have been a different world. Projecting the most destructive of those ancient behaviors onto modern times is not only misguided, it is short-sighted and inaccurate. Ingvar desires influence. He uses the discontented among us to gain it."

"He wouldn't be the first malcontent to foment discord for personal gain," Nora said.

"He would not."

"Unless Magnus Dahl buys into Ingvar's nonsense, none of this will happen. I thought Magnus was a peaceful sort of guy as far as Vikings go."

"Would you risk your nation on that hope alone?"

She would not. "You're monitoring Magnus. Anything concerning pop up?"

"Only his recent audience with members of his family and the prime minister. I have been told Magnus's rhetoric took a harder edge during this conversation. He also discussed a more ephemeral topic, which is unlike him."

"I thought this was a private meeting."

"I am a policeman, Agent Doyle."

That made her grin. "And a good one. What do you mean by *ephemeral?*"

"Magnus made statements to the effect that Odin now favors his movement. The Scandinavians have never explicitly advocated for reunification of Norway, Denmark and Sweden. Rather, their focus has been on preserving our shared heritage. The favor of Norse gods has not factored into their efforts, and the fact that he has mentioned it now is a concern. Suggesting Odin – one of the most prominent gods – not only favors The Scandinavians, but that the time for change is near? This is a new level of rhetoric."

"Okay, you convinced me. Something fishy is going on. What are you doing about it?"

"Continuing to listen, and to prepare. We will be ready to combat this nationalistic fervor if it becomes a threat." He paused. "A greater threat, that is."

Nora let the silence drag on. "Is there more?"

"There is. This is speculation on my part. Magnus Dahl is the king's first cousin and only relative since our queen died in a terrible skiing accident. The king has not remarried, and he and the queen had no children, so should he die without remarrying and producing an heir, Magnus will take the throne."

That changes things. "You think Magnus has his eyes on the throne?"

"I believe the potential exists for another person – an extremist – to ingratiate himself with the man who has a realistic chance of becoming king of Norway. I must also consider Magnus's relationship with his college roommate, Ola Hanche.

"In truth the monarchy is ceremonial. The Storting, our parliament, controls the nation, and Ola Hanche is presently the most powerful man in the Storting. It is not widely advertised, but Ola is a member of

The Scandinavians. Two such like-minded men working together could prove dangerous."

Nora leaned back in her chair. "You could have an ugly situation if Ingvar cozies up to Magnus. Who's to say what he'll do if he becomes king?"

"If you want to test a man's character, give him power."

A chill ran up Nora's arms. "Abraham Lincoln said that."

"Now you understand my concerns."

Detective Henning promised to update Nora on anything he learned, and Nora did the same. She did not tell him about Harry and Sara's search in and around Norway. That card remained up her sleeve, though right now felt like a good time to warn them.

Harry answered her call quickly. "What's up?" he asked.

"Are you with Sara?" Harry said he was and that she could hear them talking. "There may be other people following the Viking trail you're on."

A long pause. Too long. "What makes you say that?"

Nora's innate sense of distrust sent up a warning flash. One she had to ignore. Harry was her partner now. "I just spoke with a friend in the Norwegian police. Those drinking horns have attracted attention from unlikely people. Powerful people."

"Like who?"

"Someone close to the Norwegian royal family." She detailed everything, starting with the dead trafficker Wilhelm's ties to The Scandinavians and to Magnus Dahl, relative of the king of Norway and university roommate of Norwegian prime minister Ola Hanche.

"Would the king send thugs after us?"

"Doubtful," Nora said. "This isn't confirmed, but my contact suspects Magnus and The Scandinavians have ties to more radical parts of the reunification movement. Hard-line nationalists, led by a real piece of work named Ingvar Larsen."

Sara cut in. "You're not going to believe this, but I'm holding Ingvar's driver's license right now."

Nora nearly dropped the phone. "His *what?*"

Harry responded. "His license. We've been busy."

Nora sat in amazement as Harry related their axe battle on Visby Island, how they'd escaped to the Swedish mainland and then traveled to Norway and the ancient Viking fortress in front of them. "The axe you found points you to this castle?"

"It's called Gungnir Castle," Sara said. "Gungnir being the name of Odin's spear. The trail led us to this fortress. Beyond that, I don't know. We are only just now getting here."

"I'll let you get to it, then," Nora said. "Let me know if I can help."

"Wait," Harry said before she could hang up. He spoke rapidly. "I need to talk to you after we figure out what's in this castle," he said. "It's about the Morellos. You know they're having issues with their Brooklyn neighbors."

"The Albanians," Nora said. "I'm aware."

"I may have a way to stop the trouble." He looked at Sara. "It would require bending a few rules."

"It's interesting you say that. I was speaking with my mother recently."

"That's good," Harry said hesitantly.

"She reminded me the world is rarely black and white. I've had a hard time thinking that way. It's a lot easier when you can tell the good guys and bad guys apart."

"The world doesn't work like that," Harry said.

"Sometimes we do the wrong thing for the right reason if we believe it's justified. Is that the sort of thing you're thinking about?"

"It is."

"Then I'm listening."

"Let's talk later. After Sara and I find the site of Odin's power in Norway."

"Good plan. Stay focused on what's in front of you." A beat passed. "I think you told me that."

"I probably did."

"Don't lose that axe or whatever else you find. You're on my team this time, remember?"

"You can have the glory on this one. We're a team. We've got each other's backs." He took a breath. "Even when it's not black and white."

"Call if you need anything. I have friends in Norway. And Sara?"

"Yes?" Sara said.

"Keep him out of trouble."

"I promise nothing of the sort."

Chapter 18

Avaldsnes, Norway

Harry stuck the phone in his pocket and pointed at the crumbling fortress in front of them. "Now what?"

Sara raised an eyebrow. "Want to tell me what that was about?"

"The Morello stuff?" Harry hesitated. "Later – I promise. It's an idea I'm still thinking through."

Sara didn't seem to like it, but apparently she was now choosing her battles. "Do you see what I mean about Nora? She's trying to help."

"I know, I know. We're a team, even if sometimes I want to scream at her." His mouth tightened. "She's too stubborn."

Sara chuckled. "Know anyone else like that?"

"Not funny."

"We're all challenging in our own ways. Even me."

"That's the truth."

"That's enough out of you." Sara pointed to the series of buildings hundreds of yards away, the structures huddled together as though to ward off the wind. Some still appeared suitable for habitation. Others were no more than empty shells pockmarked with holes. A three-story stone church stood over everything else. "The main buildings of Avaldsnes Kongsgård estate are over there. Whoever controlled the fortress controlled the strait, a major thoroughfare for traders up and down the coast. Lots of traders paying taxes to the lord of the fortress."

Archways supported an exterior wall that was now mostly fallen down, though several turrets remained above the fortress's main door. A crenellated battlement topped the entrance. The wooden doors meant to hold marauding hordes at bay had long ago rotted, leaving the doorway wide open. Arrow slits were cut in the stone wall running the entire length of the fortress's front portion. The rear portion of the castle had been built atop the cliffside, which was at a nearly vertical angle. The ground was over twenty feet above the water, with the fortress wall another twenty feet above that. The wall stretched across hundreds of yards, from one edge of the cliff to another in a massive half-circle.

Sara watched him studying the walls. "They carved switchback stairs into the cliffside, and they had docks on the strait. If an army approached on land, the fortress's inhabitants could escape over the water."

"What if the intruders had a navy?"

"In addition to an army? Then the fortress might fall. Still, this was an incredibly stout fortress."

"It also ties back to Odin. Is there a shrine inside?"

She marched off. "Follow me."

As they approached the fortress Harry asked a question. "How much has this place been studied?"

"Extensively. Nothing has been found suggesting it is part of a hidden Visigoth path." Her eyes sparkled. "Which is excellent news."

"It's a big fortress. Lots of places to hide things that no one was looking to find."

"We have it to ourselves today," Sara said. She pointed to the fields surrounding them. "Nobody else wants to visit when it's so windy outside. If anyone comes, we stay out of their way."

"Who owns this place? The city?"

"The village oversees it." Again she pointed into the distance. "A dying village with few resources. We shouldn't have any trouble from them."

"Where do we start?"

"At this exterior wall." Sara led him toward the cliff edge, perhaps fifty yards from where the ground fell away in a sheer drop to the strait. "You'll see why I believe the battle-axe pointed us to this fortress. Oh, and there's the name as well."

He hazarded a guess. "Avaldsnes Fortress?"

"Not quite. This is Gungnir Castle, though it's more appropriate to refer to Viking castles as fortresses. Any true castles they possessed were not built until long after Ataulf and the Visigoths were in Valhalla."

"You said Gungnir is the name of Odin's spear."

"You have more of a tie to Odin than you realize." She led him closer to the cliff edge.

"How so?"

"Wednesday derives from the Middle English *Wednesdei*, which came from the Old English *Wodnesdaeg*. It means *day of Woden*. Odin is actually a modern form of the god's original name. Woden."

"A day of the week? That's neat." He looked at the wall rising above them. "Is Odin's spear around here?"

"We're almost there."

Sara pointed farther down the stone wall. Harry stopped, squinted, then began walking faster. "Why didn't you tell me this was here?" he asked.

"I thought you'd enjoy the surprise."

And surprise it was. The fortress wall in front of them was more than ragged stone and crumbled mortar. This section was a shrine dedicated to a towering, bearded man carrying a spear. Fifteen feet tall, the man wore a flowing cloak and wide-brimmed hat. One eye was a mass of scars. The spear he leaned on stood taller than him. "This is beautiful," Harry said, craning his neck to look up at it. "They carved this into the wall."

"It's the largest free-standing representation of Odin in the world," Sara said. "It makes sense the castle is named for Odin's spear."

"I'm buying your theory." Harry rubbed a hand on his chin as he studied the towering god. "Question is, where do we look next? Inside the fortress?"

Sara didn't respond. She walked closer to the wall, not turning when she responded. "We stay right here. Look at Odin's spear."

Harry turned his head sideways. "There are runes running up the spear shaft. They're so small I missed them."

"As did I until now." She was quiet for a moment. "Harry, I can read these."

"Of course you can."

"No, you don't get it. These aren't standard runes. It's Ataulf's code. This is a marker. Move aside while I decode them."

Bracing himself against the harsh wind, Harry kept watch as she studied the spear, head angled to read the faint runestones running the length it. Harry stuck both hands in his pockets and bounced from foot to foot. Clouds covered the sun and took the chill up a notch.

Sara's voice snapped him out of surveillance mode. "I'm glad we brought the axe. Listen to what this says." Sara began reading the coded runes.

Thor's axe in this site of Odin's Noregr power leads to the hammer. Ataulf honors Thor by following his greatest treasure.

Harry rubbed warmth into his fingers. "This fortress is Odin's *Noregr* power. We're in the right place." He scanned the drawing. "I don't see an axe. Only the spear."

"It's a large fortress. The axe may be inside."

"Unless they're talking about the axe in our car."

Sara shook her head. "I doubt it. It says *in this site,* not *before* it. Let's go inside."

Harry tilted his head back again to take in the shrine. A message left in plain sight, if you knew how to read it.

"These are some of the thickest walls I've ever seen." They were walking through the main fortress entrance.

Harry actually looked at the walls for the first time. "You're not kidding. These are at least ten feet thick."

"But only on this side of the fortress." She patiently pointed to the closest wall, the one they'd been walking beside until they arrived at the gate. "The opposite wall is barely half as thick."

"Maybe they did this side first and then ran short of stone?"

"I doubt it," Sara said. "This is odd."

Harry looked back over his shoulder as they passed beneath the arched entranceway and entered the fortress. Nobody in sight. They still had the place to themselves. "It's bigger than I realized," he said. "And open."

The fortress walls had one asset in abundance: open space. There was a central tower where the fortress lord would have resided, the remains of a mead hall and several smaller buildings of which little remained beyond foundation stones and crumbled walls. Grass covered nearly the entire grounds, though at the lord's manor flagstones encircled the central structure to keep the mud and muck at bay. Steps were built along the interior walls to allow defenders access to the ramparts above. Harry aimed toward one of them.

"Let's go up on the walkway."

"Help me check the lower level first," Sara said. She pointed toward the thicker wall. "You go that way. I'll go the opposite. Check the wall for anything that could be related to Odin or an axe. An engraving, a statue, a marker. Or it may be something else entirely."

"Thanks for the hints."

She offered him a choice word and turned away. Left to himself, Harry closed his eyes. *Forget about the letters for now. They're not going anywhere. Sara needs you.*

The thought of letting her down got his feet moving. Sara had come across an ocean and stayed at his side far longer than any reasonable person should. He could return the favor and help her now. If he were being truthful, it's what his father would expect him to do. If they found another step on the Visigoth path, all the better.

Harry studied the wall as he walked alongside it. The curving path led him back toward the cliff, closer to the pungent ocean and the waves cresting up and down the shore. He covered the distance in fifteen minutes, stopping where the castle wall ran just along the coastline. He passed more staircases leading up to the rampart walkways, at the top of which he knew he'd find a clear view of the strait and waters beyond. He did not climb up.

He saw Sara heading toward him. "Find anything?" Harry asked as he finished checking his last few feet of wall. "I didn't."

"Nothing on my side either." Sara walked past him and up the staircase. "Some of these steps are in poor condition. Be careful."

She turned at the top and headed down the walkway. Harry followed her up the stairs, turned the other way and got to work. The wind up here was gusting in spurts that made his eyes water. He allowed himself a moment to appreciate the vast expanse of water stretching to the horizon ahead, and the flowing green fields of the sparsely populated Norwegian countryside. No wonder Ataulf's people had decided to make this their homeland for a time.

A search of the upper level left him empty-handed as he came to the end of the coastline wall and turned back inland. Harry grabbed hold of the stones when he reached a low-slung part of the crenellated defenses, leaned over the edge, and looked straight down at the carving. *There you are.* Odin waited a few steps ahead. A hunch itching in his gut made Harry's feet move quickly. This was why he'd wanted to come up to this level first. To the spot where the tip of Odin's spear pointed to the rampart walkway. Right about...*here.*

Harry blinked away the tears from a particularly strong gust of wind. The cold creeping into his bones vanished. "Sara," he shouted, and let the wind carry his words. "Come look at this."

Sara practically sprinted around the walkway. "What is it?" she asked, skidding to a stop.

"Odin's carving is on the other side of this wall," Harry said. "The tip of his spear points right to where I'm standing."

"You'd better not have made me run over here for that."

"No. I made you run for this." He stepped back and pointed at the stone he'd been standing in front of. There was a small carving in the wall, cut into the stone at knee height. He'd almost missed it, assuming the marks came from weathering over centuries. Only these lines were too regular, too perfect. Peering closer, they could see an image of a tiny, double-headed axe, carved into the stone by a skilled craftsman.

"It looks like the axe we found," Sara said. "The four-pointed top is identical. It must be the same one."

"It's not just the axe." Harry traced a faint line running around the carving. Far around it, in a winding loop. "This line looks familiar."

Sara leaned back from the stone. "The line is almost too faint to see." Her head snapped around and she fixed him with a questioning look. "Why do you say it's familiar? It's a large circle."

"Not a circle. One side is flat, and this other side comes nearly to a point." He traced the not-quite-a-circle surrounding the axe. "This is the same shape as the fortress walls."

Lines creased her forehead. Then Sara's lips fell open before her eyes did the same. "Oh, my. It *does*."

Harry felt lighter on his feet. "It's a map. Figure out where that axe is on the map, and I bet we find something interesting."

She punched his thigh with the sort of blow you learned in self-defense class. "Brilliant work. This flat side represents the coastline wall. The pointed side is the front gate, which means the axe carving points us over there." She pointed to her right, toward the front entrance. "We don't know if it's the upper or lower level."

"My money is on the top level," Harry said. He raised his eyebrows as Sara turned and took off without waiting. "Keep going," he called out when she stopped to inspect the stones. "It's nearly at the end." He sprinted off after her.

Sara stayed one step ahead of him the entire way until they approached the spot where the walkway curved around to cross over the front entrance. Harry followed closely – too close, for when she stopped mid-stride and dropped to one knee she turned into a perfect tripping hazard. Harry didn't stop in time, smacking into her and flipping up and over to crash onto the stone walkway.

"Watch it," she growled. "And get back here. I found it."

Harry scrambled up, dusted himself off and knelt by her side. "I was right."

It wasn't at ground level. No, what they sought waited up here, cut into the exterior wall. "It's a hole," he said.

"Natural holes don't look like plus signs."

An image every schoolchild around the world knew had been cut into the rock. The plus sign, signifying addition. Harry knelt and touched the carving. He stuck his finger inside one of its grooves. "It's deep. They really dug it out." He kept wiggling his finger. The hole wasn't only deep. It was more than that. "It's open inside here."

"What do you mean?"

"It's almost like this stone is hollow. Look at the top of it. Can you see any marks, anything to suggest the stone isn't one solid rock?"

She stood. She didn't respond. Harry kept poking around. "What do you see?" he asked.

"Stand up and look."

He did, looking down on the battlement's uppermost stone, down to the Odin carving below. "It looks as though this specific stone was cut in half and then placed back together." Sara scraped a fine layer of grime from the line showing this stone had been sliced in half, making it all the more apparent. "Why?" She leaned over the stones on either side. "None of the other stones look to be put together in the same fashion. It certainly wouldn't make them stronger. Perhaps this one broke and the hole is from repairing it?"

"I don't think so." An image of the burial chamber flashed across his mind. An object left lying atop the table. "I need the axe," he said.

"Why?"

"Do you remember what's carved on top of it?"

She drew in a sharp breath. "A shape that looks like a *plus sign*."

"That may fit into this hole. Ataulf created a scepter to unlock the runestone." A silent *boom* came to mind. "He may have left the battle-axe for a similar reason. It's solid gold. The four-sided top looks like it could fit this hole in this wall." Harry shook his head. "You know what my dad said about coincidences."

"They don't happen in the field. I'll get the axe."

Harry grabbed her arm as she made to leave. "I'll get it. You stay here. I want to see if anyone's around." The memory of Jacob Pedersen and Ingvar Larsen catching them unaware loomed large as he ran back to the car, finding no signs of intruders other than cows grazing in the distance and the faint putter of a far-off engine. It faded as he opened the car and pulled out the fearsome battle-axe, then hurried back inside and climbed the staircase to rejoin Sara. "Watch out," he said.

Sara stood to one side as Harry hefted it, angling the axe so the four-sided top piece could slide into the hole. He held his breath, nudging it ever so slightly when the axe's top piece caught and refused to go in. A wiggle, the sound of metal scraping on stone, and it slid like a key into a lock. The entire top piece disappeared into the hole, stopping short just as the axe blade touched stone. "It's a perfect fit," Harry said.

"Does it turn?"

He took a step back for leverage, the wide walkway offering room to work with. He held the axe handle and twisted. Nothing. He tried again with no result, his hands slipping as he turned. "I can't get good leverage on this handle."

"Use the knob at the bottom."

The handle base had a thick knob, and the designs in the metal would give him extra purchase to grip. Harry wiped his hands on his shirt, took fresh hold of the axe, and started twisting again. Nothing happened, so he pushed harder, moving to the side so he could lean into it. Metal scraped on rock inside the stone. "It's moving," he said through gritted teeth.

Sara grabbed hold of the axe handle with both hands and started twisting as well, leaning back as she pulled, the weight of both their bodies slowly forcing the axe further around. He could feel it turning inside until, without warning, the entire handle twisted. Rocks cracked and a thundering crash shook the castle walls, the ground rumbling as the ancient Viking mechanism finally revealed what it had hidden for centuries.

The walkway stones beneath their feet opened and Harry went weightless, tumbling into darkness, reaching for Sara as they fell into the void.

Chapter 19

Gotland, Sweden

Dying leaves rustled on tree branches. A dog barked in the distance. Two men sat together on a bench, shoulder to shoulder. One of the men was Jacob Pedersen. He balanced a laptop on his knee, and at this moment he was using every ounce of self-control he possessed. It wasn't enough. He turned to the man beside him. "I will break your jaw if you do not stop talking."

Ingvar Larsen must have seen the truth in Jacob's eyes. He closed his mouth.

"Thank you." Jacob turned back to the computer screen in front of them. "As you were saying, Magnus?"

A digital image of Magnus Dahl stared back at them, his features tight. "You two are my chosen allies. Put aside your differences."

Jacob bit off a retort about how Ingvar could use a good punch or three. "We have, sir."

Magnus looked at Ingvar. "As I was saying, you cannot use such methods. Attacking two Americans we do not know will not happen again."

"It is for a worthy cause," Ingvar offered.

"You must use discretion. I do not know who this Harry Fox person is." Magnus's contact at Interpol had identified the passport used to rent the car Jacob and Ingvar had followed from the burial mound to the nearby runestone. "He may have ties to law enforcement. My Interpol source cannot say either way."

Jacob lifted his collar against the brisk Swedish wind. He and Ingvar had spent the night searching for the American and his female colleague, who had not only bested them at the runestone, but flattened their car tires and left them stranded. Niko Sparv had eventually come to get them, but now he was en route back to Oslo, while Jacob and Ingvar were forced to wait for the local police to provide them with replacement identification due to their wallets having been stolen. The paperwork had been delivered an hour ago, helped mightily by Magnus's influence.

"He knew to steal our wallets, to flatten our tires," Jacob said. "There is more to this man than it seems."

Ingvar spoke again. "You are correct." He looked at Magnus while he spoke. "I made a poor decision. I apologize. I only meant to further the interests of a reunited Scandinavia. To make our dream a reality."

Jacob was too stunned to respond. Ingvar Larsen had never apologized for anything.

"Thank you," Magnus said. "Your dedication to our shared cause is appreciated. I know how the fervor to change the future can make a person act out of character."

Jacob's blood pressure rose again. How could Magnus believe this drivel? Ingvar worried only about increasing his legions of vitriol-spewing thugs who antagonized anyone not on their side. The idea of Ingvar's hooligans working with The Scandinavians was crazy. Jacob pulled at his beard. Or was it?

"I held the axe for several seconds," Ingvar said. "There was writing on both sides."

Magnus leaned closer to the screen. "Go on."

Ingvar recited one line from memory. "*King Ataulf's axe, a gift from Thor, who gave Ataulf's people power to defeat the White God and make his power theirs.*"

"I'm not certain what this means," Ingvar said. "The phrase inscribed on the opposite side, though, is intriguing."

Ataulf honors Theodosius as Thor honors his father. Thor commanded Ataulf's people to return his earthly might to the site of Odin's power in Noregr.

"What about it drew your attention?" Magnus asked.

"The final words. *Noregr* is Norway. What in Norway could be the *site of Odin's power?* More importantly, what is *Odin's power?*" Ingvar waited a beat, then put his hand out, as though gripping an object. "His spear."

"I'm not aware of any Norwegian locations tied to his spear."

"The name of Odin's spear is *Gungnir*. Which is also the name of a fortress." Ingvar gave a brief description of the location and how it dated to Viking times.

"You two must go there and determine whether Ingvar is correct," Magnus said. "The Americans may already have deciphered the battle-axe message."

"I will make a call," Ingvar said. He stood, then hesitated. "To confirm my information is accurate." Ingvar said he would meet Jacob at the car and left.

Only after Ingvar had walked away did Jacob speak. "I have concerns about Ingvar."

Lines creased Magnus's forehead. "As do I. His actions trouble me. Attacking the Americans was short-sighted, and it jeopardized your mission."

"Do you trust him?"

Magnus looked past Jacob, to a place only he could see. "I do. What you think about him may be true, yet we face a larger challenge, one we cannot tackle alone. Ingvar is a true Scandinavian. We must find a way to work together."

Our movement. That encapsulated why Magnus would succeed. Jacob's heart thudded a little faster. It wasn't just one man. This was bigger. Their movement would turn a nation around, rip it out of the ill-conceived present and into a strong new future where Viking ideals reigned and Scandinavians stood united. Magnus would make it happen precisely because it wasn't about him. It was about *all* of them. Including Ingvar Larsen and his followers. If Magnus believed they needed an alliance with men such as Ingvar, then Jacob would embrace it.

"I understand," Jacob said. "We will work together."

"Good. You are wise to be cautious. Help Ingvar understand when to act and when to wait. This is a journey, a path we must be willing to follow to the end, no matter how long."

Magnus Dahl had led them this far. Jacob would follow him to the end. "Then I must be going. We will be in touch." Jacob ended the call, closed the laptop and stood from the bench. Fallen leaves rustled beneath his feet as he hurried toward their parked car.

Ingvar slipped a phone into his pocket as Jacob approached. "Ready to go?" he asked.

"Yes," Jacob said. "We head to the ferry?"

"And from there to Stockholm airport. The flight to Haugesund in Norway is less than two hours. From there it is slightly more than an hour to Gungnir Castle in Avaldsnes. That is where we continue our search." Ingvar opened his door. "Hurry. The Americans already have too much of a lead."

Jacob put his hand on the door, stopping it from opening enough for Ingvar to slide in. The smaller man's eyes narrowed.

"Listen to me." Jacob took his hand off the door. Ingvar shrank back. "We are in this together. You and me. For Scandinavia." The words didn't taste as sour as he imagined they would. He stuck a hand out. "While I may not agree with your tactics, I understand we cannot afford to lose."

Ingvar looked at Jacob's hand as though it held a gun. His eyes went back to Jacob's face, then to his hand again. Only after several long moments did Ingvar's face soften. "Thank you. My passion for this cause can overwhelm me," Ingvar said as he pumped Jacob's hand. "We are a team."

"A team works together." Jacob's words had a hard edge as he pulled his hand free and got behind the wheel. Ingvar climbed into the passenger seat, and Jacob fired the engine and veered out into traffic.

"What do you expect to find?" Jacob asked him once they were underway.

"I only know Gungnir Castle is the *site of Odin's power* in Norway and that we must hope any message Ataulf's people left for us has withstood the passage of time." Now his voice rose, and Jacob got a glimpse of the obsessive, inspired little man who lit a flame in so many others. Even if that flame ignited passions Jacob would rather see doused. "We will find it if it exists," he said quickly. "Our path will lead us to Odin's power, for we are Odin's true warriors, and we will retake what is rightfully ours."

The hair on Jacob's neck stood up. He looked at Ingvar, then turned back to the road and pressed the gas pedal a little harder.

Chapter 20

Avaldsnes, Norway

The underworld was a place of absolute darkness. And pain. Lots of pain.

Harry Fox blinked against the dark. A dagger bit into his back. Several tiny daggers, each biting into his skin but not slicing through. He twisted away from the pain and smacked his head on something sharp. White lights exploded all around him, his blindness now lit with shooting stars.

Stop. Think. The lights cleared and darkness returned. He tested one arm, then the other. Both ached, both worked. He squinted. A strip of faint gray light cut across the blackness around him. A *moving* strip of gray light. His eyes widened. *Clouds.*

It came back in a flash. The axe turning in Gungnir Castle's wall. The walkway collapsing beneath him. Sara falling into nothing with him.

"Sara?" A hacking cough overtook him. Dust filled the air, caked his throat. He wasn't dead, not yet. The walkway they'd fallen through was atop the thicker castle wall, the one with Odin's image carved on it.

The *thick* castle wall. Why was it so much bigger? Not for defense. It was *hollow*, and now they were inside it. He sat up like a shot and wished he hadn't. "Ugh, my head."

Sara's voice pierced the dark. "Are you okay?" He said he was. "Then get up."

Blinding light stabbed his eyes. Harry shielded his face from the intolerable brightness. "What *is* that?"

"A flashlight." Her hand grabbed his arm and hauled him upright. He promptly fell back, barking his knee on something hard. "Stand up. We didn't fall that far."

Harry's eyes slowly adjusted to the light. The world came into focus, now all sharp rocks and broken stones, one of which he'd just banged his knee against. Rubble underfoot made him stumble again before he finally gained a solid foothold. Sara kept a grip on his arm until he steadied. He looked above to the narrow strip of moving sky. "We fell twenty feet."

"Rolled, more like it. We're on a staircase."

The murky shapes around him got sharper as the world came into focus. They stood on the remains of the walkway, which had collapsed when Harry turned the battle-axe. "The axe was a key," he said. "It opened this." His brow furrowed. "Which leads to what?"

"To a hidden chamber inside the castle's exterior wall." Sara aimed her light at the ground, kicking a stone aside. "The walkway opened into this staircase. It hasn't been opened for centuries. I suspect that's why it partially collapsed."

He dug his flashlight out of his pocket and aimed it back toward the sliver of gray sky. A wooden mechanism, decrepit with age, had allowed the false stone walkway to open to what should have been a smooth descent onto the staircase below. Age had rotted the ropes supporting it, however, and the stone walkway had partially collapsed, sending Harry and Sara tumbling down a staircase buried inside the thick, hollow wall. The daggers in his back had been some smaller stones, though in truth those same stones may have stopped him from tumbling farther down the steps. He aimed his light toward the bottom. They went a *long* way down.

"Why would they have constructed a false wall?" Sara asked the air.

"Let's find out." Harry kicked a rock out of the way and began descending.

If he thought it was dark at the stop, it was impenetrable going down, as though a black velvet curtain lay across everything. His light hardly pierced the gloom, motes dancing in the beam and dust mushrooming under his boots. The steps led down at a sharp angle. No writing or symbols on the walls, which were rough mortar and stone. Well-constructed, as no wind whistled through cracks, and there wasn't a water-stain to be found.

After descending the roughly three stories they hadn't fallen, the staircase brought them to a stone floor. "This is the foundation," Harry said. "These walls on either side are the interior and exterior. Somebody went to a lot of trouble to hide this place."

The passageway was ten feet wide, though it felt much smaller when Harry craned his neck to look up at the nearly invisible opening forty feet overhead. Several ropes hung down from the ceiling far above, remnants of the mechanism that raised and lowered the entranceway. The ropes swayed gently as he watched. Harry turned to study the walls. "What's this?"

A wooden taper stuck out of a metal sconce attached to the wall. Additional sconces ran the length of the wall at eye level for as far as his flashlight beam carried. "It's a torch." Harry pulled a lighter from his pocket. "Aim your light over here," he told Sara.

He slid his flashlight into a pocket, grabbed hold of the wooden taper and lifted it from the sconce. A sharp scent caught his nose. "Smells like accelerant," he said. "Watch this."

His lighter flared, flame touched treated wood, and sparks erupted as whatever devil's pitch the Vikings used on their torches burst into a low flame. "Good stuff," Harry said. "I'm going to light more of them."

"There may be flammable materials in here," Sara said. "Let me look around first."

"The Vikings wouldn't have put these here if lighting them would burn the place down." Still, she had a point. Caution really wasn't his strong suit. "Here, take one." He reached for the next taper as a mark on the wall caught his eye. "Hang on." He leaned closer. A line ran along the stone wall, straight behind the torches. Above the line a series of holes had been cut into the wall behind each sconce, likely for air flow. Harry reached out and touched the line. "It's some kind of string. Coated with the same stuff as these torches. And look at the wall. Those are scorch marks on the stone. This string has been lit before." He didn't wait for Sara to respond, touching his burning torch to the string. Fibers sizzled as it caught and the flame sprinted down the wall. Each torch popped and crackled as the burning line of fire came alive behind it and set the torch alight. In seconds the narrow chamber went from gloomy dark to a flame-lit burnt orange. Shadows danced on the stone walls as the torches sputtered and flared, gaining strength to spew dark smoke upward where it disappeared into the upper recesses of the cavern. Harry's eyes took a moment to adjust. A moment longer than Sara's.

"Oh my."

He was still blinking as she moved away. "What is it?" he called out. She offered no response. Harry followed her deeper into the chamber and found her standing in front of a wide table. She was leaning over it, preventing him from seeing what had her eye. "What are you – wow."

He looked up at two ten-foot-tall limestone warriors standing guard. Each statue held a massive sword in the air with one hand and a gigantic round shield in the other. Their beards and biceps were the stuff of legend. A third towering figure stood between the warriors and looked down on Harry, fearsome enough to stop him in his tracks.

"That would be Odin," Sara said. "A different image than the one outside. He's carrying his spear, Gungnir, and he also has one eye missing. It's a classic depiction."

"What's Odin holding in his other hand?" Harry tilted his head. "Those look like horns."

"I believe he's holding this." She moved aside so Harry could see what was on the table.

"It's a helmet," Harry said. "A warrior's helmet. Made of gold."

Sara walked around the table, leaning closer to inspect it by the light of her torch. "A ceremonial helmet. This would have never been used in battle."

Words evaded him. The polished metal monstrosity flashed under the torchlight, its long cheekpieces connecting to a pointed nose guard bordered by two eyeholes for the user. A user intent on raiding and pillaging his way across Europe, perhaps. Or standing in the center of a Viking shield wall while hellish opponents bore down on him. If a man big enough to wear this massive piece of armor didn't scare them witless, the pointed metal horns sprouting from either side of his head would do the trick.

"Then this is a symbolic piece." He waved an arm to encompass the huge carving of Odin behind her, the raised table and burning torches. "Used for worship, maybe?"

"Vikings didn't worship gods as Christians did, remember?"

"Right."

"Though I don't think you're wrong. This is a sacred place. For honoring gods and fallen kings." She touched the helmet. "Like King Ataulf. Look here."

Harry skirted the thick wooden table and stood beside her. "There's writing on the helmet." He studied it a moment longer. "Is that Ataulf's code?"

"It is." Her lips moved silently as she translated the now familiar runes. "Listen to this."

The helmet of Ataulf, brother of Alaric, two kings who proved the true gods. Odin and Thor defeated the false god through their servants, Ataulf and Alaric, who recovered Thor's hammer for all eternity after the White God fell, taking his most powerful treasure for their own.

We honor Odin in this fortress and sing of his victories as we wait to meet him in Valhalla to prepare for Ragnarök. While Odin's guards protect this helmet and the Viking homestead in Noregr, Odin has wandered on to be with Thor and his hammer. They rest until Valhalla with King Ataulf and his treasure on the isle where Odin closed his eye and where his dark companions hold sway.

This helmet guides us to Thor's power. Honor Mímir and follow his creed if you seek Thor. Those who do not will join him.

"That's the third time we've read about Thor's hammer." Harry ran through the prior two messages from Ataulf in his head. "And again he mentions this *White God*. Which could be any number of deities."

"Look at the first portion. It talks about how *after the White God fell*, Ataulf and Alaric took *his most powerful treasure*. Do you have any idea how many different gods and goddesses the people living under Roman rule worshipped? Hundreds. A number of them were worshipped for centuries even before Romans arrived." Sara shook her head. "It's impossible to narrow down what god he means."

"Let's work with what we have." Another of his father's quips. "Thor's hammer. It must be real, and an object or idea they value highly."

Sara turned to him, her eyes glowing in the torchlight. "If we're correct, then a prize really does wait at the end of this path. A treasure the Vikings held dear."

"So Thor and his hammer are with Odin." Harry raised an arm to indicate the carving of Odin looking down on them, along with the two stone statues on either side. "While his guards keep watch over the helmet."

"Odin is often pictured in the guise of a traveler, or *wanderer*. A wide-brimmed hat, his spear used as a walking stick, and in traveler's robes. It says he *wandered on to be with Thor*." Now Sara's brow furrowed. "How does this tell us where to go?"

The same question Harry had. "Any chance you know where *Odin closed his eye and where his dark companions hold sway*?"

"That's quite a bit to dissect. Think like a Viking."

"I could put the helmet on."

She did not laugh. "I know who his *dark companions* are. In Nordic lore Odin had animal companions who brought him information from around the world. Wolves and ravens."

"His dark companions are ravens." Harry's thoughts flashed back several months to an ancient Greek warrior and the society protecting his legacy. "What is it with us and ravens?"

"Perhaps they are watching out for us too. I suggest we follow their guidance. This talks about an *isle*."

"No shortage of those around here."

"True, but are any associated with ravens?" she asked. Harry shrugged. "Maybe the answer is in this message." Sara frowned. "This line jumps out. *Where Odin closed his eye.* Why would a man with only one eye close it? He wouldn't be able to see."

"Unless that's the point. My guess is we're looking for something that's hard to see, or maybe a place you can't see easily."

"Such as a valley, or an island hidden from view. Behind another island, perhaps." Her teeth flashed. "An island only Vikings would refer to in this way."

"Sounds like a good homework project."

"As you said, there are hundreds of islands in this region. Any one of them could be the location."

Harry leaned over until his face was inches from the helmet. "What about this last part? Mimir and his creed and all that. Sounds ominous."

Sara didn't answer. She stood there, arms crossed on her chest, shadows flitting across her body. He let her think. "Mimir is an odd reference," Sara finally said. "He's the Norse god of knowledge and wisdom."

"You've heard of him? There are so many Norse gods I can't keep them all straight."

"Which is nothing compared to Egyptian gods. There are approximately one thousand four hundred of them."

Harry blinked. "Right."

"Mimir represents knowledge and wisdom. He's unique in that most Norse gods are tied to war, seafaring or power. Traditional Viking values. Mimir's different. He carried a quill and book." She shifted her weight from one foot to the other. "The last line worries me. If we fail to *honor Mimir and follow his creed*, we may find trouble. In Norse myth Mimir was eventually beheaded. Odin retrieved the head and carried it with him."

"He must have really liked the guy."

"Mimir shared secret knowledge with Odin after his beheading, so he was of great use."

The Viking mythology was nothing if not consistent. "Did the Norse have any happy stories?"

"If you consider feasting, fighting and quaffing endless mugs of ale fun, then yes."

"There are worse fates." Harry pointed to a part of the altar or podium or whatever this raised structure was meant to be. "What's that for?"

A circular stone handle rose out of the ground adjacent to the table. It looked like a broom handle. Or perhaps an ancient helmet-holder. "I have no idea," Sara said. "It may be part of their ceremony."

"Or the priest just put his hat on it."

"Don't touch it. I don't want to find out what happens if you push it." Sara had turned away to look up at Odin. "Perhaps there are other messages on the walls. The Vikings carved these statues for a purpose."

She may have been looking at the walls, but Harry's attention went elsewhere. The helmet's outside already told them where to go next. What about the inside? "I'll check in here." He lifted the helmet from its perch atop the stone table.

"Wait!"

She latched onto his arm a moment after the helmet came off the table. "What?" Harry turned toward her. "I want to see if there's writing on the inside."

Sara's words tumbled out in a breathless rush. "I said don't touch anything."

"Why not?"

A distant *crack* split the air, as though something massive had shifted, but the sound was muffled by a layer of stone between them and whatever had moved. A sound that Harry realized too late was the noise of another mechanism being activated by a man who had foolishly lifted the Viking helmet off the table.

The noise blanched Sara's face of color. "That's why." Then the ground shook.

Movement caught Harry's eye and he shouted, "Get down!" He dropped the helmet and dove at Sara, knocking her to the ground as the massive stone Viking statue behind her came alive and swung its sword. The air *whooshed* across his back as the sword whipped around faster than should have been possible. It missed lopping her head off by inches.

Harry lifted his head. "I had no idea—"

That was all he got out before Sara pulled him down again as the sword spun back around at full speed, taking another swipe at any would-be grave robbers before coming back once more. He grabbed hold of Sara and rolled, spinning end-over-end with her until they were out of harm's way. Behind them, the second Viking statue's sword swung mercilessly as well, over and over, in a deadly slashing motion.

"Time to go," Sara said. She pushed him off and got to her feet.

"One second." Harry lay flat on the quaking ground as he reached back, staying below the arcing sword until he reached the helmet and dragged it clear. "Now we can leave."

The two of them scrambled away.

Sara hit the brakes a few feet later and wouldn't budge. "Hear that?"

"Hear what? *Come on.*" This wasn't the first time he'd been stuck in a living nightmare designed by ancient engineers. These things didn't tend to get better with time.

"Wait." She tilted her head, listening. "It sounds like *liquid.* Sloshing around."

Harry went still. *Hang on.* Slowly he turned, his eyes drawn to the flickering torches. "The holes."

"What holes?"

"Behind the torches," he said. His eyes narrowed as he looked back toward the cutting statues. He could make out the sound Sara had mentioned now, and it seemed to be coming from back by the statues. "I thought they were air holes." A dark line formed on the wall as he watched, as though someone were pouring ink from the holes. It began as a trickle that rapidly increased to a stream, then finally into a spray. Harry's chest went cold. "Run!"

Oil sprayed out of the farthest hole, shooting through the torch flame nearest to it to become a flamethrower. More oil shot out of the next hole down, then the next as well. Liquid fire filled the air as Harry shoved Sara toward the steps. A tremendous wave of searing heat gave chase as they ran, scorching his neck as the burning air scratched his lungs and a filmy black smoke filled the chamber. One of the hanging ropes smacked him in the face as they ran.

"It's too fast," he shouted, head on a swivel. The flaming holes came to life faster now, the oil pouring from what must have been a storage tank hidden behind Odin's carving, shooting out to catch fire and incinerate intruders. They were only halfway to the stairs — they'd never make it before the oil jets caught them. Ducking down would only mean a rain of fire consumed them from above.

Another rope smacked him in the face. *The ropes.* "Grab a rope and climb."

Sara did as he said, grabbing the closest hanging rope and hauling herself up, hand over hand. Another one hung steps ahead of him. Harry hooked the helmet into the back of his waistband as he took a running leap and grabbed hold of the dangling rope. Pulling with the strength born of flames touching his backside, he climbed up and up, smoke choking his lungs and stinging his eyes. Harry glanced down at the raging inferno that just moments before had been a dark, cool chamber.

"Are you okay?" he shouted.

"This rope isn't sturdy," Sara yelled back. "It's going to break."

His rope wasn't much better. The frayed fibers had unraveled in some spots, and as he climbed the rope made an ominous creaking noise under his weight. "Move fast," he yelled back. "There can't be that much oil in these walls."

He had no idea how much oil there was. This inferno could rage all night for all he knew, choking the life from their lungs even if they managed to avoid the flames. A vision of hell roiled below as fire danced and churned beneath a dark cloud of oily smoke. It was like looking down on a storm cloud raining Satan's fire.

Sara shouted across the fiery chasm between them. "My rope is breaking."

Sure enough, rope fibers frayed and split as he looked up and down her lifeline. With a *snap* she dropped half a foot, sliding down even farther until it held fast. "Kick your feet," he yelled back. "Swing toward me. Mine's holding. I'll grab you."

In truth his rope was doing nothing of the sort; his hold was feeling more tenuous by the second. Flames licked at the bottom portion of Sara's rope now. He blinked, and the flames began climbing. "The fire's coming," he shouted. "Start swinging."

Frantic kicks back and forth got her moving, then momentum took her in growing arcs, a pendulum gaining steam. All the while the fire beneath her intensified, licking at the ancient rope.

"Reach out." Harry held his rope with one hand as he leaned out, reaching for Sara. Her outstretched arm stopped inches short of his fingers. Back she went, her eyes white in the dense smoke that swallowed her. She would swing back, he knew, and he took a wild guess at the timing, kicking his legs away from her, trying to swing out so that when she reappeared he'd be close enough to grab her hand and stop her from plummeting into the fiery abyss.

He swung away, reached the end of his range and gave a hard kick as he turned back toward where Sara should be. On he went, the smoke parting as he punched through it, going faster until he slowed nearly to a stop at the top of his arc, suspended in the darkness, reaching for her hand. It never appeared.

Sara screamed through the smoke. "Harry!"

He leaned farther as the world stopped for a heartbeat. Then he swung back. Sara's hand appeared through the smoke.

"Don't kick again," he shouted as he flew back. With both hands on the rope and the helmet digging into his back, he kicked away from Sara with both legs as though he were trying to make a swing go higher, nearly throwing himself off the rope with his own momentum. His hands stung as he hurtled backwards through the smoke. Out and up he went, and then he kicked back toward Sara, aiming for the spot in the murk where she should appear.

"It's breaking!" she called out.

He couldn't see her. He could barely see his hand in front of him. "Jump to me," he shouted.

Time slowed, decelerating as he approached the end of his arc, leaning through the searing heat, searching for a hand, a finger, anything of hers that he could grasp to save her from this nightmare. He strained his eyes, desperate for a sign of her, as he slowed once more at the top of the arc, reaching into the void. But there was no sign of Sara. He gave an agonizing cry as he started swinging away again.

Then there was a scream and Sara tumbled towards him through the billowing smoke, falling, careening toward him, the frayed remains of her rope still clenched in one hand, her mouth open and shouting as she fell.

"Got you!" Harry shouted as he snatched her out of the burning air, wrapped an arm around her chest and pulled her to him. "Grab my rope," he yelled. She fumbled until one hand found the rope, then the other.

The rope jerked. Fibers snapped. They descended a foot. "It's breaking," Sara shouted.

"Get ready!" Harry released his hold on Sara. "Jump for the steps when we swing back," he yelled.

In his mind, he was calculating frantically, trying to remember whether they had run far enough back down the narrow chamber to make reaching the steps possible. Not like they had any other options.

They swung back and the rope gained speed as it moved through the bottom of its arc and up again. "Kick," he shouted. "Then jump."

She did, and he watched her leap away like a spider, arms and legs spread. He sucked in a lungful of smoke as he shouted for Sara to aim for the stairs.

And then the rope broke.

Harry's shout turned to a strangled choke of terror as he fell through the burning air to the conflagration below.

Chapter 21

Brooklyn

Joey stepped out of his car and into a familiar nightmare. One he'd lived through not a week earlier. Tendrils of smoke drifting from dark rubble. Broken glass crunching underfoot, sparkling in the late fall sun. The broken shell of a building in front of him, encircled by yellow tape as blue lights flashed silently on police cars. Joey ignored the eyes following his every step. He didn't react as the uniformed officers putting up traffic barricades leaned close and spoke in low tones to each other. *That's him. The Morello kid.*

Joey stopped in front of what used to be the entrance to a pizza shop in the heart of Morello turf. A place that had been there for as long as anyone could remember. It did a respectable business, a shop that looked like countless others in the city. A shop that did much more than sell pizza. The operation's true purpose was to shield a countinghouse from prying eyes, to provide a secure location where Joey's crew could count, store and eventually distribute the cash Joey's city-wide operation generated. This system was, in many ways, the blood that kept the Morello family heart beating.

"I'm sorry, sir." A uniformed officer looked at Joey as he spoke. "You have to stay behind the yellow tape."

"I own this place," Joey said.

The cop's mouth was a hard line. "You still need to stay back. For your safety."

Joey stood still, counting down the seconds in his head. He made it to *six*.

"I'll handle this, officer." A hand clapped on the young cop's shoulder. "The fellas across the street could use a hand with traffic control."

The young cop looked over his shoulder and his back straightened. "Yes, sir."

"Thanks, Paul." Joey offered his hand to NYPD Captain Paul Hill, head of the local precinct and a man whose father had known Vincent Morello since they were kids running around this very block.

"He's a good kid," Paul said. "A bit ambitious."

"My father said you were like that. Now look at you. Running the place."

"Hard work still pays off," Paul said. He took a breath. "Loyalty too."

"My father also said you were a man we could count on," Joey said. "Same as your father."

"May they rest in peace," Paul said as both men crossed themselves. "Your father was kind to everyone in the neighborhood." Paul took a long, casual look around and didn't find anyone too close. "I'll never forget what your father did for my cousin."

"My father was more than happy to take care of the hospital bills." Joey turned his gaze toward the ruin of the pizza parlor. "Any idea what happened?"

Paul chewed on his lip for a moment. "I was about to ask you the same thing. It looks like a gas leak. I talked to one of the guys who handles scenes like this. He said there's evidence of an accelerant." Paul leaned closer. "And the gas line was tampered with."

"This was intentional."

Paul nodded. "There are casualties inside."

Joey was kicking at the broken bricks beside his feet. He stopped mid-kick. "Where?"

"In the rear," Paul said. The next words were a long time coming. "It's a strange setup for a pizza place, Joey. The back is walled off. It's almost like the rear wasn't part of the shop."

Joey kept any emotion out of his voice. "What did you find back there, Paul?"

"Two bodies. Both male, middle age. Killed instantly in the blast."

"Gabe and Dom." Joey shook his head. "They were friends."

"There's something else," Paul said. "The big safe in the back. Did you have anything in there?"

Joey blinked. "Perhaps."

Paul shoved his hands in his coat pockets. "If you did, it's gone. Whatever it was. The safe door is hanging open and there's nothing inside."

The sidewalk seemed to shift beneath Joey's feet. It took him two tries to get his question out. "Empty? Are you certain?"

"I'm sure."

This should have been impossible. "Gabe or Dom would never have given up the combination."

Five million dollars. That's what had been in the safe. This pizza parlor was the central location where Morello money went before cleaning, locked in a massive bank safe his father had bought. Impenetrable. Only five people knew its combination. Joey, of course. Gabe and Dom. And two of Joey's attorneys, who knew the combination numbers but didn't know what they were for.

Paul turned as a morgue van arrived. "This scene will be locked down for a while. I'll have someone notify you as soon as it's released." He stepped closer to Joey. "A word of advice, from an old friend? You lost something today. Two friends, but maybe something else too. Whatever it was is gone. Don't fill my streets with bodies as payback. I can only protect you so far." Paul turned and left, barking orders at several uniformed officers nearby.

Cops milled about. Firefighters stood near their trucks, all dressed up with precious little to do. A coroner's vehicle had parked halfway up the curb in the middle of the bustle, the driver heading inside to examine two bodies, certainly not his first of the day. Despite the stream of people moving around him, Joey had never felt so alone.

Five million dollars. The cash to make his operation run. This wasn't merely another washing operation hit. No, this was targeted. Intentional. Whoever did this knew exactly what they were doing. Joey couldn't run his operation for long without cash. His men were loyal, but they had to put food on the table. Taking that much liquidity out of his cashflow made him vulnerable. Another hit like this and he'd soon be out of business.

Joey turned back to his car. Mack waited behind the wheel as he slid into the rear seat. "We need to go home, Mack."

"You got it, boss."

Mack pulled into traffic as Joey rolled his neck. It sounded like a bowl of Rice Krispies. Losing the money wasn't the biggest challenge right now. He could eventually recover from that. The real problem was that now he had less than two weeks to bring down Altin Cana – without starting a war – or else he'd never lead the New York families. That was a failure from which he'd never recover.

The city rolled past outside his window. *Focus, Joey. No time to feel sorry for yourself now. Figure out how to take care of Altin Cana. Then worry about cashflow.* Joey pulled out his phone and dialed the number for his top capo. "George, we need a meeting. All the capos."

George Fazzini had grown up at Joey's side, been in more scraps and tussles with him than Joey could remember. He was one of Joey's most trusted men, up there with Mack and Harry Fox. "You got it, boss." A pause. "Is it true they hit the pizza parlor?"

Word traveled fast. "Yeah, it's true."

"What about Gabe and Dom?"

"It's not good, George. Get the others together."

Joey clicked off. The ride home passed in a blur, as did the intervening hour while his capos, the men who handled the day-to-day operations of the Morello empire, gathered at Joey's compound in the heart of Brooklyn. Everyone sat in the conference room that held several poker tables and a bar. Mack sat in a chair by the door, a loaded shotgun in his lap. Joey looked around. There weren't enough of them left. Not enough men to handle what was to come.

Joey finished the espresso in front of him. "I have bad news. The pizza parlor was hit. Gabe and Dom are dead. Whoever did this emptied the safe." The men rustled, chairs moved, but no one spoke. "We lost about five million."

George was the first to speak up. "Who has the stones to do it?"

Joey didn't have proof. "I know who it was. So do you."

"The Canas." George balled one hand into a fist. "We need to go after those Albanians, show them what happens when you mess with us." The other men murmured in agreement.

Joey raised a hand. "I would love nothing more. But right now we can't."

"Why not?" George indicated the men gathered. "We'll go after them. Tonight. I'll be the first one through the door."

"I know you would, George. All of you would. I wish it was that easy. The problem is that if we do that, Altin Cana wins."

Thunderclouds crossed George's face. "They win if we sit here and do nothing. We look weak."

The room went silent. Joey kept his eyes on the table as a fan whirled overhead. He twisted his empty espresso cup and finally looked up. "What did you say?"

George, to his credit, didn't look away. "We need to fight back, boss." His voice lowered. "When you say so."

Joey didn't blink. "That's right, George. When I say so." He listened to the whirring of the fan for a while. "I'd love nothing more than to pour gas all over the Cana headquarters and toss in a match, but if I do that, we lose."

George tried to dig himself out of the hole. "Sounds like a good plan to me, boss. I got a bunch of matches." The other men chuckled.

"We can't use the old ways now. My father built this family using his muscles *and* his mind. I need to do the same." He tapped the side of his head. "We need to be smarter than those chumps. I'm getting proof of what they did – to me *and* my father – and when I have enough, then we strike back. We hit them hard, and then we never have to deal with the Albanians again. We take them down, and then we take their turf. We'll work alongside the other families, the way it was before. The way it will be again."

Hands thumped the table in agreement. Joey waited until the hubbub subsided. "All of you, go to your crews. Keep them on a tight leash. No attacks, no trouble. Anyone kills a Cana man, they answer to me. Understand?"

The capos said they did and departed in silence. Joey waited until everyone had left before he stood and headed to his office. Mack followed him in.

"Take a load off, Mack," Joey told him. "I have some calls to make."

The big man settled into an oversized lounge chair near the door and flicked on one of the televisions, keeping the sound low. He set the shotgun in his lap. Joey pulled out his cell phone and pulled up the cryptic text message from Harry Fox.

I might have a way to get rid of our mutual problems. No stiffs. More to come.

What was Harry planning? His friend had pulled plenty of rabbits out of his hat, but this would top them all. Was he really counting on Harry Fox to solve the Cana problem from across an ocean, all while chasing some Viking artifact? Joey shook his head as he dialed Harry's number. *Some boss I am. Counting on a relics man to save the family.*

The call went straight to voicemail. Joey tried again. Same result. He frowned, tapping the phone against his desk. Where are you, Harry? What's up your sleeve?

Chapter 22

Oslo, Norway

The ancient village had come to life. People in decidedly non-Viking attire filled the village center, surrounded by wooden buildings topped with thatched roofs. Several television cameras were set up in an area roped off for media coverage, directly alongside a hastily erected presentation stage. A podium stood in the center, bright spotlights blinking on and off overhead as technicians tested the microphones on top of it. All the normal fuss that came with Magnus Dahl's quarterly address to The Scandinavians. Having it outside in the chilly early winter air only added to the festive occasion, as the group's members came from around the country to spend a day in their village, many wearing period costumes and enjoying roasted meats washed down with large mugs – or in some cases, horns – of ale. It was a celebration.

Magnus wore a casual sweater and jacket. His office in the mead hall afforded privacy as he reviewed his notes, noise filtering in from the growing crowd outside. Tonight's speech would be special.

"Any nerves?"

Magnus looked up from his speech toward the familiar voice near the door. "Never," he replied. "Come in, come in."

A man he'd known since college slipped into the office, closing the door behind him. "I have given a few speeches of my own." Prime Minister Ola Hanche walked over to Magnus's desk. "The best ones keep your nerves alive, if only for a moment."

Magnus gathered up the papers and glanced at his watch. "It is nearly time to go."

Ola put a hand on Magnus's shoulder. "Believe in yourself. If you don't, no one else will."

"I have never lacked confidence."

"Then we have nothing to worry about." Ola flashed a politician's smile. "It is our night, Magnus. Tonight we light the kindling for a roaring fire. A fire worthy of the gods."

"Perhaps." Magnus stood. "Perhaps not. It is hard to say."

Ola pretended to be offended. "I thought you had confidence."

"I do. Yet I am also realistic. Our movement is large, yes, but so is our ambition. To reunite Scandinavia will take decades. Tonight may be the start, but we must understand it is only that. A beginning." He shrugged. "To believe otherwise is foolish. A clear head is needed now. You of all people must know this."

Ola chuckled. "People think I am the born leader. You, Magnus. You see the future. You *create* the future, because you have a plan. A plan to change this nation."

"It is already in motion," Magnus said. "We are merely guiding the change with a touch here, a push there. Tonight is one step of many."

"One only you can lead." Ola lowered his voice. "This is *your* destiny. To lead people to a new Scandinavia. Is it not what you have always wanted?"

Magnus couldn't put a specific date on it, but years of promoting the ties he felt to his heritage, of showing people where they came from in order to make them proud, to inspire them to greater heights – those years had changed him. Not long ago, he would have privately said the dream of a united Scandinavia was merely that. A dream. Now he knew they could come true. Why else would Odin and Thor have left this trail for him? Now was Magnus's time.

"Embrace this night," Ola said. "Share your message. It cannot fail. Even now your men have found the next message from Odin. They will succeed – I know it. Because they believe in you."

Magnus had used his connections with the government to track

Harry Fox's passport activity. The American had flown to western Norway, to an airport south of Avaldsnes. Jacob and Ingvar would be arriving there soon. They would soon learn whether Gungnir Castle was the *site of Odin's power* in Norway, and if it was where Thor's hammer waited for Magnus. Whatever the Viking kings had gone to such lengths to hide must tie to the Vikings' true power, to the force that had led them to become the most feared people in the world. A force Magnus could use to stir his people toward their destiny.

"Yes," Magnus said. "They will."

Ola slapped Magnus's chest. "The crowd is large. Give them the message they need."

The noise of the throng gathered outside filtered in as Ola opened the door and walked out, fading again when it closed. Magnus dropped his gaze to an object on his desk. A chess piece carved from walrus ivory, discovered in the dirt on a Norwegian farm. Magnus had purchased this single piece at great personal expense and considered it a bargain, as the farmer's family had later sold the remaining pieces to Norway's national museum. Magnus's piece was the only one in private hands, and the museum had made a substantial offer to acquire it, for a chess set required both kings.

A thousand years ago this king had been carved by an unknown Viking of uncommon skill. The king stood with a sword in one hand and a book in the other. Its pointed crown, decorated with tiny diamonds, proclaimed his status, while the weapon showed his strength. The book conveyed an understanding of his people and his purpose. A king who offered his people leadership and protection. A king who knew what his people needed.

The noise of the crowd's anticipation rumbled through the walls, across the floor, and arced up Magnus's body. Perhaps Ola was right: maybe this was his time.

Magnus touched the chess piece. He closed his eyes, listening for Thor, for Odin, asking for a sign. His eyes remained closed. And Thor spoke to him.

Now.

So be it. Magnus stood and walked outside, through the mead hall to where the cool air wrapped him in a welcome embrace. He stood at the edge of the crowd, where a few people spotted him, tapping their neighbors to point him out. Several called his name. Magnus hardly felt the ground beneath his feet, barely heard the greetings. He seemed to float, propelled toward the stage, lifted up the steps by Odin's will. Applause erupted. He spoke, and the words came not from him, but from a higher place.

What seemed mere seconds later Magnus pounded the lectern and thanked his audience for coming, and as his speech ended, the crowd reacted with joy greater than any he'd coaxed from them before. Chants competed for his attention, the voices of his familiar Scandinavians joining with those of so many newcomers until they spoke as one. *Magnus. Magnus. Magnus.*

Ola replaced Magnus on stage. Strong hands shepherded Magnus past people clamoring for his attention and back into his office, where he could think, could plan. Could prepare to *lead.* The speech had gone well, but this one had been different. The air had seemed charged with an energy he couldn't quite describe, and one aspect stood out above all others. What was it?

Magnus had received the sign he asked Odin for. As he'd urged the crowd to believe in a future where Scandinavians lived together again as one nation, a sign had arrived.

Magnus had been speaking when motion drew his eyes to the top of the mead hall, to the peak of the pointed roof that looked out over the open square. A bird settled on its farthest edge, backlit by a nearly full moon when it landed, as though to listen to Magnus. Not just any bird. A raven.

A raven had come to watch.

The magical creature who symbolized war and battle for Vikings. But this bird had not landed in their village by chance. Odin had sent it. Its presence signified that he, Magnus, was to lead these gathered

Vikings in a new battle. One to reunite Scandinavia. Of this, Magnus was absolutely certain.

"What a night!" Ola boomed as he walked into the office.

"Yes." The euphoria filling Magnus's head had not receded. "Quite a crowd."

"Did you notice how many of Larsen's people attended?" Ola continued. "Their energy was unlike anything we have seen."

Ingvar Larsen's people. "They were waving flags." Magnus frowned, a sense of unease in his chest. "I did not recognize the symbols. I need to know what they mean." Another image came back. "Did they all come in matching clothes?"

"Many of them dressed in similar colors."

"That must stop. We are not a cult."

Ola hesitated. "No, we are not. I will have a word with Ingvar. They listen to him."

"I will speak to him." Ingvar's followers were known for their unquestioning devotion to the man. If Magnus made it clear that Ingvar's people would be welcomed into The Scandinavians with several conditions, they would listen. "Their chanting was," Magnus searched for the right word, "intense."

"Praising Thor, Odin and Viking values."

Ola had a point.

"We have always created a family atmosphere," Magnus said. "I would like to see it stay that way."

"Mention it to Ingvar. He will see to it." Ola put his hands behind his back. "Or perhaps you should give that directive at your next speech."

"I do not have any speeches scheduled."

Ola leaned against the corner of Magnus's desk, arms crossed. He flashed the quick smile of a born politician. "Your time has come, Magnus. Now. Not tomorrow, not next week. You must act or it will pass you by." His gaze bored into Magnus. "I have seen careers rise and fall in a matter of days. You must act. The gods have seen fit to offer this chance. Take it."

Yesterday Magnus would have laughed if Ola had told him the gods offered this chance. Ola was a politician. Hyperbole came with the job. But Magnus wasn't ordained by the gods to lead his people. He was one of them, a man who shared his beliefs with others, and helped them rediscover the forgotten ways. Not a messenger of the gods.

Or was he? He thought of the raven again. "You recommend another speech." It wasn't a question.

"A rally," Ola said. "To our cause. To *your* cause."

"My cause is Scandinavia."

"Yes. You must embrace the new members. Welcome them into the fold. Your tent is growing, Magnus. Set the course."

It made sense. The crowds. The treasure Jacob and Ingvar pursued. Above all, the raven. An omen that portended success. The gods intended for Magnus to lead his people to a new homeland.

"I will hold a rally." He opened his computer and fired off an email to The Scandinavians' secretary. An order to notify the press of another speech – a rally – with time and location to be provided shortly. "We will need national coverage."

"Leave that to me," Ola said.

"I must speak with Jacob and Ingvar." Their quest had now taken on even greater importance. Thor's hammer, whatever form it took, would confirm his path and prove that the gods favored him.

"They must not fail." Ola's finger thumped on the desktop. "Success also requires alliances, such as the one you now form with Ingvar." He scrutinized Magnus. "I understand the arrangement gives you concern."

"In certain ways."

"Reuniting Scandinavia requires an army. You must make alliances to find yours." His finger crashed down again. "Bring Ingvar and his people into your army, and control them. As a leader does."

Magnus nodded slowly. "As a leader does."

Chapter 23

Harry tried to scream as he fell, but there was no air. There was nothing.

He hit the ground, landing on hot stones. No flames.

"On fire!"

Sara's voice reached his ears, twisted and muffled by the smoke and his rattled brain. "What?" Harry tried to stand, made it to one knee and then crashed back down. Each breath was torture, acidic air scorching his windpipe. "Sara?" He tried to scream, to shout for her, but it came out as nothing more than a croak. "Where are you?"

Her voice was much closer this time, the words no longer garbled. "You're on fire!"

He looked down. Flames surrounded his ankles. "I'm on fire!"

Air whooshed as he bent down and smacked his pantlegs. The flames leapt off under his touch, some flying into the air before vanishing into nothing, other tiny ones sticking to his fingers until he flicked them off.

A rough hand grabbed his shoulder. "Stand still." Sara had found him through the smoky haze. Now she administered a beating, pounding on his legs and arms until the flames went out. "There," she said. "That's all of it."

Harry sucked in dirty air and hacked up half a lung, though his coughing seemed to clear a patch of air around him. More than a patch, in truth. He could see more clearly with every passing second. Another moment and a breeze wafted across his face, carrying the smoke with it until he realized Sara had her shirt off and was waving it around to fan the air. The white undershirt she wore looked to have been doused in creosote. Harry stood up as it hit him. "The oil. The oil finally ran out."

Harry pulled his shirt off and began waving it as well. Soon their tiny oasis of breathable air grew bigger, and it wasn't long until the haze around them dissipated. The torches alongside the walls still burned, but with less ferocity now. "The oil inside the wall ran out."

"Some of it got on our clothes." Sara stopped waving her shirt around and put it back on. "That's how I got this hole." She tapped a charred circle on her top. "And why your pants caught."

Harry looked down. His clothing, while decidedly grimy, sported no new holes. "There must be ventilation holes in here," he said. "Or we'd have suffocated."

"The Vikings would have wanted to be able to come back in here." She buttoned up her shirt, or what was left of it. Her eyes burned hot enough to ignite a new blaze. "*After* anyone who tried to steal their helmet was roasted."

"How was I supposed to know it would turn this place into a volcano?"

A sticky residue covered parts of the floor. Sara stepped over the mess, headed toward the steps. "What is it you always said about being in a hurry?"

Harry groaned. "My father said it, and there are two parts. 'Don't move too quickly. Unless you have to, then don't stop.'"

"We didn't have to move quickly." Sara picked up the helmet that had sprung the trap that had nearly turned them into charred meat. "This helmet itself wasn't going to hurt us."

He skipped over the sludge and took it from her, turning it upside down. "I picked it up to see if there was anything written inside." The light from the torches reflected inside the metal. There was no padding to protect the warrior's head. No writing either. "Nothing." Harry resisted an urge to chuck the helmet across the cavern. "I almost killed us for nothing."

Sara pointed over his shoulder to the platform. "They didn't give us any clues."

Harry looked at the platform. "That stick." He snapped his fingers. "It's not a hat stand for this helmet. That's what the table is for." He looked to the bottom of the stone pole. "The bottom is hinged, which means it moves." He looked at the table again. "I bet it's a safety catch. Like a safety on a firearm. Then the Vikings could pick up the helmet and fire wouldn't come out of the walls."

"Good thing to notice *before* you picked it up." Sara took the helmet from him and read the inscription on the outside of it again. "Oh, my. I missed it."

"Missed what?"

"The meaning of this inscription. The Vikings warned us not to move the helmet." Harry raised an eyebrow, so she pointed to a specific phrase in the engraving. "Right here. *Honor Mimir and follow his creed if you seek Thor.* We're following the path to Thor's hammer. We had to *honor Mimir.*" She shook her head.

"Assume I'm not an expert on Norse mythology."

"Mimir is the Norse god of knowledge, wisdom and writing. One of the very few Norse gods to be associated with writing, as the Vikings preserved their history primarily through oral traditions. *Mimir* is the message."

"It's telling us to write something down," Harry said. "Not to take the helmet." He pursed his lips. "That's a good one. I need to read more mythology books."

"As do I. We nearly joined Mimir in the afterlife."

He rested his hands on her shoulders. "We're still alive. A close call, sure, but we made it out." He tapped the inscription on Ataulf's helmet. "And now we're looking for an isle with ties to ravens. One Vikings considered difficult to find. Or at least part of it is hard to find."

"Time for some research."

He followed Sara up the stairs, through the dark smoke and dim light, until they were free of the grim chamber and Harry inhaled the deepest breath of his life. The actual clouds overhead had dissipated enough for sunlight to paint the countryside and turn the distant whitecaps into a shimmering blanket. He took another breath, coughed, and the hellish residue of Odin's chamber began to leave his lungs. Did it leave his mind? No chance of that. He'd remember that seething fire reaching up to grab him for a long time.

His pocket buzzed. "My phone still works," he said, yanking it out and staring at the screen. "It's Nora." He connected the call as they walked down the exterior fortress wall steps and began crossing the courtyard. "What's going on?"

"Where are you?"

"Still in Avaldsnes. We just found King Ataulf's helmet."

"Does that matter?"

Her forthright nature never failed to warm his insides. "Yes." A quick recap of their near-incineration and the message on Ataulf's helmet whetted her appetite. "Now we're trying to unravel the helmet message."

His phone buzzed again. A text message from Joey. It could wait.

"Any guesses what it means?" Nora asked.

"Ask Sara." Harry put the call on speaker and Nora repeated the question.

"None yet," Sara said. "I need to do some research before I can say more."

"What's *Thor's hammer*?" Nora asked. "It keeps coming up."

"We believe it's an object or idea so important to Alaric's descendants that they created a quest to protect it. I'm not sure beyond that."

Harry knew Sara had an idea of the truth, but she wasn't sharing yet. He could also tell Nora was bursting with other questions, but she kept them to herself. "Keep me in the loop," she said.

"We will," Harry said.

"One more thing. There have been developments in Norway."

"Did you find the person who killed Wilhelm?" Harry asked.

"Not yet. We will. This is about The Scandinavians."

The wind picked up as they exited Gungnir Castle's front gate. "Magnus Dahl's group."

"They had a large rally last night. I received word of it this morning."

"Is that unusual?" Harry asked.

"For them to have a gathering? No. What's unusual is Magnus's speech. Normally he tells stories about great Vikings, encourages people to help in their communities. Normal things for a historical organization. Nothing overtly political."

"The same Vikings who pillaged and plundered most of Europe."

"He doesn't go in for that stuff," Nora said. "Until last night. He didn't exactly advocate for plundering yet, but this time he leaned hard into the political angle. Much more so than ever before."

"It was bound to happen sooner or later," Sara said as they approached their car. "Norway's heritage is strongly linked to the Vikings. If he wants to shift Norway's course toward the past, he needs to wade into politics at some point."

"He shouldn't do it with the people who joined last night."

They stopped at the parked car. Harry popped the trunk so Sara could put their newfound helmet inside. "What people?" Harry asked as he watched a gray car the color of cloudy skies pull off the main road and head toward the castle parking lot.

"Ingvar Larsen and his followers."

"He's trouble," Sara said.

"Ingvar's followers are fanatics," Nora said. "Nationalists who believe people who don't look or think like them should be kicked out of Norway."

"Nationalism is rising around the world," Harry said. "No surprise there are people like that in Norway. Or that they'd show up to a Scandinavians event. They're probably trying to co-opt the spotlight and play off Magnus's popularity."

"I wish that were the case," Nora said. "Magnus seemed to embrace them last night. He talked of a return to their Scandinavian roots and Viking heritage. Working together to achieve a reunited homeland."

"Did he say that explicitly?" Harry asked.

"Yes and no, which worries me. His language was just vague enough to give him plausible deniability. The problem is he's smart enough to realize this. That, and he didn't denounce the extremism of Ingvar's people, who made up at least half his audience. Magnus has to understand the implications of what he said – and what he didn't say."

Sara jumped in. "So your contact in Oslo thinks this could be a turn on his part. A shift from the peaceful, historical-loving Magnus to a darker version of The Scandinavians."

"You got it."

The gray car that had been coming toward the castle parking lot changed course and headed farther upriver, away from where Harry and Sara stood.

"Did any reporters ask Magnus about it?" Sara asked.

"He claimed his speech was nothing out of the ordinary. Which it certainly was." Nora let out a long breath. "He announced plans for more speeches. Magnus has never been a man who sought the public's attention, not to this degree. He's speaking again this week, near Oslo at an old Viking battleground."

Sara rested a hand on the helmet. "The word *ominous* comes to mind."

"Among others," Nora said. "There's another piece. Prime Minister Ola Hanche also spoke at the rally last night."

"Brazen of him," Sara said.

"Hard to say what to make of it," Nora said. "Perhaps Magnus really isn't trying to fire up Ingvar's lunatics. Like I said, it's out of character for the man. Either I'm reading too much into this or something has changed in Magnus's world. You two may be in danger if it's the latter."

"A man willing to court Ingvar Larsen's followers is dangerous," Harry said.

"One more thing." Nora cleared her throat. "Last night Magnus referenced an idea he's never mentioned before. That The Scandinavians are the chosen people. Chosen by the ancient gods."

Sara didn't see the issue. "Their beliefs have always been tied to Norse mythology. That's not as concerning as him aligning with Ingvar's people."

"Magnus said a sign of Thor's favor would soon come for all to see."

"That does sound kinda crazy," Harry said.

"Agreed," Nora said. "Keep your eyes open. I have friends in Oslo if you need help."

Harry promised they would and clicked off. "What do you think?" he asked Sara.

He looked down at the artifacts in the trunk as she turned to look at several birds riding air currents off shore.

"I think only a fool believes in coincidence," she replied. "First Ingvar Larsen tries to kill us, then he infiltrates Magnus Dahl's organization, putting him not only in a position to co-opt The Scandinavians, but also close to the most powerful elected official in Norway."

"Magnus seems too smart to let Ingvar twist him around."

"You'd be surprised what power does to people. Ola Hanche has power. Magnus Dahl isn't far from the throne. Ceremonial or not, combine the two and you could have real trouble."

"You know what I really don't want to see them get their hands on?" He reached in and tapped the helmet. "The same thing Magnus mentioned. Thor's hammer. Talk about a rallying call for their messed-up alliance."

"We need to find it first." She stuck a hand out.

He straightened and slapped her five. "Right on. Did you figure out the helmet code?"

The light on her face flickered. "No, not yet." She reached in and took out the helmet, then closed the trunk and walked around to the passenger side door. Harry pulled the keys out of his pocket and walked to the driver's side.

"I'll drive while you research."

Harry climbed in behind the wheel and started the engine. The metal headgear rested on the floor by Sara's feet as she pulled out her phone.

"A colleague at Trier University is a professor of Folklore and Mythology. He'll know experts in Scandinavian myth to help our search."

Harry put the car in gear and their tires crunched softly over the gravel lot. Clouds had returned to blot out the remaining weak sunlight. A row of shrubs lined the parking area along one side. Harry came to a red sign and slowed to a stop. "I'm heading back to Avaldsnes," he said. "Closer to the airport if we have to fly somewhere."

Sara didn't answer. He looked away from the sign, watching her type into her phone. "Hello? Earth to Sara."

"Yes, yes." She waved a hand. "I need a minute."

"As you command." Harry touched the gas. Getting her attention while she was on the chase for information was useless. That doggedness was why she made an excellent partner.

A gray blur moved at the edge of his vision. Harry blinked, twisting his head as he pulled onto the main road. The gray object was coming at him too quickly to react. Harry blinked again as a part of his brain he didn't understand made him smash the gas pedal.

Too late. The gray sedan rammed into the back of Harry's car. Metal crunched, glass shattered, and as his world spun Harry realized he hadn't heard any tires squealing.

The fields outside twisted. Sara screamed, then a blanket covered his ears as the world went silent. The scent of burnt powder filled the car. They spun in silent slow motion, how many times he couldn't say, then an invisible fist cracked off the side of his head and a dark curtain covered his vision.

The dark curtain slowly lifted. A dull pain flashed on the side of his face. Harry blinked, his vision slowly clearing from a pinpoint until he could see the world once more. The sun had come back out to shimmer off broken glass in his lap. Warm liquid ran down the bridge of his nose. He reached up to touch it. Or tried to, at least. One arm wouldn't move due to the seatbelt pulled tight across his shoulder. Why couldn't he work it free? As he puzzled over this, a red dot appeared on the white pillow in front of him. *The airbag.* It had deployed and filled the car with the acrid odor of burnt powder. A deflating white airbag now sporting one, no, make that two drops of blood. Blood dripping from the tip of his nose.

"Wake up."

A distant voice reached his ears. His cheek stung again and the world seemed to shimmer. Harry twisted against the seatbelt holding him tight. His mouth opened. He wanted to say *stop*, but the word came out as a mumble. Another smack to his face got his blood up. "Stop it," Harry said.

"He's awake." A voice Harry recognized.

Harry twisted against the seatbelt again, turning himself just enough to see who was hitting him. His eyes narrowed, sending a shooting pain through his skull. *Ingvar Larsen.*

Ingvar held out a cell phone. "Do not lose this," he said. "I will call in twenty-four hours. You will tell us where to find Thor's hammer. If we find it before you, or if you do not answer, it does not go well for her. Bring the helmet when you come." Ingvar set the phone on the dashboard. "Do not waste time sitting here."

Who was *her*? Harry tried to shout questions at Ingvar as the man walked out of sight, but his lips were thick and nothing came out. He twisted once more, struggling to get free from the wretched seatbelt. Pain half-blinded him as he turned his head toward the other side of the car. To an empty passenger seat.

Sara. Ingvar had Sara.

"Wait!" he cried hoarsely as he turned back to where Ingvar had disappeared. He watched helplessly through the spiderwebbed windshield as a car drove in front of him, a light-gray car with a banged-up front end from where it had smashed into Harry's car. Another man sat behind the wheel. Harry squinted to see him through the broken window. Jacob Pedersen, the other man who had assaulted them at the runestone. Ingvar sat in back, Sara's head lolling against one shoulder.

That was the last image he had before the driver gunned the engine and the car sped off in the direction of Avaldsnes. Harry gave one last heave against the seatbelt, shouting for help as he finally wrenched his arm free. Ignoring the splitting pain behind his eyes, he turned his head in every direction. Nobody in sight. He looked around for something to cut the seatbelt. The tempered window glass had worked as intended, shattering into a million tiny useless pieces.

Metal flashed on the seat beside him. *The helmet.* This helmet with pointed horns sprouting from each side.

Harry grabbed the helmet, cursed to color the air around him, then managed to get a grip on one horn and used it as a knife to slice through his seatbelt. Once freed he dropped the helmet and shoved the air bag out of his face.

He had to get to Sara, find their car before they got away. He would take those bastards out. One horn in the chest for each man who had taken her. He reached down to find the car keys still in the ignition. He twisted them. The engine sputtered. He tried again. It caught, the engine churning and the car leaping forward as he stomped on the gas.

An ear-splitting shriek filled the air as tortured metal protested. The car lurched ahead only to stop. He tried again. Same result. Harry pounded on the steering wheel and sent a wave of white-hot pain up his arms. *Stop.* Raging at the car wouldn't help Sara.

He threw it into park, opened his door and fell out. It took several seconds to gain his feet. What he found sent him back to his knees. The rear half of the car had been bashed in, the rear driver's side tire twisted in a way that told Harry this car wouldn't be driving anywhere.

The road was deserted. No convenient cars waited to offer him a ride. No motorcycles sitting around with the keys tucked under the saddlebag. There was nothing and no one at all to help him catch the car speeding away with Sara in tow. Harry was stuck, alone outside a Viking fortress, with no help closer than an ocean away. And he had just twenty-four hours to fix it all.

His jaw tightened. Fine. Ingvar Larsen had just made his last mistake. Harry pulled out his phone and dialed a number.

"Nora? I need your help."

Chapter 24

Oslo, Norway

"You did *what?*" Magnus shouted into his phone.

Ingvar Larsen answered softly. "We did what was necessary."

"You kidnapped her." Magnus Dahl pounded his desk hard enough to rattle the walls. "Let her go."

"I cannot."

Magnus ground his teeth. "What did you say?"

"She is the key to finding Thor's hammer."

Magnus sat back heavily in his chair as the truth hit him. Ingvar Larsen was not a Scandinavian. He was a terrorist. "The hammer will be of no use to you in prison."

Ingvar laughed. "You think I will go to prison? Impossible. Not with you on my side."

"I have no control over the legal system."

Ingvar's voice grew hard. "Not yet. Soon you will control it all. You are Magnus Dahl. Cousin to the king. His only male relative."

"My cousin is in fine health. He will remarry, have children. They will be his heirs to the throne."

"Perhaps. Or perhaps he will not, and eventually he will die without children. What then? Your family will not relinquish the throne. *You* will take the throne."

"Do not say such things."

"Even if it does not happen, you are still Magnus Dahl, close friend of Prime Minister Hanche. His power is undeniable. As is his dedication to our cause."

"*My* cause does not include kidnapping innocent women."

"Innocent? She is a thief, a threat to our Scandinavian history. This *Hamed* woman…" Ingvar practically spat the name out. "She steals our artifacts, ruins our culture. No, she is not innocent. She and Harry Fox are the enemy. And both are thieves. Do not forget, the helmet was in his car."

A helmet Magnus dearly wanted. To share with the world. To possess, as a Viking. Ingvar's detainment of the woman could be seen differently in light of these facts. "Who is this woman?"

"Sara Hamed. An Egyptologist from Germany."

"Who came to Norway with an American."

"Yes. And both are criminals I should take to the police."

Any empty threat if ever there was one. "Where you will be arrested for kidnapping," Magnus said.

"Jacob is my witness. I never detained her, and I will inform the police of her theft. I am a patriot preserving our homeland. The police should thank me."

Magnus was quiet for a moment. "I do not agree with your methods," he said at last. "Yet if they can help find Thor's hammer, we must use them. It is my duty to protect the sacred relic. Where is it?"

"We will know within twenty-four hours."

"Regardless of whether we find anything, the woman must then be released. We will count this as a misunderstanding." Inspiration struck. "I will meet you at the airport south of Avaldsnes," he told Ingvar. "Wait for my call."

He clicked off and immediately called Ola Hanche. The spark of an idea had come to him, bringing with it an image of a man standing in the dark – not alone, but surrounded by a sea of fellow believers. They all looked to that single man. It was Magnus.

Ola answered quickly. "Magnus."

"I need your advice." Magnus began to outline his plan, suggesting he might be interested in running for national office if this next speech and the ones to come after it were well received. Would he stand a chance of being elected to the Storting? Would Ola support him? If it happened, how much power could they wield together?

"Enough to change the direction of the country," Ola said without hesitation, and then his voice dropped. "There is also the matter of your royal blood. The king's lack of an heir will only become more of an issue as time passes. Long may he live," Ola said quickly. "I hope a suitable successor exists when his reign is over. A successor the nation may not yet realize is the right choice."

Magnus shook his head in wonder. Why had he never considered this before? Even if he never became king, Magnus had a unique chance to help shift the national narrative through the Storting. "Long may he live," Magnus said.

"Know this. Working together, we would be unstoppable."

Magnus went still. *We, with me as the leader.* Was that the raven's message – that Magnus should take charge of Norway's destiny in the Storting?

Only time would tell. Magnus thanked Ola and hung up. Now he saw the truth. Only one path waited. To make his vision a reality, Magnus needed Thor's hammer.

Chapter 25

Avaldsnes, Norway

"You need to call the police," Nora said. "Don't think about doing anything else. You're risking her life."

Harry had recapped everything leading to Sara's kidnapping and asked for Nora's help. The help she'd promised. And, as it turned out, help she couldn't provide. "The police will make a mess of this," Harry said. "They're too slow. I have less than a day."

"Until what?"

Good question. "The same people who tried to cut my head off with an ancient axe might do the same to her. I'm not risking her safety by calling their bluff. Sara is a college professor. She never signed up for this." He didn't voice the other reason in his head. The one about possibly losing her, even if he managed to get her back.

"I agree."

"What? You just said you wouldn't help me."

"I said I *can't* help you in an official capacity. I work for the city of New York and there's little they can do. That doesn't mean I *won't* help you."

"Then start helping."

"You're calling the wrong person. I might bend the laws to do the right thing for Sara, but that's not good enough. We need someone who can smash them to bits."

Of course. "Joey Morello."

"Took you long enough. Call him. If anyone ever asks, I didn't say any of this. Odds are he has connections in Norway, people who can get you what you need fast."

Harry thought for a moment. What did he need? A gun, which made him cringe. Guns were the tools of people who didn't prepare. And he had to get ahead of Ingvar and Magnus. Take the fight to them. "Since when did you become so open to me working with Joey?"

"Not long ago, someone reminded me of the value of doing not what's convenient, but what's right. It would be *convenient* for me to tell you I can't help and wish you luck. The *right* thing to do is help Sara because she's part of the team. Which means calling Joey Morello."

"I doubt your father told you that."

"Not my father. Someone else I trust."

Harry sent out a silent thank you to that person, whoever it was.

Nora continued. "Once you find her – and you will – then you call the police. I can have my contact in Oslo help with the response."

"I'll let you know." His phone buzzed as another text from Joey came through. "One more thing about Joey. You know about the trouble between Joey and Altin Cana."

"You mean the brewing gangland war. What about it?"

"I told you I might have a way to stop it."

"A way you never explained."

"I'd need your help."

"Harry, if you can stop those gangsters from turning my streets into a shooting gallery, I'm all ears."

"I want your help charging Altin Cana with tax evasion."

The silence was deafening. For a while, Nora's breathing was the only sound that came through the phone. He waited. "I told you I only bend the law. I don't break it. I can't help you."

Harry didn't respond. Her silence, combined with the way she had spoken, told him there was a lot of churning happening in her head right now. His gut said to keep quiet.

A beat later she resumed talking. "Even if I wanted to help find the evidence, I'm not a tax attorney."

"Your father handles tax matters. He said so when we were in his office last month."

Nora made a noise somewhere between a grunt and a growl. "He's an attorney for the city, Harry. He has to play by the rules."

"He's an attorney," Harry fired back. "He can make the rules say what he wants."

An even longer silence this time. "Say I go to my father and tell him I have proof of Altin Cana evading taxes, or whatever sort of tax malfeasance you're alleging. Do you have any proof?"

A minor point. "I'll get it."

"You want my help? Tell me what you have."

In truth, nothing, but there was no way he'd reveal that. "I'm working on it," he said. His jaw tightened. What was it they said about necessity? It was the mother of invention. Perhaps this problem called for a solution that didn't yet exist.

"It may not be tax fraud," Harry continued, the idea taking shape as he spoke. "But I can get you proof Altin Cana is guilty of *something*. Murder. Extortion. Something good."

"You don't have anything, do you?"

"I will. I'll get it to you soon. Today I'm going to save Sara, remember?" He said it with enough spice to send a message.

"Once you really have proof, give it to me when you and Sara are safe. If it's real, I promise I'll talk to my father about charges against Altin Cana. I assure you he would like nothing more than to put Altin in jail for a long time."

This might work. Now all he needed was proof. "I'll call you when this is finished," he assured her. He clicked off and opened Joey's message. Two words. *Call me.*

Joey could wait another minute. Harry tapped out a message to a woman who had connections stretching from New York to Sydney and back again. A woman who happened to be New York's biggest fence of black-market goods. Rose Leroux.

He needed an expert in Norse mythology. Given Rose's work often required knowledge of the arcane and unusual, she paid a number of experts to consult with her on certain topics. Rose would definitely know someone who could help.

Harry left her a voicemail saying he needed such an expert, and he needed them right now. Rose would get back to him quickly, he knew. She always did. Now, what did Joey want?

Harry looked up toward the closest building in sight. A farmhouse with cows grazing outside of it. He started walking toward it as he dialed Joey's number. No sense in standing around here any longer. The wind snuck down his grimy, charred shirt as he moved.

Joey answered. "Where are you?"

"Still in Norway. I have a problem."

"Hold on." Other voices were in the background. They faded moments later, then Joey came back on. "Tell me what's going on."

Joey sounded a bit off. "Everything okay?" Harry asked.

"I'm in the middle of something," Joey said. "Something big."

"What's going on?" Harry asked.

Joey sounded like a man at the end of his rope. "The Canas hit our pizza shop. They killed Gabe and Dom, then emptied the safe. Made it look like another accidental explosion so I can't prove it was them."

"How much did you lose?"

"Five million in cash."

A single-engine plane buzzed slowly overhead as Harry walked. "That's a lot of cash."

"I'm in trouble. The family heads gave me two weeks to avenge my father's death and prove I can handle Altin Cana. I have no chance of being elected as the boss if I don't deal with him. I know you said you had a plan for this, but I'm making a move. Tonight."

Chapter 26

Brooklyn

A fist pounded on the door to Joey's office.

Joey pulled the phone from his ear and covered the mouthpiece. "One second." He put the phone against his ear again and spoke to Harry. "We're going after Altin tonight."

"Gio Sabella warned you not to start a war," Harry said. "It sounds like that's what you're doing."

More pounding on the door. "Hold on," he told Harry, then walked over and opened it. Mack stood outside. "What is it?"

"We're ready."

"Give me five minutes," Joey said. Mack disappeared down the hallway. Joey closed the door again, then put the call on speaker, freeing his hands to check his weapon once more. "We're taking the fight to Altin Cana," he continued. "Tonight."

"Gio won't like that."

"Gio Sabella isn't avenging his father." He spat the words out as he pulled his pistol from his shoulder holster. "I am, and it's happening tonight."

"Good men will die if you go through with this. Your men."

Joey looked out of his office window at the tree his father used to admire as the seasons passed. Harry Fox had a talent for cutting to the heart of things. "I know. But it must be done. I'm out of time. I'll never be respected if I let Altin Cana kill my father *and* tear my operation down piece by piece."

Harry's response was nearly lost in the sound of whistling wind. "There's another way to do it. But I need time."

"Are you in a wind tunnel?"

"I'm walking to the closest farmhouse. I need a ride back to town. Sara's been kidnapped."

Joey nearly dropped his gun. "Who took her?"

"Men who are probably working for Magnus Dahl." Joey stood slack-jawed as Harry told him the story, from a Norwegian nationalist named Ingvar Larsen who had also tried to chop Harry's head off, to an ancient helmet and a room full of flamethrowing walls, to a car crash and Sara's abduction. The words tumbled at him so fast Joey's head spun. "I need your help to save her," Harry finished.

"Anything."

"You know anyone in Norway who can get me a gun and a car?"

Joey racked his brain. "Yeah, I know a guy. Might take a few hours to get them to you."

"I have twenty-three left to save Sara."

"I'll take care of it."

"I have faith in you," Harry said. "But enough about my problems. Let's talk about Altin Cana. What exactly are you doing tonight?"

"We're going to Altin's counting houses. I paid off one of his guys. He told me where Altin keeps his cash."

"You sure you can trust this guy?"

"I paid him enough to be sure," Joey said. "And I'm keeping him here until we get back. If he lied, he doesn't go home."

"Smart move with the guy. Not so smart with the plan."

"What would you do?"

"You say you bought a guy in Altin's operation?" Joey said he did. "That's the key. You have the right idea, but you're asking the wrong questions."

"Which questions are the right ones?"

"I read a book on my flight over here," Harry said. "About Al Capone."

"What does that have to do with me?"

"You know what eventually brought Capone down? Other than syphilis, I mean." Harry paused. "Taxes. The feds never pinned a single murder, extortion or weapons charge on him. What finally got him in court were charges of tax evasion."

"You want to send the I.R.S. after Altin Cana?"

"No. I want to use your inside man to find proof Altin Cana isn't paying his taxes. We know he's responsible for killing your father, but we can't prove it. How close to Altin is this guy?"

"Very."

"So we'll use him to find proof to bring Altin down."

"I doubt he keeps a black book of all his finances lying around."

"If we can't find the proof, we create it. There's only one rule in this game. You have to win."

Joey closed the pistol's slide. He did not eject the magazine. "You're serious."

"We can do it, Joey. Trust me."

Could they? Months had passed since this had all begun, but justice remained unserved. It was past time to launch an attack and give Altin the payback he deserved. Would it show Gio Sabella and the other family heads that Joey Morello was his father's heir and the man to lead them? Joey couldn't say. But it needed to be done. Done now.

A finger of doubt prodded at Joey. Harry had offered another option. No guarantees, but another choice. He should at least consider it, but his gut said waiting could make him look even weaker. That was why they had to attack. Tonight.

"I do, Harry. Trust you. But that's not enough. I can't wait any longer while Altin destroys us."

"Give me a week," Harry said. "If we don't have what we need to bring Altin down by then, go for it. Do whatever you have to. But not tonight. You can show the families what an intelligent leader does." His words softened. "The way your father did."

"My father wasn't afraid of a fight."

"He also made it his last resort. You know that."

What Harry said was true. But still… "It's too late, Harry. I only have two weeks."

"Give me one of them." More wind whistled on the phone and Harry raised his voice to be heard over it. "Even if I'm wrong, it keeps your men alive for one more week. Think about it, Joey. Some of them are going to die. You want to be a true leader? Show your men you care about them. Don't sacrifice lives because you feel trapped. Do what Vincent would do."

The words plunged into Joey's chest. Harry was right. Vincent Morello had only resorted to violence when absolutely necessary. Joey rubbed his chin. *Do what Vincent would do.* "Okay. I'm calling it off. You have one week."

"I won't let you down."

"I know you won't. Now find Sara, figure out what the hell Thor's hammer is, and then get back to New York. I'll have this inside man ready to do what you say."

Joey hung up and walked to the conference room where his men had gathered. Every eye turned to him as he stopped in the middle of the room.

"It's off. We're not going tonight." A questioning rumble filled the air. "There's a better way," Joey said. "We're going to take Altin Cana down, and we're not going to need a single bullet to do it."

Chapter 27

Stars pierced through the night's black veil, brighter than any New York lights. Distant ships floated on the dark North Sea off to one side, while the scenic Norwegian coastal lands were nearly invisible on the other. Several lighthouses and their swirling beacons warned sailors where land jutted into the sea. Harry's phone told him he was minutes away from the Maloy Bridge, which connected the Norwegian mainland with the island of Vagsoy, roughly five hours north of where Sara had been kidnapped at Gungnir Castle. Five hours Harry had covered in record time after he'd managed to find a phone and call a cab from near where his totaled car remained.

Joey Morello's contact had met him in the nearby town. Two cars had pulled up outside the café where Harry had been waiting. One driver had exited his vehicle, leaving the door open for Harry to slide behind the wheel. His eyes had locked on Harry's from beneath the brim of a weathered flat cap. "Under the front seat," the man said, and then he slid into the passenger seat of the second car and the men drove off.

Under the seat was the pistol Joey had promised, along with an extra magazine of ammunition. The petrol tank had been topped off. Harry had put the vehicle into drive and motored for the highway, turned north and pressed the pedal down until he reached a slightly reckless speed. The winding road hugging Norway's western coast had taken him north toward an island he'd never heard of, where he hoped to find the answer to bringing Sara home safely. Where, if the Norse scholar from New York was correct, it had waited for over a thousand years.

Vagsoy Island. Or rather, a much smaller island off the coast of Vagsoy. An island protected by strict environmental regulations due to the scores of pied ravens that nested there. A critically endangered subspecies of raven, the pied raven lived in only three places, all on western shorelines of European nations, all without human population. The birds had survived only in locations inhospitable to human habitation. Harry had learned this when he spoke with Rose Leroux's contact, a college professor with the utterly non-Norse name of Manny Diaz. Professor Diaz was one of America's leading experts on Norse mythology, and he worked at Columbia University in New York.

Harry had chatted to Manny Diaz while he waited for Joey's friends to bring him a vehicle, telling Professor Diaz that he worked for Rose Leroux, but keeping the details deliberately vague. Diaz had listened as Harry offered a half-true story about a Viking mystery he needed to unravel. The clues left by King Ataulf's people were recounted faithfully. How Harry came to have these clues remained a mystery, and to his credit, Professor Diaz didn't ask where Harry had come by his information.

Harry had barely got through the relevant lines inscribed on Ataulf's helmet before Diaz jumped in. According to Diaz, the *isle where his dark companions hold sway* suggested an island off Norway's coast, small and largely forgotten, but tied to Norse myth. It was called Pai Island due to the presence of the endangered pied ravens. In Viking times it was called Usynlig Island for the same reason.

Pied ravens had lived on this rocky patch as far back as Ataulf's time. *Usynlig* meant *unseeing*, a name bestowed by the Vikings, who believed Odin had closed his one eye while painting this type of raven and accidentally mixed white paint with black to create a bird that had a combination of both black and white feathers. Vikings viewed the pied ravens as positive omens any time they were sighted, signaling the gods' approval and suggesting success in all endeavors.

Harry asked if there were any other islands where these birds could be found. Diaz told him there was none so intertwined with Viking lore as Usynlig Island: another Norse myth held that Odin stopped to rest on the island during a visit to the realm of man. This story, which had been relegated to the back pages of Norse history, provided yet another link between Odin and the island. That was enough for Harry.

The stubble on Harry's chin rustled as he scratched it. One other piece from his chat with Professor Diaz gave him hope. According to yet another Viking legend, Pai Island was home to spectral beings: ghosts. Ghosts who didn't take kindly to visitors. The story held that a Viking ship had sunk on its rocky shores during a long-ago storm. Having died not in battle, but in a storm, the dead sailors were cursed to wander the island for eternity, their ghosts supposedly taking out their fury at being denied a place in Valhalla on anyone who came to the island. Stories of people visiting the island but never returning had been handed down through the generations. The combination of sacred ravens and murderous ghosts kept visitors away from the island.

Harry smiled. He did love a good ghost story.

Warning lights ran along the top and bottom of the Maloy Bridge as Harry drove off the mainland. Ancillary islands to the right and left were a sharp contrast in geography; one appeared to leap from the sea as though Poseidon had thrust his fist skyward, while the other offered a gentle rise to distant hills. Lights dotted the hilly island, coming from a small village whose few inhabitants were tucked in for the night.

Smaller islands were visible as dark patches against the sparkling sea ahead. Copious moonlight gave Harry a clear view of Pai Island, a hunk of rock with sloping sides rising perhaps fifty feet in the air. The sloped terrain formed a circular ridge around the entire island, then dropped down into a valley that sat just below the ridgeline. The tips of the tallest trees were just visible above the line. Waves frothed white around the narrow beaches surrounding Pai, and not a single light was present on it. Not surprising, as people were forbidden from setting foot on the rock without a permit from the Norwegian government.

If Odin had indeed come through here on his travels, Harry expected to find a remnant. Not left by Odin, of course, but by the Vikings who revered the island as holy ground. Hopefully they hadn't installed flamethrowers to protect this one.

Village lights faded into his rearview mirror as he drove off the bridge and on to Vagsoy. A stretch of sea stood between Vagsoy and Pai island. His car couldn't get there, of course, but boats were in no short supply on Vagsoy. Seemingly every house and structure along the coast had a dock, and boats were plentiful. The fact he had little experience operating a boat didn't matter. He wasn't going far, and he wouldn't need the boat for long. In fact, he planned to have it back to the owner before they ever knew it had gone missing.

Harry parked his car at the side of a road near the water. A distant dog barked as he tucked the pistol and ammunition into his pockets and headed for a narrow strip of beach ahead. He kept his head down, careful to avoid any lights as he passed the first three boats, all nice-sized fishing vessels that looked sturdy enough to handle the choppy waters. The sort of boats with at least rudimentary security systems. Rocky sand crunched beneath his boots as he narrowed his eyes at the dock ahead. *That'll do.*

He knelt to tie an already-tied shoelace and looked around. No movement. Harry walked to the small dock and strode out to the craft that had grabbed his attention, descended the dock ladder, and stepped into the boat. His arms went out to keep his balance as soft waves slapped off the hull.

It was a lightweight, flat fishing boat, hardly ideal for venturing into unfamiliar waters, but it was perfect for Harry. No more than fifteen feet from stem to stern, the craft sported a single engine mounted on the rear, controlled by means of a handle attached to the motor. The sort of motor you could jumpstart, if only you knew how. Which, thanks to his father, Harry did.

A minute's work with a Swiss Army knife he'd purchased in Avaldsnes opened a panel on the motor to reveal the inner wiring.

Another two minutes until he had the wires stripped, then he touched the proper ones together. The engine sputtered. Another tap and it caught, the roar like a gunshot on the night air. He loosed the mooring lines, flipped the boat fenders up and over the edge, then engaged the motor. The boat shot ahead. He laid off the throttle, getting his borrowed craft under control, then aimed for Pai Island.

The wind had been merely biting on land. Out here it was a bone-chilling beast, and his upturned collar did nothing to keep it at bay. Tears blurred his vision as he upped the throttle, the boat cutting through the calm waters toward the shoreline a quarter-mile distant. The rectangular island stretched several hundred yards on its long sides, and not much more than a hundred and fifty yards on the short sides. The rocky face looking toward the mainland wasn't quite sheer, and he suspected he could ascend it without climbing gear.

He bounced over the water without illuminating the craft's navigation lights, easing off the throttle as he approached a shore outlined by moonlight. A shore he couldn't run aground on less he damage the motor. Puttering along, he pushed forward until it seemed he was close enough to slide overboard and touch bottom when he landed. The boat had a small anchor he could carry to shore and hook over a sturdy rock to keep it from floating away. A little further. *That should do it.* Once he was close enough to keep his upper body from a dunk in the freezing water, he cut the throttle, checked that the anchor was attached to a bow cleat, then leapt overboard.

Harry sank like a stone, his feet hitting nothing as he dropped into the frigid ocean. An involuntary shudder wracked his body and he nearly swallowed a gallon of water before kicking up until he broke the surface. *Damn. I thought it wasn't so deep.*

Teeth chattering, cursing himself for being so dumb, he reached over the gunwale, grabbed the anchor and swam for shore until his feet touched the bottom and he was able to half-paddle, half-walk his way to the beach. A shelf must run along the shoreline right under where he'd stopped. The rocky sand crunched beneath his boots as he came ashore and found a suitable rock on which to anchor the stolen craft. Behind him, the village lights twinkled merrily on the shore of Vagsoy Island, revealing nothing amiss. No flashlights racing around, no blue lights of police cars flickering as officers and an outraged owner searched for a stolen boat. Wet and irritable as Harry was, he was still in the game.

The sandy beach turned to rocky soil as he walked farther up the beach. Patches of evergreen trees twice his height dotted the shoreline, and it was toward these that he moved. Harry flicked his light on once he had the trees at his back, moving fast and keeping the light aimed at the ground. Once he made it to a thicker patch of trees he stuck the flashlight between his teeth and pulled out the pistol. Water drained out when he worked the slide, but it looked fine. Same with the magazine.

The ground sloped upward toward the ridgeline above him. Halfway up the fifty-foot hillside he put the light away and navigated the uneven ground by moonlight alone, darting from tree to tree. The activity got his blood pumping enough so that by the time he reached the ridgeline the worst of his shakes had vanished. Then he stepped up and walked into a brick wall of racing wind.

He could hardly move. The wind was strong enough to push him back a step before he dropped low to get beneath it. He leaned into the gusting gale, his feet slipping on the grass for one step, two steps. One more and then, as quickly as it had started, the blowing onslaught ceased.

The ground dipped beneath his feet and Harry descended the interior rim of this rocky bowl, out of the wind's reach. He went down to one knee and took stock. Trees some twenty feet tall reached up to the very lip of the ridge, the grass underfoot thicker inside the island's protected interior. Clusters of trees dotted the ground, which ran down to a plateau, one hidden from view until he'd crested the ridge. Harry stopped at the first copse and hunkered down at the base of the thickest trunk.

The loud, unearthly croaking of ravens protested this intrusion, the eerie noise making Harry wonder why they didn't call it a *murder* of ravens. No crows could make this kind of skin-crawling racket. Thankfully, the birds stayed where they were, not venturing down to peck at his eyes or ears. *I should have brought a bigger knife.* A serious one. Something to wave at any bird brave enough to come for his head.

The island's interior stretched out before him, the ground running down for perhaps thirty feet, then sloping away from him, leading to a valley at the far end, with another steep hillside rising to the ridge behind it. His watch told him around five hours of darkness remained. *Think, Harry. You've been in enough places like this. Where would a Viking hide something in here?* A better question sprang to mind. *What* would a Viking hide?

He closed his eyes and ran through the writing on Ataulf's helmet again.

The helmet of Ataulf, brother of Alaric, two kings who proved the true gods. Odin and Thor defeated the false god through their servants, Ataulf and Alaric, who recovered Thor's hammer for all eternity after the White God fell, taking his most powerful treasure for their own.

He was searching for a hammer. *Thor's hammer*, one that came from this *White God.* Harry had thrown the name out to Professor Diaz during their talk, but Diaz, like Sara, had said trying to pick one god from among the hundreds worshipped by those under Roman rule was impossible.

Fine. I'm looking for a hammer. Probably a big one. If Ataulf and his people held true to form, there would be a marker indicating Harry was in the right spot. He considered the helmet's second paragraph.

We honor Odin in this fortress and sing of his victories as we wait to meet him in Valhalla to prepare for Ragnarök. While Odin's guards protect this helmet and the Viking homestead in Noregr, Odin has wandered on to be with Thor and his hammer. They rest until Valhalla with King Ataulf and his treasure on the isle where Odin closed his eye and where his dark companions hold sway.

Pai Island fit the description. Harry was in the right place. He could *feel* it. Then there was the part about honoring *Mimir*, the god who preferred quills to axes. Mimir had been important in the castle; here, though, not so much.

Harry opened his eyes. One spot in the interior grabbed his attention. He stood and started walking. Time to find that hammer.

The valley narrowed rapidly at the end near where he stood, the ground below rising out of it to form a perfect access ramp – if you considered a ramp of loose gravel a perfect ramp, that is. So, Harry did his best impression of a surfer and tried to slide his way down the steep slope to the valley floor. Halfway down, things were going well. That's when his foot caught and Harry went ass over elbows in a tumble that deposited him face first on the grass covering the valley's floor.

He cursed loud enough to light the night sky as he stood and brushed dirt from his clothes. A boulder rising to his waist stood off to one side. Harry swallowed. A few more feet to the right and his head would have smacked off that rock. He pulled out his flashlight and swung the beam from side to side; the valley walls rose about twenty feet high. A rough line of trees filled the interior of this bowl on either side, though none ran down the center, as though they had been cleared long ago to offer a line of sight from one end to the other and never again taken root. So far, the Vikings had always left a marker or sign that gave direction about where to look next. The markers had all been hidden, but hidden in plain sight.

The few hours he had left weren't enough for him to inspect every nook and cranny in this valley. Might as well start at the back. He turned. The ramp down which he'd fallen seemed like nothing more than an access point for the valley. Same with the valley walls to either side. No writing on them, no Viking imagery. He even checked the boulder on which he'd nearly brained himself. A well-rounded boulder, smooth and plain and unhelpful.

He aimed his light between the trees toward the far end of the valley. The rock wall that formed its end was perhaps one hundred yards distant. He would have to go around the perimeter, checking the exterior walls as he went. Trees hemmed him in on one side as he walked, moving his flashlight slowly to scan the ground and the walls on either side of him. Branches he could scarcely make out in the darkness above bounced as he passed, dozens of glittering eyes reflected in his light when he aimed it upward. He swallowed and forced himself to keep checking the exterior walls, trying and failing to ignore the feeling of a hundred angry birds glaring with accusation.

Several ledges and jagged shards of stone warranted a second look as he moved on. All proved natural, and several had ravens perched on them, the black birds shouting their odd *kruk kruk* call when he got too close. Harry stepped back to get a better look at the upper reaches of the wall, moving between an opening in the row of trees. He took another step back. His foot caught on something and he stumbled back several steps before regaining his balance. What the heck? He shone his flashlight at his feet. A channel ran down the valley's middle, a slight depression he hadn't seen until now. Probably from water runoff after it came down the ramp. He leaned closer. This channel seemed off. It looked too perfect, too straight. Almost as though it were a man-made drain. Now the hairs rose on his neck. A drain to *where*?

Easy, Harry. Finish checking the walls first. He stepped across the channel and went past the trees to search the wall in front of him, still finding nothing of interest. The wall was a blank stone face until he reached the corner, where it turned at a sharp angle and ran across the face of the valley. The valley walls were several feet higher all around, for the floor had sloped gently downward as he'd moved. One step at a time, Harry moved closer to the middle until he reached the channel. He stepped into the slight depression. He shone his light onto the wall at the valley's base, on the other side of which the sea waited.

Thick grass covered nearly every inch of this wall, bulging out from the rock face in tufts and clumps. For some reason, this was the only wall with any sort of grass or plant sprouting from it. Odd. He reached up, took hold of a patch and pulled. It held. Steadying himself against the wall with his other hand, Harry grabbed tight and ripped the grass off the rock wall. Dirt flew, grass fell, and a chunk of sod fell to the ground. He rubbed at the bit of dirt still clinging to the wall. He felt the sharp tang of salt air on his tongue as a thin line came into view. A line carved into the rock.

I knew it. Someone had planted grass on the wall. It didn't grow on any other rock faces in the valley, only this far one. Could Ataulf's descendants have carved the line on this rock wall before concealing it beneath a layer of transplanted grass? Over time the grass had grown thick, covering the line. His breath came faster. This confirmed Pai Island was the right place. But what was on this wall?

Grass and dirt flew as he ripped the grass away. Anything in arm's reach was flung aside so he could follow the carved line along the rock face. It ran at eye level for several feet before splitting in two, one carrying on parallel to the ground, the other moving vertically toward Harry's feet. He followed the one at eye level, pulling more dirt off until he'd revealed a line ten paces long. More vertical lines ran down from it at intervals of about four feet, forming five rectangles as tall as him. He kept tearing dirt from inside the lines to reveal more blank rock and nothing else. Two rectangles were exposed. Three to go. Halfway down the middle rectangle he went still.

Runes. Harry blinked. Runes were carved into the wall. He scrubbed at them to remove the last bits of earth. Sure enough, Viking runes had been cut into the center of the rectangle. Harry angled his head. Not merely runes. No, these were in Ataulf's code. Runes Harry could read. Or at least he thought he could.

"Tyr." One word. Nothing more. A word Harry recognized. Or rather, a name. "Tyr is the Norse god of war." He stepped back to look at the rectangles. *This is familiar.* Harry reached for the horizontal upper line and pulled grass from above it. Seconds later his hands stopped moving. The carving didn't stop at the horizontal line. Not by a long shot.

"Those are helmets."

Curved lines with points sprouting on either side had been carved above the horizontal line. Horned Viking battle helmets of the style he and Sara had found before nearly dousing themselves in burning oil. He took a step back and looked at his handiwork. The rectangles were more than just random shapes. "These are *shields*."

Five in a row, with a Viking warrior standing behind each. He pulled down more dirt to reveal the entire scene. A row of shields held by fearsome warriors. *A shield wall.*

The famed defensive tactic preferred by Vikings through history. Warriors standing shoulder to shoulder would overlap the edges of their shields to form a wall. Here, the five warriors stood with shields overlapped, the only clue a single word on the center shield. *Tyr.*

What did it mean? Harry stood in front of the middle shield and stepped back. His foot caught on the shallow channel again. That dumb ditch was going to get him killed. Why was it even here? Water runoff didn't make much sense given the rain would drain through the dirt anyway. The interior would never fill like an actual bowl, and even if it did nobody lived here.

Harry turned and looked down the length of the channel, between the two rows of trees filled with glittering eyes. Back to where he'd fallen down the ramp as he entered the valley. The channel ran all the way back to the base of the ramp. He started walking, his light pointed down at the channel as he walked directly down the middle of it, back to where it started. When he reached the end and looked up, he wasn't just standing in front of the ramp. The channel led directly to the smooth boulder he'd nearly brained himself on.

The boulder had centuries of grime and dirt on it, along with no small amount of moss. Off it all came, Harry throwing dirt and moss to the ground the same as he had with the grass on the wall. This time the truth revealed itself much faster: there were gouges in the boulder, lines he recognized by feel before he ever saw them. They spelled out the same name he'd seen minutes earlier across the canyon, written in Ataulf's code.

"Tyr," he said out loud. The same word had been carved into this boulder as on the shield wall opposite it. Why the god of war? Harry looked down at the boulder. He looked back at the far wall. The boulder. The channel. The wall. War.

That's it. "A battle." This setup was meant to be a battle. Harry dropped to the ground and began digging, tearing earth out from beneath the boulder, dirt and stone that had kept it in place on the flat ground for centuries. Below the gritty earth he found a rock lying in front of the boulder, right where the channel ran up to the boulder's bottom – a single chiseled stone that acted like a chock holding the rock in place. This wedge of rock kept the boulder from moving. Where? He turned. Down the channel carved for that very purpose.

"Smash the shield wall. That's what Ataulf wants to happen." Break it down to continue the path. He grabbed the stone wedge in both hands, gritted his teeth and pulled. The rock held firm as he redoubled his efforts, feet sliding on the grass and the rock scraping his fingers. He held fast, heels digging in and a cry rising almost from his gut, a scream of rage and anger and despair, until the stone wedge shifted and gave him hope enough to keep pulling. He drew in a breath and unleashed a guttural yell, filling this hidden raven sanctuary with a noise like thunder. He heard the harsh sound of a thousand ravens' answering cries – and then it happened.

The wedge came free and Harry flew backwards, landing on his seat in the dirt. He sat up and wiped his forehead, looked down at his hands, which had been scraped raw by the stone wedge. A grinding noise caught his ear. What was that?

Movement flashed at the edge of his vision and Harry twisted to one side as the boulder crunched past inches from his head and began rolling down the channel. It moved slowly now, but he knew it was heavy enough to smash him flat. The ground rumbled as it passed and then gained speed, crunching and grinding down the channel on a collision course with the stoic warriors forming the shield wall ahead. Harry jumped up and gave chase, slapping his palms against the rock and pushing it faster and faster. Moments before impact he realized the collision could be massive, so he skidded to a halt and half-raised an arm to cover his face. The boulder slammed into the shield wall, steamrolling the carved warriors in a thunderclap of stone wrecking stone as it smashed through the rock barrier without slowing at all. The entire stone face collapsed and clouds of dust and debris filled the air. Harry stood without moving until the rumbling noise of the rolling stone ceased and the last chunk of wall rattled down. Now the ravens lost their minds, cawing and cackling and letting Harry know exactly how they felt about him as he ventured closer to the remains of the wall. A wall that had crumbled to leave a most unusual hole.

The hole formed a large square. Not a rough one, but a shape too exact to be created by nature. He picked up one of the fallen hillside pieces, turning it over so the moonlight illuminated it. The surface was covered in crevices. *Toolmarks.*

This wasn't a natural rock face. It was a stone wall, constructed by human hands and designed to hide an opening cut into the hillside. Harry aimed his flashlight into the opening; it was wide enough to drive a vehicle through. He stepped to the threshold. Nothing moved in the blackness. No sounds came out. The sound of the ocean, shifting beyond these island walls, reverberated through his head, the dirt beneath his feet seeming to crunch and crackle like firecrackers with each move he made. He licked dry lips and walked into the hole.

The floor sloped downwards as he stepped inside. His light revealed a large natural cavern, made larger by tools. Down he walked until the entrance behind him stood above head level. The boulder he'd sent into battle with the shield wall waited at the bottom, lodged securely against the wall. The ramp turned in on itself now. Harry walked on, descending even deeper into a blackness so absolute he started taking smaller steps lest an abyss be waiting ahead. His light swept back and forth, over the ground and up the walls, finding nothing of interest. No carvings, no markings, nothing at all. Another step down and that changed.

A torch had been mounted on the wall. The same sort of torch from inside Gungnir Castle. There were no strings running behind it, though, and he made doubly sure to check for any oil holes that would turn it into a flamethrower. With relief, he concluded that it was only a torch to light the way. He left it there and moved ahead, coming to a black space with an overwhelming sense of *openness*. He shone his flashlight upward. The ceiling sloped up, while the ramp continued down. Whatever this place was, it *felt* huge. Harry kept going, his light slowly revealing more than an empty cavern. His jaw dropped open. *No way*.

In front of him sat a Viking hideaway.

He looked at his watch and blinked hard. Only an hour remained until sunrise. It would take him that long to get back to his stolen boat and motor across the water to return the craft. *Ten minutes*, he told himself. *That's all*. His footsteps echoed in the cavern as he strode into the darkness.

Ten minutes later and not a second more, he came back up the cavern ramp at a run, stopping briefly by the imbedded boulder before racing up the exit ramp, into the island's bowl. Ravens chattered by the hundreds as he sped between the rows of trees. Part one of his rescue plan was in place. The second part…well, he might need to say a prayer to the right gods tonight.

The night's black sky had purpled at the edges as he scaled the interior slope, hopped over the upper ridge and half-fell, half-ran down to the shore where his boat waited. He grabbed the anchor, gritting his teeth as he dove into the frigid water, pulling himself along with rapid strokes until he was against the little hull and then up and over the gunwale and inside the boat. Up came the anchor, the motor fired, and the bow aimed for land as his mind churned. *It could work. I can do this.* A final thought snuck in. *Sara won't believe what we found.*

Chapter 28

Vagsoy, Norway

Harry shot up as though the bed were electrified. Sun crept through the blinds. *Where am I?* Furiously rubbing away the fog of sleep, he looked around, mind working overtime to assemble the puzzle of disjointed memories. Returning the stolen boat and sneaking back to his car. Driving across Maloy Bridge and back to the mainland to find a hotel. Circling the hotel after taking a room to check if anyone was on his tail, then crashing into bed certain he'd never sleep after what he'd discovered on Usynlig Island.

After that, nothing. Until he'd shot out of bed a moment ago, fully clothed and utterly confused. He was in Norway, on the mainland across from Vagsoy Island. The phone next to him – a flip phone, as if anyone had those anymore – was fully charged and should ring within the next hour. Ingvar Larsen would demand Harry tell him the next step on Ataulf's trail, a path he couldn't follow on his own, which was why he'd kidnapped Sara to force Harry's hand. Ingvar thought he had the upper hand. Harry smiled grimly. He couldn't have been more wrong.

Time to move. He desperately needed a shower, coffee, and a strong drink. Experience told him to hurry the first two and hold the third. There would be time for that later, once Sara could join him.

He caught sight of himself in the mirror across from the bed. He needed new clothes, as the ones on his back were basically rags. A scalding hot shower brought him back to life, and a run to a café for coffee made him feel fully human once more. Sparse traffic crawled the streets, while pedestrians kept their collars up against the ceaseless ocean wind coming off the water. The café windows creaked with each gust as Harry sat at a table by the window and watched the world go by without seeing it, for the wind blowing outside had nothing on the churning inside his head.

Ingvar Larsen would call in the next few hours. Harry's plan was like using duct tape to fix a rocket engine and hoping it all worked out. Terrible, but the best he could do. The island waited right across the water, though it might as well have been on the moon for all the good it did Harry now. He couldn't risk anyone seeing him pilot another boat out there, as that would bring questions, and questions put Sara in danger. Ingvar had boxed Harry into a corner, leaving him without allies, forced to rely on himself to fix this mess. All it would take was for a plan made up on the fly in the middle of the night on a deserted island to work.

The first step in his plan had been taken in the Viking cavern he'd uncovered last night. The next one came right now. He finished his coffee and pushed through the café doors, headed for a clothing store and then to a boat rental shop several streets down. A short while later Harry wore new clothes and held the keys to a boat nearly identical to the one he'd borrowed last night. He found the boat, hopped aboard, checked for and found an anchor inside, then motored away from the quayside shop toward a series of docks in the distance. He went past the private ones until he reached a public dock farther down, where he tied up before walking back the way he'd come, past the private docks, scanning the properties until he found what he was looking for. A house in front of one empty dock had a mailbox with envelopes and flyers filling it. *Perfect.* Harry went back to his boat and putted back to the empty dock in front of the house with the overloaded mailbox, tied off and got back on dry land. Chances were these people weren't coming home today. He only needed a place to keep the boat safe until Ingvar called.

He went back to his hotel. Nothing to do now but wait. Harry secured the room's deadbolt behind him, fell onto the bed, and closed his eyes. Worrying didn't help anything. Maybe he could snatch another hour of sleep.

His eyes had barely closed when the flip phone rattled and banged on the table beside him. *So much for sleeping.* He flipped the device open. "Yeah?"

Ingvar Larsen's voice filled his ear. "Have you found it?"

"I know where to go next."

"I am listening."

Harry stared at himself in the mirror as he spoke. "The helmet points to an island. Pai, across from a town called Vagsoy. The Vikings called it *Usynlig*."

Ingvar's words came faster. "I know it."

"Ataulf's people left something behind."

"You went to the island? What did you find?"

"Come see for yourself. It's protected because of the ravens that live there, so we can't go out during the day without a permit."

"A permit is no problem."

"You really want people seeing us go out there? Trust me, that's a bad idea." A pause. "You'll understand when you get there."

"Tell me what you found."

"No chance." Now for the hard play. "Bring Sara to me or I'm calling every news station where someone speaks English to tell them what I found."

Ingvar's words were leaden. "You will not do that."

"Why not? I have zero faith you'll let her go otherwise."

"If you make us lose this treasure, Sara dies. And then you will die, no matter how long it takes. We are many. You are two."

"You'd kill her over an old relic? Very manly of you."

"It is not my choice. This is our destiny. I will do whatever is necessary to right the wrongs done to my people."

This guy was a piece of work. "Okay, Ingvar. I'm sure it's your destiny. If you want it so bad, you let Sara go. Then I'll tell you how to find what Ataulf left behind."

"You will tell me how to find it right now or she dies. No more warnings."

He'd never expected Ingvar to agree to it anyway. "No deal. You meet me at the island. Bring Sara. I show you how to find what Ataulf left, then we leave. I don't care what you do with it after that." He also had no faith Ingvar would follow through on this deal, but it was his only shot.

"Agreed. We will be there in an hour."

"Not during the day. No one can see us, remember? Meet me there after the sun goes down. Bring flashlights."

"We will be waiting."

Harry was halfway to the door before Ingvar clicked off. Chances were this flip phone had been used to track Harry's movements the entire time, so while it was unlikely Ingvar knew he'd been to Pai Island, they probably had a rough idea of where he'd been and would figure it out eventually. Which meant Harry needed to get out to the island and in position before his adversaries managed to find a boat and make it across the water. He stopped outside the hotel to tuck his car keys under a wheel well, then headed for the dock where he'd tied up his rental boat. He climbed in, fired up the engine and headed out to sea, steering the small craft out and around Usynlig Island so nobody on shore could see his true destination. Only once the island hid him from view did he double back and gun it for a sheltered bay on the far side, tucking his boat behind a rock along the shore. Safely anchored, he managed to make it onto dry land without getting more than his feet wet.

Getting to a place where he could climb the exterior hill required going around to the landward side of the island and retracing his path up and over the ridge. He kept low, counting on the dark clothes he'd purchased to hide him from anyone on shore. He didn't look back until he'd cleared the rim. Nothing looked out of place. No boats racing for the island, no cars careering toward a dock. Ingvar and his cronies hadn't made it here yet.

He turned and slid down the ramp, managing to stay on his feet the entire way before hitting the ground at a run and following the narrow channel leading to the decimated shield wall. Into the cavern, where he slipped on a headlamp purchased at the boat shop, allowing him to keep both hands free as he went to Tyr's stone and knelt beside it briefly before jumping up again and heading for the torch attached to the wall. The first of several torches, he'd discovered, dry and sturdy Viking lights that would serve him well shortly. A Zippo came out of his pocket and fired on the first try. He glanced at his watch. Time to go.

Back through the cavern entrance, across the island's open interior and up the hillside ramp. He poked his head cautiously above the ridgeline. A sizable vessel churned the water between Pai Island and the mainland, a craft built for speed, not fishing. Two men stood on the deck, with a woman seated in front of them. The captain stood behind the wheel, a big man with a serious beard. Harry squinted as the boat approached and the captain's face became clear. Magnus Dahl, cousin to the king, head of The Scandinavians. A man with everything to lose, yet he had still come to this island with two thugs and a kidnapped German national in tow. Magnus Dahl was playing for keeps.

Harry waited until their boat was nearly at the shoreline before standing. One of the men pointed as he spotted Harry. It was Jacob Pedersen, standing alongside Ingvar Larsen. Sara, seated in front of them, looked up as well. His chest tightened as their eyes locked. He shifted his gaze to Pedersen and Larsen and swore softly under his breath. *You picked a fight with the wrong guy.* The world already had enough provocateur nationalist turds like Ingvar. Maybe Ingvar should stay on this island and live among the Viking relics he so desperately wanted to co-opt. Permanently.

Down the ramp he went once more. Magnus and his crew could figure out how to get up here on their own. Harry touched the ceramic knuckledusters in his back pocket, then left them alone. Better to keep those in reserve if things got sticky. The image of Sara sitting in that boat came back and his jaw tightened. *When* they got sticky.

It took the wannabe Vikings twenty minutes to appear at the ridgeline. Harry sat on a rock at the bottom, watching them watch him.

"Keep moving," Magnus barked from the rear of the little procession as Ingvar stopped at the ridge and looked down. His eyes got big when he realized the only way down was the slippery rock slide at his feet. "We cannot stay in sight," Magnus said. "Go."

Did Jacob give Ingvar a nudge? It sure looked like it to Harry in the instant before Ingvar fell down the rocky embankment and landed in a heap in the dirt, close to where Harry was waiting. Jacob came next, sliding and flailing wildly, followed by Sara, with Magnus on her heels. Ingvar was up and dusting himself off by the time Magnus got down, and whatever Nordic insults he was grumbling ceased when Magnus raised a hand.

"You cannot wait at the top," Magnus said in English. "We may be seen."

Ingvar glared knives at Jacob, who shrugged.

"It is not worth the risk," Jacob said. "You disagree?"

"I do not," Ingvar said, his tone far from conciliatory. He turned to Harry and brightened considerably. "Where is it?"

"Let her go."

Magnus turned to Sara and then jerked his chin toward Harry. "You may go. No one is restrained here."

Sara didn't run, didn't cry out. She walked over to Harry with her head high, turning on a heel when she reached him to glare at her former captors. "This is not how it should be done." She directed the vitriol at Magnus.

"I hope to put this all behind us," he said. "We are working together. You are unhappy, which I understand."

"Bit of an understatement, don't you think?" Harry tilted his head as he spoke. "Never thought I'd see a man like you involved in a sordid affair like this."

Magnus didn't flinch. "We cannot choose when destiny comes for us. We can only respond. I realize you do not understand what this means for our nation. What we require is your assistance. Afterward, I promise, you will be free to leave."

Ingvar Larsen clearly held his tongue at that.

"Why don't I believe you?" Harry asked. "What if we tell the world about what's here? That won't help your cause."

"What is here?" Ingvar blurted out. "Tell me." He glanced at Magnus. "Tell us."

Magnus raised a hand. "Be calm," he told Ingvar before turning to Harry. "Consider this a diplomatic situation. I am in a position of power. I also have something you want." He indicated Sara. "In exchange for your assistance, you receive her. My security is assured due to the fact we will find you if this incident ever becomes public knowledge. I have thousands of associates. You do not. And please do not try anything stupid." Magnus looked at Jacob Pedersen, who displayed a pistol. "I hope this situation is resolved with cool heads."

"How unemotional of you."

"I would prefer if you were not involved. However, that cannot be helped." Magnus seemed unfazed by it all. "It is nothing personal."

"It's personal for me. Because of you."

"We have never met before," Magnus said. "I do not understand."

"Think back two decades to an artifacts deal in America. A statue of Zeus and a notebook supposedly belonging to Archimedes." Magnus's great, bushy eyebrows came together for a second, then went up. "You remember," Harry said. "The Zeus statue was authentic. You or your men, I'm not sure which, hired an expert to confirm it. You tried to force the expert to authenticate the notebook as well. Too bad it was a fake. That's where it would have ended, except the deal went south, and everyone was arrested."

Ingvar Larsen stared at Magnus. "What is he talking about?"

Magnus waved a hand to quiet the man, then turned his attention back to Harry. "How does this concern you?"

Harry took a long step toward Magnus. Longer than he meant to. The big man's bushy beard nearly tickled Harry's chin. "The expert was tricked into coming to the sale. After the cops arrested him, he denied having anything to do with the deal. He didn't even know it was happening. Then a big-shot attorney arrives, meets with the expert, and suddenly his story changes. Now the expert takes the fall. For everyone."

"I do not see how this affects you."

"The cops only charged the expert and everyone else walked, got on with their lives. The expert didn't. His life fell apart." Nothing else in the world mattered right now. Not the Viking relic, not the gun in Jacob Pedersen's hand, none of it. Harry stuck a finger in Magnus's face. "That expert was my father."

The big man rocked back a fraction. The wind blew, the sound of waves washed softly over the island, and Magnus Dahl looked at Harry Fox. "I am sorry," he finally said. "I did not know."

"How couldn't you?" Harry jabbed his finger at Magnus again. Sara's hand touched his shoulder. "Those were your guys who hired him. They set him up."

"Your father was not the only man betrayed that day." Clouds ran across the big man's face as he looked to the sky and back through the decades. "The same men betrayed my trust."

"Shocker," Harry said. "You hired a bunch of thugs."

"I hired a team of recovery specialists." Now Magnus turned the full weight of his gaze on Harry. "Men like you."

"They're nothing like me." It sounded hollow even to his ears.

"The men located a statue of Zeus, as contracted. They failed to acquire the Archimedes piece. Instead of admitting this failure, however, they forged a document. An expert's authentication was required to complete payment. I played no part in hiring your father. I only required the expert to be impartial and unknown to anyone involved."

"He had no idea he was working with people like you."

Magnus let it pass. "I am sorry for what happened."

Harry forced himself to speak in level tones. "Your attorney threatened my father. When the cops first questioned him, he told the truth. Then your lawyer shows up, speaks to my father in private, and all of a sudden, he changes his story. My father took the fall for everyone."

"I hired an attorney for the other men *before* I knew they had deceived me. I never told him to speak with the expert. I never spoke with him at all."

That made no sense. "Those guys you hired were calling the shots? No way. Your lawyer wouldn't have listened to them, not when you were paying the bills."

"That is what I told him to do. To handle it."

"So he set this all up on his own? No attorney would tell guys he'd never met to frame someone else." At least he didn't think they would.

"I agree," Magnus said. Harry frowned. "One of the men I hired likely suggested it."

"And your lawyer went with it?"

"The attorneys I hire are aware of what is required. To make a problem go away. If my attorney did not know the men he represented, perhaps the recovery specialists told him your father was the one behind it all. My attorney would not know."

"He could have called you."

"That is never part of the arrangement."

The wind left Harry's sails. Could it be true? It sounded plausible. The artifact hunters had looked out for their own skin and convinced Magnus's attorney to pass a threat to Fred Fox. Whatever it was, it had convinced Fred to take the blame.

"What happened to the guys who tried to swindle you?" Harry asked.

The clouds on Magnus's face darkened. "I made certain they would never try to cheat anyone again."

Harry knew the man was speaking the truth now. "Good. Although it doesn't make you blameless."

"No, it does not." Now Magnus looked at Harry with something close to understanding. Sadness, even? "To show you what sort of man I am, I will prove to you I did not participate in framing your father."

"How in the world could you prove that to me?"

"I have the original report on the artifacts stating the statue is genuine and the notebook is a fake. Your father gave it to the men I hired. I obtained the report before they disappeared. It proves your father evaluated both artifacts properly. There is a notarized signature to show the date is before he was arrested."

The artifact hunters must have sent Fred enough information to compile a report before the deal went down. He wouldn't have had much time, but if a report existed showing Fred said the statue was a fake *before* the cops showed up, that would clear his name. Harry leaned into Sara, grabbing her shoulder. *I can clear my dad's name.*

"I believe you want the report," Magnus said.

"Where is it?" Harry asked.

"In a safe deposit box. Here." Magnus handed him a phone. "Type your number. I will send you the bank name, the address, the box number and passcode."

"Don't I need a key?"

"It is not that type of bank."

Harry took the phone and put his number in. Magnus took it back, typed away, and moments later a message arrived on Harry's phone. "How do I know you're not making this up?"

"You do not. However, it is the best offer I can make. You help us follow Ataulf's path. I help with your father. Do we have an understanding?"

As if he had any choice. "We do."

"Good." Magnus looked away from Harry and took in the island's interior. "What have you discovered?"

Harry pointed at the channel by their feet. "See this? Follow it." He took Sara's hand and strode off down the channel, leaving Magnus and his men to catch up. "There was a boulder back there." Harry pointed over his shoulder to where they had just been standing. "It had the word *Tyr* carved into it."

"Tyr is the Norse god of war," Sara said. "Who carved it, and why?"

"Ataulf's descendants carved it," Harry said.

Ingvar came running up to Harry's side. "Where is the rock? It may contain other insights, other guidance from our forefathers."

"I pushed it out of the way."

That made Ingvar stop in his tracks. "You pushed a boulder?"

"Wasn't easy."

A meaty hand clamped on to Harry's shoulder none too softly. He came to a quick halt and turned to find Magnus Dahl looking down at him from above some impressive nostrils. "Speak directly."

"I am." Harry shrugged out of Magnus's grip on the second try. "A boulder was sitting at the bottom of the hill you came down. Which, if you're paying attention, is also where this channel by our feet begins."

Magnus looked up at where the boulder had been, and then back down in the direction they were headed. "There is a cave at the other end of the channel."

"It wasn't a cave until last night," Harry said. "It used to be a rock face with grass covering it. Grass deliberately planted to conceal a carving."

"What carving?"

Harry tried to watch each of their captors at once. "A shield wall."

In the distance, the ravens suddenly burst into a noisy chorus of cackling. All three ersatz Vikings started as though blasted by wind.

"Impossible," Magnus said. "It could not have remained undiscovered for so long."

Harry looked at Ingvar, the only man on this island shorter than him. "Ask your little buddy here," he told Magnus. "Seems like he knows his history."

242

Ingvar's face colored. "Be careful with your tongue." He turned to Magnus. "The heathen is correct. This island has long been considered haunted. Fear of the spirits living here and the remote location keep many away, as does the protected status. If this carving was hidden as he says, I believe that is why it has been undiscovered for so long."

Magnus pulled at his beard. He looked at the channel, down to the rock wall, then back at Harry. "You pushed a boulder through a rock wall?"

Harry shrugged. "Wasn't hard once I got it rolling." He started walking again. "I'll show you."

Several birds took flight as they walked, flitting around one of the few trees before settling back down, almost invisible in the foliage. Once they stood in front of the entrance, Harry let go of Sara's hand for a moment and strapped the headlamp on.

"Look at those pieces." He took Sara's hand again and pointed with his other hand to a stack of jagged rocks on the ground. "You can see parts of the shield wall carving on them. I picked them up after the boulder smashed through."

Ingvar jumped toward the pile and grabbed one. "I see it," he said, then picked up another. "This is part of a helmet."

"There were five warriors in a row," Harry said. "*Tyr* was carved into the center shield. I realized it meant for me to make war."

"A true Viking message," Ingvar said.

"The interesting stuff is inside." Harry flicked on his headlamp. "You'll need flashlights."

He waited as the men pulled out their lights and then, one by one, crossed the threshold. "It doubles back halfway down." Flashlight beams ran in front of him and soon revealed the boulder.

Ingvar was first past, followed by Magnus and Jacob. Harry hung back while they looked at the big, uninteresting rock. "I have no idea where the carved word is," Harry said.

"Here – it is here." Ingvar aimed his light at it. "Tyr. Exactly as he said. Carved by the hands of our ancestors."

Harry let the men look for another few seconds. "The good stuff is further down."

All three men turned at once and headed quickly down the path. None noticed Harry duck by the boulder, then stand up again, both hands shuffling behind his back. "There are torches on the wall," he said a moment later. "They'll be pretty bright if we light them."

Magnus inspected the unburnt torch. "How do you know?"

"Gungnir Castle had the same kind."

Magnus didn't say anything as he lifted the first torch off the wall. "Did you bring a lighter?" he asked Harry. Harry's new Zippo came out, the torch caught, and a familiar, otherworldly glow lit the cavern.

"I think this is a temple," Harry said. "The cavern is perfect for hiding a place like this."

The ceiling quickly rose to a height of thirty feet as they walked down the entrance ramp. What had been smooth stone before the ramp turned became roughly carved steps, while the cavern opened on either side until the room was over a hundred feet wide. It stretched on for that long as well, a massive underground opening hidden inside this tiny island. Darkness remained off to the right. The left, though, demanded attention.

Magnus's voice boomed. "Odin." He walked faster, pointing ahead with his torch. "Odin is on the wall."

Sara's hand slipped free from his. She moved ahead, now shoulder to shoulder with her kidnappers as all four of them stood with necks craned, looking up at the one-eyed god in all his glory. Gone was the berobed, unassuming bearded man. Now Odin stood ten feet tall, carved into the wall running the cavern's length. He wore a winged helmet and carried a massive spear and decorated shield, while a deadly sword hung from his hip. A chainmail vest, reinforced pants and protective boots replaced his flowing robe. One raven sat on his shoulder, while another stood on the shield. The missing eye was a ragged scar on his face.

"Go up on the platform if you want a better look." Harry gestured to a flat area in front of Odin. "There's writing on the wall beside him."

The three men and Sara stampeded toward the carving. Harry reached for Sara's hand, missed it, then cursed to himself. Of course she'd go running along with the rest.

They all stopped in front of the wall beside Odin. Runes were carved into the wall, small enough you couldn't see them until Harry lit a nearby torch hanging on the wall. A short series of familiar runes Harry had inspected last night. Sara spoke first.

"It's in Ataulf's code."

Ingvar fumbled with his coat. "I will translate the runes."

Sara's lips moved silently as Ingvar produced a pen and paper. She let him find the first rune and write it down before speaking again. "Save your energy. I can read it."

Magnus looked away from the wall. "You can?"

"I cracked the code several artifacts ago," she said. "That's why Harry got here before you."

Harry chuckled. *That's my girl.*

"What does it say?" Magnus asked.

"It's a plea. From Ataulf." She began reading aloud.

Here King Ataulf rests, waiting for a worthy Viking to commune with Odin. King Ataulf has prepared for his journey. His ship will set sail when the Viking who speaks to Odin offers tribute to convince Odin to reunite Ataulf and Theodosius, Ataulf's treasure.

Use Thor's hammer to send King Ataulf to be with his son. Send the hammer with King Ataulf so Odin may retrieve it on the journey. This is King Ataulf's final wish. Only a true Viking will send King Ataulf to be with his son by sending his ship through the wall born of Roman knowledge to hide King Ataulf and Theodosius as they waited for you, the Viking to reunite them forever.

Until Hel.

Her words echoed off the cavern walls. Harry sidled closer to Sara until he could touch her arm. "That's what I got from it too."

Magnus twisted to look at Harry. "You already translated this?"

"Last night. Don't worry, I didn't touch anything." He took Sara's hand and pulled her back a step. "I think I know what it means."

"I understand it." Ingvar stopped scribbling madly in the notebook and stepped close to the wall, where he stood tracing the runes with a finger. "King Ataulf has a ship. It is a metaphor for his journey to Valhalla. He wishes to find his son and his treasure, but requires a tribute to Odin."

Sara and Harry locked eyes. They said nothing.

"Thor's hammer is here," Ingvar said. "It must be. The hammer will send Ataulf to Valhalla."

"Wait." Magnus pointed to another section of writing on the wall. "What does this say?"

"It's about what happened to Ataulf's descendants," Harry said. "At least I think it is."

"It is," Sara said. "It's their story. It explains why Ataulf's ship has been here for so long, and why nobody knew about the path they left behind until we found the drinking horns."

"Read it," Magnus said.

"It says that Ataulf's descendants searched for a way to reunite Ataulf with Theodosius. They couldn't find one, so they left a trail for future Vikings to follow. A hedge against them not succeeding. They didn't want to leave Ataulf separated from his son forever." Sara read the next line. "Wow. It's a good thing they left the trail."

"Why?" Magnus asked.

"These Vikings left their lands here to fight with Harald Sigurdsson." Her voice softened. "That's why they never came back."

Why did Harry know that name? "Who's Harald Sigurdsson?"

Magnus responded. "The king of Norway defeated at the Battle of Stamford Bridge. It was the end of the Viking age. Harald's army was slaughtered."

"Which left no one alive to reunite Ataulf and Theodosius," Harry said. "It makes sense."

"It was a tragedy," Magnus said, then looked at Harry. "One that is in the past. Where is the hammer?"

"Beats me," Harry said. He walked right up to Magnus's chest, glaring at the bearded man. Harry lifted his arm. He pointed past one big shoulder, toward the darkness in the cavern they hadn't yet explored. A darkness from which came the soft sounds of lapping water. "You should turn around."

Torches, flashlights and a headlamp pushed back the dark. Water sparkled ahead, a pool with a dark shape floating on it. A shape that transformed into an impossible vision under their lights. Magnus took a step back and nearly bowled Harry over. "It cannot be."

Harry regained his footing. "Your buddy Ingvar was wrong. The message is talking about a real ship. *That* ship."

A broad-hulled Viking longship floated in front of them. Water lapped at the ground not far beyond the platform they stood on, shielded by a darkness so total none of the new visitors had noted the water's edge when they entered. Harry had only found it last night after he'd backed up on the platform for a better look at Odin and nearly fallen into the water. Forty feet from end to end, the wooden longship had a mast standing fifteen feet high, while openings for oars dotted the sides. The bow and stern had been decorated with animal carvings, each rising into curled designs taller than a man.

"Incredible." Magnus stepped to the water's edge. "It is anchored in place. There must be an opening under the sea to allow water in."

"Take a look at that wall," Harry said. "It's fake. Ataulf's people built it as camouflage for this boat."

"Our ancestors were more advanced builders than anyone knows," Ingvar said. "A match for any civilization in history."

"No," Sara said. "They didn't discover this building technique on their own."

Ingvar aimed his pen at Sara. "You are wrong. They built this wall."

"Only because Romans showed them how." Sara inclined her head to the runes. "The message tells us. What do you think *the wall born of*

Roman knowledge means? They're talking about this wall, which the boat needs to go through to get to sea. The Visigoths took more than jewels and gold from Rome. They also took knowledge."

Magnus looked askance at Ingvar. "What is your interpretation of the message?" he asked Sara.

"I believe this ship is prepared to sail, but not ready to launch. Not until Odin is convinced to accept Thor's hammer as tribute so that Ataulf and Theodosius may be rejoined."

"Why would they not be together?"

Harry jumped in before she could respond. "Theodosius died as a child. He didn't die in battle."

Ingvar wasn't entirely stupid. "That means Theodosius could not go to Valhalla."

"That's right," Harry said. His eyes flicked to Sara for an instant, catching her gaze. "Ataulf needed someone to commune with the gods, a person with enough pull to convince Odin to let Theodosius in even though he didn't die in battle. Sounds like he wasn't convinced Odin would listen to him."

"Ataulf required a true Viking," Ingvar said. "He likely asked Odin to guide him, and this is the path he chose." Ingvar grabbed Magnus's arm. "We are those Vikings. You have done it."

Magnus hadn't done much of anything except ruin Harry's life, but Harry kept that to himself. "If you think so, then you'd better take a closer look at that ship."

"What does the end of the message mean?" Jacob asked as everyone's head turned. "The part that says *Until Hel.*"

"I have seen it used before," Sara said before anyone else could speak. "As a Viking blessing."

Harry moved to the water's edge. "The water gets deep quickly. You can use this to get on the ship." He put his foot on a massive plank. One end of the plank rested on the boat's side, the other on the shore. Both ends were secured in place by iron bolts, which he'd checked several times last night before tempting fate by crossing the shaky contraption. "Go out there and take a look, but I wouldn't touch anything."

Magnus and his men jostled each other as they leapt onto the plank. Harry stopped Sara from following. "You see what I'm doing?" he asked in a whisper.

"They don't understand," she said. "Theodosius cannot enter Valhalla. Ataulf wants to join him in Hel. That's what *Until Hel* truly means."

"There's a puzzle on the boat. Follow my—"

"Wait." Ingvar's voice filled the cavern. He stared at Harry and Sara from halfway across the bridge, must have seen their heads bowed so close together. "Go back."

"Why?" Magnus asked, still walking.

"This could be a trap," Ingvar said. He shoved Jacob back toward land. "Go back, go back."

Harry put a hand up as they came back across. "What am I going to do, push you out to sea?"

"Do not trust them," Ingvar spat. "Their kind always lie."

Sara made it from Harry's side to Ingvar's face in a flash. "What *kind* are we? The kind who kidnap people? Or the kind who wave guns in people's faces? Or perhaps the kind who espouse racial hatred and thinly veiled misogyny?"

Ingvar Larsen backed up in the face of this onslaught, backed up so fast he tripped over his feet and landed flat on his ass. Sara gave him no room.

"Which is it? You bully the weak, find lost souls and feed them a diet of lies, filling them with misplaced anger, all in the name of serving your needs. The only person you care about is yourself. A horrid, hateful little man with no real power who cannot stand on his own two feet." Now Ingvar had a hand up to ward her off. Sara faked a punch at the man and he yelped. "You have excellent taste in colleagues," Sara told Magnus.

Sara went back to Harry's side. Magnus's face could have melted iron. "Get up, Ingvar." He made no move to help the man. "She is right. They have no weapons and are outnumbered. There is no trap here."

"Do not listen to her." Ingvar took several long moments to gain his feet. "My only concern is your safety. We are so close to finding Thor's hammer, to bringing back the world we had. I cannot risk this failing. We need you, Magnus. To lead us. Forgive me if I have been harsh, but it must be done."

"What a toad," Sara said under her breath. Harry chuckled.

Ingvar glared at them, his mouth pinched and eyes narrowed. Magnus considered Ingvar's position for a moment. "I appreciate your concern, Ingvar. But we must treat our opponents with respect. It is the Viking way."

Harry hadn't kept still while all this went down. He'd moved closer to Magnus, keeping one hand behind his back, going slowly so nobody noticed. Magnus stood an arm's length away, half facing him. Jacob and Ingvar were across from them, with Sara in between. Harry's fingers closed on cool metal. *Enough of this nonsense.*

"Nobody move." Harry spoke calmly, the way you should when you're pointing a gun at someone. The pistol in his hand was aimed at Magnus. A pistol he'd left under the boulder, the one Joey's contact had provided yesterday. A pistol Harry sincerely hoped not to fire. "Take your gun out," he said to Jacob. "Slowly. Now toss it at Sara's feet."

Ingvar Larsen raised his hands as Jacob followed orders. "Do not shoot us," Ingvar whined. "Do not shoot him."

"All I want to do is leave. Sara, throw that gun in the water." A splash came from the darkness as she threw Jacob's firearm away. "We're leaving now. You can have what's on that boat."

"It is difficult to bargain when you have a gun pointed at me," Magnus said.

"Now you know how it feels." The big man said nothing. "You know who I work for?" Harry asked. Magnus said he didn't. "Ask around. You'll find out. Trust me, you don't want trouble with us. You leave me alone and we'll leave you alone. Deal?"

Magnus looked at his colleagues before he responded. "It is a deal."

Harry closed his eyes. *Finally.* He kept the gun on Magnus as he backed away. He reached for Sara's hand while Jacob and Ingvar glared at him.

"I'm taking the helmet," Sara said. "I'll send it to a Norwegian museum once I'm done studying it."

"No." Ingvar actually stamped his foot. Harry bit back a laugh. "Magnus requires it to reunite Scandinavia. You will not take it."

"I'm sick of criminals like you winning," she said. "You don't get everything this time."

The men said nothing. Harry kept backing up. Why did she have to bring this up now? Magnus could have the stupid helmet for all he cared. Good riddance. But Sara never backed down, not from anyone. He was only fooling himself thinking she'd start now.

Harry half-turned to look at her. "You sure about—"

"Watch out!"

Sara cried out as the first footsteps reached Harry's ears. He turned to see a dark shape hurtling through the air toward him. Jacob had gone airborne, aiming for Harry's chest. Harry aimed the gun, his finger on the trigger. He hesitated.

BOOM. Thunder rocked the cavern. Jacob slammed into him as hot pain seared through his bicep. The full weight of the bigger man threw him backwards to the ground, knocking the breath from him, as the gun went flying. The air flew from his lungs, the rocks scraped his back. Sara's cries mixed with the echoes of the gunshot – and then a man's hoarse yells drowned her out.

"What did you do?" Magnus shouted, his voice ragged with anguish. Harry scrambled, twisting to get free of Jacob. A red-hot poker had scalded his arm. He pushed and shoved at the man on top of him. A trickle of warm liquid dribbled against his cheek and he tasted copper. Harry went still.

"Jacob!" Magnus shouted frantically. "Jacob, can you hear me?"

Harry heard the clattering of footsteps and then the weight pressing him down was lifted away as though by magic. Harry twisted to look for the gun. Where had it gone?

"Jacob, speak to me," Magnus said, lowering Jacob gently to the ground.

Red stained the front of Magnus's shirt. Harry looked down at himself and saw the same stains on his own. He traced a finger over the slick, warm wetness and his arm shouted again. He looked at his bicep. There was a searing red welt on the flesh, but no bullet hole. So where was the blood coming from? He touched the wet spot on his shirt again. The blood was not Harry's, but Jacob's. *Ingvar shot Jacob.*

Harry sat up. His eyes narrowed. *My gun.* It had landed next to where Magnus was now crouched over Jacob. The big man turned toward where Harry was looking, spotted the weapon and hurled it into the water.

"I did not mean to." Ingvar's face was ashen, his words soft. "He jumped in front of me."

"Jacob." Magnus leaned over his friend. "Talk to me." He shook Jacob's shoulder. No response. "Look at me." A slap echoed off Jacob's cheek. Nothing.

"I did not mean to," Ingvar said again. He looked at the gun in his hand as though mystified about how it had gotten there.

Magnus shook, smacked and pleaded with Jacob until his voice rang off the cavern roof. The fallen man lay still, blood beginning to pool under his body. In the flickering light, Harry could see a huge, jagged hole in his chest. Magnus held Jacob's corpse as though it were a toy, then slowly sat back on his heels, his face a mask of grief. He gently touched Jacob's head and whispered in Norwegian. "*Till Valhalla.*"

Magnus stood and stepped toward Ingvar. "He jumped in front of me," Ingvar said, unable to take his eyes off the body. "An accident."

Ingvar seemed to shrink in on himself now. He stood silently, staring at the body of his comrade. Finally, he tore his eyes from the corpse and turned to look at the man looming in front of him. Magnus slammed his fist into Ingvar's face. Ingvar fell straight back, arms out, feet splayed. He bounced once on the rocky ground and lay still.

"I will break you in half if you reach for his gun," Magnus said to Harry, his voice low and dangerous. "Do not move."

Harry didn't move as Magnus knelt and retrieved Ingvar's pistol. At least Magnus had the decency not to aim it at him. "Now, tell me where to find the helmet." The words dropped like stones in the silence.

"Is he dead?" Sara asked.

"The location of the helmet," Magnus said. "Or I shoot her." He aimed the gun at Sara.

A half-second passed. Magnus pulled the trigger. Sparks flashed off the ground beside her.

"Wait, wait!" Harry shouted over the whining in his ears. "Take the dumb helmet. It's in my car on the mainland."

"Where are the keys?" Magnus asked.

"In the wheel well. "Magnus then demanded the boat keys, so Harry reached into his pocket and threw them over. "If you are lying, you will regret it." Harry assured him he wasn't. "Now, tell me about Thor's hammer."

The lump of meat named Ingvar let out a pitiful moan. Seems Magnus's blow hadn't killed him after all.

"Like I said, there's a puzzle on the boat." Harry pointed at the makeshift bridge Ingvar had thought to be a trap. "You have to walk aboard to see it."

Magnus flicked the pistol barrel. "You go first."

Ingvar groaned again, stirring as he tried to get up. He only made it to a seated position. "You punched me," he said.

Magnus didn't look at him. "You killed my friend."

Harry shook his head, refusing to step onto the gangplank. "I'm not leaving her on land with that guy."

"Ingvar is coming with us. Aren't you, Ingvar?"

Ingvar didn't look like he could walk, much less cross a shaky bridge onto the boat. He glared at Magnus from the ground. "We cannot leave her here. She will run."

"She will not leave this man. I can tell." Magnus turned to Sara. "Run if you wish. It is of no consequence. You are on an island with no way to operate the boats. Good luck if you choose to swim."

"You'll die of hypothermia before you get to land," Harry said. "Don't try it."

"You think I would leave?" Sara asked.

Even with a gun trained on him while stuck in a cavern with two zealots and no way out, he smirked. "Never."

"Enough," Magnus said. "The boat. You go first." He gestured with the gun again.

Harry shrugged, giving the pistol a wide berth as he headed for the bridge. "Watch your head on the boat," he said. "There are ropes all over the place. I think they keep the boat from running aground or smashing against the rock wall."

His second time across the bridge was no more fun than the first. Really no more than a few planks bound together, the bridge shifted as he walked, groaning and bouncing as Magnus and then Ingvar followed suit. He used the boat's rail as a handhold and vaulted down to the deck. Ropes stretched from the rail into the darkness above and beyond. He hadn't seen an anchor chain running off the boat into the water. Probably no reason for it with all these extra support ropes.

Harry felt Magnus's presence a moment before his boots smacked on the deck. "It is amazing." He stood at Harry's shoulder now, still holding the gun, still twice Harry's size. "Exactly as I pictured it."

Benches for oarsmen ran along either side of the flat-bottomed vessel, with oars stowed against the hull. The single mast stretching toward the cavern ceiling had a rolled sail at the top. Dark rope and some sort of tar-covered insulation ran along the interior of the boat, attached to the underside of the rail. They had boarded amidships. Harry pointed to the stern and the massive rudder.

"There's nothing back there but the rudder." Now he pointed to the bow, which was aimed for the towering cliffside wall that protected the boat and hid this cavern. "The puzzle is this way."

He set off, with the two men close behind him. Dark ropes running down either side of the center walkway guided them to the bow. As in the stern, no rowing benches had been placed here, leaving the front open, perhaps to offer a clear line of vision, or a place for the Viking warriors to gather before storming an unfortunate village. However, Ataulf's people had clearly had other ideas. This bow served another purpose: the final stop on Ataulf's path.

"This is the puzzle I'm talking about," Harry said. "Oh, and there's the hammer you want."

Two stone columns stood in the stern in front of them, rising to Harry's waist and no thicker around than his thigh. A box sat between the pillars. An object sat atop it. Magnus spoke first.

"A gold hammer."

"Thor's hammer," Harry said. "Check out the tablet beside it."

Ingvar tried to sneak past Magnus, who stuck out an arm and made it clear he would not pass. "What have you touched?" Magnus demanded.

"Nothing," Harry said. "I was on this boat for less than a minute last night. It was dark, I had to get back to land, and I couldn't risk missing your call. You'd kidnapped Sara, remember?"

Magnus ignored him. "Did you read the tablet?"

"It's in Ataulf's code."

"What does it say?"

"Let me read it," Ingvar said. "We cannot trust him."

"I cannot even trust you with a gun," Magnus said. "So far, this man has told me the truth about everything."

"He also tried to shoot you."

Magnus's brow furrowed. "I have not forgotten. He is not one of us, true. Yet enemies often prove useful."

Ingvar aimed his light at the hammer. "Truly the hammer of a god."

That it was. A hammer constructed entirely of gold. It lay on the box, shining with a dull intensity. Intricate carvings covered the handle;

the rectangular head was big enough to smash an enemy flat. The entire hammer was longer than Harry's forearm. A hammer big enough for a god.

Ingvar reached for the hammer.

"I wouldn't do that," Harry said. "Read the tablet first."

Ingvar aimed his light at the rune-covered stone tablet resting beside the hammer. "Did you translate it?" Ingvar asked.

"I have it in my pocket." He slowly removed the folded piece of paper on which he'd scribbled a translation. He offered it to Magnus. The bearded man's eyes went wide as he read.

"Follow along," Harry told Ingvar. "Confirm what it says." Magnus slowly read the words aloud, allowing Ingvar time to translate.

Here lies Mjolnir. Odin now agrees to accept King Ataulf's offering. Valhalla waits for the strong and worthy Viking who speaks with Odin to reunite King Ataulf with Theodosius.

Send Mjolnir to Odin by striking the pillar where King Ataulf and Theodosius will live until the world ends. Only a true Viking may send them. If no worthy Viking uses Thor's hammer, King Ataulf kneels before Odin and asks to live with his son forever.

He offers the hammer of the White God taken from Rome. Thor's hammer proves King Ataulf is favored by the gods. The emperor took their symbol of seven candles to prove his worth. King Ataulf showed the god's favor his people by taking it from Rome and creating Mjolnir and Thor's helmet.

"Mjolnir," Magnus said with reverence. "Thor's hammer. It is truly here."

"Ataulf made it using the treasure taken from Rome," Ingvar said. "The *White God's symbol of seven candles.* Do you realize what this weapon is?"

"This hammer *used* to be the second temple menorah stolen by Emperor Vespasian," Harry said. "Same as the helmet. Ataulf melted it down and made Norse objects to show that his gods were superior to the Roman and Jewish ones." He spread his arms wide. "There it is. All you have to do is fulfill his last request and you're done."

The air went still. Harry didn't let himself think lest hope sneak past his defenses. Part one of his rescue plan was in the water. Part two was now in play. "You going to do it or not? Look at those two columns. There are words written on them."

Magnus stood over the stone columns. "This one says *Valhalla.* The other says *Hel.*"

"It is a test," Ingvar said. "Only a true Viking knows where to send Ataulf. He is a king. He must go to Valhalla."

"The hammer is proof." Magnus ignored Ingvar, his hands dropping to his sides as he spoke. Which meant the gun wasn't aimed toward Harry. "Proof our gods are the true gods. We are the chosen people."

"Yes." Ingvar took a step toward the hammer. "We must take this, Magnus. Use it to show we are the chosen Viking leaders and that we Vikings are foremost in the world. Not the Jews. Not the Christians. Their gods failed them. Vikings sit atop the world order."

"You're going to leave Ataulf's final wish unfulfilled?" Harry asked. "Not very Viking of you."

Ingvar spat invective while Magnus frowned. "He is right," he said. "Ataulf led us here. We must respect his wishes."

"You cannot lose the hammer," Ingvar protested. "It must come with us."

"Ataulf wishes it to be an offering to Odin," Magnus said. "Who are we to disobey?"

"That is not why Odin brought us here. He sent me to guide you, to join our people. He wants us to have the hammer and helmet." Ingvar's eyes went wide, spittle flying from his mouth. "It is the only way. You cannot believe this heathen."

Magnus couldn't take his eyes off the hammer. "Perhaps. The gods will give us a sign. Should I take the hammer, or should it be sacrificed?" He was speaking almost to himself now.

"Follow his wishes and then take the hammer," Ingvar said. "Send

Ataulf to Valhalla."

Magnus didn't have quite the same feverish glow as Ingvar, Harry noticed, at least not yet. Maybe that was why he had stopped to think. "Where will Ataulf go?" He looked around. "Is this ship the embodiment of his spirit?"

Harry chimed in. "Nope. Look behind the pillars. Way up front at the edge of the bow."

Ingvar's light went up. Magnus walked around the pillars, to what at first glance appeared to be the inside of the hull. Only when he was on top of it did Magnus realize it was actually a short wall built to keep two objects safe, to stop them from sliding as the boat shifted. "Coffins," Magnus said.

"Silver coffins," Harry said quickly. "A big one and a little one. Check out the names on top."

"Ataulf and Theodosius. They are together."

"In silver coffins, which is what we read on the horns that started all this. Ataulf and his son are here in body, but they need to get to Valhalla in spirit." He emphasized the last part. "They need you to make it happen."

Ingvar started to speak. Magnus raised a hand to quiet him. "Mr. Fox is right. I am to lead our people into the future. To reunite the broken lands of Scandinavia into one. How can I do that if I fail to honor King Ataulf's wishes?"

"You must have the hammer," Ingvar said. "We cannot lose it now."

"Odin will show me a sign if I am meant to have the hammer. But I must send Ataulf and his son to the gods." His eyes narrowed as he looked over at Harry again. "How will it happen?"

"Smash the pillar," Harry said. "The noise will signal Odin. Look at this cave." He waved an arm around the exterior. "It's like a giant megaphone to the gods."

The men looked around. Harry stole a glance at the dark ropes running along the bow wall, encircling the entire ship. Magnus and

Ingvar hadn't seemed to notice them. Same as they hadn't noticed the incredible number of ropes mooring this ship in such calm waters. He took a step back. One step closer to the bridge off this boat.

"Is he correct?" Magnus asked Ingvar. "It is logical."

Ingvar spat at the deck. "He is a godless wretch. If he is correct, it is mere luck."

"You'd better use the hammer," Harry said to Magnus. "Not sure your buddy could pick it up."

Ingvar's pinched features turned serpentine in the moving shadows. A welt was forming on the side of his face. "Odin will appreciate a human sacrifice," Ingvar said. "We should offer this heathen."

"Vikings didn't practice human sacrifice," Harry fired back.

"Only in times of war." Ingvar's teeth flashed. "Enemy soldiers could be offered to the gods as tribute for victories in battle. We are in a mortal struggle for the soul of Scandinavia. It is only right we honor Odin by consecrating your soul and sending it to him."

The only way that would happen was if Magnus shot him, Harry knew. He could take Ingvar, no problem. Magnus, though, was a big problem. "Very sporting of you," Harry said. "Shooting an unarmed man."

Magnus didn't say anything. He kept his eyes on the hammer. The boat creaked, ropes overhead protested, and Harry swayed gently with the craft as Magnus moved toward the hammer, reaching for the golden handle. A tiny spark of static electricity flashed when his skin touched metal. "I feel it," he said softly.

Feel what? The last thing Harry needed was Magnus buying into Ingvar's nonsense and going off the deep end. He still had a chance. A chance to fix this, to get Sara out of here unharmed.

Magnus pulled his hand back. "It feels *alive*," he said. "The metal. I can feel the power. The history of our people."

"We must sacrifice him," Ingvar said. "To assure Odin's favor."

Would this little turd ever shut up?

Magnus reached for the hammer again, then suddenly drew back.

"What is on the pillar?" he asked sharply, his fingers inches from the handle. "On the *Valhalla* pillar?"

Damn. Harry's headlamp had inadvertently lit the top of the pillar Magnus intended to hit. The gritty coating neither Magnus nor Ingvar had yet noticed became apparent now under the light. A coating Harry had seen last night. "It's rough," Harry said quickly. "I think it's from the moisture in here."

Magnus rubbed a hand over it. "Yes, it is." Now he touched the *Hel* column. "This one is not."

"You think they had quality control for stone masons back then?" Harry asked.

Magnus didn't respond. He seemed troubled by it. "Is it a sign?" A silence ensued. Harry looked back at the bridge. If he made it to the bridge, he could dive off and swim to shore. Except first he'd have to sprint down the middle of the ship in a straight line, making him an easy target for Magnus's pistol. *That Viking had better be a terrible shot.*

"Odin will tell me." Magnus reached for the hammer. "He is close, in this cave. Waiting for me to prove my worth." He stood still, eyes closed, and Harry could have sworn he seemed to grow bigger, to fill more space than even a man his size should.

"Take this." Magnus opened his eyes and handed the gun to Ingvar. "Do not shoot him. Yet." He turned back to the hammer and grabbed it with both hands. "I can feel them, Ingvar. Odin and Thor both." He lifted the hammer and there was a sound of metal clinking. "There is a chain holding it to the ship," Magnus said, puzzled. "Why?"

"In case you try to steal it without carrying out Ataulf's final wish," Harry said. "The chain will break if you smash the right pillar. Look how it's attached at the bottom."

"You are correct." Dark shadows raced across Magnus's face as he hefted the massive hammer. He grunted, lifting it in front of his chest. "The hammer of a king," Magnus said. "Sent from the gods."

The boat rocked. Ingvar tried to keep the gun aimed at Harry. The torches on shore burned brighter, turning the golden hammer in

Magnus's hands into a living creature, every whorl and curve seeming to twist and slide across the surface, as though it were an apparition sent from the heavens. Magnus lifted it overhead. His eyes were not those of a man with his feet on the ground.

His voice filled the cavern. "The gods are with us. A new beginning has arrived. A new Scandinavia!"

Holding the giant hammer high, Magnus turned toward the pillars, stepped forward, and brought it down with a roar that shook the boat and nearly blew out the torches onshore. Harry couldn't move, couldn't breathe as the hammer fell swift and hard as a lightning bolt to strike the pillar in front of him. The *Valhalla* pillar.

The pillar exploded. Fire erupted, spewing in all directions. Magnus's beard caught fire as he loosed a guttural cry, twisting and turning in a whirling ball of flame. Ingvar Larsen backed away from the tornado of death, tripped on a bench and tumbled into the water. Magnus slapped at his own face, screaming and beating the flames out on his beard. Thor's hammer flashed as it landed on the deck. Magnus dropped and rolled with fearsome speed, smothering the flames and collapsing the little wall that concealed the two silver coffins. Exposed now, they glowed in the orange light.

Harry caught all this in one look as he turned and ran. It had played out exactly as he had hoped. The rough surface on Ataulf's *Valhalla* pillar had had nothing to do with the wet cave; rather, it was a dry chemical mixture akin to gunpowder. Harry knew because he'd scraped a sample off yesterday and taken it with him. The sharp odor it had given off made him think it might be flammable. A check with his lighter had confirmed the substance might as well have been black powder. Magnus smashing the hammer on it had been like a firing pin hitting the primer.

The only question now was how big of an explosion was coming next.

Ataulf had never wanted to go to Valhalla. Valhalla was reserved for those who died in battle. Illness and old age sent a Viking to Hel, and

Theodosius had died of disease. Magnus should have hit the *Hel* pillar instead.

Harry had also checked out the ropes hanging everywhere before leaving last night, and it had appeared that activating the pillar would cause the ropes to begin a coordinated series of movements that would somehow affect the ship, given their placement and number. What it would do he'd had no idea, but it shouldn't be this.

The entire ship had caught fire, and Harry realized unhappily that this was what the dark ropes and tarry insulation were for: to burn if the wrong column were hit and sparks flew. One way or another, Ataulf and Theodosius were journeying to the afterlife together. If a false Viking arrived who had not persuaded Odin to accept Ataulf's bribe, it seemed Ataulf was taking his chances on a flaming ship and human offerings instead. Maybe the *Hel* pillar gave everyone a chance to get off the ship. Too late to find out now.

A line of fire encircled the craft, blazing beneath the rail and down the center. Flames danced on ropes running from the boat into the darkness ahead and above. Harry raised an arm against the searing heat and shouted. "Sara, get out of here."

"Harry!" Her voice cut through thick smoke stinging his eyes. "Get off the boat."

"I'm working on it," he yelled back, making his way across the smoking deck to where the top of the little gangplank lay. A nagging feeling made him stop. He turned, peering through the flames, back to where Magnus had fallen. Cursing himself, Harry ran back through the flames. If that big guy was still alive, Harry could throw him over the edge, give him a fighting chance. No way he could carry Magnus back to land, though.

A crack like the earth splitting made his brain rattle. Harry didn't look up to see what it was. No time. Dodging twisting flames while leaping over burning ropes didn't leave room for error. The ship shifted under his feet as he ran, and Harry reached out to steady himself without thinking. The burning board he touched made his skin sizzle and curses fly. His feet kept pumping and he burst through a curtain of smoke to where he'd last seen Magnus.

The man had vanished. Harry spun around in time to catch a glimpse of dull yellow moving jerkily through the dark smoke. *The hammer.* Magnus was trying to get off this deathtrap with the hammer in tow. Harry leapt a burning bench and came face-to-shoulder with Magnus Dahl. Magnus turned as though a ghost had appeared, and then, overbalanced by the weight of the huge hammer, he stumbled over a chunk of burning timber and fell toward the rail. The boat shifted again as Magnus flailed his arms, struggling to regain his balance. Thor's hammer dropped heavily from his grasp. Magnus regained his footing and scrambled to his feet, rising like an apparition through the hellfire, beard singed black and face distorted by the shimmering heat. He turned to Harry. His mouth opened, but his words were drowned out by a tremendous *crack* that split the air.

There was a whoosh of wind as a massive boulder, bigger than a car and falling like a comet, plummeted through the space in front of him. It punched a phone booth-sized hole through the ship, smashing Magnus flat on its way to the bottom of the lagoon. Harry stared, open-mouthed, at the gaping hole where Magnus had stood before vanishing under a thousand pounds of stone.

Harry fell back and looked up, then scrambled to his feet again in horror. The ceiling was collapsing, chunks of rock and rubble raining down. A crack of light appeared ahead of the ship. Then another. Harry looked wildly around. *No* – the ceiling wasn't breaking. The *far wall* was coming apart, chunks of it splitting away and falling into the water with a rattle like artillery fire. Burning ropes snapped and twirled through the air as the ship gave a mighty groan and jerked ahead. More ropes snapped and the burning boat lurched forward again.

Of course. Harry scooped up the hammer then leapt across the new hole in the deck on a dead run for the rickety bridge, which was no doubt in the process of collapsing as the boat tried to pull away from shore, free of the mooring ropes and soon without anything between it and the open seas. This, then, was Ataulf's backup plan. That's why he had left a final test in the form of two pillars. The ace up his sleeve. His final chance at convincing Odin to reunite him with Theodosius in Hel.

This hammer was *heavy*. Harry strained and sweated as he hugged the golden relic to his chest with two hands, trying to keep his feet moving. He half-ran, half-staggered down the boat's center until the exit ramp appeared ahead, by some miracle still attached to the boat. He took the ramp at full speed. The board bounced and bucked as he ran full tilt down its length, as though it were trying to toss him into the water to be crushed by the falling boulders. Flaming ropes whipped and snapped around him, lit now with a deadly luminescent glow from the accelerant that had been soaked into their fibers. Thick, choking smoke filled the cavern.

"Harry!"

Sara was standing at the bottom of the collapsing ramp, yelling his name, using her voice to guide him. Clutching the massive hammer to his chest, he pulled oily air into protesting lungs and shouted back to her. "Get out of the way."

That's when the ramp split in half. One second he was about to crush Sara as he plowed down the ramp with his burden; the next, he landed chest-first in water that was, thankfully, mere feet deep. The hammer had saved him, he thought incredulously, spitting seawater out of his mouth. It had changed his center of gravity as he fell so that, instead of plunging feet-first into the lagoon, he'd done a belly-flop. It stung like crazy, and looked less than graceful, but by some miracle he hadn't broken an ankle. Or worse.

Hands lugged him upright in the water. "Are you hurt?" Sara asked breathlessly.

He reached into the water, swallowed a horrid mouthful, then rose to his feet, coughing and spitting. "I got it." He held out the hammer and nearly dropped it. "Magnus had it. Then he got smashed by a rock."

Sara pulled him toward dry land. "What's happening?" She had to raise her voice over the din of the flames and splitting rock.

"There are two pillars on the boat." Harry made it onto the edge of the lagoon, set the hammer down and went to one knee, trying to catch his breath. Before getting back up he checked his neck. The amulet was still there. "One marked *Hel*, one marked *Valhalla*," Harry said as he stood. "We need to get out of here." He gave Sara a push toward the exit, picked up the hammer and set off after her. "Magnus had to smash one of the pillars to reunite Ataulf with Theodosius," he said, coming up behind her. "The *Valhalla* pillar had something like gunpowder on it, and the whole ship was soaked in fuel."

Sara stopped running. "He hit *Valhalla?* Why?"

"I didn't remind him that Theodosius actually went to Hel."

"You *tricked* them?"

"Only way I could see me getting off that boat. That nutjob Ingvar had the gun. He wanted to shoot me."

"You are brilliant." She stood where she was, brow furrowed in thought.

"I try." He pushed past her. "Ataulf and Theodosius were in coffins on the ship. Now they're getting a Viking send-off to convince Odin to let them spend eternity together." He moved off. "Come on. This place is done for."

Sara didn't move. The wheels in her head were too busy churning. "It's a backup plan. The pillars, the ship. All of it."

"Right," Harry said, stopping to face her. "The hammer was chained so you had to hit a pillar to break it loose. If a treasure hunter or false Viking found this place, chances are they'd hit the wrong pillar and trigger the trap." He indicated the chaos around them. "That far wall is collapsing. It's the same sort of wall I broke down to get in here. A fake wall built using Roman technique. It's been hiding this ship for nearly a thousand years."

"Amazing." Sara marveled at the hellscape.

"We're going to be here for a thousand years if we don't get out."

The snap of burning rope and the rumble of falling stone intensified.

Then a deafening roar filled the cavern as half the far wall gave way, revealing a dark gray sky and whitecapped seas beyond. The jagged split racing down what remained of the wall told Harry this place had little time left, and that King Ataulf's burning ship was on its way home.

The exit ramp waited ahead. "Come on, Sara!" At last she started to move again. Harry charged toward the ramp and Sara caught up just as a car-sized rock broke away and smacked down in front of them, forcing them to veer around it.

There was a roar like a cannon blast in the shaking cavern and sparks flew off the rock.

"Stop!" Another cannon shot. More sparks flew beside Harry's feet. "You will stop."

Harry twisted. Ingvar Larsen stood behind them, blood smeared across his head, water dripping from his sodden clothes. Magnus's gun aimed at Harry's chest. "Give me the hammer."

"When we get outside," Harry said. "You want to die in here?"

"Give it to me, you godless swine." Ingvar stepped closer with each word. "Thor wants me to have it. Odin has chosen *me*, the last surviving Viking. I must have it."

"Outside," Harry said. "Put that gun down or we all die here." He looked at Sara and mouthed the word *run*. She shook her head.

Ingvar tilted his head. He pushed limp hair out of his eye and fresh blood flowed down his cheek. "No. I will not die here. It is not my destiny." He raised the gun. "It is yours."

Harry closed his eyes and ducked. A gunshot boomed and the hammer jerked in his hands, smacking him in the face. *He shot the hammer.*

He opened his eyes. Ingvar looked at the gun, then back at Harry. He raised the gun again. Harry screamed and charged.

The incoherent battle cry of a Viking erupted from his lungs, filling the cavern, his rage so hot and pure the flames around him faded to nothing as Harry ran at the man pointing a gun at him and raised the hammer as though it were a sword ready to slice Ingvar in two. Ingvar's finger tightened on the trigger an instant before a fist-sized rock smacked off his head, new blood flowed, and the gun boomed.

Harry threw the hammer as Ingvar's shot went wide, hurled it with every ounce of his strength at Ingvar's head, shouting and falling all at once as the golden weapon spun around and around. It missed Ingvar by a hair, flying farther than should have been possible until it bounced off a fallen stone and sailed toward the wall with Ataulf's final message carved on it, finally tumbling to a halt in front of the encoded runes.

Ingvar, half-stunned from the rock, watched it all the way. He shook his head and gave chase, ignoring the cracking cave walls and flames shooting all around.

"Time to go." Sara latched onto Harry's arm and tugged him toward the exit. He looked back through the smoke and flames and rubble and saw Ingvar Larsen bending down to retrieve Thor's golden hammer. Harry froze as the man lifted it above his head and loosed a triumphant cry.

With a deafening roar, the runestone wall cracked. A circular chunk of rock broke free from the ceiling, rolling down the wall and racing toward the man holding the hammer aloft. A man whose mouth was still open in a battle cry as the boulder crashed down and smashed him flat.

"Seen enough?" Sara clenched Harry's shoulder. "I have."

He tore his eyes away from the carnage. Her smoke-stained cheeks and bloodshot eyes were the most beautiful thing he'd ever seen. He grabbed her hand and they raced toward the open skies above.

Epilogue

Brooklyn
The Next Week

Harry stood outside his front door. His hand hovered over the knob. He'd knocked twice, counted to five and knocked again. He couldn't surprise Sara, not after what had happened when he'd walked in unannounced yesterday. She'd been asleep on the couch. Suffice it to say, Sara did not take kindly to surprises.

He knocked again just to be sure, then opened the door. "Sara?" He waited on the threshold. "It's me."

"I'm in here." Her voice was softer than usual.

He found her on the couch once more, this time sitting with a book open on her lap, staring at him. A shotgun was within easy reach on the table. He also noted a clear path to the rear door, currently closed and locked with two new deadbolts he'd installed yesterday. "How's it going?" he asked.

"I'm fine." She looked to either side, to the windows with their drawn blinds. "How's Joey?"

"Fine." The lie flowed smoothly off his lips. Harry had stepped outside a short while ago to take Joey's call and ended up taking a long walk around the block. Joey Morello was not fine. Not at all. Gio Sabella, head of the Sabella family and an old friend of Joey's father, was now in line to be the next boss of the bosses. A position he didn't truly want, but he was the senior-most man left standing after Vincent

Morello's murder, and the families needed to ensure peace. Gio would be a caretaker, warming the throne while the true backstabbing began. All bets were off as to what came next.

"Nora texted," Harry said. "She's stopping by in a bit. Wants to see how you're doing." In truth Harry had asked her to come, partly to check on Sara and partly to feel her out on his plan to save the Morellos. Harry and Sara had just delivered to Nora's team their recovery of the year – an authentic Viking helmet made of the same gold as the Temple Menorah, though of course no one could prove that unless they excavated several million tons of rock from a buried cavern off Norway's coast.

Nora's team didn't make the headlines with this one, as that would require explaining how they came into possession of the helmet, but the goodwill she earned with the Norwegian authorities was impossible to measure. Suffice to say Nora's unit would never lack for funding again, and Nora was suddenly receiving a lot more respect from the district attorney. Harry heard she'd even gotten an invite to one of the mayor's private parties. Regardless, recovering the drinking horns was a major coup, one they could trumpet in the papers, and Nora had always reminded him that the district attorney loved nothing more than positive press. Even more so when he didn't have to work for it.

"I'm fine," Sara said. The same empty response.

"Given any thought to the museum's offer?" Harry moved to sit by her and she flinched. He remained standing. "It's a heck of an institution."

"I'm still thinking about it." She crossed her arms on her chest. "I don't know."

The muted noise of neighborhood traffic crept into their silence. His thoughts went back a few days, to Vagsoy Island. Sara had been fine once they'd made it out of the collapsing cave. She'd looked on in wonder as an authentic Viking burial ship floated out to sea through the newly created hole in the island's exterior, blazing brightly enough to cast light on the shore behind them. Of course the massive inferno floating off the town's coast had brought countless rescue vessels and police boats, so the moment was brief, but Sara had been more excited than anything. To be alive, to be part of history, to see it with Harry.

That had all changed once they'd taken a circuitous route back to the mainland and headed home. She'd fallen silent on the plane, sleeping fitfully until they landed in New York two days ago. Sara had slept at his place, but had woken with a start in the early morning hours that nearly stopped Harry's heart. She'd come downstairs, turned all the lights on, and to his astonishment, pulled his shotgun out of the closet and sat down on the couch with it resting beside her. He'd gone back to bed for a few uneasy hours of sleep and then come downstairs when the sun rose to find her still there. She'd slept all through the next day and night, only to return to the couch and shotgun, a habit which carried on through today. Any attempt to engage her in discussion brought only short responses. Until she'd brought up the American Museum of Natural History's offer of employment.

"What do you think?" he'd asked when she reminded him it was on the table.

"I'm an Egyptologist at a small university in Germany. This would be a massive step for my career." A pause. "It would require relocating to the States."

Those seven words said enough for seven thousand. Relocation to New York, to Harry's city. Did she want to live near – or perhaps with – a man responsible for her kidnapping? She clearly didn't have the answer right now.

"You have time," he said.

Sara changed the subject. "I spoke with a former classmate of mine who works for the largest historical society in America. She is pushing for an article to be written on your father. To tell everyone he's truly innocent."

"Thank you." It was the best Harry could hope for. Before leaving Norway he'd retrieved the file from Magnus's private bank, the original evaluation Fred had produced showing only the statue of Zeus was real.

The notarization on it showed Fred had created the report before his arrest, which proved beyond a shred of a doubt that he'd been framed.

Fred Fox had been convicted decades ago, however. No prosecutor wanted to hear about such an old case now. No judge wanted to deal with new evidence. It could take years to clear Fred's name in a court of law. But if Harry could do it in the court of professional opinion first, the legal review would be much easier, and probably happen a heck of a lot sooner. An article placed by a prominent historical society in a leading journal could make that happen.

"It may take a while," Sara said. "Theirs is a slow-moving world."

"We'll stick with it."

Harry sat down across from her and reached for a letter on the table in front of her. Not a letter. *The* letter. The letter his father had been reading before he left for Rome. A letter written in Arabic. In his mother's handwriting.

"I still can't believe it," Harry said. "My mother was alive and he never told me."

"The letter proves she was alive at one point," Sara said. "I realize how much this means to you, but don't let hope cloud your reason."

He set the letter down. "It's infuriating because it doesn't say anything. It's all fluff. *I miss you. I hope our son is well.* All the generic stuff any mom would say. Nothing to tell me where she is now, when the letter was written, anything at all."

"It tells you that your mother loved you." Sara's voice softened. "That is not nothing."

Harry ran a hand over his face. He'd been so certain the letter would be the break they needed, would reveal the truth behind why his father had lied about his mother dying, why he had hidden the real story from Harry. Instead, he'd found nothing but more questions. The letter provided so little detail it was virtually worthless. He might be able to restore Fred's reputation now, but the letter gave zero help in uncovering the truth behind why Fred had let Dani go and never told Harry about it.

Harry sat up straighter. "I'm not quitting yet," he said. "I had an idea. One I'm going to test right now."

Sara looked interested in life for the first time in days. "What idea?"

"Hang tight." He dialed Jessica Barnes's number. "It's a long shot," Harry said as the phone rang. "Like everything else we do these days."

That got a ghost of a smile from her. The phone rang and rang until it went to voicemail. Little surprise, given Jessica had told him more than once how much she did not miss ringing phones. Harry left a message asking her to call him back. A half-beat later, knocking sounded on his front door.

Sara reached for the shotgun. "Easy," Harry said. "It's probably Nora Doyle. Who else knocks like your door disrespected them?" He stood. Sara kept her hand next to the firearm.

Harry opened the door. "Nora. You look nice."

Nora Doyle stood in the doorway. The flowing black dress hanging off one shoulder went all the way to her ankles, while the heels she wore probably cost more than Harry wanted to know and looked like torture devices of the highest order. A delicately embroidered shawl covered her shoulders and neck to ward off the chill. "I'm headed to a party for the mayor this afternoon." Nora *click-clacked* her way in. "Glad to see you back in one piece. I read the news reports about Magnus Dahl. Amazing how much press a dead man gets when he's related to the royal family *and* responsible for finding a lost Viking longboat. Which he set on fire."

Harry had told her the entire story. "He had a little help with the fire."

"Glad no one said much about that Larsen fellow going missing. He's despicable." She clapped a hand on his shoulder and looked past him. "Hello, Sara."

"Good to see you," Sara said. She did not get up.

"Nice accessory." Nora indicated the shotgun. "Right up my alley."

Sara looked at the gun. "I never felt the need for a firearm before."

"Getting kidnapped will do that to you." Nora sat beside Sara, ignoring Sara's flinch, and wrapped her in a hug. "It will pass."

"I hope so." Sara's voice was soft again. "I truly do."

Harry's phone buzzed. "It's Detective Barnes." He walked into the kitchen as Nora spoke to Sara in low tones. "Jessica, thanks for calling me back."

"You need something?"

Her frankness warmed his heart, which had started beating faster. "Your memory."

"Fat lot of good that will do you."

"Humor me. You heard the man's voice at the crime scene. The man who paid Connor O'Sullivan to misidentify the body."

"A man of average height and build whose face I never saw."

"That's the guy. You heard his voice. Nothing else."

"So what? Doesn't help us."

Harry's chest pounded. His skin felt tight. "Would you recognize it if you heard it again?"

"What are you getting at, Fox?"

"Would you recognize his voice if you heard it again? I'm serious."

She didn't hesitate. "Yes. You never forget your early cases. And to be clear, my memory is fine."

It was more than fine. Everyone Harry spoke to who knew Jessica Barnes said she was one of the best cops around. What made a good cop great? Paying attention to the details, which meant *remembering* them. "You somewhere quiet?"

"I was reading a book until you bothered me. Yes, it's quiet."

"Then listen up. Tell me if this is the voice of the man who bribed Connor O'Sullivan."

Harry grabbed his tablet and pulled up a saved voicemail. One of the many he still had, backed up on several devices in case the ones on his phone vanished. Voicemails from a person he would never speak with again.

"Hey, Harry, it's me. I'll be a few minutes late to dinner. Order me the usual if you get this. See you soon."

The message ended. A quick gust of wind made his kitchen window creak. Harry swallowed, his throat dry. "Did you hear it?" he asked.

"Play it again." He did. "One more time," Jessica ordered. Only after a third time through did she answer. "I'll be damned."

Harry nearly broke his phone in half. "What?"

"That's him," Jessica said. "That's the voice I heard under the bridge. The man who bribed Connor."

"Are you certain?"

"Nothing's certain in life, kid. But I'm pretty darn sure it's the same guy. Who is he?"

Harry could barely get the words out. "My dad. I'll call you back."

He clicked off as the world pushed him down, forcing him against a wall under the weight of it all. *Impossible.* Why would Fred be at Dani's supposed murder scene, and why would he bribe the detective to misidentify a body? How did he know the body would be there? Was he the fake brother who had lied to the coroner and identified the body?

"Why?" It was all he could say, all he could think. "*Why?*"

A scream ripped the air. *Sara.*

Harry raced back into the living room, nearly tangling his legs in a pair of kitchen stools as he slid around the corner. "What's wrong?" he shouted.

Sara was sitting rigid on the couch. Nora sat beside her, turned toward her now, alarm on her face. "What?" she asked Sara. "What is it?"

Sara pointed at Nora's chest. "Your shawl. Take it off."

"My shawl?"

"Yes," Sara said quickly. "Take it off."

Nora's mouth tightened to a hard line. She grabbed one end of the flowing cloth and lifted it to reveal her dress's neckline. Gold flashed and Harry's chest froze. "No."

"What's wrong?" Nora looked at the jewelry around her neck. "Is it my necklace?"

Harry tried to respond. The words wouldn't come. He took one step closer, then another, the only thing in the universe was that golden circle resting on Nora's chest. Gold decorated with a bluish-green material. *It can't be.*

"It's a medallion," Nora said. "A bit gaudy, sure, but that's it."

"No." Harry found his voice. "It's not a medallion."

"What's wrong with you? It's gold, and this blue-green stuff is called faience." She lifted the circular object from her skin. "It's an Egyptian style. These markings are supposed to be hieroglyphs." Nora's eyes narrowed. "What's going on?"

Harry didn't answer. He looked at Sara, who stood for the first time all day and walked over to him. She touched his neck. He didn't move, so she reached down his shirt and pulled out an object Harry only ever let a very few people see. His amulet. She turned it toward Nora.

Nora's head jerked back. "You have the same medallion?"

"It's an amulet," Harry said. "My father's amulet. It's the only thing he left me."

"This is what Harry and I have been searching for," Sara said. "The amulet revealed a trail we followed around the world. A trail left by Mark Antony and Cleopatra."

"You're telling me that is a real Egyptian artifact?" Nora stared at Harry's amulet and then down at the amulet between her own fingers. "It can't be."

"It is," Sara said. "I believe yours is as well."

Harry's mind had ground to a halt. He could only ask one question. "Where did you get it?"

Nora's words seemed to float on the air. "From my mother."

THE END

Author's Note

Rome was not built in a day. Nor did it fall in one. The fall of the Western Roman Empire – the western provinces of the Roman Empire and not to be confused with the Eastern Roman, or Byzantine, Empire – occurred over hundreds of years and has been widely studied and argued. For the purposes of this summary, I will begin in the year 376, when large numbers of Goths and other non-Romans entered the empire. Why did they arrive? The Huns drove them from their lands. Attila is the man most often associated with the Huns and their tribal empire, but the truth – as always – is more complicated than saying Attila the Hun was directly responsible for the collapse of the Western Roman Empire. Attila was one of several Hun leaders whose warring ways caused the Gothic exodus.

The Western Roman Empire would be embroiled in two destructive civil wars for the next twenty years, distracting the rival armies vying for control of Rome and generally forgetting about the growing Goth problem. Spoiler alert, this does not end well for our Roman friends. Centuries earlier the incoming Goths would have been exterminated. Now the Roman armies were too busy battling each other to worry about the growing threat, and several decades later the Western Roman Emperor effectively had no control over what were generously still called the Roman territories.

Enter Alaric I, King of the Visigoths (*Chapter 3*). In 408 his army laid siege to Rome, only leaving after the city paid an incredible ransom. Two years later several battles ensued between the previously placated Visigoths and what remained of the Roman armies. Alaric again laid siege to Rome, only to fall back until he was attacked by a small Roman force. His army laid siege to Rome for a third time, ultimately sacking the eternal city in 410 to pillage and plunder for three full days. This was to be Alaric's greatest triumph, for after several months spent ravaging the Roman countryside, he died of illness and his brother-in-law Ataulf was elected king of the Visigoths. The two are not brothers, a change I made for the purposes of telling this story.

Rome truly was not conquered for twelve hundred years (*Chapter 3*). Under Ataulf's leadership, the Visigoths did not go to Scandinavia, but migrated to what we now call Portugal. Though a storied and legendary civilization, Visigoths are not the forerunners of Vikings. The Visigoths eventually assimilated with the Hispano-Roman population of Spain over time, morphing as all cultures do from one label to the next.

The Viking people had a large and shifting religious identity, including the well-known afterlife vision of being carried off to Valhalla by Valkyries, where fallen warriors and nobles would do battle each day, with the dead rising after the battle ended to feast in a great hall with friends and enemies alike under the leadership of Odin until the time came for a final battle at Odin's side against a supernatural enemy (*Chapter 3*). However, not all Vikings went to Valhalla. Those who died of natural causes went to Hel, which is nothing like the Christian version. There are numerous ways a Viking could end up in Hel (from quite a few sources) but on the whole it wasn't a bad place, often described as somewhat positive. People didn't try to avoid Hel by any means. It was, however, not Valhalla. If Ataulf wanted to reunite with his son, he would have had a tough time of it, for as a King he would have a first-class ticket to Odin's hall. His son, Theodosius would not. Everything detailed regarding Valhalla and Hel is true based on my source material, though the fact of the matter is none of this mattered to Visigoths, whose culture had an entirely different belief system – I subbed in Viking beliefs for Visigoth ones for the purposes of the story.

Viking runestones are a rich source of information about their culture. Many stand to this day, though the stone Sara references as being in Germany (*Chapter 6*) and confirming the Visigoths stole the

Temple Menorah is fiction. However, all the factual information about the menorah is accurate based on historical sources referenced in my research for this story. Gotland was truly a major trade center (*Chapter 6*), but not until around the year 700, three centuries after Ataulf died. As some of the most skilled navigators to ever live, it is no surprise Vikings truly did find new trade routes using the Baltic Sea and various rivers to avoid Arab trade and military dominance in the region. The runestone Harry and Sara visit on Gotland is a figment of my imagination, though there are several of the Viking stones on Gotland, but none about a ship called Orn sinking off the coastline. That being said, Sweden's largest island is not devoid of mystery. If you ever want to go for a treasure hunt, know that in 1999 nearly two hundred pounds of Viking precious metal was unearthed, a legendary find known as the Spillings Hoard.

Chapter 12: Viking burial chambers are often built in the same fashion as the one Harry and Sara uncover on Gotland (*Chapter* 12), what resemble mounds in the earth truly hiding the final resting place of a great Viking *jarl* or warrior. Over three hundred gravesites exist on the island, though to the best of my knowledge none tied to Ataulf have been discovered – yet. While the mounds and my descriptions are rooted in fact, no record exists regarding Viking beliefs that people, be they royalty like King Ataulf or a common Viking, could retrieve objects from a burial chamber dedicated to them. The version of Viking belief used as the basis for my story allows for only those goods or items buried with a Viking in their actual grave to be carried with them to the afterlife. Having a secondary or honorary burial chamber with additional supplies is an invention of my own.

A central idea to the story revolves around a deity Harry and Sara investigate, one referred to as the White God (*Chapter 13*). If you read this far, you'll know whose name that is in this story. However, the truth of the matter is that the term White God has been used for all the references listed in this story, including a Viking god called Heimdall.

Harry and Sara get into trouble on the Avaldsnes Kongsgård estate

(*Chapter* 18), which was a king's estate and is likely the oldest royal residence in Norway. The estate dates to 872 AD and is located on a scenic spot of land overlooking the Karmsund strait, chosen for the strategic location and proximity to existing trading posts at the time. There is no structure called Gungnir castle on the grounds, and in fact there are not many structures left at all beyond ruins and a functioning church built in 1250. I created the castle for this story, basing the design and layout on the Peel Castle partial ruins, located on the Isle of Mann and which used to be Viking buildings. Gungnir is truly the name of Odin's spear. Additionally, Odin is the namesake for day of the week Wednesday, which derives from the Germanic name for Odin, *Wodanaz* – meaning "lord of the frenzy". So if anyone ever asks if you have a case of the Wednesdays, you're probably having a good time.

One long-standing myth regarding Vikings relates to their helmets. When we think of these battle accessories, the first thing that often comes to mind are great horns jutting from each side (*Chapter 20*). Vikings didn't really have horned helmets. They never existed. The idea of horns is a modern invention, most likely originating in Scandinavian art two centuries ago. Though Vikings did not have horned helmets, the decorative pieces were used by cultures in the Bronze Age near the Mediterranean coastal area, but those were created two thousand years ago, well before the first Viking decided to plunder and pillage anywhere. My depiction of the Norse god Mimir includes a quill, which is not true. His quill is made up to help with the story, and because I thought it was neat. Mimir is truly the Norse god of knowledge and wisdom, one who tended to get short shrift in the stories I reviewed during my research. I hope he would approve of my depiction.

Magnus Dahl's interesting chess piece on his desk (*Chapter 22*) is based on the Lewis chessmen, a set of walrus ivory and whale tooth gaming pieces discovered in 1831 in Scotland. Only one of the 79 chess pieces is in private hands, with most being in the British Museum and a handful displayed in the National Museum of Scotland. The existence of these pieces suggest, but do not prove, that Vikings played chess. I choose to believe Vikings did play chess, and their favorite pieces were whoever was attacking at that moment in the game.

If you ever visit Vagsoy in Norway, you will not see Pai Island hard off the coast. The scene of Harry and Sara's ultimate triumph and Ataulf's funerary boat (*Chapter 27*) is fictional, for Pai Island does not exist. Sadly, the pied ravens who gave this fictional island its name went extinct in 1902. I also created the Viking myth of Odin's blind eye causing the pied ravens white coloring, though the birds truly did have such coloring and appeared as described.

Thank you for joining me on this journey, and I look forward to sharing more of Harry's adventures with you soon.

Andrew Clawson
March 2023

Excerpt from *The Pharaoh's Amulet*

Visit Andrew's website for more information and purchase details.

andrewclawson.com

Chapter 1

Brooklyn

A water bottle nearly killed Harry Fox.

It got him as he moved silently through the darkness of an old candy factory in a quiet corner of Brooklyn. A factory now permanently under construction thanks to the machinations of Altin Cana. Plastic sheets hung from the ceiling. Wooden boards were nailed to the floor in place of railings and around open stairwells. The elevator door hung slightly open though inviting daredevils to peek inside. And a plastic water bottle waited on the scuffed concrete floor as Harry slipped from shadow to shadow, invisible in the darkness.

Harry slid past a window and moved with purpose down the hall to a turn ahead. Frigid night air gusted through an opening in the exterior wall, one covered with black plastic sheeting that snapped in the breeze. Clouds covered the moon to leave him moving blind. He picked up the pace, reaching for the flipping sheet to pull it back and let a sliver of light in. Plastic crunched underfoot.

The full water bottled he'd stepped on sent him hurtling forward, arms flailing for balance as he crashed into something in the darkness, something sturdy which sent him closer to a gaping hole in the wall where a window should have been, a hole three stories above hard concrete with nothing to save him. Harry grabbed at the sheeting as his momentum threw him forward, into the thick black sheeting. He grabbed it with two hands. A gust of wind sent the thick sheeting between his legs, tripping him up so he twisted and fell backward through the hole and plummeted into night's cold embrace.

The sheeting tore as he fell, popping free from the nails holding it in place as Harry plunged toward the sidewalk in a halting fall, each nail holding him for an instant before his weight proved too much. One, two, three *pops* and he went sideways until an invisible fist punched him in the kidney and stopped him cold.

His body went numb. Harry gasped for air that wouldn't come. He'd have screamed if he could make a sound. Instinct took over and he threw an arm out to grab whatever hit him, finding an unlit floodlight stuck to the exterior wall. Bigger than his head, bolted to the brickwork, he latched onto it in a death grip and took his weight off the thick black sheeting now halfway torn off the wall. Harry closed his eyes and went still. *Maybe they didn't see me.*

Seconds passed. No shouts of alarm, no pounding footsteps. And best of all, no gunshots. Harry opened one eye, then the other. His nose pressed against a brick wall. One arm wrapped around the massive floodlight, the other kept bunched sheeting under an elbow. Sheeting which had stopped ripping. He leaned back from the brickwork. The opening he'd fallen through was only a few feet to his side. If he could get a hand through it, maybe he could haul himself back into the building and avoid becoming a greasy spot on the concrete below.

The *smack* of a heavy steel door banging open sounded beneath him. A man walked out of the building to stand on the side landing. A lighter flashed, his cigarette caught, and the guard Harry desperately hoped to avoid leaned against a railing directly beneath him to have a cigarette.

His arms shouted in protest. The floodlight casing jabbed his side. Harry clenched his jaw and tried to plaster himself against the wall. *Don't move.* If he kept quiet, the guard may not look up. That's all it would take for Harry to find himself in the clutches of Altin Cana, the last person in the world Harry wanted to see tonight. Albanian gangsters like Altin didn't take kindly to people breaking into their buildings, doubly so when they did so planning to steal a rare cultural artifact. An artifact Altin Cana stood to make a lot of money from when he sold it.

A newspaper delivery truck rumbled past. Harry looked down to see the guard's head turn to follow it. Harry's heart thudded as an eternity passed. Finally a swirling ember twirled when the guard flicked his butt onto the street and went back inside, the steel door banging closed once more.

Air burst from Harry's lungs. How long he'd been holding that breath he had no idea. A few more gulps of frigid air got his nerve up. One hand kept a tenuous grip on the plastic sheeting. His other arm draped the floodlight. He bit the sheeting to keep it from flying away, reaching for the opening as his armpit threatened to rip in half on the floodlight. The window opening waited just out of reach.

He grabbed the sheeting to give his other arm a break. Another *pop* as a nail tore loose and the plastic shifted. Lose a few more nails and he'd be stuck on this floodlight until the fire department showed up. Which he could only hope happened before Altin Cana's guards spotted him. Another try to reach the opening cost him two more nails. Harry Fox pressed his forehead against the brick wall and cursed the woman who'd put him in this mess. A woman who had saved his life in more ways than one. *Last time I ever help you out.* Nora Doyle was in for an earful if he survived this mess.

Harry frowned. Complaining wouldn't get him out of this. He looked at the sheet, about ready to come down if he pulled too hard. It couldn't hold his weight long enough for him to climb back over to the opening. Harry adjusted his grip on the floodlight casing, the only sturdy handhold available. He paused. The plastic sheeting couldn't hold his weight. But this floodlight could.

An idea took root. *It might work.* Harry leaned away from the wall, judging angles and distance. Yes, it might. If he played it just right. Before common sense could intervene he pushed his toes into tiny grooves on the brickwork and scrambled up, the tips of his boots catching just enough to get him moving vertically as he pulled on the sheeting and did the most awkward one-armed pull-up to clamber up the wall, one nail in holding the sheeting popping loose as his feet churned and arm twisted until he pushed himself up as the sheet ripped free. Harry flung his torso over the floodlight and collapsed.

Black sheeting fluttered to the sidewalk as Harry lay across the metal casing, chest heaving. The floodlight groaned. It may have shifted an inch, or that may have been his terror talking, but the fact remained a floodlight wasn't meant to hold a grown man's weight. With nothing to grab but the brick wall, he got one food atop the light fixture, balancing with the skill of a doomed man until his other foot jammed beside the first and he was crouching on the casing, arms splayed to either side, fingers glued to the grooves between bricks in a desperate dance to stay upright.

The window opening was only a few feet away. What seemed like a short jump only moments ago now loomed large. If he could push off the casing, and if it held long enough, he should be able to grab the opening and pull himself up to safety. Unless he bounced off the wall as he jumped, or lost his grip trying to haul himself inside. He shook his head. No time to think like that. He had this. Harry laughed without humor. *I've made it out of tougher spots.*

A bolt sprung loose from the casing and his foot slipped. One hand shot out and left a trail of blood across the brickwork, his fingers shredded as he barely kept his balance. The floodlight screeched and another bolt clanged as he lowered himself and aimed at the opening. A city bus rumbled past, a distant ambulance siren blared, and Harry jumped.

The floodlight snapped off, stealing half his momentum. A moment passed where the world slowed, gravity reaching for him and not quite grabbing hold as he half-flew, half-fell toward the opening mere feet ahead, arms out and fingers reaching for the concrete floor. He leaned closer, mouth open, and one hand grabbed the lip and latched on. His other hand grabbed for purchase. And missed.

He crashed into the wall. His face smacked bricks right below the opening, brain rattling as he slammed into the wall and skidded along it, hanging by one hand to swing pendulum-like across the wall. Raw fingers on his free hand scrabbled for a hold on the floor, getting one finger on before it slipped free and his other hand slipped across the floor as his weight kept moving. His legs splayed out to slow the deadly swinging, his shoulder ready to break as he reached up and finally got a second hand on the floor and pulled, chin and nose and who knew what else grinding over the rough brick until he flipped himself up and into the building, falling flat on his back.

Harry gulped frigid air until his arms stopped shaking. *Nothing to it.* He sat up, rubbed a hand over his face, and had to bite off a scream as the salty sweat hit his cuts and scrapes from the brickwork. Another minute passed before he stood and looked down the darkened hallway. No guards in sight, no footsteps sounding down the hall. He was still in the game.

Harry hugged what would have been the inside wall if this place had walls. Instead he kept close to standing studs, as far away from the windowless frames on the exterior wall as he could get. Unlike most people who entered a building, Harry had come in from the very top and needed to work his way down to the basement, which required passing at least a few of Altin Cana's guards. The Albanian crime boss kept his valuables in the basement of this permanently under-construction building. According to the city this old factory would eventually become an apartment building, though Altin had other ideas. Every year he moved the building from one shell company to another, selling it to himself at a profit and artificially increasing the value with each transaction. Each sale required new paperwork to be filed, delaying any construction from ever happening and letting Altin use it for his true purpose. A safe house for storing whatever he wanted to keep hidden from prying eyes.

Including a marble bust depicting Philip of Macedon. A bust commissioned by his son, Alexander the Great, and the only surviving image of Philip in the world. A bust recently acquired by Altin Cana's right-hand man, a man named Stefan Rudovic who wanted fewer things more in life than to see Harry Fox dead. Stealing the bust from Altin's safehouse cut Stefan deeply. However, Harry had other reasons for risking his life to get the hunk of marble.

Reasons which didn't matter one bit if Altin's guards captured him tonight. Harry made it to a stairwell entrance, easing the heavy metal door open with minimal squeaking and heading down to the second level. The walls in here were thankfully intact, concealing him from view and keeping the cold night air at bay. Harry tiptoed down to the next landing, opened a door and snuck into the factory's second level. It looked much like the upper floor, all plastic sheets and open windows and construction debris lying around, stuff he could trip over and an ankle if he was lucky, his neck if he wasn't. The upper two floors were truly a construction zone meant to hide the true wealth waiting below, tucked behind a false wall in a dark corner of the basement where no inspectors cared to look.

Harry knew this because his boss had a man on his payroll inside Altin's operation. The inside man told Harry about this safe house, about the guards patrolling the first floor and the basement, and how it was a fool's errand to try and get in. Unless that fool was willing to do something, well, foolish. Like sliding down an empty elevator shaft to access the basement level, then climbing back up it to escape via the same way he'd come in: jumping across rooftops. Harry wanted nothing to do with it. Until he realized it was the only way to save his oldest friend in the world.

Harry gritted his teeth. *Joey better appreciate this.*

The elevator shaft ran down the building's center. A wooden barricade had been erected in front of the closed doors, so Harry pulled the small crowbar he'd brought for this purpose from his pocket and used it to lever a board loose. That let him lean through and use his crowbar to pull the doors open. They clanged and banged, Harry went still, and silence met his waiting ear. Nobody had heard him. At least he hoped not.

Braided steel cables dangled in front of him. The elevator itself had been removed, leaving the cables to sway gently when he touched them. He leaned out over the shaft, looking up and down to find an empty black hole above and below. A headlamp came out of his other pocket. It went on his head and Harry selected the red-light setting before feeling around the corner of the door, his aching fingers finding and latching on to a metal ladder running the length of the shaft. It held steady when he stepped off solid ground and onto a rung with one foot, then the other.

Red light let him keep some of his night vision while also emitting a lower light signature than normal light. No need to give the bad guys a better chance of spotting him. Or a better target to shoot at. Halfway down he stopped, turning an ear toward the blackness below and hearing nothing of concern. He wiped the sweat off his brow and threw his hand back to flick it off. His hand got stuck. *What the heck is that?*

He turned to find a rope dangling behind him. Two ropes, actually, side-by-side and strung tight next to the braided metal cords which moved the missing elevator up and down. What were those ropes doing in here? They stretched far into the distance above and below. He pulled on one. It barely moved. Why they'd be in here he had no idea. He pulled his hand free and kept descending until his feet hit the basement floor. He promptly tripped over a wooden box on the floor. Biting off a curse, he moved to kick the box before noticing the two ropes tied to it. Ropes which disappeared into the darkness above. He pulled on one and the box moved. Workers had rigged a contraption to carry tools or other small objects up and down the shaft via a pulley system anchored at the top of the shaft. Harry stepped over the box, the closed doors in front of him.

This would be the trickiest part. The inside man said this shafted faced toward away from where the guards usually sat, so if Harry opened it quietly he could most likely get into the floor undetected. The word *usually* didn't sit well with Harry, but it was the best of several bad options. Pry open the elevator door, get behind the false wall and make his way out with the marble bust in tow. Easy as could be. In theory, that is. As Harry stuck his crowbar between the elevator doors and slowly levered them open, it didn't seem so easy any longer. He flicked his headlamp off.

The doors cracked several inches, enough to peer through them. Nothing moved outside, no footsteps sounded, no cries of alarm rang out. Another few inches, then several more, and he could stick his head out. The basement was shrouded in darkness, the only light coming through a handful of street-level windows near the ceiling. Harry left the doors open as he climbed out of the shaft. If any guards happened past he'd have to chance it they didn't realize those doors should be closed, not open. Besides, he didn't plan on staying here for long.

The false wall was off to his right, next to one of those massive tool chests called a job box. This basement looked much like the rest of the place, sheeting and boards and construction material everywhere. The furnace hummed somewhere in the distance, while pipes ran across the ceiling in every direction before disappearing into the walls. He peered around the central elevator shaft toward the front exit. Light snuck around a partially-open door, along with the sounds of a television. It seemed a soccer game was on, the announcers shouting rapid-fire in Spanish.

He put the shaft between him and the open door before turning in his headlamp. The job box waited right where it was supposed to be. Harry stood in front of the wall to one side of the box and ran his hands over what looked like damp stones. Felt like them, too, except some of the stones weren't quite damp. They were cool, but dry. Almost as though they weren't real stones, but imitation. His fingernail caught in an invisible crack in the mortar between a specific stone, one with a barely-noticeable cut on it. The stone his informant told him to look for. Harry leaned on the stone, pushing with his entire weight. It held for a moment, he pushed harder, and with a *click* it slid into the wall.

An entire section of the wall swung inward. A hidden door made to look like the basement wall opened into a curtain of utter black. Harry stepped forward, stopping with his foot inches off the ground. He stepped back. No need to walk into a booby trap. He'd done that before and it never ended well. The light on his headlamp switched from red to white when he pressed a button, washing out in front of him to light up the hidden room. Harry did a double-take.

"That's a Roman shield."

A towering rectangular shield stood in front of him. He'd seen shields like that before, mostly in museums, a few in private collections. A Roman soldier had once carried the shield as he marched with his legion over a thousand years ago. The shield should never have been in a basement like this. It shouldn't, but here it was, and he knew who was responsible. Likely the same man who brought the Chinese vase here, the one sitting next to the Roman shield. And the pair of samurai swords on another table to his side, both of which looked authentic and sharp enough to slice through limbs.

Stefan Rudovic. A man he'd last seen in Greece, limping away after attacking Harry inside an ancient Greek temple. Stefan must have recovered from the broken ankle and was back in the black market antiquities trade. Harry's jaw tightened. Stefan would be after Harry with murder in his heart if he realized Harry had stolen the marble bust from this hiding place.

He pushed that worry aside and focused on the reason he'd come. Philip had fathered the most successful general in history, and now the only accepted portrait of him in the world sat in a dark Brooklyn basement. The fine-grained marble carving stood a foot high, the aristocratic nose and tight lips seeming to judge Harry as he reached for the bust, while the sturdy jawline shouted manliness. Even Alexander the Great must have paused when this man came calling. The bust went into a bag Harry had tucked into one pocket, a specially-designed bag with straps he put over his shoulders and cinched tight, then did the same with a strap around his waist. Now he could run if need be and the awkward bust wouldn't slow him down. Much.

He ignored the other tables in the room and headed back for the hidden door. Ancient Roman coins and what looked like actual gold ingots were left behind as he flicked his light back to red and went through the open door, closing it behind him. Maybe Altin Cana and his goons wouldn't even know the bust was missing before Harry put it to good use. Ending the Canas war on his employer, in this case.

The bust pressed tight against his back. Harry touched the knuckledusters tucked into one pocket, one accessory he never committed crimes without, then moved quickly back to the elevator shaft. Climb back to the third floor, head out onto the fire escape, then up to the roof where he could retrace his path across the top of several buildings to safety. Quickly, quietly, and without anyone knowing he was here.

Harry stepped around the elevator shaft toward the doors. A man stood in front of them.

"Hey, Albi." The man's back was to Harry as he called out. "Did you open this door?"

Harry didn't move. The man hadn't heard him, mustn't have heard the hidden door close moments ago. The man kept staring at the open elevator doors. He reached a hesitant hand out to touch them.

"Albi." The man raised his voice, yelling toward where the sound of Spanish soccer announcers came from. "Did you open this door?"

"Always talking, Rudi. Be quiet, the match is on." Albi finally responded, shouting through the room's dor. "I cannot hear over your loud mouth."

Rudi mumbled something about Albi's mother under his tongue. "Who opened this door?" he asked softly, as though the door would respond.

The door said nothing. Harry did. "I opened it."

Rudi spun around, just as Harry expected. By now the knuckledusters were on his hand, which he balled into a fist that flew directly at Rudi's chin. The Albanian gangster never saw it coming, never had a chance. Harry's fist landed with a resounding *crack* and

Rudi went down in a heap. So much for slipping out unnoticed.

Rudi would be up and moving shortly. Harry knelt beside the unconscious man and frisked him. The pistol he found in Rudi's waistband was tossed in one direction, the magazine with its bullets the other. Never make it easy on someone trying to shoot you. Harry grabbed the nearest ladder rung and sprinted up the ladder, nearly to the first floor when Albi's voice filtered up the shaft.

"Rudi?" Harry passed the first-floor elevator doors and kept climbing. Now Albi was really shouting. "Rudi, what are you talking about?"

The closed second-floor doors were in front of him when Albi found his friend. "Rudi, what happened?" The sound an open palm made when striking a cheek. "Rudi, wake up." Groaning followed. Harry accelerated, trying to keep his feet from smacking on the rungs, for the sound of each step banged in the tube of an elevator shaft like hammers striking. Albi didn't miss it. "What is that noise?"

"He hit me." Rudi was awake. "Where did he go?"

"Quiet." Albi shushed his wounded friend. "Do you hear that?"

Harry went still halfway between the second and third floors. Albi's voice filled the sudden silence. "It stopped." *Click.* Light filled the shaft and Harry flew up the ladder. Too late. "There he is!"

To continue the story, visit Andrew Clawson's website at andrewclawson.com.

GET YOUR COPY OF THE HARRY FOX STORY
THE NAPOLEON CIPHER,
AVAILABLE EXCLUSIVELY FOR MY VIP READER LIST

Sharing the writing journey with my readers is a special privilege. I love connecting with anyone who reads my stories, and one way I accomplish that is through my mailing list. I only send notices of new releases or the occasional special offer related to my novels.

If you sign up for my VIP reader mailing list, I'll send you a copy of *The Napoleon Cipher*, the Harry Fox adventure that's not sold in any store. You can get your copy of this exclusive novel by signing up on my website.

Did you enjoy this story? Let people know

Reviews are the most effective way to get my books noticed. I'm one guy, a small fish in a massive pond. Over time, I hope to change that, and I would love your help. The best thing you could do to help spread the word is leave a review on your platform of choice.

Honest reviews are like gold. If you've enjoyed this book I would be so grateful if you could take a few minutes leaving a review, short or long.

Thank you very much.

Also by Andrew Clawson

The Parker Chase Series
A Patriot's Betrayal
The Crowns Vengeance
Dark Tides Rising
A Republic of Shadows
A Hollow Throne
A Tsar's Gold

The TURN Series
TURN: The Conflict Lands
TURN: A New Dawn
TURN: Endangered

Harry Fox Adventures
The Arthurian Relic
The Emerald Tablet
The Celtic Quest
The Achilles Legend
The Pagan Hammer
The Pharaoh's Amulet
The Thracian Idol
The Antikythera Code

About the Author

Andrew Clawson is the author of multiple series, including the Parker Chase and TURN thrillers, as well as the Harry Fox adventures.

You can find him at his website, AndrewClawson.com

or you can connect with him on Instagram at andrew.clawson

on Twitter at @clawsonbooks

on Facebook at facebook.com/AndrewClawsonnovels

and you can always send him an email at:
andrew@andrewclawson.com.